CECILIA

Frances Burney

CECILIA

OR

MEMOIRS OF AN HEIRESS

VOLUME I

BIBLIOBAZAAR

CECILIA

PREFACE

"Fanny's Cecilia came out last summer, and is as much liked and read, I believe, as any book ever was," wrote Charlotte Burney in Jan. 1783. "She had 250 pounds for it from Payne and Cadell. Most people say she ought to have had a thousand. It is now going into the third edition, though Payne owns that they printed two thousand at the first edition, and Lowndes told me five hundred was the common number for a novel."[1] The manuscript of *Cecilia* was submitted to Dr Burney and Mr Crisp during its composition, and their suggestions were in some cases adopted, as we learn from the *Diary*. Dr Johnson was not consulted, but a desire at once to imitate and to please him evidently controlled the work.

Under these circumstances it is naturally less fresh and spontaneous than *Evelina*, but it is more mature. The touch is surer and the plot more elaborate. We cannot to-day fully appreciate the "conflict scene between mother and son," for which, Miss Burney tells us, the book was written; but the pictures of eighteenth century affectations are all alive, and the story is thoroughly absorbing, except, perhaps, in the last book.

Miss Burney often took the name of her characters from her acquaintances, and it seems probable that some of the "types" in *Cecilia* are also drawn from real life. The title of Miss Austen's *Pride and Prejudice* was borrowed from *Cecilia*, and some points of resemblance may be traced between the two novels.

---

1 *The Early Diary of Frances Burney, with a selection from her correspondence, and from the journals of her sisters Susan and Charlotte Burney.* Edited by Annie Raine Ellis. 1889. Vol. II. p. 307.

The present edition is reprinted from:—

CECILIA, or, Memoirs of an Heiress. By the author of Evelina. In five volumes. London: Printed for T. Payne and Son, at the Newsgate, and T. Cadell in the Strand. MDCCLXXXII. R. B. J.

THE RIGHT HON. EDMUND BURKE TO MISS F. BURNEY. (AFTER READING CECILIA.)

Madam,—I should feel exceedingly to blame if I could refuse to myself the natural satisfaction, and to you the just but poor return, of my best thanks for the very great instruction and entertainment I have received from the new present you have bestowed on the public. There are few—I believe I may say fairly there are none at all—that will not find themselves better informed concerning human nature, and their stock of observation enriched, by reading your "Cecilia." They certainly will, let their experience in life and manners be what it may. The arrogance of age must submit to be taught by youth. You have crowded into a few small volumes an incredible variety of characters; most of them well planned, well supported, and well contrasted with each other. If there be any fault in this respect, it is one in which you are in no great danger of being imitated. Justly as your characters are drawn, perhaps they are too numerous. But I beg pardon; I fear it is quite in vain to preach economy to those who are come young to excessive and sudden opulence.

I might trespass on your delicacy if I should fill my letter to you with what I fill my conversation to others. I should be troublesome to you alone if I should tell you all I feel and think on the natural vein of humour, the tender pathetic, the comprehensive and noble moral, and the sagacious observation, that appear quite throughout that extraordinary performance.

In an age distinguished by producing extraordinary women, I hardly dare to tell you where my opinion would place you amongst them. I respect your modesty, that will not endure the commendations which your merit forces from everybody.

I have the honour to be, with great gratitude, respect, and esteem, madam, your most obedient and most humble servant,

EDM. BURKE
WHITEHALL, *July 19, 1782.*

My best compliments and congratulations to Dr Burney on the great honour acquired to his family.

ADVERTISEMENT.

The indulgence shewn by the Public to Evelina, which, unpatronized, unaided, and unowned, past through Four Editions in one Year, has encouraged its Author to risk this SECOND attempt. The animation of success is too universally acknowledged, to make the writer of the following sheets dread much censure of temerity; though the precariousness of any power to give pleasure, suppresses all vanity of confidence, and sends CECILIA into the world with scarce more hope, though far more encouragement, than attended her highly-honoured predecessor, Evelina.

July, 1782

BOOK I

CHAPTER I

A JOURNEY.

"Peace to the spirits of my honoured parents, respected be their remains, and immortalized their virtues! may time, while it moulders their frail relicks to dust, commit to tradition the record of their goodness; and Oh, may their orphan-descendant be influenced through life by the remembrance of their purity, and be solaced in death, that by her it was unsullied!"

Such was the secret prayer with which the only survivor of the Beverley family quitted the abode of her youth, and residence of her forefathers; while tears of recollecting sorrow filled her eyes, and obstructed the last view of her native town which had excited them.

Cecilia, this fair traveller, had lately entered into the one-and-twentieth year of her age. Her ancestors had been rich farmers in the county of Suffolk, though her father, in whom a spirit of elegance had supplanted the rapacity of wealth, had spent his time as a private country gentleman, satisfied, without increasing his store, to live upon what he inherited from the labours of his predecessors. She had lost him in her early youth, and her mother had not long survived him. They had bequeathed to her 10,000 pounds, and consigned her to the care of the Dean of—, her uncle. With this gentleman, in whom, by various contingencies, the accumulated possessions of a rising and prosperous family were centred, she had passed the last four years of her life; and a few weeks only had yet elapsed since his death, which, by depriving her of her last relation, made her heiress to an estate of 3000 pounds per annum; with no other restriction than that of annexing her name, if she married, to the disposal of her hand and her riches.

But though thus largely indebted to fortune, to nature she had yet greater obligations: her form was elegant, her heart was liberal; her countenance announced the intelligence of her mind, her complexion varied with every emotion of her soul, and her eyes, the heralds of her speech, now beamed with understanding and now glistened with sensibility.

For the short period of her minority, the management of her fortune and the care of her person, had by the Dean been entrusted to three guardians, among whom her own choice was to settle her residence: but her mind, saddened by the loss of all her natural friends, coveted to regain its serenity in the quietness of the country, and in the bosom of an aged and maternal counsellor, whom she loved as her mother, and to whom she had been known from her childhood.

The Deanery, indeed, she was obliged to relinquish, a long repining expectant being eager, by entering it, to bequeath to another the anxiety and suspense he had suffered himself; though probably without much impatience to shorten their duration in favour of the next successor; but the house of Mrs Charlton, her benevolent friend, was open for her reception, and the alleviating tenderness of her conversation took from her all wish of changing it.

Here she had dwelt since the interment of her uncle; and here, from the affectionate gratitude of her disposition, she had perhaps been content to dwell till her own, had not her guardians interfered to remove her.

Reluctantly she complied; she quitted her early companions, the friend she most revered, and the spot which contained the relicks of all she had yet lived to lament; and, accompanied by one of her guardians, and attended by two servants, she began her journey from Bury to London.

Mr Harrel, this gentleman, though in the prime of his life, though gay, fashionable and splendid, had been appointed by her uncle to be one of her trustees; a choice which had for object the peculiar gratification of his niece, whose most favourite young friend Mr Harrel had married, and in whose house he therefore knew she would most wish to live.

Whatever good-nature could dictate or politeness suggest to dispel her melancholy, Mr Harrel failed not to urge; and Cecilia, in whose disposition sweetness was tempered with dignity, and gentleness with fortitude, suffered not his kind offices to seem ineffectual; she kissed her hand at the last glimpse a friendly hill afforded of her native town, and made an effort to forget the regret with which she lost sight of it. She revived her spirits by plans of future happiness, dwelt upon the delight with which she should meet her young friend, and, by accepting his consolation, amply rewarded his trouble.

Her serenity, however, had yet another, though milder trial to undergo, since another friend was yet to be met, and another farewell was yet to be taken.

At the distance of seven miles from Bury resided Mr Monckton, the richest and most powerful man in that neighbourhood, at whose house Cecilia and her guardian were invited to breakfast in their journey.

Mr Monckton, who was the younger son of a noble family, was a man of parts, information and sagacity; to great native strength of mind he added a penetrating knowledge of the world, and to faculties the most skilful of investigating the character of every other, a dissimulation the most profound in concealing his own. In the bloom of his youth, impatient for wealth and ambitious of power, he had tied himself to a rich dowager of quality, whose age, though sixty-seven, was but among the smaller species of her evil properties, her disposition being far more repulsive than her wrinkles. An inequality of years so considerable, had led him to expect that the fortune he had thus acquired, would speedily be released from the burthen with which it was at present incumbered; but his expectations proved as vain as they were mercenary, and his lady was not more the dupe of his protestations than he was himself of his own purposes. Ten years he had been married to her, yet her health was good, and her faculties were unimpaired; eagerly he had watched for her dissolution, yet his eagerness had injured no health but his own! So short-sighted is selfish cunning, that in aiming no further than at the gratification of the present moment, it obscures the evils of the future, while it impedes the perception of integrity and honour.

His ardour, however, to attain the blessed period of returning liberty, deprived him neither of spirit nor inclination for intermediate enjoyment; he knew the world too well to incur its censure by ill-treating the woman to whom he was indebted for the rank he held in it; he saw her, indeed, but seldom, yet he had the decency, alike in avoiding as in meeting her, to shew no abatement of civility and good breeding: but, having thus sacrificed to ambition all possibility of happiness in domestic life, he turned his thoughts to those other methods of procuring it, which he had so dearly purchased the power of essaying.

The resources of pleasure to the possessors of wealth are only to be cut off by the satiety of which they are productive: a satiety which the vigorous mind of Mr Monckton had not yet suffered him to experience; his time, therefore, was either devoted to the expensive amusements of the metropolis, or spent in the country among the gayest of its diversions.

The little knowledge of fashionable manners and of the characters of the times of which Cecilia was yet mistress, she had gathered at the house of this gentleman, with whom the Dean her uncle had been intimately connected: for as he preserved to the world the same appearance of decency he supported to his wife, he was everywhere well received, and being but partially known, was extremely respected: the world, with its wonted facility, repaying his circumspect attention to its laws, by silencing the voice of censure, guarding his character from impeachment, and his name from reproach.

Cecilia had been known to him half her life; she had been caressed in his house as a beautiful child, and her presence was now solicited there as an amiable acquaintance. Her visits, indeed, had by no means been frequent, as the ill-humour of Lady Margaret Monckton had rendered them painful to her; yet the opportunities they had afforded her of mixing with people of fashion, had served to prepare her for the new scenes in which she was soon to be a performer.

Mr Monckton, in return, had always been a welcome guest at the Deanery; his conversation was to Cecilia a never-failing source of information, as his knowledge of life and manners enabled him to start those subjects of which she was most ignorant; and her mind, copious for the admission and intelligent for the arrangement of knowledge, received all new ideas with avidity.

Pleasure given in society, like money lent in usury, returns with interest to those who dispense it: and the discourse of Mr Monckton conferred not a greater favour upon Cecilia than her attention to it repaid. And thus, the speaker and the hearer being mutually gratified, they had always met with complacency, and commonly parted with regret.

This reciprocation of pleasure had, however, produced different effects upon their minds; the ideas of Cecilia were enlarged, while the reflections of Mr Monckton were embittered. He here saw an object who to all the advantages of that wealth he had so highly prized, added youth, beauty, and intelligence; though much her senior, he was by no means of an age to render his addressing her an impropriety, and the entertainment she received from his conversation, persuaded him that her good opinion might with ease be improved into a regard the most partial. He regretted the venal rapacity with which he had sacrificed himself to a woman he abhorred, and his wishes for her final decay became daily more fervent. He knew that the acquaintance of Cecilia was confined to a circle of which he was himself the principal ornament, that she had rejected all the proposals of marriage which had hitherto been made to her, and, as he had sedulously watched her from her earliest years, he had reason to believe that her heart had escaped any dangerous impression. This being her situation, he had long looked upon her as his future property; as such he had indulged his admiration, and as such he had already appropriated her estate, though he had not more vigilantly inspected into her sentiments, than he had guarded his own from a similar scrutiny.

The death of the Dean her uncle had, indeed, much alarmed him; he grieved at her leaving Suffolk, where he considered himself the first man, alike in parts and in consequence, and he dreaded her residing in London, where he foresaw that numerous rivals, equal to himself in talents and in riches, would speedily surround her; rivals, too, youthful and sanguine, not shackled by present ties, but at liberty to solicit her immediate acceptance. Beauty and independence, rarely found together, would attract a crowd of suitors at once brilliant and assiduous; and the house of Mr Harrel was eminent for its elegance and gaiety; but yet, undaunted by danger, and confiding in his own powers, he determined to pursue the project he had formed, not fearing by address and perseverance to ensure its success.

CHAPTER II

AN ARGUMENT.

Mr Monckton had, at this time, a party of company assembled at his house for the purpose of spending the Christmas holidays. He waited with anxiety the arrival of Cecilia, and flew to hand her from the chaise before Mr Harrel could alight. He observed the melancholy of her countenance, and was much pleased to find that her London journey had so little power to charm her. He conducted her to the breakfast parlour, where Lady Margaret and his friends expected her.

Lady Margaret received her with a coldness that bordered upon incivility; irascible by nature and jealous by situation, the appearance of beauty alarmed, and of chearfulness disgusted her. She regarded with watchful suspicion whoever was addressed by her husband, and having marked his frequent attendance at the Deanery, she had singled out Cecilia for the object of her peculiar antipathy; while Cecilia, perceiving her aversion though ignorant of its cause, took care to avoid all intercourse with her but what ceremony exacted, and pitied in secret the unfortunate lot of her friend.

The company now present consisted of one lady and several gentlemen.

Miss Bennet, the lady, was in every sense of the phrase, the humble companion of Lady Margaret; she was low-born, meanly educated, and narrow-minded; a stranger alike to innate merit or acquired accomplishments, yet skilful in the art of flattery, and an adept in every species of low cunning. With no other view in life than the attainment of affluence without labour, she was not more the slave of the mistress of the house, than the tool of its master; receiving indignity without murmur, and submitting to contempt as a thing of course.

Among the gentlemen, the most conspicuous, by means of his dress, was Mr Aresby, a captain in the militia; a young man who having frequently heard the words red-coat and gallantry put together, imagined the conjunction not merely customary, but honourable, and therefore, without even pretending to think of the service of his country, he considered a cockade as a badge of politeness, and wore it but to mark his devotion to the ladies, whom he held himself equipped to conquer, and bound to adore.

The next who by forwardness the most officious took care to be noticed, was Mr Morrice, a young lawyer, who, though rising in his profession, owed his success neither to distinguished abilities, nor to skill-supplying industry, but to the art of uniting suppleness to others with confidence in himself. To a reverence of rank, talents, and fortune the most profound, he joined an assurance in his own merit, which no superiority could depress; and with a presumption which encouraged him to aim at all things, he blended a good-humour that no mortification could lessen. And while by the pliability of his disposition he avoided making enemies, by his readiness to oblige, he learned the surest way of making friends by becoming useful to them.

There were also some neighbouring squires; and there was one old gentleman, who, without seeming to notice any of the company, sat frowning in a corner.

But the principal figure in the circle was Mr Belfield, a tall, thin young man, whose face was all animation, and whose eyes sparkled with intelligence. He had been intended by his father for trade, but his spirit, soaring above the occupation for which he was designed, from repining led him to resist, and from resisting, to rebel. He eloped from his friends, and contrived to enter the army. But, fond of the polite arts, and eager for the acquirement of knowledge, he found not this way of life much better adapted to his inclination than that from which he had escaped; he soon grew weary of it, was reconciled to his father, and entered at the Temple. But here, too volatile for serious study, and too gay for laborious application, he made little progress: and the same quickness of parts and vigour of imagination which united with prudence, or accompanied by judgment, might have raised him to the head of his profession, being unhappily associated with fickleness and caprice, served only to impede his improvement, and obstruct his preferment. And now, with little business, and that little neglected, a small fortune, and that fortune daily becoming less, the admiration of the world, but that admiration ending simply in civility, he lived an unsettled and unprofitable life, generally caressed, and universally sought, yet careless of his interest and thoughtless of the future; devoting his time to company, his income to dissipation, and his heart to the Muses.

"I bring you," said Mr Monckton, as he attended Cecilia into the room, "a subject of sorrow in a young lady who never gave disturbance to her friends but in quitting them."

"If sorrow," cried Mr Belfield, darting upon her his piercing eyes, "wears in your part of the world a form such as this, who would wish to change it for a view of joy?"

"She's divinely handsome, indeed!" cried the Captain, affecting an involuntary exclamation.

Meantime, Cecilia, who was placed next to the lady of the house, quietly began her breakfast; Mr Morrice, the young lawyer, with the most easy freedom, seating himself at her side, while Mr Monckton was elsewhere arranging the rest of his guests, in order to secure that place for himself.

Mr Morrice, without ceremony, attacked his fair neighbour; he talked of her journey, and the prospects of gaiety which it opened to her view; but by these finding her unmoved, he changed his theme, and expatiated upon the delights of the spot she was quitting. Studious to recommend himself to her notice, and indifferent by what means, one moment he flippantly extolled the entertainments of the town; and the next, rapturously described the charms of the country. A word, a look sufficed to mark her approbation or dissent, which he no sooner discovered, than he slided into her opinion, with as much facility and satisfaction as if it had originally been his own.

Mr Monckton, suppressing his chagrin, waited some time in expectation that when this young man saw he was standing, he would yield to him his chair: but the remark was not made, and the resignation was not thought of. The Captain, too, regarding the lady as his natural property for the morning, perceived with indignation by whom he was supplanted; while the company in general, saw with much surprize, the place they had severally foreborne to occupy from respect to their host, thus familiarly seized upon by the man who, in the whole room, had the least claim, either from age or rank, to consult nothing but his own inclination.

Mr Monckton, however, when he found that delicacy and good manners had no weight with his guest, thought it most expedient to allow them none with himself; and therefore, disguising his displeasure under an appearance of facetiousness, he called out, "Come, Morrice, you that love Christmas sports, what say you to the game of move-all?"

"I like it of all things!" answered Morrice, and starting from his chair, he skipped to another.

"So should I too," cried Mr Monckton, instantly taking his place, "were I to remove from any seat but this."

Morrice, though he felt himself outwitted, was the first to laugh, and seemed as happy in the change as Mr Monckton himself.

Mr Monckton now, addressing himself to Cecilia, said, "We are going to lose you, and you seem concerned at leaving us; yet, in a very few months you will forget Bury, forget its inhabitants, and forget its environs."

"If you think so," answered Cecilia, "must I not thence infer that Bury, its inhabitants, and its environs, will in a very few months forget me?"

"Ay, ay, and so much the better!" said Lady Margaret, muttering between her teeth, "so much the better!" "I am sorry you think so, madam," cried Cecilia, colouring at her ill-breeding.

"You will find," said Mr Monckton, affecting the same ignorance of her meaning that Cecilia really felt, "as you mix with the world, you will find that Lady Margaret has but expressed what by almost every body is thought: to neglect old friends, and to court new acquaintance, though perhaps not yet avowedly delivered as a precept from parents to children, is nevertheless so universally recommended by example, that those who act differently, incur general censure for affecting singularity."

"It is happy then, for me," answered Cecilia, "that neither my actions nor myself will be sufficiently known to attract public observation."

"You intend, then, madam," said Mr Belfield, "in defiance of these maxims of the world, to be guided by the light of your own understanding."

"And such," returned Mr Monckton, "at first setting out in life, is the intention of every one. The closet reasoner is always refined in his sentiments, and always confident in his virtue; but when he mixes with the world, when he thinks less and acts more, he soon finds the necessity of accommodating himself to such customs as are already received, and of pursuing quietly the track that is already marked out."

"But not," exclaimed Mr Belfield, "if he has the least grain of spirit! the beaten track will be the last that a man of parts will deign to tread,

> For common rules were ne'er designed
> Directors of a noble mind."

"A pernicious maxim! a most pernicious maxim!" cried the old gentleman, who sat frowning in a corner of the room.

"Deviations from common rules," said Mr Monckton, without taking any notice of this interruption, "when they proceed from genius, are not merely pardonable, but admirable; and you, Belfield, have a peculiar right to plead their merits; but so little genius as there is in the world, you must surely grant that pleas of this sort are very rarely to be urged."

"And why rarely," cried Belfield, "but because your general rules, your appropriated customs, your settled forms, are but so many absurd arrangements to impede not merely the progress of genius, but the use of understanding? If man dared act for himself, if neither worldly views, contracted prejudices, eternal precepts, nor compulsive examples, swayed his better reason and impelled his conduct, how noble indeed would he be! *how infinite in faculties! in apprehension how like a God!*"[2]

"All this," answered Mr Monckton, "is but the doctrine of a lively imagination, that looks upon impossibilities simply as difficulties, and upon difficulties as mere invitations to victory. But experience teaches another lesson; experience shows that the opposition of an individual to a community is always dangerous in the operation, and seldom successful in the event;—never, indeed, without a concurrence strange as desirable, of fortunate circumstances with great abilities."

"And why is this," returned Belfield, "but because the attempt is so seldom made? The pitiful prevalence of general conformity extirpates genius, and murders originality; the man is brought up, not as if he were 'the noblest work of God,' but as a mere ductile machine of human formation: he is early taught that he must neither consult his understanding, nor pursue his inclinations, lest, unhappily for his commerce with the world, his understanding should be averse to fools, and provoke him to despise them; and his inclinations to the tyranny of perpetual restraint, and give him courage to abjure it."

"I am ready enough to allow," answered Mr Monckton, "that an eccentric genius, such, for example, as yours, may murmur at the

---

2 Hamlet.

tediousness of complying with the customs of the world, and wish, unconfined, and at large, to range through life without any settled plan or prudential restriction; but would you, therefore, grant the same licence to every one? would you wish to see the world peopled with defiers of order, and contemners of established forms? and not merely excuse the irregularities resulting from uncommon parts, but encourage those, also, to lead, who without blundering cannot even follow?"

"I would have *all* men," replied Belfield, "whether philosophers or ideots, act for themselves. Every one would then appear what he is; enterprize would be encouraged, and imitation abolished; genius would feel its superiority, and folly its insignificance; and then, and then only, should we cease to be surfeited with that eternal sameness of manner and appearance which at present runs through all ranks of men."

"Petrifying dull work this, *mon ami!*" said the Captain, in a whisper to Morrice, "*de grace*, start some new game."

"With all my heart," answered he; and then, suddenly jumping up, exclaimed, "A hare! a hare!"

"Where?—where?—which way?" and all the gentlemen arose, and ran to different windows, except the master of the house, the object of whose pursuit was already near him.

Morrice, with much pretended earnestness, flew from window to window, to trace footsteps upon the turf which he knew had not printed it: yet, never inattentive to his own interest, when he perceived in the midst of the combustion he had raised, that Lady Margaret was incensed at the noise it produced, he artfully gave over his search, and seating himself in a chair next to her, eagerly offered to assist her with cakes, chocolate, or whatever the table afforded.

He had, however, effectually broken up the conversation; and breakfast being over, Mr Harrel ordered his chaise, and Cecilia arose to take leave.

And now not without some difficulty could Mr Monckton disguise the uneasy fears which her departure occasioned him. Taking her hand, "I suppose," he said, "you will not permit an old friend to visit you in town, lest the sight of him should prove a disagreeable memorial of the time you will soon regret having wasted in the country?"

"Why will you say this, Mr Monckton?" cried Cecilia; "I am sure you cannot think it."

"These profound studiers of mankind, madam," said Belfield, "are mighty sorry champions for constancy or friendship. They wage war with all expectations but of depravity, and grant no quarter even to the purest designs, where they think there will be any temptation to deviate from them."

"Temptation," said Mr Monckton, "is very easy of resistance in theory; but if you reflect upon the great change of situation Miss Beverley will experience, upon the new scenes she will see, the new acquaintance she must make, and the new connections she may form, you will not wonder at the anxiety of a friend for her welfare."

"But I presume," cried Belfield, with a laugh, "Miss Beverley does not mean to convey her person to town, and leave her understanding locked up, with other natural curiosities, in the country? Why, therefore, may not the same discernment regulate her adoption of new acquaintance, and choice of new connections, that guided her selection of old ones? Do you suppose that because she is to take leave of you, she is to take leave of herself?"

"Where fortune smiles upon youth and beauty," answered Mr Monckton, "do you think it nothing that their fair possessor should make a sudden transition of situation from the quietness of a retired life in the country, to the gaiety of a splendid town residence?"

"Where fortune *frowns* upon youth and beauty," returned Belfield, "they may not irrationally excite commiseration; but where nature and chance unite their forces to bless the same object, what room there may be for alarm or lamentation I confess I cannot divine."

"What!" cried Mr Monckton, with some emotion, "are there not sharpers, fortune-hunters, sycophants, wretches of all sorts and denominations, who watch the approach of the rich and unwary, feed upon their inexperience, and prey upon their property?"

"Come, come," cried Mr Harrel, "it is time I should hasten my fair ward away, if this is your method of describing the place she is going to live in."

"Is it possible," cried the Captain, advancing to Cecilia, "that this lady has never yet tried the town?" and then, lowering his voice, and smiling languishingly in her face, he added, "Can anything so divinely handsome have been immured in the country? Ah! *quelle honte!* do you make it a principle to be so cruel?"

Cecilia, thinking such a compliment merited not any other notice than a slight bow, turned to Lady Margaret, and said, "Should your ladyship be in town this winter, may I expect the honour of hearing where I may wait upon you?"

"I don't know whether I shall go or not," answered the old lady, with her usual ungraciousness.

Cecilia would now have hastened away, but Mr Monckton, stopping her, again expressed his fears of the consequences of her journey; "Be upon your guard," he cried, "with all new acquaintance; judge nobody from appearances; form no friendship rashly; take time to look about you, and remember you can make no alteration in your way of life, without greater probability of faring worse, than chance of faring better. Keep therefore as you are, and the more you see of others, the more you will rejoice that you neither resemble nor are connected with them."

"This from you, Mr Monckton!" cried Belfield, "what is become of your conformity system? I thought all the world was to be alike, or only so much the worse for any variation?"

"I spoke," said Mr Monckton, "of the world in general, not of this lady in particular; and who that knows, who that sees her, would not wish it were possible she might continue in every respect exactly and unalterably what she is at present?"

"I find," said Cecilia, "you are determined that flattery at least, should I meet with it, shall owe no pernicious effects to its novelty."

"Well, Miss Beverley," cried Mr Harrel, "will you now venture to accompany me to town? Or has Mr Monckton frightened you from proceeding any farther?"

"If," replied Cecilia, "I felt no more sorrow in quitting my friends, than I feel terror in venturing to London, with how light a heart should I make the journey!"

"Brava!" cried Belfield, "I am happy to find the discourse of Mr Monckton has not intimidated you, nor prevailed upon you to deplore your condition in having the accumulated misery of being young, fair and affluent."

"Alas! poor thing!" exclaimed the old gentleman who sat in the corner, fixing his eyes upon Cecilia with an expression of mingled grief and pity.

Cecilia started, but no one else paid him any attention.

The usual ceremonies of leave-taking now followed, and the Captain, with most obsequious reverence, advanced to conduct Cecilia to the carriage; but in the midst of the dumb eloquence of his bows and smiles, Mr Morrice, affecting not to perceive his design, skipped gaily between them, and, without any previous formality, seized the hand of Cecilia himself; failing not, however, to temper the freedom of his action by a look of respect the most profound.

The Captain shrugged and retired. But Mr Monckton, enraged at his assurance, and determined it should nothing avail him, exclaimed, "Why how now, Morrice, do you take away the privilege of my house?"

"True, true;" answered Morrice, "you members of parliament have an undoubted right to be tenacious of your privileges." Then, bowing with a look of veneration to Cecilia, he resigned her hand with an air of as much happiness as he had taken it.

Mr Monckton, in leading her to the chaise, again begged permission to wait upon her in town: Mr Harrel took the hint, and entreated him to consider his house as his own; and Cecilia, gratefully thanking him for his solicitude in her welfare, added, "And I hope, sir, you will honour me with your counsel and admonitions with respect to my future conduct, whenever you have the goodness to let me see you."

This was precisely his wish. He begged, in return, that she would treat him with confidence, and then suffered the chaise to drive off.

CHAPTER III

AN ARRIVAL.

As soon as they lost sight of the house, Cecilia expressed her surprise at the behaviour of the old gentleman who sat in the corner, whose general silence, seclusion from the company, and absence of mind, had strongly excited her curiosity.

Mr Harrel could give her very little satisfaction: he told her that he had twice or thrice met him in public places, where everybody remarked the singularity of his manners and appearance, but that he had never discoursed with anyone to whom he seemed known; and that he was as much surprised as herself in seeing so strange a character at the house of Mr Monckton.

The conversation then turned upon the family they had just quitted, and Cecilia warmly declared the good opinion she had of Mr Monckton, the obligations she owed to him for the interest which, from her childhood, he had always taken in her affairs; and her hopes of reaping much instruction from the friendship of a man who had so extensive a knowledge of the world.

Mr Harrel professed himself well satisfied that she should have such a counsellor; for though but little acquainted with him, he knew he was a man of fortune and fashion, and well esteemed in the world. They mutually compassionated his unhappy situation in domestic life, and Cecilia innocently expressed her concern at the dislike Lady Margaret seemed to have taken to her; a dislike which Mr Harrel naturally enough imputed to her youth and beauty, yet without suspecting any cause more cogent than a general jealousy of attractions of which she had herself so long outlived the possession.

As their journey drew near to its conclusion, all the uneasy and disagreeable sensations which in the bosom of Cecilia had accompanied its commencement, gave way to the expectation of quick approaching happiness in again meeting her favourite young friend.

Mrs Harrel had in childhood been her playmate, and in youth her school-fellow; a similarity of disposition with respect to sweetness of temper, had early rendered them dear to each other, though the resemblance extended no farther, Mrs Harrel having no pretensions to the wit or understanding of her friend; but she was amiable and obliging, and therefore sufficiently deserving affection, though neither blazing with attractions which laid claim to admiration, nor endowed with those superior qualities which mingle respect in the love they inspire.

From the time of her marriage, which was near three years, she had entirely quitted Suffolk, and had had no intercourse with Cecilia but by letter. She was now just returned from Violet Bank, the name given by Mr Harrel to a villa about twelve miles from London, where with a large party of company she had spent the Christmas holidays.

Their meeting was tender and affectionate; the sensibility of Cecilia's heart flowed from her eyes, and the gladness of Mrs Harrel's dimpled her cheeks.

As soon as their mutual salutations, expressions of kindness, and general inquiries had been made, Mrs Harrel begged to lead her to the drawing-room, "where," she added, "you will see some of my friends, who are impatient to be presented to you."

"I could have wished," said Cecilia, "after so long an absence, to have passed this first evening alone with you."

"They are all people who particularly desired to see you," she answered, "and I had them by way of entertaining you, as I was afraid you would be out of spirits at leaving Bury."

Cecilia, finding the kindness of her intentions, forbore any further expostulation, and quietly followed her to the drawing-room. But as the door was opened, she was struck with amazement upon finding that the apartment, which was spacious, lighted with brilliancy, and decorated with magnificence, was more than half filled with company, every one of which was dressed with gaiety and profusion.

Cecilia, who from the word friends, expected to have seen a small and private party, selected for the purpose of social converse, started involuntarily at the sight before her, and had hardly courage to proceed.

Mrs Harrel, however, took her hand and introduced her to the whole company, who were all severally named to her; a ceremonial which though not merely agreeable but even necessary to those who live in the gay world, in order to obviate distressing mistakes, or unfortunate implications in discourse, would by Cecilia have been willingly dispensed with, since to her their names were as new as their persons, and since knowing nothing of their histories, parties or connections, she could to nothing allude: it therefore served but to heighten her colour and increase her embarrassment.

A native dignity of mind, however, which had early taught her to distinguish modesty from bashfulness, enabled her in a short time to conquer her surprise, and recover her composure. She entreated Mrs Harrel to apologise for her appearance, and being seated between two young ladies, endeavoured to seem reconciled to it herself.

Nor was this very difficult; for while her dress, which she had not changed since her journey, joined to the novelty of her face, attracted general observation, the report of her fortune, which had preceded her entrance, secured to her general respect. She soon found, too, that a company was not necessarily formidable because full dressed, that familiarity could be united with magnificence, and that though to her, every one seemed attired to walk in a procession, or to grace a drawing-room, no formality was assumed, and no solemnity was affected: every one was without restraint, even rank obtained but little distinction; ease was the general plan, and entertainment the general pursuit.

Cecilia, though new to London, which city the ill-health of her uncle had hitherto prevented her seeing, was yet no stranger to company; she had passed her time in retirement, but not in obscurity, since for some years past she had presided at the table of the Dean, who was visited by the first people of the county in which he lived: and notwithstanding his parties, which were frequent though small, and elegant though private, had not prepared her for the splendour or the diversity of a London assembly, they yet, by initiating her in the practical rules of good breeding, had taught her to subdue the timid fears of total inexperience, and to repress the bashful feelings of shamefaced awkwardness; fears and feelings which rather call for compassion than admiration, and which, except in extreme youth, serve but to degrade the modesty they indicate.

She regarded, therefore, the two young ladies between whom she was seated, rather with a wish of addressing, than a shyness of being attacked by them; but the elder, Miss Larolles, was earnestly engaged in discourse with a gentleman, and the younger, Miss Leeson, totally discouraged her, by the invariable silence and gravity with which from time to time she met her eyes.

Uninterrupted, therefore, except by occasional speeches from Mr and Mrs Harrel, she spent the first part of the evening merely in surveying the company.

Nor was the company dilatory in returning her notice, since from the time of her entrance into the room, she had been the object of general regard.

The ladies took an exact inventory of her dress, and internally settled how differently they would have been attired if blessed with equal affluence.

The men disputed among themselves whether or not she was painted; and one of them asserting boldly that she rouged well, a debate ensued, which ended in a bet, and the decision was mutually agreed to depend upon the colour of her cheeks by the beginning of April, when, if unfaded by bad hours and continual dissipation, they wore the same bright bloom with which they were now glowing, her champion acknowledged that his wager would be lost.

In about half an hour the gentleman with whom Miss Larolles had been talking, left the room, and then that young lady, turning suddenly to Cecilia, exclaimed, "How odd Mr Meadows is! Do you know, he says he shan't be well enough to go to Lady Nyland's assembly! How ridiculous! as if that could hurt him."

Cecilia, surprised at an attack so little ceremonious, lent her a civil, but silent attention.

"You shall be there, shan't you?" she added.

"No, ma'am, I have not the honour of being at all known to her ladyship."

"Oh, there's nothing in that," returned she, "for Mrs Harrel can acquaint her you are here, and then, you know, she'll send you a ticket, and then you can go."

"A ticket?" repeated Cecilia, "does Lady Nyland only admit her company with tickets?"

"Oh, lord!" cried Miss Larolles, laughing immoderately, "don't you know what I mean? Why, a ticket is only a visiting card, with a name upon it; but we all call them tickets now."

Cecilia thanked her for the information, and then Miss Larolles enquired how many miles she had travelled since morning?

"Seventy-three," answered Cecilia, "which I hope will plead my apology for being so little dressed."

"Oh, you're vastly well," returned the other, "and for my part, I never think about dress. But only conceive what happened to me last year! Do you know I came to town the twentieth of March! was not that horrid provoking?"

"Perhaps so," said Cecilia, "but I am sure I cannot tell why."

"Not tell why?" repeated Miss Larolles, "why, don't you know it was the very night of the grand private masquerade at Lord Darien's? I would not have missed it for the whole universe. I never travelled in such an agony in my life: we did not get to town till monstrous late, and then do you know I had neither a ticket nor a habit! Only conceive what a distress! well, I sent to every creature I knew for a ticket, but they all said there was not one to be had; so I was just like a mad creature—but about ten or eleven o'clock, a young lady of my particular acquaintance, by the greatest good luck in the world happened to be taken suddenly ill; so she sent me her ticket,—was not that delightful?"

"For *her*, extremely!" said Cecilia, laughing.

"Well," she continued, "then I was almost out of my wits with joy; and I went about, and got one of the sweetest dresses you ever saw. If you'll call upon me some morning, I'll shew it you."

Cecilia, not prepared for an invitation so abrupt, bowed without speaking, and Miss Larolles, too happy in talking herself to be offended at the silence of another, continued her narration.

"Well, but now comes the vilest part of the business; do you know, when everything else was ready, I could not get my hair-dresser! I sent all over the town,—he was nowhere to be found; I thought I should have died with vexation; I assure you I cried so that if I had not gone in a mask, I should have been ashamed to be seen. And so, after all this monstrous fatigue, I was forced to have my hair dressed by my own maid, quite in a common way; was not it cruelly mortifying?"

"Why yes," answered Cecilia, "I should think it was almost sufficient to make you regret the illness of the young lady who sent you her ticket."

They were now interrupted by Mrs Harrel, who advanced to them followed by a young man of a serious aspect and modest demeanour, and said, "I am happy to see you both so well engaged; but my brother has been reproaching me with presenting everybody to Miss Beverley but himself."

"I cannot hope," said Mr Arnott, "that I have any place in the recollection of Miss Beverley, but long as I have been absent from Suffolk, and unfortunate as I was in not seeing her during my last visit there, I am yet sure, even at this distance of time, grown and formed as she is, I should instantly have known her."

"Amazing!" cried an elderly gentleman, in a tone of irony, who was standing near them, "for the face is a very common one!"

"I remember well," said Cecilia, "that when you left Suffolk I thought I had lost my best friend."

"Is that possible?" cried Mr Arnott, with a look of much delight.

"Yes, indeed, and not without reason, for in all disputes you were my advocate; in all plays, my companion; and in all difficulties, my assistant."

"Madam," cried the same gentleman, "if you liked him because he was your advocate, companion, and assistant, pray like me too, for I am ready to become all three at once."

"You are very good," said Cecilia, laughing, "but at present I find no want of any defender."

"That's pity," he returned, "for Mr Arnott seems to me very willing to act the same parts over again with you."

"But for that purpose he must return to the days of his childhood."

"Ah, would to heaven it were possible!" cried Mr Arnott, "for they were the happiest of my life."

"After such a confession," said his companion, "surely you will let him attempt to renew them? 'tis but taking a walk backwards; and though it is very early in life for Mr Arnott to sigh for that retrograde motion, which, in the regular course of things, we shall all in our turns desire, yet with such a motive as recovering Miss Beverley for a playfellow, who can wonder that he anticipates in youth the hopeless wishes of age?"

Here Miss Larolles, who was one of that numerous tribe of young ladies to whom all conversation is irksome in which they are not themselves engaged, quitted her place, of which Mr Gosport, Cecilia's new acquaintance, immediately took possession.

"Is it utterly impossible," continued this gentleman, "that I should assist in procuring Mr Arnott such a renovation? Is there no subaltern part I can perform to facilitate the project? for I will either *hide* or *seek* with any boy in the parish; and for a *Q in the corner*, there is none more celebrated."

"I have no doubt, sir," answered Cecilia, "of your accomplishments; and I should be not a little entertained with the surprize of the company if you could persuade yourself to display them." "And what," cried he, "could the company do half so well as to rise also, and join in the sport? it would but interrupt some tale of scandal, or some description of a *toupee*. Active wit, however despicable when compared with intellectual, is yet surely better than the insignificant click-clack of modish conversation," casting his eyes towards Miss Larolles, "or even the pensive dullness of affected silence," changing their direction towards Miss Leeson.

Cecilia, though surprised at an attack upon the society her friend had selected, by one who was admitted to make a part of it, felt its justice too strongly to be offended at its severity.

"I have often wished," he continued, "that when large parties are collected, as here, without any possible reason why they might not as well be separated, something could be proposed in which each person might innocently take a share: for surely after the first half-hour, they can find little new to observe in the dress of their neighbours, or to display in their own; and with whatever seeming gaiety they may contrive to fill up the middle and end of the evening, by wire-drawing the comments afforded by the beginning, they are yet so miserably fatigued, that if they have not four or five places to run to every night, they suffer nearly as much from weariness of their friends in company, as they would do from weariness of themselves in solitude."

Here, by the general breaking up of the party, the conversation was interrupted, and Mr Gosport was obliged to make his exit; not much to the regret of Cecilia, who was impatient to be alone with Mrs Harrel.

The rest of the evening, therefore, was spent much more to her satisfaction; it was devoted to friendship, to mutual enquiries, to kind congratulations, and endearing recollections; and though it was late when she retired, she retired with reluctance.

CHAPTER IV

A SKETCH OF HIGH LIFE.

Eager to renew a conversation which had afforded her so much pleasure, Cecilia, neither sensible of fatigue from her change of hours nor her journey, arose with the light, and as soon as she was dressed, hastened to the breakfast apartment.

She had not, however, been more impatient to enter than she soon became to quit it; for though not much surprized to find herself there before her friend, her ardour for waiting her arrival was somewhat chilled, upon finding the fire but just lighted, the room cold, and the servants still employed in putting it in order.

At 10 o'clock she made another attempt: the room was then better prepared for her reception, but still it was empty. Again she was retiring, when the appearance of Mr Arnott stopped her.

He expressed his surprize at her early rising, in a manner that marked the pleasure it gave to him; and then, returning to the conversation of the preceding evening, he expatiated with warmth and feeling upon the happiness of his boyish days, remembered every circumstance belonging to the plays in which they had formerly been companions, and dwelt upon every incident with a minuteness of delight that shewed his unwillingness ever to have done with the subject.

This discourse detained her till they were joined by Mrs Harrel, and then another, more gay and more general succeeded to it.

During their breakfast, Miss Larolles was announced as a visitor to Cecilia, to whom she immediately advanced with the intimacy of an old acquaintance, taking her hand, and assuring her she could no longer defer the honour of waiting upon her.

Cecilia, much amazed at this warmth of civility from one to whom she was almost a stranger, received her compliment rather coldly; but Miss Larolles, without consulting her looks, or attending to her manner, proceeded to express the earnest desire she had long had to be known to her; to hope they should meet very often; to declare nothing could make her so happy; and to beg leave to recommend to her notice her own milliner.

"I assure you," she continued, "she has all Paris in her disposal; the sweetest caps! the most beautiful trimmings! and her ribbons are quite divine! It is the most dangerous thing you can conceive to go near her; I never trust myself in her room but I am sure to be ruined. If you please, I'll take you to her this morning."

"If her acquaintance is so ruinous," said Cecilia, "I think I had better avoid it."

"Oh, impossible! there's no such thing as living without her. To be sure she's shockingly dear, that I must own; but then who can wonder? She makes such sweet things, 'tis impossible to pay her too much for them."

Mrs Harrel now joining in the recommendation, the party was agreed upon, and accompanied by Mr Arnott, the ladies proceeded to the house of the milliner.

Here the raptures of Miss Larolles were again excited: she viewed the finery displayed with delight inexpressible, enquired who were the intended possessors, heard their names with envy, and sighed with all the bitterness of mortification that she was unable to order home almost everything she looked at.

Having finished their business here, they proceeded to various other dress manufacturers, in whose praises Miss Larolles was almost equally eloquent, and to appropriate whose goods she was almost equally earnest: and then, after attending this loquacious young lady to her father's house, Mrs Harrel and Cecilia returned to their own.

Cecilia rejoiced at the separation, and congratulated herself that the rest of the day might be spent alone with her friend.

"Why, no," said Mrs Harrel, "not absolutely alone, for I expect some company at night."

"Company again to-night?"

"Nay, don't be frightened, for it will be a very small party; not more than fifteen or twenty in all."

"Is that so small a party?" said Cecilia, smiling; "and how short a time since would you, as well as I, have reckoned it a large one!"

"Oh, you mean when I lived in the country," returned Mrs Harrel; "but what in the world could I know of parties or company then?"

"Not much, indeed," said Cecilia, "as my present ignorance shews."

They then parted to dress for dinner.

The company of this evening were again all strangers to Cecilia, except Miss Leeson, who was seated next to her, and whose frigid looks again compelled her to observe the same silence she so resolutely practised herself. Yet not the less was her internal surprise that a lady who seemed determined neither to give nor receive any entertainment, should repeatedly chuse to show herself in a company with no part of which she associated.

Mr Arnott, who contrived to occupy the seat on her other side, suffered not the silence with which her fair neighbour had infected her to spread any further: he talked, indeed, upon no new subject; and upon the old one, of their former sports and amusements, he had already exhausted all that was worth being mentioned; but not yet had he exhausted the pleasure he received from the theme; it seemed always fresh and always enchanting to him; it employed his thoughts, regaled his imagination, and enlivened his discourse. Cecilia in vain tried to change it for another; he quitted it only by compulsion, and returned to it with redoubled eagerness.

When the company was retired, and Mr Arnott only remained with the ladies, Cecilia, with no little surprise, inquired for Mr Harrel, observing that she had not seen him the whole day.

"O!" cried his lady, "don't think of wondering at that, for it happens continually. He dines at home, indeed, in general, but otherwise I should see nothing of him at all."

"Indeed? why, how does he fill up his time?"

"That I am sure I cannot tell, for he never consults me about it; but I suppose much in the same way that other people do."

"Ah, Priscilla!" cried Cecilia, with some earnestness, "how little did I ever expect to see you so much a fine lady!"

"A fine lady?" repeated Mrs Harrel; "why, what is it I do? Don't I live exactly like every body else that mixes at all with the world?"

"You, Miss Beverley," said Mr Arnott in a low voice, "will I hope give to the world an example, not take one from it."

Soon after, they separated for the night.

The next morning, Cecilia took care to fill up her time more advantageously, than in wandering about the house in search of a companion she now expected not to find: she got together her books, arranged them to her fancy, and secured to herself for the future occupation of her leisure hours, the exhaustless fund of entertainment which reading, that richest, highest, and noblest source of intellectual enjoyment, perpetually affords.

While they were yet at breakfast, they were again visited by Miss Larolles. "I am come," cried she, eagerly, "to run away with you both to my Lord Belgrade's sale. All the world will be there; and we shall go in with tickets, and you have no notion how it will be crowded."

"What is to be sold there?" said Cecilia.

"Oh, every thing you can conceive; house, stables, china, laces, horses, caps, everything in the world."

"And do you intend to buy any thing?"

"Lord, no; but one likes to see the people's things."

Cecilia then begged they would excuse her attendance.

"O, by no means!" cried Miss Larolles; "you must go, I assure you; there'll be such a monstrous crowd as you never saw in your life. I dare say we shall be half squeezed to death."

"That," said Cecilia, "is an inducement which you must not expect will have much weight with a poor rustic just out of the country: it must require all the polish of a long residence in the metropolis to make it attractive."

"O but do go, for I assure you it will be the best sale we shall have this season. I can't imagine, Mrs Harrel, what poor Lady Belgrade will do with herself; I hear the creditors have seized every thing; I really believe creditors are the cruelest set of people in the world! they have taken those beautiful buckles out of her shoes! Poor soul! I declare it will make my heart ache to see them put up. It's quite shocking, upon my word. I wonder who'll buy them. I assure you they were the prettiest fancied I ever saw. But come, if we don't go directly, there will be no getting in."

Cecilia again desired to be excused accompanying them, adding that she wished to spend the day at home.

"At home, my dear?" cried Mrs Harrel; "why we have been engaged to Mrs Mears this month, and she begged me to prevail with you to be of the party. I expect she'll call, or send you a ticket, every moment"

"How unlucky for me," said Cecilia, "that you should happen to have so many engagements just at this time! I hope, at least, there will not be any for to-morrow."

"O yes; to-morrow we go to Mrs Elton's."

"Again to-morrow? and how long is this to last?"

"O, heaven knows; I'll shew you my catalogue."

She then produced a book which contained a list of engagements for more than three weeks. "And as these," she said, "are struck off, new ones are made; and so it is we go on till after the birth-day."

When this list had been examined and commented upon by Miss Larolles, and viewed and wondered at by Cecilia, it was restored to its place, the two ladies went together to the auction, permitting Cecilia, at her repeated request, to return to her own apartment.

She returned, however, neither satisfied with the behaviour of her friend, nor pleased with her own situation: the sobriety of her education, as it had early instilled into her mind the pure dictates of religion, and strict principles of honour, had also taught her to regard continual dissipation as an introduction to vice, and unbounded extravagance as the harbinger of injustice. Long accustomed to see Mrs Harrel in the same retirement in which she had hitherto lived herself, when books were their first amusement, and the society of each other was their chief happiness, the change she now perceived in her mind and manners equally concerned and surprised her. She found her insensible to friendship, indifferent to her husband, and negligent of all social felicity. Dress, company, parties of pleasure, and public places, seemed not merely to occupy all her time; but to gratify all her wishes. Cecilia, in whose heart glowed the warmest affections and most generous virtue, was cruelly depressed and mortified by this disappointment; yet she had the good sense to determine against upbraiding her, well aware that if reproach has any power over indifference, it is only that of changing it into aversion.

Mrs Harrel, in truth, was innocent of heart, though dissipated in life; married very young, she had made an immediate transition from living in a private family and a country town, to becoming mistress of one of the most elegant houses in Portman-square, at the head of a splendid fortune, and wife to a man whose own pursuits soon showed her the little value he himself set upon domestic happiness. Immersed in the fashionable round of company and diversions, her understanding, naturally weak, was easily dazzled by the brilliancy of her situation; greedily, therefore, sucking in air impregnated with luxury and extravagance, she had soon no pleasure but to vie with some rival in elegance, and no ambition but to exceed some superior in expence.

The Dean of—in naming Mr Harrel for one of the guardians of his niece, had no other view than that of indulging her wishes by allowing her to reside in the house of her friend: he had little personal knowledge of him, but was satisfied with the nomination, because acquainted with his family, fortune, and connections, all which persuaded him to believe without further enquiry, that it was more peculiarly proper for his niece than any other he could make.

In his choice of the other two trustees he had been more prudent; the first of these, the honourable Mr Delvile, was a man of high birth and character; the second, Mr Briggs, had spent his whole life in business, in which he had already amassed an immense fortune, and had still no greater pleasure than that of encreasing it. From the high honour, therefore, of Mr Delvile, he expected the most scrupulous watchfulness that his niece should in nothing be injured, and from the experience of Mr Briggs in money matters, and his diligence in transacting business, he hoped for the most vigilant observance that her fortune, while under his care, should be turned to the best account. And thus, as far as he was able, he had equally consulted her pleasure, her security, and her pecuniary advantage.

Mrs Harrel returned home only in time to dress for the rest of the day.

When Cecilia was summoned to dinner, she found, besides her host and hostess and Mr Arnott, a gentleman she had not before seen, but who as soon as she entered the parlour, Mr Harrel presented to her, saying at the same time he was one of the most intimate of his friends.

This gentleman, Sir Robert Floyer, was about thirty years of age; his face was neither remarkable for its beauty nor its ugliness, but sufficiently distinguished by its expression of invincible assurance; his person, too, though neither striking for its grace nor its deformity, attracted notice from the insolence of his deportment. His manners, haughty and supercilious, marked the high opinion he cherished of his own importance; and his air and address, at once bold and negligent, announced his happy perfection in the character at which he aimed, that of an accomplished man of the town.

The moment Cecilia appeared, she became the object of his attention, though neither with the look of admiration due to her beauty, nor yet with that of curiosity excited by her novelty, but with the scrutinizing observation of a man on the point of making a bargain, who views with fault-seeking eyes the property he means to cheapen.

Cecilia, wholly unused to an examination so little ceremonious, shrunk abashed from his regards: but his conversation was not less displeasing to her than his looks; his principal subjects, which were horse-racing, losses at play, and disputes at gaming-tables, could afford her but little amusement, because she could not understand them; and the episodes with which they were occasionally interspersed, consisting chiefly of comparative strictures upon celebrated beauties, hints of impending bankruptcies, and witticisms upon recent divorces, were yet more disagreeable to her, because more intelligible. Wearied, therefore, with uninteresting anecdotes, and offended with injudicious subjects of pleasantry, she waited with impatience for the moment of retiring; but Mrs Harrel, less eager, because better entertained, was in no haste to remove, and therefore she was compelled to remain quiet, till they were both obliged to arise, in order to fulfil their engagement with Mrs Mears.

As they went together to the house of that lady, in Mrs Harrel's vis-a-vis, Cecilia, not doubting but their opinions concerning the Baronet would accord, instantly and openly declared her disapprobation of every thing he had uttered; but Mrs Harrel, far from confirming her expectations, only said, "I am sorry you don't like him, for he is almost always with us?"

"Do you like him, then, yourself?"

"Extremely; he is very entertaining and clever, and knows the world."

"How judiciously do you praise him!" cried Cecilia; "and how long might you deliberate before you could add another word to his panegyric!"

Mrs Harrel, satisfied to commend, without even attempting to vindicate him, was soon content to change the subject; and Cecilia, though much concerned that the husband of her friend had made so disgraceful an election of a favourite, yet hoped that the lenity of Mrs Harrel resulted from her desire to excuse his choice, not from her own approbation.

CHAPTER V

AN ASSEMBLY.

Mrs Mears, whose character was of that common sort which renders delineation superfluous, received them with the customary forms of good breeding.

Mrs Harrel soon engaged herself at a card-table; and Cecilia, who declined playing, was seated next to Miss Leeson, who arose to return the courtesy she made in advancing to her, but that past, did not again even look at her.

Cecilia, though fond of conversation and formed for society, was too diffident to attempt speaking where so little encouraged; they both, therefore, continued silent, till Sir Robert Floyer, Mr Harrel, and Mr Arnott entered the room together, and all at the same time advanced to Cecilia.

"What," cried Mr Harrel, "don't you chuse to play, Miss Beverley?"

"I flatter myself," cried Mr Arnott, "that Miss Beverley never plays at all, for then, in one thing, I shall have the honour to resemble her."

"Very seldom, indeed," answered Cecilia, "and consequently very ill."

"O, you must take a few lessons," said Mr Harrel, "Sir Robert Floyer, I am sure, will be proud to instruct you."

Sir Robert, who had placed himself opposite to her, and was staring full in her face, made a slight inclination of his head, and said, "Certainly."

"I should be a very unpromising pupil," returned Cecilia, "for I fear I should not only want diligence to improve, but desire."

"Oh, you will learn better things," said Mr Harrel; "we have had you yet but three days amongst us,—in three months we shall see the difference."

"I hope not," cried Mr Arnott, "I earnestly hope there will be none!"

Mr Harrel now joined another party; and Mr Arnott seeing no seat vacant near that of Cecilia, moved round to the back of her chair, where he patiently stood for the rest of the evening. But Sir Robert still kept his post, and still, without troubling himself to speak, kept his eyes fixed upon the same object.

Cecilia, offended by his boldness, looked a thousand ways to avoid him; but her embarrassment, by giving greater play to her features, served only to keep awake an attention which might otherwise have wearied. She was almost tempted to move her chair round and face Mr Arnott, but though she wished to shew her disapprobation of the Baronet, she had not yet been reconciled by fashion to turning her back upon the company at large, for the indulgence of conversing with some particular person: a fashion which to unaccustomed observers seems rude and repulsive, but which, when once adopted, carries with it imperceptibly its own recommendation, in the ease, convenience and freedom it promotes.

Thus disagreeably stationed, she found but little assistance from the neighbourhood of Mr Arnott, since even his own desire of conversing with her, was swallowed up by an anxious and involuntary impulse to watch the looks and motions of Sir Robert.

At length, quite tired of sitting as if merely an object to be gazed at, she determined to attempt entering into conversation with Miss Leeson.

The difficulty, however, was not inconsiderable how to make the attack; she was unacquainted with her friends and connections, uninformed of her way of thinking, or her way of life, ignorant even of the sound of her voice, and chilled by the coldness of her aspect: yet, having no other alternative, she was more willing to encounter the forbidding looks of this lady, than to continue silently abashed under the scrutinizing eyes of Sir Robert.

After much deliberation with what subject to begin, she remembered that Miss Larolles had been present the first time they had met, and thought it probable they might be acquainted with each other; and therefore, bending forward, she ventured to enquire if she had lately seen that young lady?

Miss Leeson, in a voice alike inexpressive of satisfaction or displeasure, quietly answered, "No, ma'am."

Cecilia, discouraged by this conciseness, was a few minutes silent; but the perseverance of Sir Robert in staring at her, exciting her own in trying to avoid his eyes, she exerted herself so far as to add, "Does Mrs Mears expect Miss Larolles here this evening?"

Miss Leeson, without raising her head, gravely replied, "I don't know, ma'am."

All was now to be done over again, and a new subject to be started, for she could suggest nothing further to ask concerning Miss Larolles.

Cecilia had seen, little of life, but that little she had well marked, and her observation had taught her, that among fashionable people, public places seemed a never-failing source of conversation and entertainment: upon this topic, therefore, she hoped for better success; and as to those who have spent more time in the country than in London, no place of amusement is so interesting as a theatre, she opened the subject she had so happily suggested, by an enquiry whether any new play had lately come out?

Miss Leeson, with the same dryness, only answered, "Indeed, I can't tell."

Another pause now followed, and the spirits of Cecilia were considerably dampt; but happening accidentally to recollect the name of Almack, she presently revived, and, congratulating herself that she should now be able to speak of a place too fashionable for disdain, she asked her, in a manner somewhat more assured, if she was a subscriber to his assemblies?

"Yes, ma'am."

"Do you go to them constantly?"

"No, ma'am."

Again they were both silent. And now, tired of finding the ill-success of each particular enquiry, she thought a more general one might obtain an answer less laconic, and therefore begged she would inform her what was the most fashionable place of diversion for the present season?

This question, however, cost Miss Leeson no more trouble than any which had preceded it, for she only replied, "Indeed I don't know."

Cecilia now began to sicken of her attempt, and for some minutes to give it up as hopeless; but afterwards when she reflected how frivolous were the questions she had asked, she felt more inclined to pardon the answers she had received, and in a short time to fancy she had mistaken contempt for stupidity, and to grow less angry with Miss Leeson than ashamed of herself.

This supposition excited her to make yet another trial of her talents for conversation, and therefore, summoning all the courage in her power, she modestly apologised for the liberty she was taking, and then begged her permission to enquire whether there was anything new in the literary way that she thought worth recommending?

Miss Leeson now turned her eyes towards her, with a look that implied a doubt whether she had heard right; and when the attentive attitude of Cecilia confirmed her question, surprise for a few instants took place of insensibility, and with rather more spirit than she had yet shown, she answered, "Indeed, I know nothing of the matter."

Cecilia was now utterly disconcerted; and half angry with herself, and wholly provoked with her sullen neighbour, she resolved to let nothing in future provoke her to a similar trial with so unpromising a subject.

She had not, however, much longer to endure the examination of Sir Robert, who being pretty well satisfied with staring, turned upon his heel, and was striding out of the room, when he was stopt by Mr Gosport, who for some time had been watching him.

Mr Gosport was a man of good parts, and keen satire: minute in his observations, and ironical in his expressions.

"So you don't play, Sir Robert?" he cried.

"What, here? No, I am going to Brookes's."

"But how do you like Harrel's ward? You have taken a pretty good survey of her."

"Why, faith, I don't know; but not much, I think; she's a devilish fine woman, too; but she has no spirit, no life."

"Did you try her? Have you talked to her?"

"Not I, truly!"

"Nay, then how do you mean to judge of her?"

"O, faith, that's all over, now; one never thinks of talking to the women by way of trying them."

"What other method, then, have you adopted?"

"None."

"None? Why, then, how do you go on?"

"Why, they talk to us. The women take all that trouble upon themselves now."

"And pray how long may you have commenced *fade macaroni?* For this is a part of your character with which I was not acquainted."

"Oh, hang it, 'tis not from *ton*; no, it's merely from laziness. Who the d—l will fatigue himself with dancing attendance upon the women, when keeping them at a distance makes them dance attendance upon us?"

Then stalking from him to Mr Harrel, he took him by the arm, and they left the room together.

Mr Gosport now advanced to Cecilia, and addressing her so as not to be heard by Miss Leeson, said, "I have been wishing to approach you, some time, but the fear that you are already overpowered by the loquacity of your fair neighbour makes me cautious of attempting to engage you."

"You mean," said Cecilia, "to laugh at *my* loquacity, and indeed its ill success has rendered it sufficiently ridiculous."

"Are you, then, yet to learn," cried he, "that there are certain young ladies who make it a rule never to speak but to their own cronies? Of this class is Miss Leeson, and till you get into her particular coterie, you must never expect to hear from her a word of two syllables. The TON misses, as they are called, who now infest the town, are in two divisions, the SUPERCILIOUS, and the VOLUBLE. The SUPERCILIOUS, like Miss Leeson, are silent, scornful, languid, and affected, and disdain all converse but with those of their own set: the VOLUBLE, like Miss Larolles, are flirting, communicative, restless, and familiar, and attack without the smallest ceremony, every one they think worthy their notice. But this they have in common, that at home they think of nothing but dress, abroad, of nothing but admiration, and that every where they hold in supreme contempt all but themselves."

"Probably, then," said Cecilia, "I have passed tonight, for one of the VOLUBLES; however, all the advantage has been with the SUPERCILIOUS, for I have suffered a total repulse."

"Are you sure, however, you have not talked too well for her?"

"O, a child of five years old ought to have been whipt for not talking better!"

"But it is not capacity alone you are to consult when you talk with misses of the TON; were their understandings only to be considered, they would indeed be wonderfully easy of access! in order, therefore, to render their commerce somewhat difficult, they will only be pleased by an observance of their humours: which are ever most various and most exuberant where the intellects are weakest and least cultivated. I have, however, a receipt which I have found infallible for engaging the attention of young ladies of whatsoever character or denomination."

"O, then," cried Cecilia, "pray favour me with it, for I have here an admirable opportunity to try its efficacy."

"I will give it you," he answered, "with full directions. When you meet with a young lady who seems resolutely determined not to speak, or who, if compelled by a direct question to make some answer, drily gives a brief affirmative, or coldly a laconic negative—"

"A case in point," interrupted Cecilia.

"Well, thus circumstanced," he continued, "the remedy I have to propose consists of three topics of discourse."

"Pray what are they?"

"Dress, public places, and love."

Cecilia, half surprised and half diverted, waited a fuller explanation without giving any interruption.

"These three topics," he continued, "are to answer three purposes, since there are no less than three causes from which the silence of young ladies may proceed: sorrow, affectation, and stupidity."

"Do you, then," cried Cecilia, "give nothing at all to modesty?"

"I give much to it," he answered, "as an excuse, nay almost as an equivalent for wit; but for that sullen silence which resists all encouragement, modesty is a mere pretence, not a cause."

"You must, however, be somewhat more explicit, if you mean that I should benefit from your instructions."

"Well, then," he answered, "I will briefly enumerate the three causes, with directions for the three methods of cure. To begin with sorrow. The taciturnity which really results from that is attended with an incurable absence of mind, and a total unconsciousness of the observation which it excites; upon this occasion, public places may sometimes be tried in vain, and even dress may fail; but love—"

"Are you sure, then," said Cecilia, with a laugh, "that sorrow has but that one source?"

"By no means," answered he, "for perhaps papa may have been angry, or mama may have been cross; a milliner may have sent a wrong pompoon, or a chaperon to an assembly may have been taken ill—"

"Bitter subjects of affliction, indeed! And are these all you allow us?"

"Nay, I speak but of young ladies of fashion, and what of greater importance can befall them? If, therefore, the grief of the fair patient proceeds from papa, mama, or the chaperon, then the mention of public places, those endless incentives of displeasure between the old and the young, will draw forth her complaints, and her complaints will bring their own cure, for those who lament find speedy consolation: if the milliner has occasioned the calamity, the discussion of dress will have the same effect; should both these medicines fail, love, as I said before, will be found infallible, for you will then have investigated every subject of uneasiness which a youthful female in high life can experience."

"They are greatly obliged to you," cried Cecilia, bowing, "for granting them motives of sorrow so honourable, and I thank you in the name of the whole sex."

"You, madam," said he, returning her bow, "are I hope an exception in the happiest way, that of having no sorrow at all. I come, now, to the silence of affectation, which is presently discernible by the roving of the eye round the room to see if it is heeded, by the sedulous care to avoid an accidental smile, and by the variety of disconsolate attitudes exhibited to the beholders. This species of silence has almost without exception its origin in that babyish vanity which is always gratified by exciting attention, without ever perceiving that it provokes contempt. In these cases, as nature is wholly out of the question, and the mind is guarded against its own feelings, dress and public places are almost certain of failing, but here again love is sure to vanquish; as soon as it is named, attention becomes involuntary, and in a short time a struggling simper discomposes the arrangement of the features, and then the business is presently over, for the young lady is either supporting some system, or opposing some proposition, before she is well aware that she has been cheated out of her sad silence at all."

"So much," said Cecilia, "for sorrow and for affectation. Proceed next to stupidity; for that, in all probability, I shall most frequently encounter." "That always must be heavy work," returned he, "yet the road is plain, though it is all up hill. Love, here, may be talked of without exciting any emotion, or provoking any reply, and dress may be dilated upon without producing any other effect than that of attracting a vacant stare; but public places are indubitably certain of success. Dull and heavy characters, incapable of animating from wit or from reason, because unable to keep pace with them, and void of all internal sources of entertainment, require the stimulation of shew, glare, noise, and bustle, to interest or awaken them. Talk to them of such subjects, and they adore you; no matter whether you paint to them joy or horror, let there but be action, and they are content; a battle has charms for them equal to a coronation, and a funeral amuses them as much as a wedding."

"I am much obliged to you," said Cecilia, smiling, "for these instructions; yet I must confess I know not how upon the present occasion to make use of them: public places I have already tried, but tried in vain; dress I dare not mention, as I have not yet learned its technical terms—"

"Well, but," interrupted he, "be not desperate; you have yet the third topic unessayed."

"O, that," returned she, laughing, "I leave to you."

"Pardon me," cried he; "love is a source of loquacity only with yourselves: when it is started by men, young ladies dwindle into mere listeners. *Simpering* listeners, I confess; but it is only with one another that you will discuss its merits."

At this time they were interrupted by the approach of Miss Larolles, who, tripping towards Cecilia, exclaimed, "Lord, how glad I am to see you! So you would not go to the auction! Well, you had a prodigious loss, I assure you. All the wardrobe was sold, and all Lady Belgrade's trinkets. I never saw such a collection of sweet things in my life. I was ready to cry that I could not bid for half a hundred of them. I declare I was kept in an agony the whole morning. I would not but have been there for the world. Poor Lady Belgrade! you really can't conceive how I was shocked for her. All her beautiful things sold for almost nothing. I assure you, if you had seen how they went, you would have lost all patience. It's a thousand pities you were not there."

"On the contrary," said Cecilia, "I think I had a very fortunate escape, for the loss of patience without the acquisition of the trinkets, would have been rather mortifying."

"Yes," said Mr Gosport; "but when you have lived some time longer in this commercial city, you will find the exchange of patience for mortification the most common and constant traffic amongst its inhabitants."

"Pray, have you been here long?" cried Miss Larolles, "for I have been to twenty places, wondering I did not meet with you before. But whereabouts is Mrs Mears? O, I see her now; I'm sure there's no mistaking her; I could know her by that old red gown half a mile off. Did you ever see such a frightful thing in your life? And it's never off her back. I believe she sleeps in it. I am sure I have seen her in nothing else all winter. It quite tires one's eye. She's a monstrous shocking dresser. But do you know I have met with the most provoking thing in the world this evening? I declare it has made me quite sick. I was never in such a passion in my life. You can conceive nothing like it."

"Like what?" cried Cecilia, laughing; "your passion, or your provocation?"

"Why, I'll tell you what it was, and then you shall judge if it was not quite past endurance. You must know I commissioned a particular friend of mine, Miss Moffat, to buy me a trimming when she went to Paris; well, she sent it me over about a month ago by Mr Meadows, and it's the sweetest thing you ever saw in your life; but I would not make it up, because there was not a creature in town, so I thought to bring it out quite new in about a week's time, for you know any thing does till after Christmas. Well, to-night at Lady Jane Dranet's, who should I meet but Miss Moffat! She had been in town some days, but so monstrously engaged I could never find her at home. Well, I was quite delighted to see her, for you must know she's a prodigious favourite with me, so I ran up to her in a great hurry to shake hands, and what do you think was the first thing that struck my eyes? Why, just such a trimming as my own, upon a nasty, odious gown, and half dirty! Can you conceive anything so distressing? I could have cried with pleasure."

"Why so?" said Cecilia. "If her trimming is dirty, yours will look the more delicate."

"O Lord! but it's making it seem quite an old thing! Half the town will get something like it. And I quite ruined myself to buy it. I declare, I don't think anything was ever half so mortifying. It distressed me so, I could hardly speak to her. If she had stayed a month or two longer, I should not have minded it, but it was the cruellest thing in the world to come over just now. I wish the Custom-house officers had kept all her cloaths till summer."

"The wish is tender, indeed," said Cecilia, "for a *particular friend*."

Mrs Mears now rising from the card-table, Miss Larolles tript away to pay her compliments to her.

"Here, at least," cried Cecilia, "no receipt seems requisite for the cure of silence! I would have Miss Larolles be the constant companion of Miss Leeson: they could not but agree admirably, since that SUPERCILIOUS young lady seems determined never to speak, and the VOLUBLE Miss Larolles never to be silent. Were each to borrow something of the other, how greatly would both be the better!"

"The composition would still be a sorry one," answered Mr Gosport, "for I believe they are equally weak, and equally ignorant; the only difference is, that one, though silly, is quick, the other, though deliberate, is stupid. Upon a short acquaintance, that heaviness which leaves to others the whole weight of discourse, and whole search of entertainment, is the most fatiguing, but, upon a longer intimacy, even that is less irksome and less offensive, than the flippancy which hears nothing but itself."

Mrs Harrel arose now to depart, and Cecilia, not more tired of the beginning of the evening than entertained with its conclusion, was handed to the carriage by Mr Arnott.

CHAPTER VI

A BREAKFAST.

The next morning, during breakfast, a servant acquainted Cecilia that a young gentleman was in the hall, who begged to speak with her. She desired he might be admitted; and Mrs Harrel, laughing, asked if she ought not to quit the room; while Mr Arnott, with even more than his usual gravity, directed his eye towards the door to watch who should enter.

Neither of them, however, received any satisfaction when it was opened, for the gentleman who made his appearance was unknown to both: but great was the amazement of Cecilia, though little her emotion, when she saw Mr Morrice!

He came forward with an air of the most profound respect for the company in general, and obsequiously advancing to Cecilia, made an earnest enquiry into her health after her journey, and hoped she had heard good news from her friends in the country.

Mrs Harrel, naturally concluding both from his visit and behaviour, that he was an acquaintance of some intimacy, very civilly offered him a seat and some breakfast, which, very frankly, he accepted. But Mr Arnott, who already felt the anxiety of a rising passion which was too full of veneration to be sanguine, looked at him with uneasiness, and waited his departure with impatience.

Cecilia began to imagine he had been commissioned to call upon her with some message from Mr Monckton: for she knew not how to suppose that merely and accidentally having spent an hour or two in the same room with her, would authorize a visiting acquaintance. Mr Morrice, however, had a faculty the most happy of reconciling his pretensions to his inclination; and therefore she soon found that the pretence she had suggested appeared to him unnecessary. To lead, however, to the subject from which she expected his excuse, she enquired how long he had left Suffolk?

"But yesterday noon, ma'am," he answered, "or I should certainly have taken the liberty to wait upon you before."

Cecilia, who had only been perplexing herself to devise some reason why he came at all, now looked at him with a grave surprize, which would totally have abashed a man whose courage had been less, or whose expectations had been greater; but Mr Morrice, though he had hazarded every danger upon the slightest chance of hope, knew too well the weakness of his claims to be confident of success, and had been too familiar with rebuffs to be much hurt by receiving them. He might possibly have something to gain, but he knew he had nothing to lose.

"I had the pleasure," he continued, "to leave all our friends well, except poor Lady Margaret, and she has had an attack of the asthma; yet she would not have a physician, though Mr Monckton would fain have persuaded her: however, I believe the old lady knows better things." And he looked archly at Cecilia: but perceiving that the insinuation gave her nothing but disgust, he changed his tone, and added, "It is amazing how well they live together; nobody would imagine the disparity in their years. Poor old lady! Mr Monckton will really have a great loss of her when she dies."

"A loss of her!" repeated Mrs Harrel, "I am sure she is an exceeding ill-natured old woman. When I lived at Bury, I was always frightened out of my wits at the sight of her."

"Why indeed, ma'am," said Morrice, "I must own her appearance is rather against her: I had myself a great aversion to her at first sight. But the house is chearful,—very chearful; I like to spend a few days there now and then of all things. Miss Bennet, too, is agreeable enough, and—"

"Miss Bennet agreeable!" cried Mrs Harrel, "I think she's the most odious creature I ever knew in my life; a nasty, spiteful old maid!"

"Why indeed, ma'am, as you say," answered Morrice, "she is not very young; and as to her temper, I confess I know very little about it; and Mr Monckton is likely enough to try it, for he is pretty severe."

"Mr Monckton," cried Cecilia, extremely provoked at hearing him censured by a man she thought highly honoured in being permitted to approach him, "whenever *I* have been his guest, has merited from me nothing but praise and gratitude."

"O," cried Morrice, eagerly, "there is not a more worthy man in the world! he has so much wit, so much politeness! I don't know a more charming man anywhere than my friend Mr Monckton." Cecilia now perceiving that the opinions of her new acquaintance were as pliant as his bows, determined to pay him no further attention, and hoped by sitting silent to force from him the business of his visit, if any he had, or if, as she now suspected, he had none, to weary him into a retreat.

But this plan, though it would have succeeded with herself, failed with Mr Morrice, who to a stock of good humour that made him always ready to oblige others, added an equal portion of insensibility that hardened him against all indignity. Finding, therefore, that Cecilia, to whom his visit was intended, seemed already satisfied with its length, he prudently forbore to torment her; but perceiving that the lady of the house was more accessible, he quickly made a transfer of his attention, and addressed his discourse to her with as much pleasure as if his only view had been to see her, and as much ease as if he had known her all his life.

With Mrs Harrel this conduct was not injudicious; she was pleased with his assiduity, amused with his vivacity, and sufficiently satisfied with his understanding. They conversed, therefore, upon pretty equal terms, and neither of them were yet tired, when they were interrupted by Mr

Harrel, who came into the room, to ask if they had seen or heard any thing of Sir Robert Floyer?

"No," answered Mrs Harrel, "nothing at all."

"I wish he was hanged," returned he, "for he has kept me waiting this hour. He made me promise not to ride out till he called and now he'll stay till the morning is over."

"Pray where does he live, sir?" cried Morrice, starting from his seat.

"In Cavendish Square, sir," answered Mr Harrel, looking at him with much surprise.

Not a word more said Morrice, but scampered out of the room.

"Pray who is this Genius?" cried Mr Harrel, "and what has he run away for?"

"Upon my word I know nothing at all of him," said Mrs Harrel; "he is a visitor of Miss Beverley's."

"And I, too," said Cecilia, "might almost equally disclaim all knowledge of him; for though I once saw, I never was introduced to him."

She then began a relation of her meeting him at Mr Monckton's house, and had hardly concluded it, before again, and quite out of breath, he made his appearance.

"Sir Robert Floyer, sir," said he to Mr Harrel, "will be here in two minutes."

"I hope, sir," said Mr Harrel, "you have not given yourself the trouble of going to him?"

"No, sir, it has given me nothing but pleasure; a run these cold mornings is the thing I like best."

"Sir, you are extremely good," said Mr Harrel, "but I had not the least intention of your taking such a walk upon my account."

He then begged him to be seated, to rest himself, and to take some refreshment; which civilities he received without scruple.

"But, Miss Beverley," said Mr Harrel, turning suddenly to Cecilia, "you don't tell me what you think of my friend?"

"What friend, sir?"

"Why, Sir Robert Floyer; I observed he never quitted you a moment while he stayed at Mrs Mears."

"His stay, however, was too short," said Cecilia, "to allow me to form a fair opinion of him."

"But perhaps," cried Morrice," it was long enough to allow you to form a *foul* one."

Cecilia could not forbear laughing to hear the truth thus accidentally blundered out; but Mr Harrel, looking very little pleased, said, "Surely you can find no fault with him? he is one of the most fashionable men I know."

"My finding fault with him then," said Cecilia, "will only farther prove what I believe is already pretty evident, that I am yet a novice in the art of admiration."

Mr Arnott, animating at this speech, glided behind her chair, and said, "I knew you could not like him! I knew it from the turn of your mind;—I knew it even from your countenance!"

Soon after, Sir Robert Floyer arrived.

"You are a pretty fellow, a'n't you," cried Mr Harrel, "to keep me waiting so long."

"I could not come a moment sooner; I hardly expected to get here at all, for my horse has been so confounded resty I could not tell how to get him along."

"Do you come on horseback through the streets, Sir Robert?" asked Mrs Harrel.

"Sometimes; when I am lazy. But what the d—l is the matter with him I don't know; he has started at everything. I suspect there has been some foul play with him."

"Is he at the door, sir?" cried Morrice.

"Yes," answered Sir Robert.

"Then I'll tell you what's the matter with him in a minute;" and away again ran Morrice.

"What time did you get off last night, Harrel?" said Sir Robert.

"Not very early; but you were too much engaged to miss me. By the way," lowering his voice, "what do you think I lost?"

"I can't tell indeed, but I know what I gained: I have not had such a run of luck this winter."

They then went up to a window to carry on their enquiries more privately.

At the words *what do you think I lost*, Cecilia, half starting, cast her eyes uneasily upon Mrs Harrel, but perceived not the least change in her countenance. Mr Arnott, however, seemed as little pleased as herself, and from a similar sensation looked anxiously at his sister.

Morrice now returning, called out, "He's had a fall, I assure you!"

"Curse him!" cried Sir Robert, "what shall I do now? he cost me the d—l and all of money, and I have not had him a twelvemonth. Can you lend me a horse for this morning, Harrel?"

"No, I have not one that will do for you. You must send to Astley."

"Who can I send? John must take care of this."

"I'll go, sir," cried Morrice, "if you'll give me the commission."

"By no means, sir," said Sir Robert, "I can't think of giving you such an office."

"It is the thing in the world I like best," answered he; "I understand horses, and had rather go to Astley's than any where."

The matter was now settled in a few minutes, and having received his directions, and an invitation to dinner, Morrice danced off, with a heart yet lighter than his heels.

"Why, Miss Beverley," said Mr Harrel, "this friend of yours is the most obliging gentleman I ever met with; there was no avoiding asking him to dinner."

"Remember, however," said Cecilia, who was involuntarily diverted at the successful officiousness of her new acquaintance, "that if you receive him henceforth as your guest, he obtains admission through his own merits, and not through my interest."

At dinner, Morrice, who failed not to accept the invitation of Mr Harrel, was the gayest, and indeed the happiest man in the company: the effort he had made to fasten himself upon Cecilia as an acquaintance, had not, it is true, from herself met with much encouragement; but he knew the chances were against him when he made the trial, and therefore the prospect of gaining admission into such a house as Mr Harrel's, was not only sufficient to make amends for what scarcely amounted to a disappointment, but a subject of serious comfort from the credit of the connection, and of internal exultation at his own management and address.

In the evening, the ladies, as usual, went to a private assembly, and, as usual, were attended to it by Mr Arnott. The other gentlemen had engagements elsewhere.

CHAPTER VII

A PROJECT.

Several days passed on nearly in the same manner; the mornings were all spent in gossipping, shopping and dressing, and the evenings were regularly appropriated to public places, or large parties of company.

Meanwhile Mr Arnott lived almost entirely in Portman Square; he slept, indeed, at his own lodgings, but he boarded wholly with Mr Harrel, whose house he never for a moment quitted till night, except to attend Cecilia and his sister in their visitings and rambles.

Mr Arnott was a young man of unexceptionable character, and of a disposition mild, serious and benignant: his principles and blameless conduct obtained the universal esteem of the world, but his manners, which were rather too precise, joined to an uncommon gravity of countenance and demeanour, made his society rather permitted as a duty, than sought as a pleasure.

The charms of Cecilia had forcibly, suddenly and deeply penetrated his heart; he only lived in her presence, away from her he hardly existed: the emotions she excited were rather those of adoration than of love, for he gazed upon her beauty till he thought her more than human, and hung upon her accents till all speech seemed impertinent to him but her own. Yet so small were his expectations of success, that not even to his sister did he hint at the situation of his heart: happy in an easy access to her, he contented himself with seeing, hearing and watching her, beyond which bounds he formed not any plan, and scarce indulged any hope.

Sir Robert Floyer, too, was a frequent visitor in Portman Square, where he dined almost daily. Cecilia was chagrined at seeing so much of him, and provoked to find herself almost constantly the object of his unrestrained examination; she was, however, far more seriously concerned for Mrs Harrel, when she discovered that this favourite friend of her husband was an unprincipled spendthrift, and an extravagant gamester, for as he was the inseparable companion of Mr Harrel, she dreaded the consequence both of his influence and his example.

She saw, too, with an amazement that daily increased, the fatigue, yet fascination of a life of pleasure: Mr Harrel seemed to consider his own house merely as an hotel, where at any hour of the night he might disturb the family to claim admittance, where letters and messages might be left for him, where he dined when no other dinner was offered him, and where, when he made an appointment, he was to be met with. His lady, too, though more at home, was not therefore more solitary; her acquaintance were numerous, expensive and idle, and every moment not actually spent in company, was scrupulously devoted to making arrangements for that purpose.

In a short time Cecilia, who every day had hoped that the next would afford her greater satisfaction, but who every day found the present no better than the former, began to grow weary of eternally running the same round, and to sicken at the irksome repetition of unremitting yet uninteresting dissipation. She saw nobody she wished to see, as she had met with nobody for whom she could care; for though sometimes those with whom she mixed appeared to be amiable, she knew that their manners, like their persons, were in their best array, and therefore she had too much understanding to judge decisively of their characters. But what chiefly damped her hopes of forming a friendship with any of the new acquaintance to whom she was introduced, was the observation she herself made how ill the coldness of their hearts accorded with the warmth of their professions; upon every first meeting, the civilities which were shewn her, flattered her into believing she had excited a partiality that a very little time would ripen into affection; the next meeting commonly confirmed the expectation; but the third, and every future one, regularly destroyed it. She found that time added nothing to their fondness, nor intimacy to their sincerity; that the interest in her welfare which appeared to be taken at first sight, seldom, with whatever reason, increased, and often without any, abated; that the distinction she at first met with, was no effusion of kindness, but of curiosity, which is scarcely sooner gratified than satiated; and that those who lived always the life into which she had only lately been initiated, were as much harassed with it as herself, though less spirited to relinquish, and more helpless to better it, and that they coveted nothing but what was new, because they had experienced the insufficiency of whatever was familiar.

She began now to regret the loss she sustained in quitting the neighbourhood, and being deprived of the conversation of Mr Monckton, and yet more earnestly to miss the affection and sigh for the society of Mrs Charlton, the lady with whom she had long and happily resided at Bury; for she was very soon compelled to give up all expectation of renewing the felicity of her earlier years, by being restored to the friendship of Mrs Harrel, in whom she had mistaken the kindness of childish intimacy for the sincerity of chosen affection; and though she saw her credulous error with mortification and displeasure, she regretted it with tenderness and sorrow. "What, at last," cried she, "is human felicity, who has tasted, and where is it to be found? If I, who, to others, seem marked out for even a partial possession of it,—distinguished by fortune, caressed by the world, brought into the circle of high life, and surrounded with splendour, seek without finding it, yet losing, scarce know how I miss it!"

Ashamed upon reflection to believe she was considered as an object of envy by others, while repining and discontented herself, she determined no longer to be the only one insensible to the blessings within her reach, but by projecting and adopting some plan of conduct better suited to her taste and feelings than the frivolous insipidity of her present life, to make at once a more spirited and more worthy use of the affluence, freedom, and power which she possessed.

A scheme of happiness at once rational and refined soon presented itself to her imagination. She purposed, for the basis of her plan, to become mistress of her own time, and with this view, to drop all idle and uninteresting acquaintance, who, while they contribute neither to use nor pleasure, make so large a part of the community, that they may properly be called the underminers of existence; she could then shew some taste and discernment in her choice of friends, and she resolved to select such only as by their piety could elevate her mind, by their knowledge improve her understanding, or by their accomplishments and manners delight her affections. This regulation, if strictly adhered to, would soon relieve her from the fatigue of receiving many visitors, and therefore she might have all the leisure she could desire for the pursuit of her favourite studies, music and reading.

Having thus, from her own estimation of human perfection, culled whatever was noblest for her society, and from her own ideas of sedentary enjoyments arranged the occupations of her hours of solitude, she felt fully satisfied with the portion of happiness which her scheme promised to herself, and began next to consider what was due from her to the world.

And not without trembling did she then look forward to the claims which the splendid income she was soon to possess would call upon her to discharge. A strong sense of DUTY, a fervent desire to ACT RIGHT, were the ruling characteristics of her mind: her affluence she therefore considered as a debt contracted with the poor, and her independence as a tie upon her liberality to pay it with interest.

Many and various, then, soothing to her spirit and grateful to her sensibility, were the scenes which her fancy delineated; now she supported an orphan, now softened the sorrows of a widow, now snatched from iniquity the feeble trembler at poverty, and now rescued from shame the proud struggler with disgrace. The prospect at once exalted her hopes,

70

and enraptured her imagination; she regarded herself as an agent of Charity, and already in idea anticipated the rewards of a good and faithful delegate; so animating are the designs of disinterested benevolence! so pure is the bliss of intellectual philanthropy!

Not immediately, however, could this plan be put in execution; the society she meant to form could not be selected in the house of another, where, though to some she might shew a preference, there were none she could reject: nor had she yet the power to indulge, according to the munificence of her wishes, the extensive generosity she projected: these purposes demanded a house of her own, and the unlimited disposal of her fortune, neither of which she could claim till she became of age. That period, however, was only eight months distant, and she pleased herself with the intention of meliorating her plan in the meantime, and preparing to put it in practice.

But though, in common with all the race of still-expecting man, she looked for that happiness in the time to come which the present failed to afford, she had yet the spirit and good sense to determine upon making every effort in her power to render her immediate way of life more useful and contented.

Her first wish, therefore, now, was to quit the house of Mr Harrel, where she neither met with entertainment nor instruction, but was perpetually mortified by seeing the total indifference of the friend in whose society she had hoped for nothing but affection.

The will of her uncle, though it obliged her while under age to live with one of her guardians, left her at liberty to chuse and to change amongst them according to her wishes or convenience: she determined, therefore, to make a visit herself to each of them, to observe their manners and way of life, and then, to the best of her judgment, decide with which she could be most contented: resolving, however, not to hint at her intention till it was ripe for execution, and then honestly to confess the reasons of her retreat.

She had acquainted them both of her journey to town the morning after her arrival. She was almost an entire stranger to each of them, as she had not seen Mr Briggs since she was nine years old, nor Mr Delvile within the time she could remember.

The very morning that she had settled her proceedings for the arrangement of this new plan, she intended to request the use of Mrs Harrel's carriage, and to make, without delay, the visits preparatory to her removal; but when she entered the parlour upon a summons to breakfast, her eagerness to quit the house gave way, for the present, to the pleasure she felt at the sight of Mr Monckton, who was just arrived from Suffolk.

She expressed her satisfaction in the most lively terms, and scrupled not to tell him she had not once been so much pleased since her journey to town, except at her first meeting with Mrs Harrel.

Mr Monckton, whose delight was infinitely superior to her own, and whose joy in seeing her was redoubled by the affectionate frankness of her reception, stifled the emotions to which her sight gave rise, and denying himself the solace of expressing his feelings, seemed much less charmed than herself at the meeting, and suffered no word nor look to escape him beyond what could be authorised by friendly civility.

He then renewed with Mrs Harrel an acquaintance which had been formed before her marriage, but which [he] had dropt when her distance from Cecilia, upon whose account alone he had thought it worth cultivation, made it no longer of use to him. She afterwards introduced her brother to him; and a conversation very interesting to both the ladies took place, concerning several families with which they had been formerly connected, as well as the neighbourhood at large in which they had lately dwelt.

Very little was the share taken by Mr Arnott in these accounts and enquiries; the unaffected joy with which Cecilia had received Mr Monckton, had struck him with a sensation of envy as involuntary as it was painful; he did not, indeed, suspect that gentleman's secret views; no reason for suspicion was obvious, and his penetration sunk not deeper than appearances; he knew, too, that he was married, and therefore no jealousy occurred to him; but still she had smiled upon him!—and he felt that to purchase for himself a smile of so much sweetness, he would have sacrificed almost all else that was valuable to him upon earth.

With an attention infinitely more accurate, Mr Monckton had returned his observations. The uneasiness of his mind was apparent, and the anxious watchfulness of his eyes plainly manifested whence it arose. From a situation, indeed, which permitted an intercourse the most constant and unrestrained with such an object as Cecilia, nothing less could be expected, and therefore he considered his admiration as inevitable; all that remained to be discovered, was the reception it had met from his fair enslaver. Nor was he here long in doubt; he soon saw that she was not merely free from all passion herself, but had so little watched Mr Arnott as to be unconscious she had inspired any.

Yet was his own serenity, though apparently unmoved, little less disturbed in secret than that of his rival; he did not think him a formidable candidate, but he dreaded the effects of intimacy, fearing she might first grow accustomed to his attentions, and then become pleased with them. He apprehended, also, the influence of his sister and of Mr Harrel in his favour; and though he had no difficulty to persuade himself that any offer he might now make would be rejected without hesitation, he knew too well the insidious properties of perseverance, to see him, without inquietude, situated so advantageously.

The morning was far advanced before he took leave, yet he found no opportunity of discoursing with Cecilia, though he impatiently desired to examine into the state of her mind, and to discover whether her London journey had added any fresh difficulties to the success of his long-concerted scheme. But as Mrs Harrel invited him to dinner, he hoped the afternoon would be more propitious to his wishes.

Cecilia, too, was eager to communicate to him her favourite project, and to receive his advice with respect to its execution. She had long been used to his counsel, and she was now more than ever solicitous to obtain it, because she considered him as the only person in London who was interested in her welfare.

He saw, however, no promise of better success when he made his appearance at dinner time, for not only Mr Arnott was already arrived, but Sir Robert Floyer, and he found Cecilia so much the object of their mutual attention, that he had still less chance than in the morning of speaking to her unheard.

Yet was he not idle; the sight of Sir Robert gave abundant employment to his penetration, which was immediately at work, to discover the motive of his visit: but this, with all his sagacity, was not easily decided; for though the constant direction of his eyes towards Cecilia, proved, at least, that he was not insensible of her beauty, his carelessness whether or not she was hurt by his examination, the little pains he took to converse with her, and the invariable assurance and negligence of his manners, seemed strongly to demonstrate an indifference to the sentiments he inspired, totally incompatible with the solicitude of affection.

In Cecilia he had nothing to observe but what his knowledge of her character prepared him to expect, a shame no less indignant than modest at the freedom with which she saw herself surveyed.

Very little, therefore, was the satisfaction which this visit procured him, for soon after dinner the ladies retired; and as they had an early engagement for the evening, the gentlemen received no summons to their tea-table. But he contrived, before they quitted the room, to make an appointment for attending them the next morning to a rehearsal of a new serious Opera.

He stayed not after their departure longer than decency required, for too much in earnest was his present pursuit, to fit him for such conversation as the house in Cecilia's absence could afford him.

CHAPTER VIII

AN OPERA REHEARSAL.

The next day, between eleven and twelve o'clock, Mr Monckton was again in Portman Square; he found, as he expected, both the ladies, and he found, as he feared, Mr Arnott prepared to be of their party. He had, however, but little time to repine at this intrusion, before he was disturbed by another, for, in a few minutes, they were joined by Sir Robert Floyer, who also declared his intention of accompanying them to the Haymarket.

Mr Monckton, to disguise his chagrin, pretended he was in great haste to set off, lest they should be too late for the overture: they were, therefore, quitting the breakfast room, when they were stopt by the appearance of Mr Morrice.

The surprise which the sight of him gave to Mr Monckton was extreme; he knew that he was unacquainted with Mr Harrel, for he remembered they were strangers to each other when they lately met at his house; he concluded, therefore, that Cecilia was the object of his visit, but he could frame no conjecture under what pretence.

The easy terms upon which he seemed with all the family by no means diminished his amazement; for when Mrs Harrel expressed some concern that she was obliged to go out, he gaily begged her not to mind him, assuring her he could not have stayed two minutes, and promising, unasked, to call again the next day: and when she added, "We would not hurry away so, only we are going to a rehearsal of an Opera," he exclaimed with quickness, "A rehearsal!—are you really? I have a great mind to go too!"

Then, perceiving Mr Monckton, he bowed to him with great respect, and enquired, with no little solemnity, how he had left Lady Margaret, hoped she was perfectly recovered from her late indisposition, and asked sundry questions with regard to her plan for the winter.

This discourse was ill constructed for rendering his presence desirable to Mr Monckton; he answered him very drily, and again pressed their departure.

"O," cried Morrice, "there's no occasion for such haste; the rehearsal does not begin till one."

"You are mistaken, sir," said Mr Monckton; "it is to begin at twelve o'clock."

"O ay, very true," returned Morrice; "I had forgot the dances, and I suppose they are to be rehearsed first. Pray, Miss Beverley, did you ever see any dances rehearsed?"

"No, sir."

"You will be excessively entertained, then, I assure you. It's the most comical thing in the world to see those signores and signoras cutting capers in a morning. And the *figuranti* will divert you beyond measure; you never saw such a shabby set in your life: but the most amusing thing is to look in their faces, for all the time they are jumping and skipping about the stage as if they could not stand still for joy, they look as sedate and as dismal as if they were so many undertaker's men."

"Not a word against dancing!" cried Sir Robert, "it's the only thing carries one to the Opera; and I am sure it's the only thing one minds at it."

The two ladies were then handed to Mrs Harrel's *vis-a-vis*; and the gentlemen, joined without further ceremony by Mr Morrice, followed them to the Haymarket.

The rehearsal was not begun, and Mrs Harrel and Cecilia secured themselves a box upon the stage, from which the gentlemen of their party took care not to be very distant.

They were soon perceived by Mr Gosport, who instantly entered into conversation with Cecilia. Miss Larolles, who with some other ladies came soon after into the next box, looked out to courtsie and nod, with her usual readiness, at Mrs Harrel, but took not any notice of Cecilia, though she made the first advances.

"What's the matter now?" cried Mr Gosport; "have you affronted your little prattling friend?"

"Not with my own knowledge," answered Cecilia; "perhaps she does not recollect me."

Just then Miss Larolles, tapping at the door, came in from the next box to speak to Mrs Harrel; with whom she stood chatting and laughing some minutes, without seeming to perceive that Cecilia was of her party.

"Why, what have you done to the poor girl?" whispered Mr Gosport; "did you talk more than herself when you saw her last?"

"Would that have been possible?" cried Cecilia; "however, I still fancy she does not know me."

She then stood up, which making Miss Larolles involuntarily turn towards her, she again courtsied; a civility which that young lady scarce deigned to return, before, bridling with an air of resentment, she hastily looked another way, and then, nodding good-humouredly at Mrs Harrel, hurried back to her party.

Cecilia, much amazed, said to Mr Gosport, "See now how great was our presumption in supposing this young lady's loquacity always at our devotion!"

"Ah, madam!" cried he, laughing, "there is no permanency, no consistency in the world! no, not even in the tongue of a VOLUBLE! and if that fails, upon what may we depend?"

"But seriously," said Cecilia, "I am sorry I have offended her, and the more because I so little know how, that I can offer her no apology."

"Will you appoint me your envoy? Shall I demand the cause of these hostilities?"

She thanked him, and he followed Miss Larolles; who was now addressing herself with great earnestness to Mr Meadows, the gentleman with whom she was conversing when Cecilia first saw her in Portman Square. He stopt a moment to let her finish her speech, which, with no little spirit, she did in these words, "I never knew anything like it in my life; but I shan't put up with such airs, I assure her!"

Mr Meadows made not any other return to her harangue, but stretching himself with a languid smile, and yawning: Mr Gosport, therefore, seizing the moment of cessation, said, "Miss Larolles, I hear a strange report about you."

"Do you?" returned she, with quickness, "pray what is it? something monstrous impertinent, I dare say,—however, I assure you it i'n't true."

"Your assurance," cried he, "carries conviction indisputable, for the report was that you had left off talking."

"O, was that all?" cried she, disappointed, "I thought it had been something about Mr Sawyer, for I declare I have been plagued so about him, I am quite sick of his name."

"And for my part, I never heard it! so fear nothing from me upon his account."

"Lord, Mr Gosport, how can you say so? I am sure you must know about the Festino that night, for it was all over the town in a moment."

"What festino?"

"Well, only conceive, how provoking!—why, I know nothing else was talked of for a month!"

"You are most formidably stout this morning! it is not two minutes since I saw you fling the gauntlet at Miss Beverley, and yet you are already prepared for another antagonist."

"O as to Miss Beverley, I must really beg you not to mention her; she has behaved so impertinently, that I don't intend ever to speak to her again."

"Why, what has she done?"

"O she's been so rude you've no notion. I'll tell you how it was. You must know I met her at Mrs Barrel's the day she came to town, and the very next morning I waited on her myself, for I would not send a ticket, because I really wished to be civil to her; well, the day after, she never came near me, though I called upon her again; however, I did not take any notice of that; but when the third day came, and I found she had not even sent me a ticket, I thought it monstrous ill bred indeed; and now there has passed more than a week, and yet she has never called: so I suppose she don't like me; so I shall drop her acquaintance."

Mr Gosport, satisfied now with the subject of her complaint, returned to Cecilia, and informed her of the heavy charge which was brought against her.

"I am glad, at least, to know my crime," said she, "for otherwise I should certainly have sinned on in ignorance, as I must confess I never thought of returning her visits: but even if I had, I should not have supposed I had yet lost much time."

"I beg your pardon there," said Mrs Harrel; "a first visit ought to be returned always by the third day."

"Then have I an unanswerable excuse," said Cecilia, "for I remember that on the third day I saw her at your house."

"O that's nothing at all to the purpose; you should have waited upon her, or sent her a ticket, just the same as if you had not seen her."

The overture was now begun, and Cecilia declined any further conversation. This was the first Opera she had ever heard, yet she was not wholly a stranger to Italian compositions, having assiduously studied music from a natural love of the art, attended all the best concerts her neighbourhood afforded, and regularly received from London the works of the best masters. But the little skill she had thus gained, served rather to increase than to lessen the surprize with which she heard the present performance,—a surprize of which the discovery of her own ignorance made not the least part. Unconscious from the little she had acquired how much was to be learnt, she was astonished to find the inadequate power of written music to convey any idea of vocal abilities: with just knowledge enough, therefore, to understand something of the difficulties, and feel much of the merit, she gave to the whole Opera an avidity of attention almost painful from its own eagerness.

But both the surprize and the pleasure which she received from the performance in general, were faint, cold, and languid, compared to the strength of those emotions when excited by Signore Pacchierotti in particular; and though not half the excellencies of that superior singer were necessary either to amaze or charm her unaccustomed ears, though the refinement of his taste and masterly originality of his genius, to be praised as they deserved, called for the judgment and knowledge of professors, yet a natural love of music in some measure supplied the place of cultivation, and what she could neither explain nor understand, she could feel and enjoy.

The opera was Artaserse; and the pleasure she received from the music was much augmented by her previous acquaintance with that interesting drama; yet, as to all noviciates in science, whatever is least complicated is most pleasing, she found herself by nothing so deeply impressed, as by the plaintive and beautiful simplicity with which Pacchierotti uttered the affecting repetition of *sono innocente*! his voice, always either sweet or impassioned, delivered those words in a tone of softness, pathos, and sensibility, that struck her with a sensation not more new than delightful.

But though she was, perhaps, the only person thus astonished, she was by no means the only one enraptured; for notwithstanding she was too earnestly engaged to remark the company in general, she could not avoid taking notice of an old gentleman who stood by one of the side scenes, against which he leant his head in a manner that concealed his face, with an evident design to be wholly absorbed in listening: and during the songs of Pacchierotti he sighed so deeply that Cecilia, struck by his uncommon sensibility to the power of music, involuntarily watched him, whenever her mind was sufficiently at liberty to attend to any emotions but its own.

As soon as the rehearsal was over, the gentlemen of Mrs Harrel's party crowded before her box; and Cecilia then perceived that the person whose musical enthusiasm had excited her curiosity, was the same old gentleman whose extraordinary behaviour had so much surprized her at the house of Mr Monckton. Her desire to obtain some information concerning him again reviving, she was beginning to make fresh enquiries, when she was interrupted by the approach of Captain Aresby.

That gentleman, advancing to her with a smile of the extremest self-complacency, after hoping, in a low voice, he had the honour of seeing her well, exclaimed, "How wretchedly empty is the town! petrifying to a degree! I believe you do not find yourself at present *obsede* by too much company?"

"*At present*, I believe the contrary!" cried Mr Gosport.

"Really!" said the Captain, unsuspicious of his sneer, "I protest I have hardly seen a soul. Have you tried the Pantheon yet, ma'am?"

"No, sir."

"Nor I; I don't know whether people go there this year. It is not a favourite *spectacle* with me; that sitting to hear the music is a horrid bore. Have you done the Festino the honour to look in there yet?"

"No, sir."

"Permit me, then, to have the honour to beg you will try it."

"O, ay, true," cried Mrs Harrel; "I have really used you very ill about that; I should have got you in for a subscriber: but Lord, I have done nothing for you yet, and you never put me in mind. There's the ancient music, and Abel's concert;—as to the opera, we may have a box between us;—but there's the ladies' concert we must try for; and there's—O Lord, fifty other places we must think of!"

"Oh times of folly and dissipation!" exclaimed a voice at some distance; "Oh mignons of idleness and luxury! What next will ye invent for the perdition of your time! How yet further will ye proceed in the annihilation of virtue!"

Everybody stared; but Mrs Harrel coolly said, "Dear, it's only the man-hater!"

"The man-hater?" repeated Cecilia, who found that the speech was made by the object of her former curiosity; "is that the name by which he is known?"

"He is known by fifty names," said Mr Monckton; "his friends call him the *moralist*; the young ladies, the *crazy-man*; the macaronies, the *bore*; in short, he is called by any and every name but his own."

"He is a most petrifying wretch, I assure you," said the Captain; "I am *obsede* by him *partout*; if I had known he had been so near, I should certainly have said nothing."

"That you have done so well," cried Mr Gosport, "that if you had known it the whole time, you could have done it no better."

The Captain, who had not heard this speech, which was rather made at him than to him, continued his address to Cecilia; "Give me leave to have the honour of hoping you intend to honour our select masquerade at the Pantheon with your presence. We shall have but five hundred tickets, and the subscription will only be three guineas and a half."

"Oh objects of penury and want!" again exclaimed the incognito; "Oh vassals of famine and distress! Come and listen to this wantonness of wealth! Come, naked and breadless as ye are, and learn how that money is consumed which to you might bring raiment and food!"

"That strange wretch," said the Captain, "ought really to be confined; I have had the honour to be *degoute* by him so often, that I think him quite obnoxious. I make it quite a principle to seal up my lips the moment I perceive him."

"Where is it, then," said Cecilia, "that you have so often met him?"

"O," answered the Captain, "*partout*; there is no greater bore about town. But the time I found him most petrifying was once when I happened to have the honour of dancing with a very young lady, who was but just come from a boarding-school, and whose friends had done me the honour to fix upon me upon the principle of first bringing her out: and while I was doing *mon possible* for killing the time, he came up, and in his particular manner, told her I had no meaning in any thing I said! I must own I never felt more tempted to be *enrage* with a person in years, in my life."

Mr Arnott now brought the ladies word that their carriage was ready, and they quitted their box: but as Cecilia had never before seen the interior parts of a theatre, Mr Monckton, hoping while they loitered to have an opportunity of talking with her, asked Morrice why he did not *shew the lions?* Morrice, always happy in being employed, declared it was *just the thing he liked best*, and begged permission to do the honours to Mrs Harrel, who, ever eager in the search of amusement, willingly accepted his offer.

They all, therefore, marched upon the stage, their own party now being the only one that remained.

"We shall make a triumphal entry here," cried Sir Robert Floyer; "the very tread of the stage half tempts me to turn actor."

"You are a rare man," said Mr Gosport, "if, at your time of life, that is a turn not already taken."

"My time of life!" repeated he; "what do you mean by that? do you take me for an old man?"

"No, sir, but I take you to be past childhood, and consequently to have served your apprenticeship to the actors you have mixed with on the great stage of the world, and, for some years at least, to have set up for yourself."

"Come," cried Morrice, "let's have a little spouting; 'twill make us warm."

"Yes," said Sir Robert, "if we spout to an animating object. If Miss Beverley will be Juliet, I am Romeo at her service."

At this moment the incognito, quitting the corner in which he had planted himself, came suddenly forward, and standing before the whole group, cast upon Cecilia a look of much compassion, and called out, "Poor simple victim! hast thou already so many pursuers? yet seest not that thou art marked for sacrifice! yet knowest not that thou art destined for prey!"

Cecilia, extremely struck by this extraordinary address, stopt short and looked much disturbed: which, when he perceived, he added, "Let the danger, not the warning affect you! discard the sycophants that surround you, seek the virtuous, relieve the poor, and save yourself from the impending destruction of unfeeling prosperity!"

Having uttered these words with vehemence and authority, he sternly passed them, and disappeared.

Cecilia, too much astonished for speech, stood for some time immoveable, revolving in her mind various conjectures upon the meaning of an exhortation so strange and so urgent.

Nor was the rest of the company much less discomposed: Sir Robert, Mr Monckton, and Mr Arnott, each conscious of their own particular plans, were each apprehensive that the warning pointed at himself: Mr Gosport was offended at being included in the general appellation of sycophants; Mrs Harrel was provoked at being interrupted in her ramble; and Captain Aresby, sickening at the very sight of him, retreated the moment he came forth.

"For heaven's sake," cried Cecilia, when somewhat recovered from her consternation, "who can this be, and what can he mean? You, Mr Monckton, must surely know something of him; it was at your house I first saw him."

"Indeed," answered Mr Monckton, "I knew almost nothing of him then, and I am but little better informed now. Belfield picked him up somewhere, and desired to bring him to my house: he called him by the name of Albany: I found him a most extraordinary character, and Belfield, who is a worshipper of originality, was very fond of him."

"He's a devilish crabbed old fellow," cried Sir Robert, "and if he goes on much longer at this confounded rate, he stands a very fair chance of getting his ears cropped."

"He is a man of the most singular conduct I have ever met with," said Mr Gosport; "he seems to hold mankind in abhorrence, yet he is never a moment alone, and at the same time that he intrudes himself into all parties, he associates with none: he is commonly a stern and silent observer of all that passes, or when he speaks, it is but to utter some sentence of rigid morality, or some bitterness of indignant reproof."

The carriage was now again announced, and Mr Monckton taking Cecilia's hand, while Mr Morrice secured to himself the honour of Mrs Harrel's, Sir Robert and Mr Gosport made their bows and departed. But though they had now quitted the stage, and arrived at the head of a small stair case by which they were to descend out of the theatre, Mr Monckton, finding all his tormentors retired, except Mr Arnott, whom he hoped to elude, could not resist making one more attempt for a few moments' conversation with Cecilia; and therefore, again applying to Morrice, he called out, "I don't think you have shewn the ladies any of the contrivances behind the scenes?"

"True," cried Morrice, "no more I have; suppose we go back?"

"I shall like it vastly," said Mrs Harrel; and back they returned.

Mr Monckton now soon found an opportunity to say to Cecilia, "Miss Beverley, what I foresaw has exactly come to pass; you are surrounded by selfish designers, by interested, double-minded people, who have nothing at heart but your fortune, and whose mercenary views, if you are not guarded against them—"

Here a loud scream from Mrs Harrel interrupted his speech; Cecilia, much alarmed, turned from him to enquire the cause, and Mr Monckton was obliged to follow her example: but his mortification was almost intolerable when he saw that lady in a violent fit of laughter, and found her scream was only occasioned by seeing Mr Morrice, in his diligence to do the honours, pull upon his own head one of the side scenes!

There was now no possibility of proposing any further delay; but Mr Monckton, in attending the ladies to their carriage, was obliged to have recourse to his utmost discretion and forbearance, in order to check his desire of reprimanding Morrice for his blundering officiousness.

Dressing, dining with company at home, and then going out with company abroad, filled up, as usual, the rest of the day.

CHAPTER IX

A SUPPLICATION.

The next morning Cecilia, at the repeated remonstrances of Mrs Harrel, consented to call upon Miss Larolles. She felt the impracticability of beginning at present the alteration in her way of life she had projected, and therefore thought it most expedient to assume no singularity till her independency should enable her to support it with consistency; yet greater than ever was her internal eagerness to better satisfy her inclination and her conscience in the disposition of her time, and the distribution of her wealth, since she had heard the emphatic charge of her unknown Mentor.

Mrs Harrel declined accompanying her in this visit, because she had appointed a surveyor to bring a plan for the inspection of Mr Harrel and herself, of a small temporary building, to be erected at Violet-Bank, for the purpose of performing plays in private the ensuing Easter.

When the street door was opened for her to get into the carriage, she was struck with the appearance of an elderly woman who was standing at some distance, and seemed shivering with cold, and who, as she descended the steps, joined her hands in an act of supplication, and advanced nearer to the carriage.

Cecilia stopt to look at her: her dress, though parsimonious, was too neat for a beggar, and she considered a moment what she could offer her. The poor woman continued to move forward, but with a slowness of pace that indicated extreme weakness; and, as she approached and raised her head, she exhibited a countenance so wretched, and a complexion so sickly, that Cecilia was impressed with horror at the sight.

With her hands still joined, and a voice that seemed fearful of its own sound, "Oh madam," she cried, "that you would but hear me!"

"Hear you!" repeated Cecilia, hastily feeling for her purse; "most certainly, and tell me how I shall assist you."

"Heaven bless you for speaking so kindly, madam!" cried the woman, with a voice more assured; "I was sadly afraid you would be angry, but I saw the carriage at the door, and I thought I would try; for I could be no worse; and distress, madam, makes very bold."

"Angry!" said Cecilia, taking a crown from her purse; "no, indeed!—who could see such wretchedness, and feel any thing but pity?"

"Oh madam," returned the poor woman, "I could almost cry to hear you talk so, though I never thought to cry again, since I left it off for my poor Billy!"

"Have you, then, lost a son?"

"Yes, madam; but he was a great deal too good to live, so I have quite left off grieving for him now."

"Come in, good woman," said Cecilia, "it is too cold to stand here, and you seem half-starved already: come in, and let me have some talk with you."

She then gave orders that the carriage should be driven round the square till she was ready, and making the woman follow her into a parlour, desired to know what she should do for her; changing, while she spoke, from a movement of encreasing compassion, the crown which she held in her hand for double that sum.

"You can do everything, madam," she answered, "if you will but plead for us to his honour: he little thinks of our distress, because he has been afflicted with none himself, and I would not be so troublesome to him, but indeed, indeed, madam, we are quite pinched for want!"

Cecilia, struck with the words, *he little thinks of our distress, because he has been afflicted with none himself*, felt again ashamed of the smallness of her intended donation, and taking from her purse another half guinea, said, "Will this assist you? Will a guinea be sufficient to you for the present?"

"I humbly thank you, madam," said the woman, curtsying low, "shall I give you a receipt?"

"A receipt?" cried Cecilia, with emotion, "for what? Alas, our accounts are by no means balanced! but I shall do more for you if I find you as deserving an object as you seem to be."

"You are very good, madam; but I only meant a receipt in part of payment."

"Payment for what? I don't understand you."

"Did his honour never tell you, madam, of our account?"

"What account?"

"Our bill, madam, for work done to the new Temple at Violet-Bank: it was the last great work my poor husband was able to do, for it was there he met with his misfortune."

"What bill? What misfortune?" cried Cecilia; "what had your husband to do at Violet-Bank?"

"He was the carpenter, madam. I thought you might have seen poor Hill the carpenter there."

"No, I never was there myself. Perhaps you mistake me for Mrs Harrel."

"Why, sure, madam, a'n't you his honour's lady?"

"No. But tell me, what is this bill?"

"'Tis a bill, madam, for very hard work, for work, madam, which I am sure will cost my husband his life; and though I have been after his honour night and day to get it, and sent him letters and petitions with an account of our misfortunes, I have never received so much as a shilling! and now the servants won't even let me wait in the hall to speak to him. Oh, madam! you who seem so good, plead to his honour in our behalf! tell him my poor husband cannot live! tell him my children are starving! and tell him my poor Billy, that used to help to keep us, is dead, and that all the work I can do by myself is not enough to maintain us!"

"Good heaven!" cried Cecilia, extremely moved, "is it then your own money for which you sue thus humbly?"

"Yes, madam, for my own just and honest money, as his honour knows, and will tell you himself."

"Impossible!" cried Cecilia, "he cannot know it; but I will take care he shall soon be informed of it. How much is the bill?"

"Two-and-twenty pounds, madam."

"What, no more?"

"Ah, madam, you gentlefolks little think how much that is to poor people! A hard working family, like mine, madam, with the help of 20 pounds will go on for a long while quite in paradise."

"Poor worthy woman!" cried Cecilia, whose eyes were filled with tears of compassion, "if 20 pounds will place you in paradise, and that 20 pounds only your just right, it is hard, indeed, that you should be kept without it; especially when your debtors are too affluent to miss it. Stay here a few moments, and I will bring you the money immediately."

Away she flew, and returned to the breakfast room, but found there only Mr Arnott, who told her that Mr Harrel was in the library, with his sister and some gentlemen. Cecilia briefly related her business, and begged he would inform Mr Harrel she wished to speak to him directly. Mr Arnott shook his head, but obeyed.

They returned together, and immediately.

"Miss Beverley," cried Mr Harrel, gaily, "I am glad you are not gone, for we want much to consult with you. Will you come up stairs?"

"Presently," answered she; "but first I must speak to you about a poor woman with whom I have accidentally been talking, who has begged me to intercede with you to pay a little debt that she thinks you have forgotten, but that probably you have never heard mentioned."

"A debt?" cried he, with an immediate change of countenance, "to whom?"

"Her name, I think, is Hill; she is wife to the carpenter you employed about a new temple at Violet-Bank."

"O, what—what, that woman?—Well, well, I'll see she shall be paid. Come, let us go to the library."

"What, with my commission so ill executed? I promised to petition for her to have the money directly."

"Pho, pho, there's no such hurry; I don't know what I have done with her bill."

"I'll run and get another."

"O upon no account! She may send another in two or three days. She deserves to wait a twelvemonth for her impertinence in troubling you at all about it."

"That was entirely accidental: but indeed you must give me leave to perform my promise and plead for her. It must be almost the same to you whether you pay such a trifle as 20 pounds now or a month hence, and to this poor woman the difference seems little short of life or death, for she tells me her husband is dying, and her children are half-famished; and though she looks an object of the cruellest want and distress herself, she appears to be their only support."

"O," cried Mr Harrel, laughing, "what a dismal tale has she been telling you! no doubt she saw you were fresh from the country! But if you give credit to all the farragos of these trumpery impostors, you will never have a moment to yourself, nor a guinea in your purse."

"This woman,"' answered Cecilia, "cannot be an impostor, she carries marks but too evident and too dreadful in her countenance of the sufferings which she relates."

"O," returned he, "when you know the town better you will soon see through tricks of this sort; a sick husband and five small children are complaints so stale now, that they serve no other purpose in the world but to make a joke."

"Those, however, who can laugh at them must have notions of merriment very different to mine. And this poor woman, whose cause I have ventured to undertake, had she no family at all, must still and indisputably be an object of pity herself, for she is so weak she can hardly crawl, and so pallid that she seems already half dead."

"All imposition, depend upon it! The moment she is out of your sight her complaints will vanish."

"Nay, sir," cried Cecilia, a little impatiently, "there is no reason to suspect such deceit, since she does not come hither as a beggar, however well the state of beggary may accord with her poverty: she only solicits the payment of a bill, and if in that there is any fraud, nothing can be so easy as detection."

Mr Harrel bit his lips at this speech, and for some instants looked much disturbed; but soon recovering himself, he negligently said, "Pray, how did she get at you?"

"I met her at the street door. But tell me, is not her bill a just one?"

"I cannot say; I have never had time to look at it."

"But you know who the woman is, and that her husband worked for you, and therefore that in all probability it is right,—do you not?"

"Yes, yes, I know who the woman is well enough; she has taken care of that, for she has pestered me every day these nine months."

Cecilia was struck dumb by this speech: hitherto she had supposed that the dissipation of his life kept him ignorant of his own injustice; but when she found he was so well informed of it, yet, with such total indifference, could suffer a poor woman to claim a just debt every day for nine months together, she was shocked and astonished beyond measure. They were both some time silent, and then Mr Harrel, yawning and stretching out his arms, indolently asked, "Pray, why does not the man come himself?"

"Did I not tell you," answered Cecilia, staring at so absent a question, "that he was very ill, and unable even to work?"

"Well, when he is better," added he, moving towards the door, "he may call, and I will talk to him."

Cecilia, all amazement at this unfeeling behaviour, turned involuntarily to Mr Arnott, with a countenance that appealed for his assistance; but

Mr Arnott hung his head, ashamed to meet her eyes, and abruptly left the room.

Meantime Mr Harrel, half-turning back, though without looking Cecilia in the face, carelessly said, "Well, won't you come?"

"No, sir," answered she, coldly.

He then returned to the library, leaving her equally displeased, surprised, and disconcerted at the conversation which had just passed between them. "Good heaven," cried she to herself, "what strange, what cruel insensibility! to suffer a wretched family to starve, from an obstinate determination to assert that they can live! to distress the poor by retaining the recompense for which alone they labour, and which at last they must have, merely from indolence, forgetfulness, or insolence! Oh how little did my uncle know, how little did I imagine to what a guardian I was entrusted!" She now felt ashamed even to return to the poor woman, though she resolved to do all in her power to soften her disappointment and relieve her distress.

But before she had quitted the room one of the servants came to tell her that his master begged the honor of her company up stairs. "Perhaps he relents!" thought she; and pleased with the hope, readily obeyed the summons.

She found him, his lady, Sir Robert Floyer, and two other gentlemen, all earnestly engaged in an argument over a large table, which was covered with plans and elevations of small buildings.

Mr Harrel immediately addressed her with an air of vivacity, and said, "You are very good for coming; we can settle nothing without your advice: pray look at these different plans for our theatre, and tell us which is the best."

Cecilia advanced not a step: the sight of plans for new edifices when the workmen were yet unpaid for old ones; the cruel wantonness of raising fresh fabrics of expensive luxury, while those so lately built had brought their neglected labourers to ruin, excited an indignation she scarce thought right to repress: while the easy sprightliness of the director of these revels, to whom but the moment before she had represented the oppression of which they made him guilty, filled her with aversion and disgust: and, recollecting the charge given her by the stranger at the Opera rehearsal, she resolved to speed her departure to another house, internally repeating, "Yes, I *will* save myself from *the impending destruction of unfeeling prosperity!*"

Mrs Harrel, surprised at her silence and extreme gravity, enquired if she was not well, and why she had put off her visit to Miss Larolles? And Sir Robert Floyer, turning suddenly to look at her, said, "Do you begin to feel the London air already?"

Cecilia endeavoured to recover her serenity, and answer these questions in her usual manner; but she persisted in declining to give any opinion at all about the plans, and, after slightly looking at them, left the room.

Mr Harrel, who knew better how to account for her behaviour than he thought proper to declare, saw with concern that she was more seriously displeased than he had believed an occurrence which he had regarded as wholly unimportant could have made her: and, therefore, desirous that she should be appeased, he followed her out of the library, and said, "Miss Beverley, will to-morrow be soon enough for your *protegee?*"

"O yes, no doubt!" answered she, most agreeably surprised by the question.

"Well, then, will you take the trouble to bid her come to me in the morning?"

Delighted at this unexpected commission, she thanked him with smiles for the office; and as she hastened down stairs to chear the poor expectant with the welcome intelligence, she framed a thousand excuses for the part he had hitherto acted, and without any difficulty, persuaded herself he began to see the faults of his conduct, and to meditate a reformation.

She was received by the poor creature she so warmly wished to serve with a countenance already so much enlivened, that she fancied Mr Harrel had himself anticipated her intended information: this, however, she found was not the case, for as soon as she heard his message, she shook her head, and said, "Ah, madam, his honour always says to-morrow! but I can better bear to be disappointed now, so I'll grumble no more; for indeed, madam, I have been blessed enough to-day to comfort me for every thing in the world, if I could but keep from thinking of poor Billy! I could bear all the rest, madam, but whenever my other troubles go off, that comes back to me so much the harder!"

"There, indeed, I can afford you no relief," said Cecilia, "but you must try to think less of him, and more of your husband and children who are now alive. To-morrow you will receive your money, and that, I hope, will raise your spirits. And pray let your husband have a physician, to tell you how to nurse and manage him; I will give you one fee for him now, and if he should want further advice, don't fear to let me know."

Cecilia had again taken out her purse, but Mrs Hill, clasping her hands, called out, "Oh madam no! I don't come here to fleece such goodness! but blessed be the hour that brought me here to-day, and if my poor Billy was alive, he should help me to thank you!"

She then told her that she was now quite rich, for while she was gone, a gentleman had come into the room, who had given her five guineas.

Cecilia, by her description, soon found this gentleman was Mr Arnott, and a charity so sympathetic with her own, failed not to raise him greatly in her favour. But as her benevolence was a stranger to that parade which is only liberal from emulation, when she found more money not immediately wanted, she put up her purse, and charging Mrs Hill to enquire for her the next morning when she came to be paid, bid her hasten back to her sick husband.

And then, again ordering the carriage to the door, she set off upon her visit to Miss Larolles, with a heart happy in the good already done, and happier still in the hope of doing more.

Miss Larolles was out, and she returned home; for she was too sanguine in her expectations from Mr Harrel, to have any desire of seeking her other guardians. The rest of the day she was more than usually civil to him, with a view to mark her approbation of his good intentions: while Mr Arnott, gratified by meeting the smiles he so much valued, thought his five guineas amply repaid, independently of the real pleasure which he took in doing good.

CHAPTER X

A PROVOCATION.

The next morning, when breakfast was over, Cecilia waited with much impatience to hear some tidings of the poor carpenter's wife; but though Mr Harrel, who had always that meal in his own room, came into his lady's at his usual hour, to see what was going forward, he did not mention her name. She therefore went into the hall herself, to enquire among the servants if Mrs Hill was yet come?

Yes, they answered, and had seen their master, and was gone.

She then returned to the breakfast room, where her eagerness to procure some information detained her, though the entrance of Sir Robert Floyer made her wish to retire. But she was wholly at a loss whether to impute to general forgetfulness, or to the failure of performing his promise, the silence of Mr Harrel upon the subject of her petition.

In a few minutes they were visited by Mr Morrice, who said he called to acquaint the ladies that the next morning there was to be a rehearsal of a very grand new dance at the Opera-House, where, though admission was difficult, if it was agreeable to them to go, he would undertake to introduce them.

Mrs Harrel happened to be engaged, and therefore declined the offer. He then turned to Cecilia, and said, "Well, ma'am, when did you see our friend Monckton?"

"Not since the rehearsal, sir."

"He is a mighty agreeable fellow," he continued, "and his house in the country is charming. One is as easy at it as at home. Were you ever there, Sir Robert?"

"Not I, truly," replied Sir Robert; "what should I go for?—to see an old woman with never a tooth in her head sitting at the top of the table! Faith, I'd go an hundred miles a day for a month never to see such a sight again."

"O but you don't know how well she does the honours," said Morrice; "and for my part, except just at meal times, I always contrive to keep out of her way."

"I wonder when she intends to die," said Mr Harrel.

"She's been a long time about it," cried Sir Robert; "but those tough old cats last for ever. We all thought she was going when Monckton married her; however, if he had not managed like a driveler, he might have broke her heart nine years ago."

"I am sure I wish he had," cried Mrs Harrel, "for she's an odious creature, and used always to make me afraid of her."

"But an old woman," answered Sir Robert, "is a person who has no sense of decency; if once she takes to living, the devil himself can't get rid of her."

"I dare say," cried Morrice, "she'll pop off before long in one of those fits of the asthma. I assure you sometimes you may hear her wheeze a mile off."

"She'll go never the sooner for that," said Sir Robert, "for I have got an old aunt of my own, who has been puffing and blowing as if she was at her last gasp ever since I can remember; and for all that, only yesterday, when I asked her doctor when she'd give up the ghost, he told me she might live these dozen years."

Cecilia was by no means sorry to have this brutal conversation interrupted by the entrance of a servant with a letter for her. She was immediately retiring to read it; but upon the petition of Mr Monckton, who just then came into the room, she only went to a window. The letter was as follows:

To Miss, at his Honour Squire Harrel's—These:
Honoured Madam,—This with my humble duty. His Honour has given me nothing. But I would not be troublesome, having wherewithal to wait, so conclude, Honoured Madam, your dutiful servant to command, till death, M. HILL.

The vexation with which Cecilia read this letter was visible to the whole company; and while Mr Arnott looked at her with a wish of enquiry he did not dare express, and Mr Monckton, under an appearance of inattention, concealed the most anxious curiosity, Mr Morrice alone had courage to interrogate her; and, pertly advancing, said, "He is a happy man who writ that letter, ma'am, for I am sure you have not read it with indifference."

"Were I the writer," said Mr Arnott, tenderly, "I am sure I should reckon myself far otherwise, for Miss Beverley seems to have read it with uneasiness."

"However, I have read it," answered she, "I assure you it is not from *any man*."

"O pray, Miss Beverley," cried Sir Robert, coming forward, "are you any better to-day?"

"No, sir, for I have not been ill."

"A little vapoured, I thought, yesterday; perhaps you want exercise."

"I wish the ladies would put themselves under my care," cried Morrice, "and take a turn round the park."

"I don't doubt you, Sir," said Mr Monckton, contemptuously, "and, but for the check of modesty, probably there is not a man here who would not wish the same."

"I could propose a much better scheme than that," said Sir Robert; "what if you all walk to Harley Street, and give me your notions of a house I am about there? what say you, Mrs Harrel?"

"O, I shall like it vastly."

"Done," cried Mr Harrel; "'tis an excellent motion."

"Come then," said Sir Robert, "let's be off. Miss Beverley, I hope you have a good warm cloak?"

"I must beg you to excuse my attending you, sir."

Mr Monckton, who had heard this proposal with the utmost dread of its success, revived at the calm steadiness with which it was declined. Mr and Mrs Harrel both teized Cecilia to consent; but the haughty Baronet, evidently more offended than hurt by her refusal, pressed the matter no further, either with her or the rest of the party, and the scheme was dropt entirely.

Mr Monckton failed not to remark this circumstance, which confirmed his suspicions, that though the proposal seemed made by chance, its design was nothing else than to obtain Cecilia's opinion concerning his house. But while this somewhat alarmed him, the unabated insolence of his carriage, and the confident defiance of his pride, still more surprized him; and notwithstanding all he observed of Cecilia, seemed to promise nothing but dislike; he could draw no other inference from his behaviour, than that if he admired, he also concluded himself sure of her.

This was not a pleasant conjecture, however little weight he allowed to it; and he resolved, by outstaying all the company, to have a few minutes' private discourse with her upon the subject.

In about half an hour, Sir Robert and Mr Harrel went out together: Mr Monckton still persevered in keeping his ground, and tried, though already weary, to keep up a general conversation; but what moved at once his wonder and his indignation was the assurance of Morrice, who seemed not only bent upon staying as long as himself, but determined, by rattling away, to make his own entertainment.

At length a servant came in to tell Mrs Harrel that a stranger, who was waiting in the house-keeper's room, begged to speak with her upon very particular business.

"O, I know," cried she, "'tis that odious John Groot: do pray, brother, try to get rid of him for me, for he comes to teize me about his bill, and I never know what to say to him."

Mr Arnott went immediately, and Mr Monckton could scarce refrain from going too, that he might entreat John Groot by no means to be satisfied without seeing Mrs Harrel herself: John Groot, however, wanted not his entreaties, as the servant soon returned to summons his lady to the conference.

But though Mr Monckton now seemed near the completion of his purpose, Morrice still remained; his vexation at this circumstance soon grew intolerable; to see himself upon the point of receiving the recompense of his perseverance, by the fortunate removal of all the obstacles in its way, and then to have it held from him by a young fellow he so much despised, and who had no entrance into the house but through his own boldness, and no inducement to stay in it but from his own impertinence, mortified him so insufferably, that it was with difficulty he even forbore from affronting him. Nor would he have scrupled a moment desiring him to leave the room, had he not prudently determined to guard with the utmost sedulity against raising any suspicions of his passion for Cecilia.

He arose, however, and was moving towards her, with the intention to occupy a part of a sofa on which she was seated, when Morrice, who was standing at the back of it, with a sudden spring which made the whole room shake, jumpt over, and sunk plump into the vacant place himself, calling out at the same time, "Come, come, what have you married men to do with young ladies? I shall seize this post for myself."

The rage of Mr Monckton at this feat, and still more at the words *married men*, almost exceeded endurance; he stopt short, and looking at him with a fierceness that overpowered his discretion, was bursting out with, "Sir, you are an—*impudent fellow*," but checking himself when he got half way, concluded with, "a very facetious gentleman!"

Morrice, who wished nothing so little as disobliging Mr Monckton, and whose behaviour was merely the result of levity and a want of early education, no sooner perceived his displeasure, than, rising with yet more agility than he had seated himself, he resumed the obsequiousness of which an uncommon flow of spirits had robbed him, and guessing no other subject for his anger than the disturbance he had made, he bowed almost to the ground, first to him, and afterwards to Cecilia, most respectfully begging pardon of them both for his frolic, and protesting he had no notion he should have made such a noise!

Mrs Harrel and Mr Arnott, now hastening back, enquired what had been the matter? Morrice, ashamed of his exploit, and frightened by the looks of Mr Monckton, made an apology with the utmost humility, and hurried away: and Mr Monckton, hopeless of any better fortune, soon did the same, gnawn with a cruel discontent which he did not dare avow, and longing. to revenge himself upon Morrice, even by personal chastisement.

CHAPTER XI

A NARRATION.

The moment Cecilia was at liberty, she sent her own servant to examine into the real situation of the carpenter and his family, and to desire his wife would call upon her as soon as she was at leisure. The account which he brought back encreased her concern for the injuries of these poor people, and determined her not to rest satisfied till she saw them redressed. He informed her that they lived in a small lodging up two pair of stairs; that there were five children, all girls, the three eldest of whom were hard at work with their mother in matting chair-bottoms, and the fourth, though a mere child, was nursing the youngest; while the poor carpenter himself was confined to his bed, in consequence of a fall from a ladder while working at Violet-Bank, by which he was covered with wounds and contusions, and an object of misery and pain.

As soon as Mrs Hill came, Cecilia sent for her into her own room, where she received her with the most compassionate tenderness, and desired to know when Mr Harrel talked of paying her?

"To-morrow, madam," she answered, shaking her head, "that is always his honour's speech: but I shall bear it while I can. However, though I dare not tell his honour, something bad will come of it, if I am not paid soon."

"Do you mean, then, to apply to the law?"

"I must not tell you, madam; but to be sure we have thought of it many a sad time and often; but still, while we could rub on, we thought it best not to make enemies: but, indeed, madam, his honour was so hardhearted this morning, that if I was not afraid you would be angry, I could not tell how to bear it; for when I told him I had no help now, for I had lost my Billy, he had the heart to say, 'So much the better, there's one the less of you.'"

"But what," cried Cecilia, extremely shocked by this unfeeling speech, "is the reason he gives for disappointing you so often?"

"He says, madam, that none of the other workmen are paid yet; and that, to be sure, is very true; but then they can all better afford to wait than we can, for we were the poorest of all, madam, and have been misfortunate from the beginning: and his honour would never have employed us, only he had run up such a bill with Mr Wright, that he would not undertake any thing more till he was paid. We were told from the first we should not get our money; but we were willing to hope for the best, for we had nothing to do, and were hard run, and had never had the offer of so good a job before; and we had a great family to keep, and many losses, and so much illness!—Oh madam! if you did but know what the poor go through!"

This speech opened to Cecilia a new view of life; that a young man could appear so gay and happy, yet be guilty of such injustice and inhumanity, that he could take pride in works which not even money had made his own, and live with undiminished splendor, when his credit itself began to fail, seemed to her incongruities so irrational, that hitherto she had supposed them impossible.

She then enquired if her husband had yet had any physician?

"Yes, madam, I humbly thank your goodness," she answered; "but I am not the poorer for that, for the gentleman was so kind he would take nothing."

"And does he give you any hopes? what does he say?"

"He says he must die, madam, but I knew that before."

"Poor woman! and what will you do then?"

"The same, madam, as I did when I lost my Billy, work on the harder!"

"Good heaven, *how severe a lot!* but tell me, why is it you seem to love your Billy so much better than the rest of your children?"

"Because, madam, he was the only boy that ever I had; he was seventeen years old, madam, and as tall and as pretty a lad! and so good, that he never cost me a wet eye till I lost him. He worked with his father, and all the folks used to say he was the better workman of the two."

"And what was the occasion of his death?"

"A consumption, madam, that wasted him quite to nothing: and he was ill a long time, and cost us a deal of money, for we spared neither for wine nor any thing that we thought would but comfort him; and we loved him so we never grudged it. But he died, madam! and if it had not been for very hard work, the loss of him would quite have broke my heart."

"Try, however, to think less of him," said Cecilia; "and depend upon my speaking again for you to Mr Harrel. You shall certainly have your money; take care, therefore, of your own health, and go home and give comfort to your sick husband."

"Oh, madam," cried the poor woman, tears streaming down her cheeks, "you don't know how touching it is to hear gentlefolks talk so kindly! And I have been used to nothing but roughness from his honour! But what I most fear, madam, is that when my husband is gone, he will be harder to deal with than ever; for a widow, madam, is always hard to be righted; and I don't expect to hold out long myself, for sickness and sorrow wear fast: and then, when we are both gone, who is to help our poor children?"

"*I will!*" cried the generous Cecilia; "I am able, and I am willing; you shall not find all the rich hardhearted, and I will try to make you some amends for the unkindness you have suffered."

The poor woman, overcome by a promise so unexpected, burst into a passionate fit of tears, and sobbed out her thanks with a violence of emotion that frightened Cecilia almost as much as it melted her. She endeavoured, by re-iterated assurances of assistance, to appease her, and solemnly pledged her own honour that she should certainly be paid the following Saturday, which was only three days distant.

Mrs Hill, when a little calmer, dried her eyes, and humbly begging her to forgive a transport which she could not restrain, most gratefully thanked her for the engagement into which she had entered, protesting that she would not be *troublesome to her goodness* as long as she could help it; "And I believe," she continued, "that if his honour will but pay me time enough for the burial, I can make shift with what I have till then. But when my poor Billy died, we were sadly off indeed, for we could not bear but bury him prettily, because it was the last we could do for him: but we could hardly scrape up enough for it, and yet we all went without our dinners to help forward, except the little one of all. But that did not much matter, for we had no great heart for eating.".

"I cannot bear this!" cried Cecilia; "you must tell me no more of your Billy; but go home, and chear your spirits, and do every thing in your power to save your husband."

"I will, madam," answered the woman, "and his dying prayers shall bless you! and all my children shall bless you, and every night they shall pray for you. And oh!"—again bursting into tears, "that Billy was but alive to pray for you too!"

Cecilia kindly endeavoured to soothe her, but the poor creature, no longer able to suppress the violence of her awakened sorrows, cried out, "I must go, madam, and pray for you at home, for now I have once begun crying again, I don't know how to have done!" and hurried away.

Cecilia determined to make once more an effort with Mr Harrel for the payment of the bill, and if that, in two days, did not succeed, to take up money for the discharge of it herself, and rest all her security for reimbursement upon the shame with which such a proceeding must overwhelm him. Offended, however, by the repulse she had already received from him, and disgusted by all she had heard of his unfeeling negligence, she knew not how to address him, and resolved upon applying again to Mr Arnott, who was already acquainted with the affair, for advice and assistance.

Mr Arnott, though extremely gratified that she consulted him, betrayed by his looks a hopelessness of success, that damped all her expectations. He promised, however, to speak to Mr Harrel upon the subject, but the promise was evidently given to oblige the fair mediatrix, without any hope of advantage to the cause.

The next morning Mrs Hill again came, and again without payment was dismissed.

Mr Arnott then, at the request of Cecilia, followed Mr Harrel into his room, to enquire into the reason of this breach of promise; they continued some time together, and when he returned to Cecilia, he told her, that his brother had assured him he would give orders to Davison, his gentleman, to let her have the money the next day.

The pleasure with which she would have heard this intelligence was much checked by the grave and cold manner in which it was communicated: she waited, therefore, with more impatience than confidence for the result of this fresh assurance.

The next morning, however, was the same as the last; Mrs Hill came, saw Davison, and was sent away.

Cecilia, to whom she related her grievances, then flew to Mr Arnott, and entreated him to enquire at least of Davison why the woman had again been disappointed.

Mr Arnott obeyed her, and brought for answer, that Davison had received no orders from his master.

"I entreat you then," cried she, with mingled eagerness and vexation, "to go, for the last time, to Mr Harrel. I am sorry to impose upon you an office so disagreeable, but I am sure you compassionate these poor people, and will serve them now with your interest, as you have already done with your purse. I only wish to know if there has been any mistake, or if these delays are merely to sicken me of petitioning."

Mr Arnott, with a repugnance to the request which he could as ill conceal as his admiration of the zealous requester, again forced himself to follow Mr Harrel. His stay was not long, and Cecilia at his return perceived that he was hurt and disconcerted. As soon as they were alone together, she begged to know what had passed? "Nothing," answered he, "that will give you any pleasure. When I entreated my brother to come to the point, he said it was his intention to pay all his workmen together, for that if he paid any one singly, all the rest would be dissatisfied."

"And why," said Cecilia, "should he not pay them at once? There can be no more comparison in the value of the money to him and to them, than, to speak with truth, there is in his and in their right to it."

"But, madam, the bills for the new house itself are none of them settled, and he says that the moment he is known to discharge an account for the Temple, he shall not have any rest for the clamours it will raise among the workmen who were employed about the house."

"How infinitely strange!" exclaimed Cecilia; "will he not, then, pay anybody?"

"Next quarter, he says, he shall pay them all, but, at present, he has a particular call for his money."

Cecilia would not trust herself to make any comments upon such an avowal, but thanking Mr Arnott for the trouble which he had taken, she determined, without any further application, to desire Mr Harrel to advance her 20 pounds the next morning, and satisfy the carpenter herself, be the risk what it might.

The following day, therefore, which was the Saturday when payment was promised, she begged an audience of Mr Harrel; which he immediately granted; but, before she could make her demand, he said to her, with an air of the utmost gaiety and good-humour, "Well, Miss Beverley, how fares it with your *protegee*? I hope, at length, she is contented. But I must beg you would charge her to keep her own counsel, as otherwise she will draw me into a scrape I shall not thank her for."

"Have you, then, paid her?" cried Cecilia, with much amazement.

"Yes; I promised you I would, you know."

This intelligence equally delighted and astonished her; she repeatedly thanked him for his attention to her petition, and, eager to communicate her success to Mr Arnott, she hastened to find him. "Now," cried she, "I shall torment you no more with painful commissions; the Hills, at last, are paid!"

"From you, madam," answered he gravely, "no commissions could be painful."

"Well, but," said Cecilia, somewhat disappointed, "you don't seem glad of this?"

"Yes," answered he, with a forced smile, "I am very glad to see you so."

"But how was it brought about? did Mr Harrel relent? or did you attack him again?"

The hesitation of his answer convinced her there was some mystery in the transaction; she began to apprehend she had been deceived, and hastily quitting the room, sent for Mrs Hill: but the moment the poor woman appeared, she was satisfied of the contrary, for, almost frantic with joy and gratitude, she immediately flung herself upon her knees, to thank her benefactress for having *seen her righted*.

Cecilia then gave her some general advice, promised to continue her friend, and offered her assistance in getting her husband into an hospital; but she told her he had already been in one many months, where he had been pronounced incurable, and therefore was desirous to spend his last days in his own lodgings.

"Well," said Cecilia, "make them as easy to him as you, can, and come to me next week, and I will try to put you in a better way of living."

She then, still greatly perplexed about Mr Arnott, sought him again, and, after various questions and conjectures, at length brought him to confess he had himself lent his brother the sum with which the Hills had been paid.

Struck with his generosity, she poured forth thanks and praises so grateful to his ears, that she soon gave him a recompense which he would have thought cheaply purchased by half his fortune.

BOOK II

CHAPTER I

A MAN OF WEALTH

The meanness with which Mr Harrel had assumed the credit, as well as accepted the assistance of Mr Arnott, increased the disgust he had already excited in Cecilia, and hastened her resolution of quitting his house; and therefore, without waiting any longer for the advice of Mr Monckton, she resolved to go instantly to her other guardians, and see what better prospects their habitations might offer.

For this purpose she borrowed one of the carriages, and gave orders to be driven into the city to the house of Mr Briggs.

She told her name, and was shewn, by a little shabby footboy, into a parlour.

Here she waited, with tolerable patience, for half an hour, but then, imagining the boy had forgotten to tell his master she was in the house, she thought it expedient to make some enquiry.

No bell, however, could she find, and therefore she went into the passage in search of the footboy; but, as she was proceeding to the head of the kitchen stairs, she was startled by hearing a man's voice from the upper part of the house exclaiming, in a furious passion, "Dare say you've filched it for a dish-clout!"

She called out, however, "Are any of Mr Briggs's servants below?"

"Anan!" answered the boy, who came to the foot of the stairs, with a knife in one hand and an old shoe, upon the sole of which he was sharpening it, in the other, "Does any one call?"

"Yes," said Cecilia, "I do; for I could not find the bell."

"O, we have no bell in the parlour," returned the boy, "master always knocks with his stick."

"I am afraid Mr Briggs is too busy to see me, and if so, I will come another time."

"No, ma'am," said the boy, "master's only looking over his things from the wash."

"Will you tell him, then, that I am waiting?"

"I has, ma'am; but master misses his shaving-rag, and he says he won't come to the Mogul till he's found it." And then he went on with sharpening his knife.

This little circumstance was at least sufficient to satisfy Cecilia that if she fixed her abode with Mr Briggs, she should not have much uneasiness to fear from the sight of extravagance and profusion.

She returned to the parlour, and after waiting another half-hour, Mr Briggs made his appearance.

Mr Briggs was a short, thick, sturdy man, with very small keen black eyes, a square face, a dark complexion, and a snub nose. His constant dress, both in winter and summer, was a snuff-colour suit of clothes, blue and white speckled worsted stockings, a plain shirt, and a bob wig. He was seldom without a stick in his hand, which he usually held to his forehead when not speaking.

This bob wig, however, to the no small amazement of Cecilia, he now brought into the room upon the forefinger of his left hand, while, with his right, he was smoothing the curls; and his head, in defiance of the coldness of the weather, was bald and uncovered.

"Well," cried he, as he entered, "did you think I should not come?"

"I was very willing, sir, to wait your leisure."

"Ay, ay, knew you had not much to do. Been looking for my shaving-rag. Going out of town; never use such a thing at home, paper does as well. Warrant Master Harrel never heard of such a thing; ever see him comb his own wig? Warrant he don't know how! never trust mine out of my hands, the boy would tear off half the hair; all one to master Harrel, I suppose. Well, which is the warmer man, that's all? Will he cast an account with me?"

Cecilia, at a loss what to say to this singular exordium, began an apology for not waiting upon him sooner.

"Ay, ay," cried he, "always gadding, no getting sight of you. Live a fine life! A pretty guardian, Master Harrel! and where's t'other? where's old Don Puffabout?"

"If you mean Mr Delvile, sir, I have not yet seen him."

"Thought so. No matter, as well not. Only tell you he's a German Duke, or a Spanish Don Ferdinand. Well, you've me! poorly off else. A couple of ignoramuses! don't know when to buy nor when to sell. No doing business with either of them. We met once or twice; all to no purpose; only heard Don Vampus count his old Grandees; how will that get interest for money? Then comes Master Harrel—twenty bows to a word,—looks at a watch,—about as big as a sixpence,—poor raw ninny!—a couple of rare guardians! Well, you've me, I say; mind that!"

Cecilia was wholly unable to devise any answer to these effusions of contempt and anger; and therefore his harangue lasted without interruption, till he had exhausted all his subjects of complaint, and emptied his mind of ill-will; and then, settling his wig, he drew a chair near her, and twinkling his little black eyes in her face, his rage subsided into the most perfect good humour; and, after peering at her some time with a look of much approbation, he said, with an arch nod, "Well, my duck, got ever a sweetheart yet?"

Cecilia laughed, and said "No."

"Ah, little rogue, don't believe you! all a fib! better speak out: come, fit I should know; a'n't you my own ward? to be sure, almost of age, but not quite, so what's that to me?"

She then, more seriously, assured him she had no intelligence of that sort to communicate.

"Well, when you have, tell, that's all. Warrant sparks enough hankering. I'll give you some advice Take care of sharpers; don't trust shoe-buckles, nothing but Bristol stones! tricks in all things. A fine gentleman sharp as another man. Never give your heart to a gold-topped cane, nothing but brass gilt over. Cheats everywhere: fleece you in a year; won't leave you a groat. But one way to be safe,—bring 'em all to me."

Cecilia thanked him for his caution, and promised not to forget his advice.

"That's the way," he continued, "bring 'em to me. Won't be bamboozled. Know their tricks. Shew 'em the odds on't. Ask for the rent-roll,—see how they look! stare like stuck pigs! got no such thing."

"Certainly, sir, that will be an excellent method of trial."

"Ay, ay, know the way! soon find if they are above par. Be sure don't mind gold waistcoats; nothing but tinsel, all shew and no substance; better leave the matter to me; take care of you myself; know where to find one will do."

She again thanked him; and, being fully satisfied with this specimen of his conversation, and unambitious of any further counsel from him, she arose to depart.

"Well," repeated he, nodding at her, with a look of much kindness, "leave it to me, I say; I'll get you a careful husband, so take no thought about the matter."

Cecilia, half-laughing, begged he would not give himself much trouble, and assured him she was not in any haste.

"All the better," said he, "good girl; no fear for you: look out myself; warrant I'll find one. Not very easy, neither! hard times! men scarce; wars and tumults! stocks low! women chargeable!—but don't fear; do our best; get you off soon."

She then returned to her carriage: full of reflection upon the scene in which she had just been engaged, and upon the strangeness of hastening from one house to avoid a vice the very want of which seemed to render another insupportable! but she now found that though luxury was more baneful in its consequences, it was less disgustful in its progress than avarice; yet, insuperably averse to both, and almost equally desirous to fly from the unjust extravagance of Mr Harrel, as from the comfortless and unnecessary parsimony of Mr Briggs, she proceeded instantly to St James's Square, convinced that her third guardian, unless exactly resembling one of the others, must inevitably be preferable to both.

CHAPTER II

A MAN OF FAMILY.

The house of Mr Delvile was grand and spacious, fitted up not with modern taste, but with the magnificence of former times; the servants were all veterans, gorgeous in their liveries, and profoundly respectful in their manners; every thing had an air of state, but of a state so gloomy, that while it inspired awe, it repressed pleasure.

Cecilia sent in her name and was admitted without difficulty, and was then ushered with great pomp through sundry apartments, and rows of servants, before she came into the presence of Mr Delvile.

He received her with an air of haughty affability which, to a spirit open and liberal as that of Cecilia, could not fail being extremely offensive; but too much occupied with the care of his own importance to penetrate into the feelings of another, he attributed the uneasiness which his reception occasioned to the overawing predominance of superior rank and consequence.

He ordered a servant to bring her a chair, while he only half rose from his own upon her entering into the room; then, waving his hand and bowing, with a motion that desired her to be seated, he said, "I am very happy, Miss Beverley, that you have found me alone; you would rarely have had the same good fortune. At this time of day I am generally in a crowd. People of large connections have not much leisure in London, especially if they see a little after their own affairs, and if their estates, like mine, are dispersed in various parts of the kingdom. However, I am glad it happened so. And I am glad, too, that you have done me the favour of calling without waiting till I sent, which I really would have done as soon as I heard of your arrival, but that the multiplicity of my engagements allowed me no respite."

A display of importance so ostentatious made Cecilia already half repent her visit, satisfied that the hope in which she had planned it would be fruitless.

Mr Delvile, still imputing to embarrassment, an inquietude of countenance that proceeded merely from disappointment, imagined her veneration was every moment increasing; and therefore, pitying a timidity which both gratified and softened him, and equally pleased with himself for inspiring, and with her for feeling it, he abated more and more of his greatness, till he became, at length, so infinitely condescending, with intention to give her courage, that he totally depressed her with mortification and chagrin.

After some general inquiries concerning her way of life, he told her that he hoped she was contented with her situation at the Harrels, adding, "If you have any thing to complain of, remember to whom you may appeal." He then asked if she had seen Mr Briggs?

"Yes, sir, I am this moment come from his house."

"I am sorry for it; his house cannot be a proper one for the reception of a young lady. When the Dean made application that I would be one of your guardians, I instantly sent him a refusal, as is my custom upon all such occasions, which indeed occur to me with a frequency extremely importunate: but the Dean was a man for whom I had really a regard, and, therefore, when I found my refusal had affected him, I suffered myself to be prevailed upon to indulge him, contrary not only to my general rule, but to my inclination."

Here he stopt, as if to receive some compliment, but Cecilia, very little disposed to pay him any, went no farther than an inclination of the head.

"I knew not, however," he continued, "at the time I was induced to give my consent, with whom I was to be associated; nor could I have imagined the Dean so little conversant with the distinctions of the world, as to disgrace me with inferior coadjutors: but the moment I learnt the state of the affair, I insisted upon withdrawing both my name and countenance."

Here again he paused; not in expectation of an answer from Cecilia, but merely to give her time to marvel in what manner he had at last been melted.

"The Dean," he resumed, "was then very ill; my displeasure, I believe, hurt him. I was sorry for it; he was a worthy man, and had not meant to offend me; in the end, I accepted his apology, and was even persuaded to accept the office. You have a right, therefore, to consider yourself as *personally* my ward, and though I do not think proper to mix much with your other guardians, I shall always be ready to serve and advise you, and much pleased to see you."

"You do me honour, sir," said Cecilia, extremely wearied of such graciousness, and rising to be gone.

"Pray sit still," said he, with a smile; "I have not many engagements for this morning. You must give me some account how you pass your time. Are you much out? The Harrels, I am told, live at a great expense. What is their establishment?"

"I don't exactly know, sir."

"They are decent sort of people, I believe; are they not?"

"I hope so, sir!"

"And they have a tolerable acquaintance, I believe: I am told so; for I know nothing of them."

"They have, at least, a very numerous one, sir."

"Well, my dear," said he, taking her hand, "now you have once ventured to come, don't be apprehensive of repeating your visits. I must introduce you to Mrs Delvile; I am sure she will be happy to shew you any kindness. Come, therefore, when you please, and without scruple. I would call upon you myself, but am fearful of being embarrassed by the people with whom you live."

He then rang his bell, and with the same ceremonies which had attended her admittance, she was conducted back to her carriage.

And here died away all hope of putting into execution, during her minority, the plan of which the formation had given her so much pleasure. She found that her present situation, however wide of her wishes, was by no means the most disagreeable in which she could be placed; she was tired, indeed, of dissipation, and shocked at the sight of unfeeling extravagance; but notwithstanding the houses of each of her other guardians were exempt from these particular vices, she saw not any prospect of happiness with either of them; vulgarity seemed leagued with avarice to drive her from the mansion of Mr Briggs, and haughtiness with ostentation to exclude her from that of Mr Delvile.

She came back, therefore, to Portman Square, disappointed in her hopes, and sick both of those whom she quitted and of those to whom she was returning; but in going to her own apartment Mrs Harrel, eagerly stopping her, begged she would come into the drawing-room, where she promised her a most agreeable surprise.

Cecilia, for an instant, imagined that some old acquaintance was just arrived out of the country; but, upon her entrance, she saw only Mr Harrel and some workmen, and found that the agreeable surprise was to proceed from the sight of an elegant Awning, prepared for one of the inner apartments, to be fixed over a long desert-table, which was to be ornamented with various devices of cut glass.

"Did you ever see any thing so beautiful in your life?" cried Mrs Harrel; "and when the table is covered with the coloured ices and those sort of things, it will be as beautiful again. We shall have it ready for Tuesday se'nnight.

"I understood you were engaged to go to the Masquerade ?"

"So we shall; only we intend to see masks at home first."

"I have some thoughts," said Mr Harrel, leading the way to another small room, "of running up a flight of steps and a little light gallery here, and so making a little Orchestra. What would such a thing come to, Mr Tomkins?"

"O, a trifle, sir," answered Mr Tomkins, "a mere nothing."

"Well, then, give orders for it, and let it be done directly. I don't care how slight it is, but pray let it be very elegant. Won't it be a great addition, Miss Beverley?"

"Indeed, sir, I don't think it seems to be very necessary," said Cecilia, who wished much to take that moment for reminding him of the debt he had contracted with Mr Arnott.

"Lord, Miss Beverley is so grave!" cried Mrs Harrel; "nothing of this sort gives her any pleasure."

"She has indeed," answered Cecilia, trying to smile, "not much taste for the pleasure of being always surrounded by workmen."

And, as soon as she was able, she retired to her room, feeling, both on the part of Mr Arnott and the Hills, a resentment at the injustice of Mr Harrel, which fixed her in the resolution of breaking through that facility of compliance, which had hitherto confined her disapprobation to her own breast, and venturing, henceforward, to mark the opinion she entertained of his conduct by consulting nothing but reason and principle in her own.

Her first effort towards this change was made immediately, in begging to be excused from accompanying Mrs Harrel to a large card assembly that evening.

Mrs Harrel, extremely surprised, asked a thousand times the reason of her refusal, imagining it to proceed from some very extraordinary cause; nor was she, without the utmost difficulty, persuaded at last that she merely meant to pass one evening by herself.

But the next day, when the refusal was repeated, she was still more incredulous; it seemed to her impossible that any one who had the power to be encircled with company, could by choice spend a second afternoon alone: and she was so urgent in her request to be entrusted with the secret, that Cecilia found no way left to appease her, but by frankly confessing she was weary of eternal visiting, and sick of living always in a crowd.

"Suppose, then," cried she, "I send for Miss Larolles to come and sit with you?"

Cecilia, not without laughing, declined this proposal, assuring her that no such assistant was necessary for her entertainment: yet it was not till after a long contention that she was able to convince her there would be no cruelty in leaving her by herself.

The following day, however, her trouble diminished; for Mrs Harrel, ceasing to be surprised, thought little more of the matter, and forbore any earnestness of solicitation: and, from that time, she suffered her to follow her own humour with very little opposition. Cecilia was much concerned to find her so unmoved; and not less disappointed at the indifference of Mr Harrel, who, being seldom of the same parties with his lady, and seeing her too rarely either to communicate or hear any domestic occurrences, far from being struck, as she had hoped, with the new way in which she passed her time, was scarce sensible of the change, and interfered not upon the subject.

Sir Robert Floyer, who continued to see her when he dined in Portman Square, often enquired what she did with herself in an evening; but never obtaining any satisfactory answer, he concluded her engagements were with people to whom he was a stranger.

Poor Mr Arnott felt the cruellest disappointment in being deprived of the happiness of attending her in her evening's expeditions, when, whether he conversed with her or not, he was sure of the indulgence of seeing and hearing her.

But the greatest sufferer from this new regulation was Mr Monckton, who, unable any longer to endure the mortifications of which his morning visits to Portman Square had been productive, determined not to trust his temper with such provocations in future, but rather to take his chance of meeting with her elsewhere: for which purpose, he assiduously frequented all public places, and sought acquaintance with every family and every person he believed to be known to the Harrels: but his patience was unrewarded, and his diligence unsuccessful; he met with her no where, and, while he continued his search, fancied every evil power was at work to lead him whither he was sure never to find her.

Meanwhile Cecilia passed her time greatly to her own satisfaction. Her first care was to assist and comfort the Hills. She went herself to their lodgings, ordered and paid for whatever the physician prescribed to the sick man, gave clothes to the children, and money and various necessaries to the wife. She found that the poor carpenter was not likely to languish much longer, and therefore, for the present, only thought of alleviating his sufferings, by procuring him such indulgences as were authorised by his physician, and enabling his family to abate so much of their labour as was requisite for obtaining time to nurse and attend him: but she meant, as soon as the last duties should be paid him, to assist his survivors in attempting to follow some better and more profitable business.

Her next solicitude was to furnish herself with a well-chosen collection of books: and this employment, which to a lover of literature, young and ardent in its pursuit, is perhaps the mind's first luxury, proved a source of entertainment so fertile and delightful that it left her nothing to wish.

She confined not her acquisitions to the limits of her present power, but, as she was laying in a stock for future as well as immediate advantage, she was restrained by no expence from gratifying her taste and her inclination. She had now entered the last year of her minority, and therefore had not any doubt that her guardians would permit her to take up whatever sum she should require for such a purpose.

And thus, in the exercise of charity, the search of knowledge, and the enjoyment of quiet, serenely in innocent philosophy passed the hours of Cecilia.

CHAPTER III

A MASQUERADE.

The first check this tranquillity received was upon the day of the masquerade, the preparations for which have been already mentioned. The whole house was then in commotion from various arrangements and improvements which were planned for almost every apartment that was to be opened for the reception of masks. Cecilia herself, however little pleased with the attendant circumstance of wantonly accumulating unnecessary debts, was not the least animated of the party: she was a stranger to every diversion of this sort, and from the novelty of the scene, hoped for uncommon satisfaction.

At noon Mrs Harrel sent for her to consult upon a new scheme which occurred to Mr Harrel, of fixing in fantastic forms some coloured lamps in the drawing-room.

While they were all discoursing this matter over, one of the servants, who had two or three times whispered some message to Mr Harrel, and then retired, said, in a voice not too low to be heard by Cecilia, "Indeed, Sir, I can't get him away."

"He's an insolent scoundrel," answered Mr Harrel; "however, if I must speak to him, I must;" and went out of the room.

Mrs Harrel still continued to exercise her fancy upon this new project, calling both upon Mr Arnott and Cecilia to admire her taste and contrivance; till they were all interrupted by the loudness of a voice from below stairs, which frequently repeated, "Sir, I can wait no longer! I have been put off till I can be put off no more!"

Startled by this, Mrs Harrel ceased her employment, and they all stood still and silent. They then heard Mr Harrel with much softness answer, "Good Mr Rawlins, have a little patience; I shall receive a large sum of money to-morrow, or next day, and you may then depend upon being paid."

"Sir," cried the man, "you have so often told me the same, that it goes just for nothing: I have had a right to it a long time, and I have a bill to make up that can't be waited for any longer."

"Certainly, Mr Rawlins," replied Mr Harrel, with still increasing gentleness, "and certainly you shall have it: nobody means to dispute your right; I only beg you to wait a day, or two days at furthest, and you may then depend upon being paid. And you shall not be the worse for obliging me; I will never employ any body else, and I shall have occasion for you very soon, as I intend to make some alterations at Violet-Bank that will be very considerable."

"Sir," said the man, still louder, "it is of no use your employing me, if I can never get my money. All my workmen must be paid whether I am or no; and so, if I must needs speak to a lawyer, why there's no help for it."

"Did you ever hear any thing so impertinent?" exclaimed Mrs Harrel; "I am sure Mr Harrel will be very much to blame, if ever he lets that man do any thing more for him."

Just then Mr Harrel appeared, and, with an air of affected unconcern, said, "Here's the most insolent rascal of a mason below stairs I ever met with in my life; he has come upon me, quite unexpectedly, with a bill of 400 pounds, and won't leave the house without the money. Brother Arnott, I wish you would do me the favour to speak to the fellow, for I could not bear to stay with him any longer."

"Do you wish me to give him a draft for the money upon my own banker?"

"That would be vastly obliging," answered Mr Harrel, "and I will give you my note for it directly. And so we shall get rid of this fellow at once:

and he shall do nothing more for me as long as he lives. I will run up a new building at Violet-Bank next summer, if only to shew him what a job he has lost."

"Pay the man at once, there's a good brother," cried Mrs Harrel, "and let's hear no more of him."

The two gentlemen then retired to another room, and Mrs Harrel, after praising the extreme good-nature of her brother, of whom she was very fond, and declaring that the mason's impertinence had quite frightened her, again returned to her plan of new decorations.

Cecilia, amazed at this indifference to the state of her husband's affairs, began to think it was her own duty to talk with her upon the subject: and therefore, after a silence so marked that Mrs Harrel enquired into its reason, she said, "Will you pardon me, my dear friend, if I own I am rather surprized to see you continue these preparations?"

"Lord, why?"

"Because any fresh unnecessary expences just now, till Mr Harrel actually receives the money he talks of—"

"Why, my dear, the expence of such a thing as this is nothing; in Mr Harrel's affairs I assure you it will not be at all felt. Besides, he expects money so soon, that it is just the same as if he had it already."

Cecilia, unwilling to be too officious, began then to express her admiration of the goodness and generosity of Mr Arnott; taking frequent occasion, in the course of her praise, to insinuate that those only can be properly liberal, who are just and economical.

She had prepared no masquerade habit for this evening, as Mrs Harrel, by whose direction she was guided, informed her it was not necessary for ladies to be masked at home, and said she should receive her company herself in a dress which she might wear upon any other occasion. Mr Harrel, also, and Mr Arnott made not any alteration in their appearance.

At about eight o'clock the business of the evening began; and before nine, there were so many masks that Cecilia wished she had herself made one of the number, as she was far more conspicuous in being almost the only female in a common dress, than any masquerade habit could have made her. The novelty of the scene, however, joined to the general air of gaiety diffused throughout the company, shortly lessened her embarrassment; and, after being somewhat familiarized to the abruptness with which the masks approached her, and the freedom with which they looked at or addressed her, the first confusion of her situation subsided, and in her curiosity to watch others, she ceased to observe how much she was watched herself.

Her expectations of entertainment were not only fulfilled but surpassed; the variety of dresses, the medley of characters, the quick succession of figures, and the ludicrous mixture of groups, kept her attention unwearied: while the conceited efforts at wit, the total thoughtlessness of consistency, and the ridiculous incongruity of the language with the appearance, were incitements to surprise and diversion without end. Even the local cant of, *Do you know me? Who are you?* and *I know you;* with the sly pointing of the finger, the arch nod of the head, and the pert squeak of the voice, though wearisome to those who frequent such assemblies, were, to her unhackneyed observation, additional subjects of amusement.

Soon after nine o'clock, every room was occupied, and the common crowd of regular masqueraders were dispersed through the various apartments. Dominos of no character, and fancy dresses of no meaning, made, as is usual at such meetings, the general herd of the company: for the rest, the men were Spaniards, chimney-sweepers, Turks, watchmen, conjurers, and old women; and the ladies, shepherdesses, orange girls, Circassians, gipseys, haymakers, and sultanas.

Cecilia had, as yet, escaped any address beyond the customary enquiry of *Do you know me?* and a few passing compliments; but when the rooms filled, and the general crowd gave general courage, she was attacked in a manner more pointed and singular.

The very first mask who approached her seemed to have nothing less in view than preventing the approach of every other: yet had he little reason to hope favour for himself, as the person he represented, of all others least alluring to the view, was the devil! He was black from head to foot, save that two red horns seemed to issue from his forehead; his face was so completely covered that the sight only of his eyes was visible, his feet were cloven, and in his right hand he held a wand the colour of fire.

Waving this wand as he advanced towards Cecilia, he cleared a semi-circular space before her chair, thrice with the most profound reverence bowed to her, thrice. turned himself around with sundry grimaces, and then fiercely planted himself at her side.

Cecilia was amused by his mummery, but felt no great delight in his guardianship, and, after a short time, arose, with intention to walk to another place; but the black gentleman, adroitly moving round her, held out his wand to obstruct her passage, and therefore, preferring captivity to resistance, she was again obliged to seat herself.

An Hotspur, who just then made his appearance, was now strutting boldly towards her; but the devil, rushing furiously forwards, placed himself immediately between them. Hotspur, putting his arms a-kimbo with an air of defiance, gave a loud stamp with his right foot, and then—marched into another room!

The victorious devil ostentatiously waved his wand, and returned to his station.

Mr Arnott, who had never moved two yards from Cecilia, knowing her too well to suppose she received any pleasure from being thus distinguished, modestly advanced to offer his assistance in releasing her from confinement; but the devil, again describing a circle with his wand, gave him three such smart raps on the head that his hair was disordered, and his face covered with powder. A general laugh succeeded, and Mr Arnott, too diffident to brave raillery, or withstand shame, retired in confusion.

The black gentleman seemed now to have all authority in his own hands, and his wand was brandished with more ferocity than ever, no one again venturing to invade the domain he thought fit to appropriate for his own.

At length, however, a Don Quixote appeared, and every mask in the room was eager to point out to him the imprisonment of Cecilia.

This Don Quixote was accoutered with tolerable exactness according to the description of the admirable Cervantes; his armour was rusty, his helmet was a barber's basin, his shield, a pewter dish, and his lance, an old sword fastened to a slim cane. His figure, tall and thin, was well adapted to the character he represented, and his mask, which depictured a lean and haggard face, worn with care, yet fiery with crazy passions, exhibited, with propriety the most striking, the knight of the doleful countenance.

The complaints against the devil with which immediately and from all quarters he was assailed, he heard with the most solemn taciturnity: after which, making a motion for general silence, he stalked majestically towards Cecilia, but stopping short of the limits prescribed by her guard, he kissed his spear in token of allegiance, and then, slowly dropping upon one knee, began the following address:

"Most incomparable Princess!—Thus humbly prostrate at the feet of your divine and ineffable beauty, graciously permit the most pitiful of your servitors, Don Quixote De la Mancha, from your high and tender grace, to salute the fair boards which sustain your corporeal machine."

Then, bending down his head, he kissed the floor; after which, raising himself upon his feet, he proceeded in his speech.

"Report, O most fair and unmatchable virgin! daringly affirmeth that a certain discourteous person, who calleth himself the devil, even now, and in thwart of your fair inclinations, keepeth and detaineth your irradiant frame in hostile thraldom. Suffer then, magnanimous and undescribable lady! that I, the most groveling of your unworthy vassals, do sift the fair truth out of this foul sieve, and obsequiously bending to your divine attractions, conjure your highness veritably to inform me, if that honourable chair which haply supports your terrestrial perfections, containeth the inimitable burthen with the free and legal consent of your celestial spirit?"

Here he ceased: and Cecilia, who laughed at this characteristic address, though she had not courage to answer it, again made an effort to quit her place, but again by the wand of her black persecutor was prevented.

This little incident was answer sufficient for the valorous knight, who indignantly exclaimed,

"Sublime Lady!—I beseech but of your exquisite mercy to refrain mouldering the clay composition of my unworthy body to impalpable dust, by the refulgence of those bright stars vulgarly called eyes, till I have lawfully wreaked my vengeance upon this unobliging caitiff, for his most disloyal obstruction of your highness's adorable pleasure."

Then, bowing low, he turned from her, and thus addressed his intended antagonist:

"Uncourtly Miscreant,—The black garment which envellopeth thy most unpleasant person, seemeth even of the most ravishing whiteness, in compare of the black bile which floateth within thy sable interior. Behold, then, my gauntlet! yet ere I deign to be the instrument of thy extirpation, O thou most mean and ignoble enemy! that the honour of Don Quixote De la Mancha may not be sullied by thy extinction, I do here confer upon thee the honour of knighthood, dubbing thee, by my own sword, Don Devil, knight of the horrible physiognomy."

He then attempted to strike his shoulder with his spear, but the black gentleman, adroitly eluding the blow, defended himself with his wand: a mock fight ensued, conducted on both sides with admirable dexterity; but Cecilia, less eager to view it than to become again a free agent, made her escape into another apartment; while the rest of the ladies, though they almost all screamed, jumped upon chairs and sofas to peep at the combat.

In conclusion, the wand of the knight of the horrible physiognomy was broken against the shield of the knight of the doleful countenance; upon which Don Quixote called out *victoria*! the whole room echoed the sound; the unfortunate new knight retired abruptly into another apartment, and the conquering Don, seizing the fragments of the weapon of his vanquished enemy went out in search of the lady for whose releasement he had fought: and the moment he found her, prostrating both himself and the trophies at her feet, he again pressed the floor with his lips, and then, slowly arising, repeated his reverences with added formality, and, without waiting her acknowledgments, gravely retired.

The moment he departed a Minerva, not stately nor austere, not marching in warlike majesty, but gay and airy,

"Tripping on light fantastic toe,"

ran up to Cecilia, and squeaked out, "Do you know me?"

"Not," answered she, instantly recollecting Miss Larolles, "by your *appearance*, I own! but by your *voice*, I think I can guess you."

"I was monstrous sorry," returned the goddess, without understanding this distinction, "that I was not at home when you called upon me. Pray, how do you like my dress? I assure you I think it's the prettiest here. But do you know there's the most shocking thing in the world happened in the next room! I really believe there's a common chimney-sweeper got in! I assure you it's enough to frighten one to death, for every time he moves the soot smells so you can't think; quite real soot, I assure you! only conceive how nasty! I declare I wish with all my heart it would suffocate him!"

Here she was interrupted by the re-appearance of *Don Devil*; who, looking around him, and perceiving that his antagonist was gone, again advanced to Cecilia: not, however, with the authority of his first approach, for with his wand he had lost much of his power; but to recompense himself for this disgrace, he had recourse to another method equally effectual for keeping his prey to himself, for he began a growling, so dismal and disagreeable, that while many of the ladies, and, among the first, the *Goddess of Wisdom and Courage*, ran away to avoid him, the men all stood aloof to watch what next was to follow.

Cecilia now became seriously uneasy; for she was made an object of general attention, yet could neither speak nor be spoken to. She could suggest no motive for behaviour so whimsical, though she imagined the only person who could have the assurance to practise it was Sir Robert Floyer.

After some time spent thus disagreeably, a white domino, who for a few minutes had been a very attentive spectator, suddenly came forward, and exclaiming, *"I'll cross him though he blast me!"* rushed upon the fiend, and grasping one of his horns, called out to a Harlequin who stood near him, "Harlequin! do you fear to fight the devil?"

"Not I truly!" answered Harlequin, whose voice immediately betrayed young Morrice, and who, issuing from the crowd, whirled himself round before the black gentleman with yet more agility than he had himself done before Cecilia, giving him, from time to time, many smart blows on his shoulders, head, and back, with his wooden sword.

The rage of *Don Devil* at this attack seemed somewhat beyond what a masquerade character rendered necessary; he foamed at the mouth with resentment, and defended himself with so much vehemence, that he soon drove poor Harlequin into another room: but, when he would have returned to his prey, the genius of pantomime, curbed, but not subdued, at the instigation of the white domino, returned to the charge, and by a perpetual rotation of attack and retreat, kept him in constant employment, pursuing him from room to room, and teazing him without cessation or mercy.

Mean time Cecilia, delighted at being released, hurried into a corner, where she hoped to breathe and look on in quiet; and the white domino having exhorted Harlequin to torment the tormentor, and keep him at bay, followed her with congratulations upon her recovered freedom.

"It is you," answered she, "I ought to thank for it, which indeed I do most heartily. I was so tired of confinement, that my mind seemed almost as little at liberty as my person."

"Your persecutor, I presume," said the domino, "is known to you."

"I hope so," answered she, "because there is one man I suspect, and I should be sorry to find there was another equally disagreeable."

"O, depend upon it," cried he, "there are many who would be happy to confine you in the same manner; neither have you much cause for complaint; you have, doubtless, been the aggressor, and played this game yourself without mercy, for I read in your face the captivity of thousands: have you, then, any right to be offended at the spirit of retaliation which one, out of such numbers has courage to exert in return?"

"I protest," cried Cecilia, "I took you for my defender! whence is it you are become my accuser?"

"From seeing the danger to which my incautious knight-errantry has exposed me; I begin, indeed, to take you for a very mischievous sort of person, and I fear the poor devil from whom I rescued you will be amply revenged for his disgrace, by finding that the first use you make of your freedom is to doom your deliverer to bondage."

Here they were disturbed by the extreme loquacity of two opposite parties: and listening attentively, they heard from one side, "My angel! fairest of creatures! goddess of my heart!" uttered in accents of rapture; while from the other, the vociferation was so violent they could distinctly hear nothing.

The white domino satisfied his curiosity by going to both parties; and then, returning to Cecilia, said, "Can you conjecture who was making those soft speeches? a Shylock! his knife all the while in his hand, and his design, doubtless, to *cut as near the heart as possible!* while the loud cackling from the other side is owing to the riotous merriment of a noisy Mentor! when next I hear a disturbance, I shall expect to see some simpering Pythagoras stunned by his talkative disciples."

"To own the truth," said Cecilia, "the almost universal neglect of the characters assumed by these masquers has been the chief source of my entertainment this evening: for at a place of this sort, the next best thing to a character well supported is a character ridiculously burlesqued."

"You cannot, then, have wanted amusement," returned the domino, "for among all the persons assembled in these apartments, I have seen only three who have seemed conscious that any change but that of dress was necessary to disguise them."

"And pray who are those?"

"A Don Quixote, a schoolmaster, and your friend the devil."

"O, call him not my friend," exclaimed Cecilia, "for indeed in or out of that garb he is particularly my aversion."

"*My* friend, then, I will call him," said the domino, "for so, were he ten devils, I must think him, since I owe to him the honour of conversing with you. And, after all, to give him his due, to which, you know, he is even proverbially entitled, he has shewn such abilities in the performance of his part, so much skill in the display of malice, and so much perseverance in the art of tormenting, that I cannot but respect his ingenuity and capacity. And, indeed, if instead of an evil genius, he had represented a guardian angel, he could not have shewn a more refined taste in his choice of an object to hover about."

Just then they were approached by a young haymaker, to whom the white domino called out, "You look as gay and as brisk as if fresh from the hay-field after only half a day's work. Pray, how is it you pretty lasses find employment for the winter"

"How?" cried she, pertly, "why, the same as for the summer!" And pleased with her own readiness at repartee, without feeling the ignorance it betrayed, she tript lightly on.

Immediately after the schoolmaster mentioned by the white domino advanced to Cecilia. His dress was merely a long wrapping gown of green stuff, a pair of red slippers, and a woollen night-cap of the same colour; while, as the symbol of his profession, he held a rod in his hand.

"Ah, fair lady," he cried, "how soothing were it to the austerity of my life, how softening to the rigidity of my manners, might I—without a *breaking out of bounds*, which I ought to be the first to discourage, and a "confusion to all order" for which the school-boy should himself chastise his master—be permitted to cast at your feet this emblem of my authority! and to forget, in the softness of your conversation, all the roughness of discipline!"

"No, no," cried Cecilia, "I will not be answerable for such corruption of taste!"

"This repulse," answered he, "is just what I feared; for alas! under what pretence could a poor miserable country pedagogue presume to approach you? Should I examine you in the dead languages, would not your living accents charm from me all power of reproof? Could I look at you, and hear a false concord? Should I doom you to water-gruel as a dunce, would not my subsequent remorse make me want it myself as a madman? Were your fair hand spread out to me for correction, should I help applying my lips to it, instead of my rat-tan? If I ordered you to be *called up*, should I ever remember to have you sent back? And if I commanded you to stand in a corner, how should I forbear following you thither myself?"

Cecilia, who had no difficulty in knowing this pretended schoolmaster for Mr Gosport, was readily beginning to propose conditions for according him her favour, when their ears were assailed by a forced phthisical cough, which they found proceeded from an apparent old woman, who was a young man in disguise, and whose hobbling gait, grunting voice, and most grievous asthmatic complaints, seemed greatly enjoyed and applauded by the company.

"How true is it, yet how inconsistent," cried the white domino, "that while we all desire to live long, we have all a horror of being old! The figure now passing is not meant to ridicule any particular person, nor to stigmatize any particular absurdity; its sole view is to expose to contempt and derision the general and natural infirmities of age! and the design is not more disgusting than impolitic; for why, while so carefully we guard from all approaches of death, should we close the only avenues to happiness in long life, respect and tenderness?"

Cecilia, delighted both by the understanding and humanity of her new acquaintance, and pleased at being joined by Mr Gosport, was beginning to be perfectly satisfied with her situation, when, creeping softly towards her, she again perceived the black gentleman.

"Ah!" cried she, with some vexation, "here comes my old tormentor! screen me from him if possible, or he will again make me his prisoner."

"Fear not," cried the white domino, "he is an evil spirit, and we will surely lay him. If one spell fails, we must try another."

Cecilia then perceiving Mr Arnott, begged he would also assist in barricading her from the fiend who so obstinately pursued her.

Mr Arnott most gratefully acceded to the proposal; and the white domino, who acted as commanding officer, assigned to each his station: he desired Cecilia would keep quietly to her seat, appointed the schoolmaster to be her guard on the left, took possession himself of the opposite post, and ordered Mr Arnott to stand centinel in front.

This arrangement being settled, the guards of the right and left wings instantly secured their places; but while Mr Arnott was considering whether it were better to face the besieged or the enemy, the arch-foe rushed suddenly before him, and laid himself down at the feet of Cecilia!

Mr Arnott, extremely disconcerted, began a serious expostulation upon the ill-breeding of this behaviour; but the devil, resting all excuse upon supporting his character, only answered by growling.

The white domino seemed to hesitate for a moment in what manner to conduct himself, and with a quickness that marked his chagrin, said to Cecilia, "You told me you knew him,—has he any right to follow you?"

"If he thinks he has," answered she, a little alarmed by his question, "this is no time to dispute it."

And then, to avoid any hazard of altercation, she discreetly forbore making further complaints, preferring any persecution to seriously remonstrating with a man of so much insolence as the Baronet.

The schoolmaster, laughing at the whole transaction, only said, "And pray, madam, after playing the devil with all mankind, what right have you to complain that one man plays the devil with you?"

"We shall, at least, fortify you," said the white domino, "from any other assailant: no three-headed Cerberus could protect you more effectually: but you will not, therefore, fancy yourself in the lower regions, for, if I mistake not, the torment of *three guardians* is nothing new to you."

"And how," said Cecilia, surprised, "should you know of my three guardians? I hope I am not quite encompassed with evil spirits!"

"No," answered he; "you will find me as inoffensive as the hue of the domino I wear;—and would I could add as insensible!"

"This black gentleman," said the schoolmaster, "who, and very innocently, I was going to call your *black-guard*, has as noble and fiend-like a disposition as I remember to have seen; for without even attempting to take any diversion himself, he seems gratified to his heart's content in excluding from it the lady he serves."

"He does me an honour I could well dispense with," said Cecilia; "but I hope he has some secret satisfaction in his situation which pays him for its apparent inconvenience."

Here the black gentleman half-raised himself, and attempted to take her hand. She started, and with much displeasure drew it back. He then growled, and again sank prostrate.

"This is a fiend," said the schoolmaster, "who to himself sayeth, *Budge not!* let his conscience never so often say *budge!* Well, fair lady, your fortifications, however, may now be deemed impregnable, since I, with a flourish of my rod, can keep off the young by recollection of the past, and since the fiend, with a jut of his foot, may keep off the old from dread of the future!"

Here a Turk, richly habited and resplendent with jewels, stalked towards Cecilia, and, having regarded her some time, called out, "I have been looking hard about me the whole evening, and, faith, I have seen nothing handsome before!"

The moment he opened his mouth, his voice, to her utter astonishment, betrayed Sir Robert Floyer! "Mercy on me," cried she aloud, and pointing to the fiend, "who, then, can this possibly be?"

"Do you not know?" cried the white domino.

"I thought I had known with certainty," answered she, "but I now find I was mistaken."

"He is a happy man," said the schoolmaster, sarcastically looking at the Turk, "who has removed your suspicions only by appearing in another character!"

"Why, what the deuce, then," exclaimed the Turk, "have you taken that black dog there for *me*?"

Before this question could be answered, an offensive smell of soot, making everybody look around the room, the chimney-sweeper already mentioned by Miss Larolles was perceived to enter it. Every way he moved a passage was cleared for him, as the company, with general disgust, retreated wherever he advanced.

He was short, and seemed somewhat incommoded by his dress; he held his soot-bag over one arm, and his shovel under the other. As soon as he espied Cecilia, whose situation was such as to prevent her eluding him, he hooted aloud, and came stumping up to her; "Ah ha," he cried, "found at last;" then, throwing down his shovel, he opened the mouth of his bag, and pointing waggishly to her head, said, "Come, shall I pop you?—a good place for naughty girls; in, I say, poke in!—cram you up the chimney."

And then he put forth his sooty hands to reach her cap.

Cecilia, though she instantly knew the dialect of her guardian Mr Briggs, was not therefore the more willing to be so handled, and started back to save herself from his touch; the white domino also came forward, and spread out his arms as a defence to her, while the devil, who was still before her, again began to growl.

"Ah ha!" cried the chimney-sweeper, laughing, "so did not know me? Poor duck! won't hurt you; don't be frightened; nothing but old guardian; all a joke!" And then, patting her cheek with his dirty hand, and nodding at her with much kindness, "Pretty dove," he added, "be of good heart! shan't be meddled with; come to see after you. Heard of your tricks; thought I'd catch you!—come o' purpose.—Poor duck! did not know me! ha! ha!—good joke enough!"

"What do you mean, you dirty dog," cried the Turk, "by touching that lady?"

"Won't tell!" answered he; "not your business. Got a good right. Who cares for pearls? Nothing but French beads." Pointing with a sneer to his turban. Then, again addressing Cecilia, "Fine doings!" he continued, "Here's a place! never saw the like before! turn a man's noddle!—All goings out; no comings in; wax candles in every room; servants thick as mushrooms! And where's the cash? Who's to pay the piper? Come to more than a guinea; warrant Master Harrel thinks that nothing!"

"A guinea?" contemptuously repeated the Turk, "and what do you suppose a guinea will do?"

"What? Why, keep a whole family handsome a week;—never spend so much myself; no, nor half neither."

"Why then, how the devil do you live? Do you beg?"

"Beg? Who should I beg of? You?—Got anything to give? Are warm?"

"Take the trouble to speak more respectfully, sir!" said the Turk, haughtily; "I see you are some low fellow, and I shall not put up with your impudence."

"Shall, shall! I say!" answered the chimneysweeper, sturdily; "Hark'ee, my duck," chucking Cecilia under the chin, "don't be cajoled, nick that spark! never mind gold trappings; none of his own; all a take-in; hired for eighteenpence; not worth a groat. Never set your heart on a fine outside, nothing within. Bristol stones won't buy stock: only wants to chouse you."

"What do you mean by that, you little old scrub!" cried the imperious Turk; "would you provoke me to soil my fingers by pulling that beastly snub nose?" For Mr Briggs had saved himself any actual mask, by merely blacking his face with soot.

"Beastly snub nose!" sputtered out the chimneysweeper in much wrath, "good nose enough; don't want a better; good as another man's. Where's the harm on't?"

"How could this blackguard get in?" cried the Turk, "I believe he's a mere common chimneysweeper out of the streets, for he's all over dirt and filth. I never saw such a dress at a masquerade before in my life."

"All the better," returned the other; "would not change. What do think it cost?"

"Cost? Why, not a crown."

"A crown? ha! ha!—a pot o' beer! Little Tom borrowed it; had it of our own sweep. Said 'twas for himself. I bid him a pint; rascal would not take less."

"Did your late uncle," said the white domino in a low voice to Cecilia, "chuse for two of your guardians Mr Harrel and Mr Briggs, to give you an early lesson upon the opposite errors of profusion and meanness?"

"My uncle?" cried Cecilia, starting, "were you acquainted with my uncle?"

"No," said he, "for my happiness I knew him not."

"You would have owed no loss of happiness to an acquaintance with him," said Cecilia, very seriously, "for he was one who dispensed to his friends nothing but good."

"Perhaps so," said the domino; "but I fear I should have found the good he dispensed through his niece not quite unmixed with evil!"

"What's here?" cried the chimney-sweeper, stumbling over the fiend, "what's this black thing? Don't like it; looks like the devil. You shan't stay with it; carry you away; take care of you myself."

He then offered Cecilia his hand; but the black gentleman, raising himself upon his knees before her, paid her, in dumb shew, the humblest devoirs, yet prevented her from removing.

"Ah ha!" cried the chimney-sweeper, significantly nodding his head, "smell a rat! a sweetheart in disguise. No bamboozling! it won't do; a'n't so soon put upon. If you've got any thing to say, tell *me*, that's the way. Where's the cash? Got ever a *rental*? Are warm? That's the point; are warm?"

The fiend, without returning any answer, continued his homage to Cecilia; at which the enraged chimney-sweeper exclaimed, "Come, come with me! won't be imposed upon; an old fox,—understand trap!"

He then again held out his hand, but Cecilia, pointing to the fiend, answered, "How can I come, sir?"

"Shew you the way," cried he, "shovel him off." And taking his shovel, he very roughly set about removing him.

The fiend then began a yell so horrid, that it disturbed the whole company; but the chimney-sweeper, only saying, "Aye, aye, blacky, growl away, blacky,—makes no odds," sturdily continued his work, and, as the fiend had no chance of resisting so coarse an antagonist without a serious struggle, he was presently compelled to change his ground.

"Warm work!" cried the victorious chimney-sweeper, taking off his wig, and wiping his head with the sleeves of his dress, "pure warm work this!"

Cecilia, once again freed from her persecutor, instantly quitted her place, almost equally desirous to escape the haughty Turk, who was peculiarly her aversion, and the facetious chimney-sweeper, whose vicinity, either on account of his dress or his conversation, was by no means desirable. She was not, however, displeased that the white domino and the schoolmaster still continued to attend her.

"Pray, look," said the white domino, as they entered another apartment, "at that figure of Hope; is there any in the room half so expressive of despondency?"

"The reason, however," answered the schoolmaster, "is obvious; that light and beautiful silver anchor upon which she reclines presents an occasion irresistible for an attitude of elegant dejection; and the assumed character is always given up where an opportunity offers to display any beauty, or manifest any perfection in the dear proper person!"

"But why," said Cecilia, "should she assume the character of *Hope*? Could she not have been equally dejected and equally elegant as Niobe, or some tragedy queen?"

"But she does not assume the character," answered the schoolmaster, "she does not even think of it: the dress is her object, and that alone fills up all her ideas. Enquire of almost any body in the room concerning the persons they seem to represent, and you will find their ignorance more gross than you can imagine; they have not once thought upon the subject; accident, or convenience, or caprice has alone directed their choice."

A tall and elegant youth now approached them, whose laurels and harp announced Apollo. The white domino immediately enquired of him if the noise and turbulence of the company had any chance of being stilled into silence and rapture by the divine music of the inspired god?

"No," answered he, pointing to the room in which was erected the new gallery, and whence, as he spoke, issued the sound of a *hautboy*, "there is a flute playing there already."

"O for a Midas," cried the white domino, "to return to this leather-eared god the disgrace he received from him!"

They now proceeded to the apartment which had been lately fitted up for refreshments, and which was so full of company that they entered it with difficulty. And here they were again joined by Minerva, who, taking Cecilia's hand, said, "Lord, how glad I am you've got away from that frightful black mask! I can't conceive who he is; nobody can find out; it's monstrous odd, but he has not spoke a word all night, and he makes such a shocking noise when people touch him, that I assure you it's enough to put one in a fright."

"And pray," cried the schoolmaster, disguising his voice, "how camest thou to take the helmet of Minerva for a fool's cap?"

"Lord, I have not," cried she, innocently, "why, the whole dress is Minerva's; don't you see?"

"My dear child," answered he, "thou couldst as well with that little figure pass for a Goliath, as with that little wit for a Pallas."

Their attention was now drawn from the goddess of wisdom to a mad Edgar, who so vehemently ran about the room calling out "Poor Tom's a cold!" that, in a short time, he was obliged to take off his mask, from an effect, not very delicate, of the heat!

Soon after, a gentleman desiring some lemonade whose toga spoke the consular dignity, though his broken English betrayed a native of France, the schoolmaster followed him, and, with reverence the most profound, began to address him in Latin; but, turning quick towards him, he gaily said, *"Monsieur, j'ai l'honneur de representer Ciceron, le grand Ciceron, pere de sa patrie! mais quoique j'ai cet honneur-la, je ne suit pas pedant!—mon dieu, Monsieur, je ne parle que le Francois dans la bonne compagnie!"* And, politely bowing, he went on.

Just then Cecilia, while looking about the room for Mrs Harrel, found herself suddenly pinched by the cheek, and hastily turning round, perceived again her friend the chimney-sweeper, who, laughing, cried, "Only me! don't be frightened. Have something to tell you;—had no luck!—got never a husband yet! can't find one! looked all over, too; sharp as a needle. Not one to be had! all catched up!"

"I am glad to hear it, sir," said Cecilia, somewhat vexed by observing the white domino attentively listening; "and I hope, therefore, you will give yourself no farther trouble."

"Pretty duck!" cried he, chucking her under the chin; "never mind, don't be cast down; get one at last. Leave it to me. Nothing under a plum; won't take up with less. Good-by, ducky, good-by! must go home now,—begin to be nodding."

And then, repeating his kind caresses, he walked away.

"Do you think, then," said the white domino, "more highly of Mr Briggs for discernment and taste than of any body?"

"I hope not!" answered she, "for low indeed should I then think of the rest of the world!"

"The commission with which he is charged," returned the domino, "has then misled me; I imagined discernment and taste might be necessary ingredients for making such a choice as your approbation would sanctify: but perhaps his skill in guarding against any fraud or deduction in the stipulation he mentioned, may be all that is requisite for the execution of his trust."

"I understand very well," said Cecilia, a little hurt, "the severity of your meaning; and if Mr Briggs had any commission but of his own suggestion, it would fill me with shame and confusion; but as that is not the case, those at least are sensations which it cannot give me."

"My meaning," cried the domino, with some earnestness, "should I express it seriously, would but prove to you the respect and admiration with which you have inspired me, and if indeed, as Mr Briggs hinted, such a prize is to be purchased by riches, I know not, from what I have seen of its merit, any sum I should think adequate to its value."

"You are determined, I see," said Cecilia, smiling, "to make most liberal amends for your asperity."

A loud clack of tongues now interrupted their discourse; and the domino, at the desire of Cecilia, for whom he had procured a seat, went forward to enquire what was the matter. But scarce had he given up his place a moment, before, to her great mortification, it was occupied by the fiend.

Again, but with the same determined silence he had hitherto preserved, he made signs of obedience and homage, and her perplexity to conjecture who he could be, or what were his motives for this persecution, became the more urgent as they seemed the less likely to be satisfied. But the fiend, who was no other than Mr Monckton, had every instant less and less encouragement to make himself known: his plan had in nothing succeeded, and his provocation at its failure had caused him the bitterest disappointment; he had intended, in the character of a tormentor, not only to pursue and hover around her himself, but he had also hoped, in the same character, to have kept at a distance all other admirers: but the violence with which he had over-acted his part, by raising her disgust and the indignation of the company, rendered his views wholly abortive while the consciousness of an extravagance for which, if discovered, he could assign no reason not liable to excite suspicions of his secret motives, reduced him to guarding a painful and most irksome silence the whole evening. And Cecilia, to whose unsuspicious mind the idea of Mr Monckton had never occurred, added continually to the cruelty of his situation, by an undisguised abhorrence of his assiduity, as well as by a manifest preference to the attendance of the white domino. All, therefore, that his disappointed scheme now left in his power, was to watch her motions, listen to her discourse, and inflict occasionally upon others some part of the chagrin with which he was tormented himself.

While they were in this situation, Harlequin, in consequence of being ridiculed by the Turk for want of agility, offered to jump over the new desert table, and desired to have a little space cleared to give room for his motions. It was in vain the people who distributed the refreshments, and who were placed at the other side of the table, expostulated upon the danger of the experiment; Morrice had a rage of enterprise untameable, and, therefore, first taking a run, he attempted the leap.

The consequence was such as might naturally be expected; he could not accomplish his purpose, but, finding himself falling, imprudently caught hold of the lately erected Awning, and pulled it entirely upon his own head, and with it the new contrived lights, which, in various forms, were fixed to it, and which all came down together.

The mischief and confusion occasioned by this exploit were very alarming, and almost dangerous; those who were near the table suffered most by the crush, but splinters of the glass flew yet further; and as the room, which was small, had been only lighted up by lamps hanging from the Awning, it was now in total darkness, except close to the door, which was still illuminated from the adjoining apartments.

The clamour of Harlequin, who was covered with glass, papier-machee, lamps and oil, the screams of the ladies, the universal buz of tongues, and the struggle between the frighted crowd which was enclosed to get out, and the curious crowd from the other apartments to get in, occasioned a disturbance and tumult equally noisy and confused. But the most serious sufferer was the unfortunate fiend, who, being nearer the table than Cecilia, was so pressed upon by the numbers which poured from it, that he found a separation unavoidable, and was unable, from the darkness and the throng, to discover whether she was still in the same place, or had made her escape into another.

She had, however, encountered the white domino, and, under his protection, was safely conveyed to a further part of the room. Her intention and desire were to quit it immediately, but at the remonstrance of her conductor, she consented to remain some time longer. "The conflict at the door," said he, "will quite overpower you. Stay here but a few minutes, and both parties will have struggled themselves tired, and you may then go without difficulty. Meantime, can you not, by this faint light, suppose me one of your guardians, Mr Briggs, for example, or, if he is too old for me, Mr Harrel, and entrust yourself to my care?"

"You seem wonderfully well acquainted with my guardians," said Cecilia; "I cannot imagine how you have had your intelligence."

"Nor can I," answered the domino, "imagine how Mr Briggs became so particularly your favourite as to be entrusted with powers to dispose of you."

"You are mistaken indeed; he is entrusted with no powers but such as his own fancy has suggested."

"But how has Mr Delvile offended you, that with him only you seem to have no commerce or communication?"

"Mr Delvile!" repeated Cecilia, still more surprised, "are you also acquainted with Mr Delvile?"

"He is certainly a man of fashion," continued the domino, "and he is also a man of honour; surely, then, he would be more pleasant for confidence and consultation than one whose only notion of happiness is money, whose only idea of excellence is avarice, and whose only conception of sense is distrust!" Here a violent outcry again interrupted their conversation; but not till Cecilia had satisfied her doubts concerning the white domino, by conjecturing he was Mr Belfield, who might easily, at the house of Mr Monckton, have gathered the little circumstances of her situation to which he alluded, and whose size and figure exactly resembled those of her new acquaintance.

The author of the former disturbance was now the occasion of the present: the fiend, having vainly traversed the room in search of Cecilia, stumbled accidentally upon Harlequin, before he was freed from the relicks of his own mischief; and unable to resist the temptation of opportunity and the impulse of revenge, he gave vent to the wrath so often excited by the blunders, forwardness, and tricks of Morrice, and inflicted upon him, with his own wooden sword, which he seized for that purpose, a chastisement the most serious and severe.

Poor Harlequin, unable to imagine any reason for this violent attack, and already cut with the glass, and bruised with the fall, spared not his lungs in making known his disapprobation of such treatment: but the fiend, regardless either of his complaints or his resistance, forbore not to belabour him till compelled by the entrance of people with lights. And then, after artfully playing sundry antics under pretence of still supporting his character, with a motion too sudden for prevention, and too rapid for pursuit, he escaped out of the room, and hurrying down stairs, threw himself into an hackney chair, which conveyed him to a place where he privately changed his dress before he returned home, bitterly repenting the experiment he had made, and conscious too late that, had he appeared in a character he might have avowed, he could, without impropriety, have attended Cecilia the whole evening. But such is deservedly the frequent fate of cunning, which, while it plots surprise and detection of others, commonly overshoots its mark, and ends in its own disgrace.

The introduction of the lights now making manifest the confusion which the frolic of Harlequin had occasioned, he was seized with such a dread of the resentment of Mr Harrel, that, forgetting blows, bruises, and wounds, not one of which were so frightful to him as reproof, he made the last exhibition of his agility by an abrupt and hasty retreat.

He had, however, no reason for apprehension, since, in every thing that regarded expence, Mr Harrel had no feeling, and his lady had no thought.

The rooms now began to empty very fast, but among the few masks yet remaining, Cecilia again perceived Don Quixote; and while, in conjunction with the white domino, she was allowing him the praise of having supported his character with more uniform propriety than any other person in the assembly, she observed him taking off his mask for the convenience of drinking some lemonade, and, looking in his face, found he was no other than Mr Belfield! Much astonished, and more than ever perplexed, she again turned to the white domino, who, seeing in her countenance a surprise of which he knew not the reason, said, half-laughing, "You think, perhaps, I shall never be gone? And indeed I am almost of the same opinion; but what can I do? Instead of growing weary by the length of my stay, my reluctance to shorten it increases with its duration; and all the methods I take, whether by speaking to you or looking at you, with a view to be satiated, only double my eagerness for looking and listening again! I must go, however; and if I am happy, I may perhaps meet with you again,—though, if I am wise, I shall never seek you more!"

And then, with the last stragglers that reluctantly disappeared, he made his exit, leaving Cecilia greatly pleased with his conversation and his manners, but extremely perplexed to account for his knowledge of her affairs and situation.

The schoolmaster had already been gone some time.

She was now earnestly pressed by the Harrels and Sir Robert, who still remained, to send to a warehouse for a dress, and accompany them to the Pantheon; but though she was not without some inclination to comply, in the hope of further prolonging the entertainment of an evening from which she had received much pleasure, she disliked the attendance of the Baronet, and felt averse to grant any request that he could make, and therefore she begged they would excuse her; and having waited to see their dresses, which were very superb, she retired to her own apartment.

A great variety of conjecture upon all that had passed, now, and till the moment that she sunk to rest, occupied her mind; the extraordinary persecution of the fiend excited at once her curiosity and amazement, while the knowledge of her affairs shown by the white domino surprised her not less, and interested her more.

CHAPTER IV

AN AFFRAY.

The next morning, during breakfast, Cecilia was informed that a gentleman desired to speak with her. She begged permission of Mrs Harrel to have him asked upstairs, and was not a little surprized when he proved to be the same old gentleman whose singular exclamations had so much struck her at Mr Monckton's, and at the rehearsal of Artaserse.

Abruptly and with a stern aspect advancing to her, "You are rich," he cried; "are you therefore worthless?"

"I hope not," answered she, in some consternation; while Mrs Harrel, believing his intention was to rob them, ran precipitately to the bell, which she rang without ceasing till two or three servants hastened into the room; by which time, being less alarmed, she only made signs to them to stay, and stood quietly herself to wait what would follow.

The old man, without attending to her, continued his dialogue with Cecilia.

"Know you then," he said, "a blameless use of riches? such a use as not only in the broad glare of day shall shine resplendent, but in the darkness of midnight, and stillness of repose, shall give you reflections unembittered, and slumbers unbroken? tell me, know you this use?"

"Not so well, perhaps," answered she, "as I ought; but I am very willing to learn better."

"Begin, then, while yet youth and inexperience, new to the callousness of power and affluence, leave something good to work upon: yesterday you saw the extravagance of luxury and folly; to-day look deeper, and see, and learn to pity, the misery of disease and penury."

He then put into her hand a paper which contained a most affecting account of the misery to which a poor and wretched family had been reduced, by sickness and various other misfortunes.

Cecilia, "open as day to melting charity," having hastily perused it, took out her purse, and offering to him three guineas, said, "You must direct me, sir, what to give if this is insufficient."

"Hast thou so much heart?" cried he, with emotion, "and has fortune, though it has cursed thee with the temptation of prosperity, not yet rooted from thy mind its native benevolence? I return in part thy liberal contribution; this," taking one guinea, "doubles my expectations; I will not, by making thy charity distress thee, accelerate the fatal hour of hardness and degeneracy."

He was then going; but Cecilia, following him, said "No, take it all! Who should assist the poor if I will not? Rich, without connections; powerful, without wants; upon whom have they any claim if not upon me?"

"True," cried he, receiving the rest, "and wise as true. Give, therefore, whilst yet thou hast the heart to give, and make, in thy days of innocence and kindness, some interest with Heaven and the poor!"

And then he disappeared.

"Why, my dear, cried Mrs Harrel, "what could induce you to give the man so much money? Don't you see he is crazy? I dare say he would have been just as well contented with sixpence."

"I know not what he is," said Cecilia, "but his manners are not more singular than his sentiments are affecting; and if he is actuated by charity to raise subscriptions for the indigent, he can surely apply to no one who ought so readily to contribute as myself."

Mr Harrel then came in, and his lady most eagerly told him the transaction.

"Scandalous!" he exclaimed; "why, this is no better than being a housebreaker! Pray give orders never to admit him again. Three guineas! I never heard so impudent a thing in my life! Indeed, Miss Beverley, you must be more discreet in future, you will else be ruined before you know where you are."

"Thus it is," said Cecilia, half smiling, "that we can all lecture one another! to-day you recommend economy to me; yesterday I with difficulty forbore recommending it to you."

"Nay," answered he, "that was quite another matter; expence incurred in the common way of a man's living is quite another thing to an extortion of this sort."

"It is another thing indeed," said she, "but I know not that it is therefore a better."

Mr Harrel made no answer: and Cecilia, privately moralizing upon the different estimates of expence and economy made by the dissipated and the charitable, soon retired to her own apartment, determined firmly to adhere to her lately adopted plan, and hoping, by the assistance of her new and very singular monitor, to extend her practice of doing good, by enlarging her knowledge of distress.

Objects are, however, never wanting for the exercise of benevolence; report soon published her liberality, and those who wished to believe it, failed not to enquire into its truth. She was soon at the head of a little band of pensioners, and, never satisfied with the generosity of her donations, found in a very short time that the common allowance of her guardians was scarce adequate to the calls of her munificence.

And thus, in acts of goodness and charity, passed undisturbed another week of the life of Cecilia: but when the fervour of self-approbation lost its novelty, the pleasure with which her new plan was begun first subsided into tranquillity, and then sunk into languor. To a heart formed for friendship and affection the charms of solitude are very short-lived; and though she had sickened of the turbulence of perpetual company, she now wearied of passing all her time by herself, and sighed for the comfort of society and the relief of communication. But she saw with astonishment the difficulty with which this was to be obtained: the endless succession of diversions, the continual rotation of assemblies, the numerousness of splendid engagements, of which, while every one complained, every one was proud to boast, so effectually impeded private meetings and friendly intercourse, that, whichever way she turned herself, all commerce seemed impracticable, but such as either led to dissipation, or accidentally flowed from it.

Yet, finding the error into which her ardour of reformation had hurried her, and that a rigid seclusion from company was productive of a lassitude as little favourable to active virtue as dissipation itself, she resolved to soften her plan, and by mingling amusement with benevolence, to try, at least, to approach that golden mean, which, like the philosopher's stone, always eludes our grasp, yet always invites our wishes.

For this purpose she desired to attend Mrs Harrel to the next Opera that should be represented.

The following Saturday, therefore, she accompanied that lady and Mrs Mears to the Haymarket, escorted by Mr Arnott.

They were very late; the Opera was begun, and even in the lobby the crowd was so great that their passage was obstructed. Here they were presently accosted by Miss Larolles, who, running up to Cecilia and taking her hand, said, "Lord, you can't conceive how glad I am to see you! why, my dear creature, where have you hid yourself these twenty ages? You are quite in luck in coming to-night, I assure you; it's the best Opera we have had this season: there's such a monstrous crowd there's no stirring. We shan't get in this half hour. The coffee-room is quite full; only come and see; is it not delightful?"

This intimation was sufficient for Mrs Harrel, whose love of the Opera was merely a love of company, fashion, and shew; and therefore to the coffee-room she readily led the way.

And here Cecilia found rather the appearance of a brilliant assembly of ladies and gentlemen, collected merely to see and to entertain one another, than of distinct and casual parties, mixing solely from necessity, and waiting only for room to enter a theatre.

The first person that addressed them was Captain Aresby, who, with his usual delicate languishment, smiled upon Cecilia, and softly whispering, "How divinely you look to-night!" proceeded to pay his compliments to some other ladies.

"Do, pray, now," cried Miss Larolles, "observe Mr Meadows! only just see where he has fixed himself! in the very best place in the room, and keeping the fire from every body! I do assure you that's always his way, and it's monstrous provoking, for if one's ever so cold, he lollops so, that one's quite starved. But you must know there's another thing he does that is quite as bad, for if he gets a seat, he never offers to move, if he sees one sinking with fatigue. And besides, if one is waiting for one's carriage two hours together, he makes it a rule never to stir a step to see for it. Only think how monstrous!"

"These are heavy complaints, indeed," said Cecilia, looking at him attentively; "I should have expected from his appearance a very different account of his gallantry, for he seems dressed with more studied elegance than anybody here."

"O yes," cried Miss Larolles, "he is the sweetest dresser in the world; he has the most delightful taste you can conceive, nobody has half so good a fancy. I assure you it's a great thing to be spoke to by him: we are all of us quite angry when he won't take any notice of us."

"Is your anger," said Cecilia, laughing, "in honour of himself or of his coat?"

"Why, Lord, don't you know all this time that he is an *ennuyé*?

"I know, at least," answered Cecilia, "that he would soon make one of me."

"O, but one is never affronted with an *ennuyé*, if he is ever so provoking, because one always knows what it means."

"Is he agreeable?"

"Why, to tell you the truth,—but pray now, don't mention it,—I think him most excessive disagreeable! He yawns in one's face every time one looks at him. I assure you sometimes I expect to see him fall fast asleep while I am talking to him, for he is so immensely absent he don't hear one half that one says; only conceive how horrid!"

"But why, then, do you encourage him? why do you take any notice of him?"

"O, every body does, I assure you, else I would not for the world; but he is so courted you have no idea. However, of all things let me advise you never to dance with him; I did once myself, and I declare I was quite distressed to death the whole time, for he was taken with such a fit of absence he knew nothing he was about, sometimes skipping and jumping with all the violence in the world, just as if he only danced for exercise, and sometimes standing quite still, or lolling against the wainscoat and gaping, and taking no more notice of me than if he had never seen me in his life!"

The Captain now, again advancing to Cecilia, said, "So you would not do us the honour to try the masquerade at the Pantheon? however, I hear you had a very brilliant spectacle at Mr Harrel's. I was quite *au desespoir* that I could not get there. I did *mon possible*, but it was quite beyond me."

"We should have been very happy," said Mrs Harrel, "to have seen you; I assure you we had some excellent masks."

"So I have heard *partout*, and I am reduced to despair that I could not have the honour of sliding in. But I was *accable* with affairs all day. Nothing could be so mortifying."

Cecilia now, growing very impatient to hear the Opera, begged to know if they might not make a trial to get into the pit?

"I fear," said the Captain, smiling as they passed him, without offering any assistance, "you will find it extreme petrifying; for my part, I confess I am not upon the principle of crowding."

The ladies, however, accompanied by Mr Arnott, made the attempt, and soon found, according to the custom of report, that the difficulty, for the pleasure of talking of it, had been considerably exaggerated. They were separated, indeed, but their accommodation was tolerably good.

Cecilia was much vexed to find the first act of the Opera almost over; but she was soon still more dissatisfied when she discovered that she had no chance of hearing the little which remained: the place she had happened to find vacant was next to a party of young ladies, who were so earnestly engaged in their own discourse, that they listened not to a note of the Opera, and so infinitely diverted with their own witticisms, that their tittering and loquacity allowed no one in their vicinity to hear better than themselves. Cecilia tried in vain to confine her attention to the singers; she was distant from the stage, and to them she was near, and her fruitless attempts all ended in chagrin and impatience.

At length she resolved to make an effort for entertainment in another way, and since the expectations which brought her to the Opera were destroyed, to try by listening to her fair neighbours, whether those who occasioned her disappointment could make her any amends.

For this purpose she turned to them wholly; yet was at first in no little perplexity to understand what was going forward, since so universal was the eagerness for talking, and so insurmountable the antipathy to listening, that every one seemed to have her wishes bounded by a continual utterance of words, without waiting for any answer, or scarce even desiring to be heard.

But when, somewhat more used to their dialect and manner, she began better to comprehend their discourse, wretchedly indeed did it supply to her the loss of the Opera. She heard nothing but descriptions of trimmings, and complaints of hair-dressers, hints of conquest that teemed with vanity, and histories of engagements which were inflated with exultation.

At the end of the act, by the crowding forward of the gentlemen to see the dance, Mrs Harrel had an opportunity of making room for her by herself, and she had then some reason to expect hearing the rest of the Opera in peace, for the company before her, consisting entirely of young men, seemed, even during the dance, fearful of speaking, lest their attention should be drawn for a moment from the stage.

But to her infinite surprize, no sooner was the second act begun, than their attention ended! they turned from the performers to each other, and entered into a whispering but gay conversation, which, though not loud enough to disturb the audience in general, kept in the ears of their neighbours a buzzing which interrupted all pleasure from the representation. Of this effect of their gaiety it seemed uncertain whether they were conscious, but very evident that they were totally careless.

The desperate resource which she had tried during the first act, of seeking entertainment from the very conversation which prevented her enjoying it, was not now even in her power: for these gentlemen, though as negligent as the young ladies had been whom they disturbed, were much more cautious whom they instructed: their language was ambiguous, and their terms, to Cecilia, were unintelligible: their subjects, indeed, required some discretion, being nothing less than a ludicrous calculation of the age and duration of jointured widows, and of the chances and expectations of unmarried young ladies.

But what more even than their talking provoked her, was finding that the moment the act was over, when she cared not if their vociferation had been incessant, one of them called out, "Come, be quiet, the dance is begun;" and then they were again all silent attention!

In the third act, however, she was more fortunate; the gentlemen again changed their places, and they were succeeded by others who came to the Opera not to hear themselves but the performers: and as soon as she was permitted to listen, the voice of Pacchierotti took from her all desire to hear any thing but itself.

During the last dance she was discovered by Sir Robert Floyer, who, sauntering down fop's alley, stationed himself by her side, and whenever the *figurante* relieved the principal dancers, turned his eyes from the stage to her face, as better worth his notice, and equally destined for his amusement.

Mr Monckton, too, who for some time had seen and watched her, now approached; he had observed with much satisfaction that her whole mind had been intent upon the performance, yet still the familiarity of Sir Robert Floyer's admiration disturbed and perplexed him; he determined, therefore, to make an effort to satisfy his doubts by examining into his intentions: and, taking him apart, before the dance was quite over, "Well," he said, "who is so handsome here as Harrel's ward?"

"Yes," answered he, calmly, "she is handsome, but I don't like her expression."

"No? why, what is the fault of it?"

"Proud, cursed proud. It is not the sort of woman I like. If one says a civil thing to her, she only wishes one at the devil for one's pains."

"O, you have tried her, then, have you? why, you are not, in general, much given to say civil things."

"Yes, you know, I said something of that sort to her once about Juliet, at the rehearsal. Was not you by?"

"What, then, was that all? and did you imagine one compliment would do your business with her?"

"O, hang it, who ever dreams of complimenting the women now? that's all at an end."

"You won't find she thinks so, though; for, as you well say, her pride is insufferable, and I, who have long known her, can assure you it does not diminish upon intimacy."

"Perhaps not,—but there's very pretty picking in 3000 pounds per annum! one would not think much of a little encumbrance upon such an estate."

"Are you quite sure the estate is so considerable? Report is mightily given to magnify."

"O, I have pretty good intelligence: though, after all, I don't know but I may be off; she'll take a confounded deal of time and trouble."

Monckton, too much a man of interest and of the world to cherish that delicacy which covets universal admiration for the object of its fondness, then artfully enlarged upon the obstacles he already apprehended, and insinuated such others as he believed would be most likely to intimidate him. But his subtlety was lost upon the impenetrable Baronet, who possessed that hard insensibility which obstinately pursues its own course, deaf to what is said, and indifferent to what is thought.

Meanwhile the ladies were now making way to the coffee-room, though very slowly on account of the crowd; and just as they got near the lobby, Cecilia perceived Mr Belfield, who, immediately making himself known to her, was offering his service to hand her out of the pit, when Sir Robert Floyer, not seeing or not heeding him, pressed forward, and said, "Will you let me have the honour, Miss Beverley, of taking care of you?"

Cecilia, to whom he grew daily more disagreeable, coldly declined his assistance, while she readily accepted that which had first been offered her by Mr Belfield.

The haughty Baronet, extremely nettled, forced his way on, and rudely stalking up to Mr Belfield, motioned with his hand for room to pass him, and said, "Make way, sir!"

"Make way for *me*, Sir!" cried Belfield, opposing him with one hand, while with the other he held Cecilia.

"You, Sir? and who are you, Sir?" demanded the Baronet, disdainfully.

"Of that, Sir, I shall give you an account whenever you please," answered Belfield, with equal scorn.

"What the devil do you mean, Sir?"

"Nothing very difficult to be understood," replied Belfield, and attempted to draw on Cecilia, who, much alarmed, was shrinking back.

Sir Robert then, swelling with rage, reproachfully turned to her, and said, "Will you suffer such an impertinent fellow as that, Miss Beverley, to have the honour of taking your hand?"

Belfield, with great indignation, demanded what he meant by the term impertinent fellow; and Sir Robert yet more insolently repeated it:

Cecilia, extremely shocked, earnestly besought them both to be quiet; but Belfield, at the repetition of this insult, hastily let go her hand and put his own upon his sword, whilst Sir Robert, taking advantage of his situation in being a step higher than his antagonist, fiercely pushed him back, and descended into the lobby.

Belfield, enraged beyond endurance, instantly drew his sword, and Sir Robert was preparing to follow his example, when Cecilia, in an agony of fright, called out, "Good Heaven! will nobody interfere?" And then a young man, forcing his way through the crowd, exclaimed, "For shame, for shame, gentlemen! is this a place for such violence?"

Belfield, endeavouring to recover himself, put up his sword, and, though in a voice half choaked with passion, said, "I thank you, Sir! I was off my guard. I beg pardon of the whole company."

Then, walking up to Sir Robert, he put into his hand a card with his name and direction, saying, "With you, Sir, I shall be happy to settle what apologies are necessary at your first leisure;" and hurried away.

Sir Robert, exclaiming aloud that he should soon teach him to whom he had been so impertinent, was immediately going to follow him, when the affrighted Cecilia again called out aloud, "Oh, stop him!—good God! will nobody stop him!"

The rapidity with which this angry scene had passed had filled her with amazement, and the evident resentment of the Baronet upon her refusing his assistance, gave her an immediate consciousness that she was herself the real cause of the quarrel; while the manner in which he was preparing to follow Mr Belfield convinced her of the desperate scene which was likely to succeed; fear, therefore, overcoming every other feeling, forced from her this exclamation before she knew what she said.

The moment she had spoken, the young man who had already interposed again rushed forward, and seizing Sir Robert by the arm, warmly remonstrated against the violence of his proceedings, and being presently seconded by other gentlemen, almost compelled him to give up his design.

Then, hastening to Cecilia, "Be not alarmed, madam," he cried, "all is over, and every body is safe."

Cecilia, finding herself thus addressed by a gentleman she had never before seen, felt extremely ashamed of having rendered her interest in the debate so apparent; she courtsied to him in some confusion, and taking hold of Mrs Harrel's arm, hurried her back into the pit, in order to quit a crowd, of which she now found herself the principal object.

Curiosity, however, was universally excited, and her retreat served but to inflame it: some of the ladies, and most of the gentlemen, upon various pretences, returned into the pit merely to look at her, and in a few minutes the report was current that the young lady who had been the occasion of the quarrel, was dying with love for Sir Robert Floyer.

Mr Monckton, who had kept by her side during the whole affair, felt thunderstruck by the emotion she had shewn; Mr Arnott too, who had never quitted her, wished himself exposed to the same danger as Sir Robert, so that he might be honoured with the same concern: but they were both too much the dupes of their own apprehensions and jealousy, to perceive that what they instantly imputed to fondness, proceeded simply from general humanity, accidentally united with the consciousness of being accessary to the quarrel.

The young stranger who had officiated as mediator between the disputants, in a few moments followed her with a glass of water, which he had brought from the coffee-room, begging her to drink it and compose herself.

Cecilia, though she declined his civility with more vexation than gratitude, perceived, as she raised her eyes to thank him, that her new friend was a young man very strikingly elegant in his address and appearance.

Miss Larolles next, who, with her party, came back into the pit, ran up to Cecilia, crying, "O my dear creature, what a monstrous shocking thing! You've no Idea how I am frightened; do you know I happened to be quite at the further end of the coffee-room when it began, and I could not get out to see what was the matter for ten ages; only conceive what a situation!"

"Would your fright, then, have been less," said Cecilia, "had you been nearer the danger?"

"O Lord no, for when I came within sight I was fifty times worse! I gave such a monstrous scream, that it quite made Mr Meadows start. I dare say he'll tell me of it these hundred years: but really when I saw them draw their swords I thought I should have died; I was so amazingly surprized you've no notion."

Here she was interrupted by the re-appearance of the active stranger, who again advancing to Cecilia, said, "I am in doubt whether the efforts I make to revive will please or irritate you, but though you rejected the last cordial I ventured to present you, perhaps you will look with a more favourable eye towards that of which I am now the herald."

Cecilia then, casting her eyes around, saw that he was followed by Sir Robert Floyer. Full of displeasure both at this introduction and at his presence, she turned hastily to Mr Arnott, and entreated him to enquire if the carriage was not yet ready.

Sir Robert, looking at her with all the exultation of new-raised vanity, said, with more softness than he had ever before addressed her, "Have you been frightened?"

"Every body, I believe was frightened," answered Cecilia, with an air of dignity intended to check his rising expectations.

"There was no sort of cause," answered he; "the fellow did not know whom he spoke [to], that was all."

"Lord, Sir Robert," cried Miss Larolles, "how could you be so shocking as to draw your sword? you can't conceive how horrid it looked."

"Why I did not draw my sword," cried he, "I only had my hand on the hilt."

"Lord, did not you, indeed! well, every body said you did, and I'm sure I thought I saw five-and-twenty swords all at once. I thought one of you would be killed every moment. It was horrid disagreeable, I assure you."

Sir Robert was now called away by some gentlemen; and Mr Monckton, earnest to be better informed of Cecilia's real sentiments, said, with affected concern, "At present this matter is merely ridiculous; I am sorry to think in how short a time it may become more important."

"Surely," cried Cecilia with quickness, "some of their friends will interfere! surely upon so trifling a subject they will not be so mad, so inexcusable, as to proceed to more serious resentment!"

"Whichever of them," said the stranger, "is most honoured by this anxiety, will be mad indeed to risk a life so valued!"

"Cannot you, Mr Monckton," continued Cecilia, too much alarmed to regard this insinuation, "speak with Mr Belfield? You are acquainted with him, I know; is it impossible you can follow him?"

"I will with pleasure do whatever you wish; but still if Sir Robert—"

"O, as to Sir Robert, Mr Harrel, I am very sure, will undertake him; I will try to see him to-night myself, and entreat him to exert all his influence."

"Ah, madam," cried the stranger, archly, and lowering his voice, "those *French beads* and *Bristol stones* have not, I find, shone in vain!"

At these words Cecilia recognised her white domino acquaintance at the masquerade; she had before recollected his voice, but was too much perturbed to consider where or when she had heard it.

"If Mr Briggs," continued he, "does not speedily come forth with his plum friend, before the glittering of swords and spears is joined to that of jewels, the glare will be so resplendent, that he will fear to come within the influence of its rays. Though, perhaps, he may only think the stronger the light, the better he shall see to count his guineas: for as

    '—in ten thousand pounds
    Ten thousand charms are centred,'

in an hundred thousand, the charms may have such magic power, that he may defy the united efforts of tinsel and knight-errantry to deliver you from the golden spell."

Here the Captain, advancing to Cecilia, said, "I have been looking for you in vain *partout*, but the crowd has been so *accablant* I was almost reduced to despair. Give me leave to hope you are now recovered from the *horreur* of this little *fracas*?"

Mr Arnott then brought intelligence that the carriage was ready. Cecilia, glad to be gone, instantly hastened to it; and, as she was conducted by Mr Monckton, most earnestly entreated him to take an active part, in endeavouring to prevent the fatal consequences with which the quarrel seemed likely to terminate.

CHAPTER V

A FASHIONABLE FRIEND.

As soon as they returned home, Cecilia begged Mrs Harrel not to
lose a moment before she tried to acquaint Mr Harrel with the state of
the affair. But that lady was too helpless to know in what manner to set
about it; she could not tell where he was, she could not conjecture where
he might be.

Cecilia then rang for his own man, and upon enquiry, heard that he
was, in all probability, at Brookes's in St James's-Street.

She then begged Mrs Harrel would write to him.

Mrs Harrel knew not what to say.

Cecilia therefore, equally quick in forming and executing her designs,
wrote to him herself, and entreated that without losing an instant he
would find out his friend Sir Robert Floyer, and endeavour to effect an
accommodation between him and Mr Belfield, with whom he had had a
dispute at the Opera-house.

The man soon returned with an answer that Mr Harrel would not fail
to obey her commands.

She determined to sit up till he came home in order to learn the event
of the negociation. She considered herself as the efficient cause of the
quarrel, yet scarce knew how or in what to blame herself; the behaviour of
Sir Robert had always been offensive to her; she disliked his manners, and
detested his boldness; and she had already shewn her intention to accept
the assistance of Mr Belfield before he had followed her with an offer

of his own. She was uncertain, indeed, whether he had remarked what had passed, but she had reason to think that, so circumstanced, to have changed her purpose, would have been construed into an encouragement that might have authorised his future presumption of her favour. All she could find to regret with regard to herself, was wanting the presence of mind to have refused the civilities of both.

Mrs Harrel, though really sorry at the state of the affair, regarded herself as so entirely unconcerned in it, that, easily wearied when out of company, she soon grew sleepy, and retired to her own room.

The anxious Cecilia, hoping every instant the return of Mr Harrel, sat up by herself: but it was not till near four o'clock in the morning that he made his appearance.

"Well, sir," cried she, the moment she saw him, "I fear by your coming home so late you have had much trouble, but I hope it has been successful?"

Great, however, was her mortification when he answered that he had not even seen the Baronet, having been engaged himself in so particular a manner, that he could not possibly break from his party till past three o'clock, at which time he drove to the house of Sir Robert, but heard that he was not yet come home.

Cecilia, though much disgusted by such a specimen of insensibility towards a man whom he pretended to call his friend, would not leave him till he had promised to arise as soon as it was light, and make an effort to recover the time lost.

She was now no longer surprised either at the debts of Mr Harrel, or at his *particular occasions* for money. She was convinced he spent half the night in gaming, and the consequences, however dreadful, were but natural. That Sir Robert Floyer also did the same was a matter of much less importance to her, but that the life of any man should through her means be endangered, disturbed her inexpressibly.

She went, however, to bed, but arose again at six o'clock, and dressed herself by candle light. In an hour's time she sent to enquire if Mr

Harrel was stirring, and hearing he was asleep, gave orders to have him called. Yet he did not rise till eight o'clock, nor could all her messages or expostulations drive him out of the house till nine.

He was scarcely gone before Mr Monckton arrived, who now for the first time had the satisfaction of finding her alone.

"You are very good for coming so early," cried she; "have you seen Mr Belfield? Have you had any conversation with him?"

Alarmed at her eagerness, and still more at seeing by her looks the sleepless night she had passed, he made at first no reply; and when, with increasing impatience, she repeated her question, he only said, "Has Belfield ever visited you since he had the honour of meeting you at my house?"

"No, never."

"Have you seen him often in public?"

"No, I have never seen him at all but the evening Mrs Harrel received masks, and last night at the Opera."

"Is it, then, for the safety of Sir Robert you are so extremely anxious?"

"It is for the safety of both; the cause of their quarrel was so trifling, that I cannot bear to think its consequence should be serious."

"But do you not wish better to one of them than to the other?"

"As a matter of justice I do, but not from any partiality: Sir Robert was undoubtedly the aggressor, and Mr Belfield, though at first too fiery, was certainly ill-used."

The candour of this speech recovered Mr Monckton from his apprehensions; and, carefully observing her looks while he spoke, he gave her the following account.

That he had hastened to Belfield's lodgings the moment he left the Opera-house, and, after repeated denials, absolutely forced himself into his room, where he was quite alone, and in much agitation: he conversed with him for more than an hour upon the subject of the quarrel, but found he so warmly resented the personal insult given him by Sir Robert, that no remonstrance had any effect in making him alter his resolution of demanding satisfaction.

"And could you bring him to consent to no compromise before you left him?" cried Cecilia.

"No; for before I got to him—the challenge had been sent."

"The challenge! good heaven!—and do you know the event?"

"I called again this morning at his lodgings, but he was not returned home."

"And was it impossible to follow him? Were there no means to discover whither he was gone?"

"None; to elude all pursuit, he went out before any body in the house was stirring, and took his servant with him."

"Have you, then, been to Sir Robert?"

"I have been to Cavendish-Square, but there, it seems, he has not appeared all night; I traced him, through his servants, from the Opera to a gaminghouse, where I found he had amused himself till this morning."

The uneasiness of Cecilia now encreased every moment; and Mr Monckton, seeing he had no other chance of satisfying her, offered his service to go again in search of both the gentlemen, and endeavour to bring her better information. She accepted the proposal with gratitude, and he departed.

Soon after she was joined by Mr Arnott, who, though seized with all the horrors of jealousy at sight of her apprehensions, was so desirous to relieve them, that without even making any merit of obliging her, he almost instantly set out upon the same errand that employed Mr Monckton, and determined not to mention his design till he found whether it would enable him to bring her good tidings.

He was scarce gone when she was told that Mr Delvile begged to have the honour of speaking to her. Surprised at this condescension, she desired he might immediately be admitted; but much was her surprise augmented, when, instead of seeing her ostentatious guardian, she again beheld her masquerade friend, the white domino.

He entreated her pardon for an intrusion neither authorised by acquaintance nor by business, though somewhat, he hoped, palliated, by his near connection with one who was privileged to take an interest in her affairs: and then, hastening to the motives which had occasioned his visit, "when I had the honour," he said, "of seeing you last night at the Opera-house, the dispute which had just happened between two gentlemen, seemed to give you an uneasiness which could not but be painful to all who observed it, and as among that number I was not the least moved, you will forgive, I hope, my eagerness to be the first to bring you intelligence that nothing fatal has happened, or is likely to happen."

"You do me, sir," said Cecilia, "much honour; and indeed you relieve me from a suspense extremely disagreeable. The accommodation, I suppose, was brought about this morning?"

"I find," answered he, smiling, "you now expect too much; but hope is never so elastic as when it springs from the ruins of terror."

"What then is the matter? Are they at last, not safe?"

"Yes, perfectly safe; but I cannot tell you they have never been in danger."

"Well, if it is now over I am contented: but you will very much oblige me, sir, if you will inform me what has passed."

"You oblige me, madam, by the honour of your commands. I saw but too much reason to apprehend that measures the most violent would follow the affray of last night; yet as I found that the quarrel had been accidental, and the offence unpremeditated, I thought it not absolutely impossible that an expeditious mediation might effect a compromise: at least it was worth trying; for though wrath slowly kindled or long nourished is sullen and intractable, the sudden anger that has not had time to impress the mind with a deep sense of injury, will, when gently managed, be sometimes appeased with the same quickness it is excited: I hoped, therefore, that some trifling concession from Sir Robert, as the aggressor,—"

"Ah sir!" cried Cecilia, "that, I fear, was not to be obtained!"

170

"Not by me, I must own," he answered; "but I was not willing to think of the difficulty, and therefore ventured to make the proposal: nor did I leave the Opera-house till I had used every possible argument to persuade Sir Robert an apology would neither stain his courage nor his reputation. But his spirit brooked not the humiliation."

"Spirit!" cried Cecilia, "how mild a word! What, then, could poor Mr Belfield resolve upon?"

"That, I believe, took him very little time to decide. I discovered, by means of a gentleman at the Opera who was acquainted with him, where he lived, and I waited upon him with an intention to offer my services towards settling the affair by arbitration: for since you call him poor Mr Belfield, I think you will permit me, without offence to his antagonist, to own that his gallantry, though too impetuous for commendation, engaged me in his interest."

"I hope you don't think," cried Cecilia, "that an offence to his antagonist must necessarily be an offence to me?"

"Whatever I may have thought," answered he, looking at her with evident surprise, "I certainly did not wish that a sympathy offensive and defensive had been concluded between you. I could not, however, gain access to Mr Belfield last night, but the affair dwelt upon my mind, and this morning I called at his lodging as soon as it was light."

"How good you have been!" cried Cecilia; "your kind offices have not, I hope, all proved ineffectual!"

"So valorous a Don Quixote," returned he, laughing, "certainly merited a faithful Esquire! He was, however, gone out, and nobody knew whither. About half an hour ago I called upon him again; he was then just returned home."

"Well, Sir?"

"I saw him; the affair was over; and in a short time he will be able, if you will allow him so much honour, to thank you for these enquiries."

"He is then wounded?"

"He is a little hurt, but Sir Robert is perfectly safe. Belfield fired first, and missed; the Baronet was not so successless."

"I am grieved to hear it, indeed! And where is the wound?"

"The ball entered his right side, and the moment he felt it, he fired his second pistol in the air. This I heard from his servant. He was brought home carefully and slowly; no surgeon had been upon the spot, but one was called to him immediately. I stayed to enquire his opinion after the wound had been dressed: he told me he had extracted the ball, and assured me Mr Belfield was not in any danger. Your alarm, madam, last night, which had always been present to me, then encouraged me to take the liberty of waiting upon you; for I concluded you could yet have had no certain intelligence, and thought it best to let the plain and simple fact out-run the probable exaggeration of rumour."

Cecilia thanked him for his attention, and Mrs Harrel then making her appearance, he arose and said, "Had my father known the honour I have had this morning of waiting upon Miss Beverley, I am sure I should have been charged with his compliments, and such a commission would somewhat have lessened the presumption of this visit; but I feared lest while I should be making interest for my credentials, the pretence of my embassy might be lost, and other couriers, less scrupulous, might obtain previous audiences, and anticipate my dispatches."

He then took his leave.

"This white domino, at last then," said Cecilia, "is the son of Mr Delvile! and thence the knowledge of my situation which gave me so much surprise:—a son how infinitely unlike his father!"

"Yes," said Mrs Harrel, "and as unlike his mother too, for I assure you she is more proud and haughty even than the old gentleman. I hate the very sight of her, for she keeps every body in such awe that there's nothing but restraint in her presence. But the son is a very pretty young man, and much admired; though I have only seen him in public, for none of the family visit here."

Mr Monckton, who now soon returned, was not a little surprised to find that all the intelligence he meant to communicate was already known: and not the more pleased to hear that the white domino, to whom before he owed no good-will, had thus officiously preceded him.

Mr Arnott, who also came just after him, had been so little satisfied with the result of his enquiries, that from the fear of encreasing Cecilia's uneasiness, he determined not to make known whither he had been; but he soon found his forbearance was of no avail, as she was already acquainted with the duel and its consequences. Yet his unremitting desire to oblige her urged him twice in the course of the same day to again call at Mr Belfield's lodgings, in order to bring her thence fresh and unsolicited intelligence.

Before breakfast was quite over, Miss Larolles, out of breath with eagerness, came to tell the news of the duel, in her way to church, as it was Sunday morning! and soon after Mrs Mears, who also was followed by other ladies, brought the same account, which by all was addressed to Cecilia, with expressions of concern that convinced her, to her infinite vexation, she was generally regarded as the person chiefly interested in the accident.

Mr Harrel did not return till late, but then seemed in very high spirits: "Miss Beverley," he cried, "I bring you news that will repay all your fright; Sir Robert is not only safe, but is come off conqueror."

"I am very sorry, Sir," answered Cecilia, extremely provoked to be thus congratulated, "that any body conquered, or any body was vanquished."

"There is no need for sorrow," cried Mr Harrel, "or for any thing but joy, for he has not killed his man; the victory, therefore, will neither cost him a flight nor a trial. To-day he means to wait upon you, and lay his laurels at your feet."

"He means, then, to take very fruitless trouble," said Cecilia, "for I have not any ambition to be so honoured."

"Ah, Miss Beverley," returned he, laughing, "this won't do now! it might have passed a little while ago, but it won't do now, I promise you!"

Cecilia, though much displeased by this accusation, found that disclaiming it only excited further raillery, and therefore prevailed upon herself to give him a quiet hearing, and scarce any reply.

At dinner, when Sir Robert arrived, the dislike she had originally taken to him, encreased already into disgust by his behaviour the preceding evening, was now fixed into the strongest aversion by the horror she conceived of his fierceness, and the indignation she felt excited by his arrogance. He seemed, from the success of this duel, to think himself raised to the highest pinnacle of human glory; triumph sat exulting on his brow; he looked down on whoever he deigned to look at all, and shewed that he thought his notice an honour, however imperious the manner in which it was accorded.

Upon Cecilia, however, he cast an eye of more complacency; he now believed her subdued, and his vanity revelled in the belief: her anxiety had so thoroughly satisfied him of her love, that she had hardly the power left to undeceive him; her silence he only attributed to admiration, her coldness to fear, and her reserve to shame.

Sickened by insolence so undisguised and unauthorised, and incensed at the triumph of his successful brutality, Cecilia with pain kept her seat, and with vexation reflected upon the necessity she was under of passing so large a portion of her time in company to which she was so extremely averse.

After dinner, when Mrs Harrel was talking of her party for the evening, of which Cecilia declined making one, Sir Robert, with a sort of proud humility, that half feared rejection, and half proclaimed an indifference to meeting it, said, "I don't much care for going further myself, if Miss Beverley will give me the honour of taking my tea with her."

Cecilia, regarding him with much surprise, answered that she had letters to write into the country, which would confine her to her own room for the rest of the evening. The Baronet, looking at his watch, instantly cried, "Faith, that is very fortunate, for I have just recollected an engagement at the other end of the town which had slipt my memory."

Soon after they were all gone, Cecilia received a note from Mrs Delvile, begging the favour of her company the next morning to breakfast. She readily accepted the invitation, though she was by no means prepared, by the character she had heard of her, to expect much pleasure from an acquaintance with that lady.

CHAPTER VI

A FAMILY PARTY.

Cecilia the next morning, between nine and ten o'clock, went to St James'-Square; she found nobody immediately ready to receive her, but in a short time was waited upon by Mr Delvile.

After the usual salutations, "Miss Beverley," he said, "I have given express orders to my people, that I may not be interrupted while I have the pleasure of passing some minutes in conversation with you before you are presented to Mrs Delvile."

And then, with an air of solemnity, he led her to a seat, and having himself taken possession of another, continued his speech.

"I have received information, from authority which I cannot doubt, that the indiscretion of certain of your admirers last Saturday at the Opera-house occasioned a disturbance which to a young woman of delicacy I should imagine must be very alarming: now as I consider myself concerned in your fame and welfare from regarding you as my ward, I think it is incumbent upon me to make enquiries into such of your affairs as become public; for I should feel in some measure disgraced myself, should it appear to the world, while you are under my guardianship, that there was any want of propriety in the direction of your conduct."

Cecilia, not much flattered by this address, gravely answered that she fancied the affair had been misrepresented to him.

"I am not much addicted," he replied, "to give ear to any thing lightly; you must therefore permit me to enquire into the merits of the cause, and then to draw my own inferences. And let me, at the same time, assure you there is no other young lady who has any right to expect such an attention from me. I must begin by begging you to inform me upon what grounds the two gentlemen in question, for such, by courtesy, I presume they are called, thought themselves entitled publicly to dispute your favour?"

"My favour, Sir!" cried Cecilia, much amazed.

"My dear," said he, with a complacency meant to give her courage, "I know the question is difficult for a young lady to answer; but be not abashed, I should be sorry to distress you, and mean to the utmost of my power to save your blushes. Do not, therefore, fear me; consider me as your guardian, and assure yourself I am perfectly well disposed to consider you as my ward. Acquaint me, then, freely, what are the pretensions of these gentlemen?"

"To me, Sir, they have, I believe, no pretensions at all."

"I see you are shy," returned he, with encreasing gentleness, "I see you cannot be easy with me; and when I consider how little you are accustomed to me, I do not wonder. But pray take courage; I think it necessary to inform myself of your affairs, and therefore I beg you will speak to me with freedom."

Cecilia, more and more mortified by this humiliating condescension, again assured him he had been misinformed, and was again, though discredited, praised for her modesty, when, to her great relief, they were interrupted by the entrance of her friend the *white domino*.

"Mortimer," said Mr Delvile, "I understand you have already had the pleasure of seeing this young lady?"

"Yes, Sir," he answered, "I have more than once had that happiness, but I have never had the honour of being introduced to her."

"Miss Beverley, then," said the father, "I must present to you Mr Mortimer Delvile, my son; and, Mortimer, in Miss Beverley I desire you will remember that you respect a ward of your father's."

"I will not, Sir," answered he, "forget an injunction my own inclinations had already out-run."

Mortimer Delvile was tall and finely formed, his features, though not handsome, were full of expression, and a noble openness of manners and address spoke the elegance of his education, and the liberality of his mind.

When this introduction was over, a more general conversation took place, till Mr Delvile, suddenly rising, said to Cecilia, "You will pardon me, Miss Beverley, if I leave you for a few minutes; one of my tenants sets out to-morrow morning for my estate in the North, and he has been two hours waiting to speak with me. But if my son is not particularly engaged, I am sure he will be so good as to do the honours of the house till his mother is ready to receive you."

And then, graciously waving his hand, he quitted the room.

"My father," cried young Delvile, "has left me an office which, could I execute it as perfectly as I shall willingly, would be performed without a fault."

"I am very sorry," said Cecilia, "that I have so much mistaken your hour of breakfast; but let me not be any restraint upon you, I shall find a book, or a newspaper, or something to fill up the time till Mrs Delvile honours me with a summons."

"You can only be a restraint upon me," answered he, "by commanding me from your presence. I breakfasted long ago, and am now just come from Mr Belfield. I had the pleasure, this morning, of being admitted into his room."

"And how, Sir, did you find him?"

"Not so well, I fear, as he thinks himself; but he was in high spirits, and surrounded by his friends, whom he was entertaining with all the gaiety of a man in full health, and entirely at his ease; though I perceived, by the frequent changes of his countenance, signs of pain and indisposition, that made me, however pleased with his conversation, think it necessary to shorten my own visit, and to hint to those who were near me the propriety of leaving him quiet."

"Did you see his surgeon, Sir?"

"No; but he told me he should only have one dressing more of his wound, and then get rid of the whole business by running into the country."

"Were you acquainted with him, Sir, before this accident?"

"No, not at all; but the little I have seen of him has strongly interested me in his favour: at Mr Harrel's masquerade, where I first met with him, I was extremely entertained by his humour,—though there, perhaps, as I had also the honour of first seeing Miss Beverley, I might be too happy to feel much difficulty in being pleased. And even at the Opera he had the advantage of finding me in the same favourable disposition, as I had long distinguished you before I had taken any notice of him. I must, however, confess I did not think his anger that evening quite without provocation,—but I beg your pardon, I may perhaps be mistaken, and you, who know the whole affair, must undoubtedly be better able to account for what happened."

Here he fixed his eyes upon Cecilia, with a look of curiosity that seemed eager to penetrate into her sentiments of the two antagonists.

"No, certainly," she answered, "he had all the provocation that ill-breeding could give him."

"And do you, madam," cried he, with much surprize, "judge of this matter with such severity?"

"No, not with severity, simply with candour."

"With candour? alas, then, poor Sir Robert! Severity were not half so bad a sign for him!"

A servant now came in, to acquaint Cecilia that Mrs Delvile waited breakfast for her.

This summons was immediately followed by the re-entrance of Mr Delvile, who, taking her hand, said he would himself present her to his lady, and with much graciousness assured her of a kind reception.

The ceremonies preceding this interview, added to the character she had already heard of Mrs Delvile, made Cecilia heartily wish it over; but, assuming all the courage in her power, she determined to support herself with a spirit that should struggle against the ostentatious superiority she was prepared to expect.

She found her seated upon a sofa, from which, however, she arose at her approach; but the moment Cecilia beheld her, all the unfavourable impressions with which she came into her presence immediately vanished, and that respect which the formalities of her introduction had failed to inspire, her air, figure, and countenance instantaneously excited.

She was not more than fifty years of age; her complection, though faded, kept the traces of its former loveliness, her eyes, though they had lost their youthful fire, retained a lustre that evinced their primeval brilliancy, and the fine symmetry of her features, still uninjured by the siege of time, not only indicated the perfection of her juvenile beauty, but still laid claim to admiration in every beholder. Her carriage was lofty and commanding; but the dignity to which high birth and conscious superiority gave rise, was so judiciously regulated by good sense, and so happily blended with politeness, that though the world at large envied or hated her, the few for whom she had herself any regard, she was infallibly certain to captivate.

The surprise and admiration with which Cecilia at the first glance was struck proved reciprocal: Mrs Delvile, though prepared for youth and beauty, expected not to see a countenance so intelligent, nor manners so well formed as those of Cecilia: thus mutually astonished and mutually pleased, their first salutations were accompanied by looks so flattering to both, that each saw in the other, an immediate prepossession in her favour, and from the moment that they met, they seemed instinctively impelled to admire.

"I have promised Miss Beverley, madam," said Mr Delvile to his lady, "that you would give her a kind reception; and I need not remind you that my promises are always held sacred."

"But I hope you have not also promised," cried she, with quickness, "that I should give *you* a kind reception, for I feel at this very moment extremely inclined to quarrel with you."

"Why so, madam?"

"For not bringing us together sooner; for now I have seen her, I already look back with regret to the time I have lost without the pleasure of knowing her."

"What a claim is this," cried young Delvile, "upon the benevolence of Miss Beverley! for if she has not now the indulgence by frequent and diligent visits to make some reparation, she must consider herself as responsible for the dissension she will occasion."

"If peace depends upon my visits," answered Cecilia, "it may immediately be proclaimed; were it to be procured only by my absence, I know not if I should so readily agree to the conditions."

"I must request of you, madam," said Mr Delvile, "that when my son and I retire, you will bestow half an hour upon this young lady, in making enquiries concerning the disturbance last Saturday at the Opera-house. I have not, myself, so much time to spare, as I have several appointments for this morning; but I am sure you will not object to the office, as I know you to be equally anxious with myself, that the minority of Miss Beverley should pass without reproach."

"Not only her minority, but her maturity," cried young Delvile, warmly, "and not only her maturity, but her decline of life will pass, I hope, not merely without reproach, but with fame and applause!"

"I hope so too;" replied Mr Delvile: "I wish her well through every stage of her life, but for her minority alone it is my business to do more than wish. For that, I feel my own honour and my own credit concerned; my honour, as I gave it to the Dean that I would superintend her conduct, and my credit, as the world is acquainted with the claim she has to my protection."

"I will not make any enquiries," said Mrs Delvile, turning to Cecilia with a sweetness that recompensed her for the haughtiness of her guardian, "till I have had some opportunity of convincing Miss Beverley, that my regard for her merits they should be answered."

"You see, Miss Beverley," said Mr Delvile, "how little reason you had to be afraid of us; Mrs Delvile is as much disposed in your favour as myself, and as desirous to be of service to you. Endeavour, therefore, to cast off this timidity, and to make yourself easy. You must come to us often; use will do more towards removing your fears, than all the encouragement we can give you."

"But what are the fears," cried Mrs Delvile, "that Miss Beverley can have to remove? unless, indeed, she apprehends her visits will make us encroachers, and that the more we are favoured with her presence, the less we shall bear her absence."

"Pray, son," said Mr Delvile, "what was the name of the person who was Sir Robert Floyer's opponent? I have again forgotten it."

"Belfield, sir."

"True; it is a name I am perfectly unacquainted with: however, he may possibly be a very good sort of man; but certainly his opposing himself to Sir Robert Floyer, a man of some family, a gentleman, rich, and allied to some people of distinction, was a rather strange circumstance: I mean not, however, to prejudge the case; I will hear it fairly stated; and am the more disposed to be cautious in what I pronounce, because I am persuaded Miss Beverley has too much sense to let my advice be thrown away upon her."

"I hope so, Sir; but with respect to the disturbance at the Opera, I know not that I have the least occasion to trouble you."

"If your measures," said he, very gravely, "are already taken, the Dean your uncle prevailed upon me to accept a very useless office; but if any thing is yet undecided, it will not, perhaps, be amiss that I should be consulted. Mean time, I will only recommend to you to consider that Mr Belfield is a person whose name nobody has heard, and that a connection with Sir Robert Floyer would certainly be very honourable for you."

"Indeed, Sir," said Cecilia, "here is some great mistake; neither of these gentlemen, I believe, think of me at all."

"They have taken, then," cried young Delvile with a laugh, "a very extraordinary method to prove their indifference!"

"The affairs of Sir Robert Floyer," continued Mr Delvile, "are indeed, I am informed, in some disorder; but he has a noble estate, and your fortune would soon clear all its incumbrances. Such an alliance, therefore, would be mutually advantageous: but what would result from a union with such a person as Mr Belfield? he is of no family, though in that, perhaps, you would not be very scrupulous; but neither has he any money; what, then, recommends him?"

"To me, Sir, nothing!" answered Cecilia.

"And to me," cried young Delvile, "almost every thing! he has wit, spirit, and understanding, talents to create admiration, and qualities, I believe, to engage esteem!"

"You speak warmly," said Mrs Delvile; "but if such is his character, he merits your earnestness. What is it you know of him?"

"Not enough, perhaps," answered he, "to coolly justify my praise; but he is one of those whose first appearance takes the mind by surprise, and leaves the judgment to make afterwards such terms as it can. Will you, madam, when he is recovered, permit me to introduce him to you?"

"Certainly;" said she, smiling; "but have a care your recommendation does not disgrace your discernment."

"This warmth of disposition, Mortimer," cried Mr Delvile, "produces nothing but difficulties and trouble: you neglect the connections I point out, and which a little attention might render serviceable as well as honourable, and run precipitately into forming such as can do you no good among people of rank, and are not only profitless in themselves, but generally lead you into expence and inconvenience. You are now of an age to correct this rashness: think, therefore, better of your own consequence, than thus idly to degrade yourself by forming friendships with every shewy adventurer that comes in your way."

"I know not, Sir," answered he, "how Mr Belfield deserves to be called an adventurer: he is not, indeed, rich; but he is in a profession where parts such as his seldom fail to acquire riches; however, as to me his wealth can be of no consequence, why should my regard to him wait for it? if he is a young man of worth and honour—"

"Mortimer," interrupted Mr Delvile, "whatever he is, we know he is not a man of rank, and whatever he may be, we know he cannot become a man of family, and consequently for Mortimer Delvile he is no companion. If you can render him any service, I shall commend your so doing; it becomes your birth, it becomes your station in life to assist individuals, and promote the general good: but never in your zeal for others forget what is due to yourself, and to the ancient and honourable house from which you are sprung."

"But can we entertain Miss Beverley with nothing better than family lectures?" cried Mrs Delvile.

"It is for me," said young Delvile, rising, "to beg pardon of Miss Beverley for having occasioned them: but when she is so good as to honour us with her company again, I hope I shall have more discretion."

He then left the room; and Mr Delvile also rising to go, said, "My dear, I commit you to very kind hands; Mrs Delvile, I am sure, will be happy to hear your story; speak to her, therefore, without reserve. And pray don't imagine that I make you over to her from any slight; on the contrary, I admire and commend your modesty very much; but my time is extremely precious, and I cannot devote so much of it to an explanation as your diffidence requires."

And then, to the great joy of Cecilia, he retired; leaving her much in doubt whether his haughtiness or his condescension humbled her most.

"These men," said Mrs Delvile, "can never comprehend the pain of a delicate female mind upon entering into explanations of this sort: I understand it, however, too well to inflict it. We will, therefore, have no explanations at all till we are better acquainted, and then if you will venture to favour me with any confidence, my best advice, and, should any be in my power, my best services shall be at your command."

"You do me, madam, much honour," answered Cecilia, "but I must assure you I have no explanation to give."

"Well, well, at present," returned Mrs Delvile, "I am content to hear that answer, as I have acquired no right to any other: but hereafter I shall hope for more openness: it is promised me by your countenance, and I mean to claim the promise by my friendship."

"Your friendship will both honour and delight me, and whatever are your enquiries, I shall always be proud to answer them; but indeed, with regard to this affair—"

"My dear Miss Beverley," interrupted Mrs Delvile, with a look of arch incredulity, "men seldom risk their lives where an escape is without hope of recompence. But we will not now say a word more upon the subject. I hope you will often favour me with your company, and by the frequency of your visits, make us both forget the shortness of our acquaintance."

Cecilia, finding her resistance only gave birth to fresh suspicion, now yielded, satisfied that a very little time must unavoidably clear up the truth. But her visit was not therefore shortened; the sudden partiality with which the figure and countenance of Mrs Delvile had impressed her, was quickly ripened into esteem by the charms of her conversation: she found her sensible, well bred, and high spirited, gifted by nature with superior talents, and polished by education and study with all the elegant embellishments of cultivation. She saw in her, indeed, some portion of the pride she had been taught to expect, but it was so much softened by elegance, and so well tempered with kindness, that it elevated her character, without rendering her manners offensive.

With such a woman, subjects of discourse could never be wanting, nor fertility of powers to make them entertaining: and so much was Cecilia delighted with her visit, that though her carriage was announced at twelve o'clock, she reluctantly concluded it at two; and in taking her leave, gladly accepted an invitation to dine with her new friend three days after; who, equally pleased with her young guest, promised before that time to return her visit.

CHAPTER VII

AN EXAMINATION.

Cecilia found Mrs Harrel eagerly waiting to hear some account how she had passed the morning, and fully persuaded that she would leave the Delviles with a determination never more, but by necessity, to see them: she was, therefore, not only surprised but disappointed, when instead of fulfilling her expectations, she assured her that she had been delighted with Mrs Delvile, whose engaging qualities amply recompensed her for the arrogance of her husband; that her visit had no fault but that of being too short, and that she had already appointed an early day for repeating it.

Mrs Harrel was evidently hurt by this praise, and Cecilia, who perceived among all her guardians a powerful disposition to hatred and jealousy, soon dropt the subject: though so much had she been charmed with Mrs Delvile, that a scheme of removal once more occurred to her, notwithstanding her dislike of her stately guardian.

At dinner, as usual, they were joined by Sir Robert Floyer, who grew more and more assiduous in his attendance, but who, this day, contrary to his general custom of remaining with the gentlemen, made his exit before the ladies left the table; and as soon as he was gone, Mr Harrel desired a private conference with Cecilia.

They went together to the drawing-room, where, after a flourishing preface upon the merits of Sir Robert Floyer, he formally acquainted her that he was commissioned by that gentleman, to make her a tender of his hand and fortune.

186

Cecilia, who had not much reason to be surprised at this overture, desired him to tell the Baronet, she was obliged to him for the honour he intended her, at the same time that she absolutely declined receiving it.

Mr Harrel, laughing, told her this answer was very well for a beginning, though it would by no means serve beyond the first day of the declaration; but when Cecilia assured him she should firmly adhere to it, he remonstrated with equal surprise and discontent upon the reasons of her refusal. She thought it sufficient to tell him that Sir Robert did not please her, but, with much raillery, he denied the assertion credit, assuring her that he was universally admired by the ladies, that she could not possibly receive a more honourable offer, and that he was reckoned by every body the finest gentleman about the town. His fortune, he added, was equally unexceptionable with his figure and his rank in life; all the world, he was certain, would approve the connexion, and the settlement made upon her should be dictated by herself.

Cecilia begged him to be satisfied with an answer which she never could change, and to spare her the enumeration of particular objections, since Sir Robert was wholly and in every respect disagreeable to her.

"What, then," cried he, "could make you so frightened for him at the Opera-house? There has been but one opinion about town ever since of your prepossession in his favour."

"I am extremely concerned to hear it; my fright was but the effect of surprise, and belonged not more to Sir Robert than to Mr Belfield."

He told her that nobody else thought the same, that her marriage with the Baronet was universally expected, and, in conclusion, notwithstanding her earnest desire that he would instantly and explicitly inform Sir Robert of her determination, he repeatedly refused to give him any final answer till she had taken more time for consideration.

Cecilia was extremely displeased at this irksome importunity, and still more chagrined to find her incautious emotion at the Opera-house, had given rise to suspicions of her harbouring a partiality for a man whom every day she more heartily disliked.

While she was deliberating in what manner she could clear up this mistake, which, after she was left alone, occupied all her thoughts, she was interrupted by the entrance of Mr. Monckton, whose joy in meeting her at length by herself exceeded not her own, for charmed as he was that he could now examine into the state of her affairs, she was not less delighted that she could make them known to him.

After mutual expressions, guarded, however, on the part of Mr. Monckton, though unreserved on that of Cecilia, of their satisfaction in being again able to converse as in former times, he asked if she would permit him, as the privilege of their long acquaintance, to speak to her with sincerity.

She assured him he could not more oblige her.

"Let me, then," said he, "enquire if yet that ardent confidence in your own steadiness, which so much disdained my fears that the change of your residence might produce a change in your sentiments, is still as unshaken as when we parted in Suffolk? Or whether experience, that foe to unpractised refinement, has already taught you the fallibility of theory?"

"When I assure you," replied Cecilia, "that your enquiry gives me no pain, I think I have sufficiently answered it, for were I conscious of any alteration, it could not but embarrass and distress me. Very far, however, from finding myself in the danger with which you threatened me, of *forgetting Bury, its inhabitants and its environs*, I think with pleasure of little else, since London, instead of bewitching, has greatly disappointed me."

"How so?" cried Mr Monckton, much delighted.

"Not," answered she, "in itself, not in its magnificence, nor in its diversions, which seem to be inexhaustible; but these, though copious as instruments of pleasure, are very shallow as sources of happiness: the disappointment, therefore, comes nearer home, and springs not from London, but from my own situation."

"Is that, then, disagreeable to you?"

"You shall yourself judge, when I have told you that from the time of my quitting your house till this very moment, when I have again the happiness of talking with you, I have never once had any conversation, society or intercourse, in which friendship or affection have had any share, or my mind has had the least interest."

She then entered into a detail of her way of life, told him how little suited to her taste was the unbounded dissipation of the Harrels, and feelingly expatiated upon the disappointment she had received from the alteration in the manners and conduct of her young friend. "In her," she continued, "had I found the companion I came prepared to meet, the companion from whom I had so lately parted, and in whose society I expected to find consolation for the loss of yours and of Mrs Charlton's, I should have complained of nothing; the very places that now tire, might then have entertained me, and all that now passes for unmeaning dissipation, might then have worn the appearance of variety and pleasure. But where the mind is wholly without interest, every thing is languid and insipid; and accustomed as I have long been to think friendship the first of human blessings, and social converse the greatest of human enjoyments, how ever can I reconcile myself to a state of careless indifference, to making acquaintance without any concern either for preserving or esteeming them, and to going on from day to day in an eager search of amusement, with no companion for the hours of retirement, and no view beyond that of passing the present moment in apparent gaiety and thoughtlessness?"

Mr Monckton, who heard these complaints with secret rapture, far from seeking to soften or remove, used his utmost endeavours to strengthen and encrease them, by artfully retracing her former way of life, and pointing out with added censures the change in it she had been lately compelled to make: "a change," he continued, "which though ruinous of your time, and detrimental to your happiness, use will, I fear, familiarize, and familiarity render pleasant."

"These suspicions, sir," said Cecilia, "mortify me greatly; and why, when far from finding me pleased, you hear nothing but repining, should you still continue to harbour them?"

"Because your trial has yet been too short to prove your firmness, and because there is nothing to which time cannot contentedly accustom us."

"I feel not much fear," said Cecilia, "of standing such a test as might fully satisfy you; but nevertheless, not to be too presumptuous, I have by no means exposed myself to all the dangers which you think surround me, for of late I have spent almost every evening at home and by myself."

This intelligence was to Mr Monckton a surprise the most agreeable he could receive. Her distaste for the amusements which were offered her greatly relieved his fears of her forming any alarming connection, and the discovery that while so anxiously he had sought her every where in public, she had quietly passed her time by her own fireside, not only re-assured him for the present, but gave him information where he might meet with her in future.

He then talked of the duel, and solicitously led her to speak [openly] of Sir Robert Floyer; and here too, his satisfaction was entire; he found her dislike of him such as his knowledge of her disposition made him expect, and she wholly removed his suspicions concerning her anxiety about the quarrel, by explaining to him her apprehensions of having occasioned it herself, from accepting the civility of Mr Belfield, at the very moment she shewed her aversion to receiving that of Sir Robert.

Neither did her confidence rest here; she acquainted him with the conversation she had just had with Mr Harrel, and begged his advice in what manner she might secure herself from further importunity.

Mr Monckton had now a new subject for his discernment. Every thing had confirmed to him the passion which Mr Arnott had conceived for Cecilia, and he had therefore concluded the interest of the Harrels would be all in his favour: other ideas now struck him; he found that Mr Arnott was given up for Sir Robert, and he determined carefully to watch the motions both of the Baronet and her young guardian, in order to discover the nature of their plans and connection. Mean time, convinced by her unaffected aversion to the proposals she had received, that she was at present in no danger from the league he suspected, he merely advised her to persevere in manifesting a calm repugnance to their solicitations, which could not fail, before long, to dishearten them both.

"But Sir," cried Cecilia, "I now fear this man as much as I dislike him, for his late fierceness and brutality, though they have encreased my disgust, make me dread to shew it. I am impatient, therefore, to have done with him, and to see him no more. And for this purpose, I wish to quit the house of Mr Harrel, where he has access at his pleasure."

"You can wish nothing more judiciously," cried he; "would you, then, return into the country?"

"That is not yet in my power; I am obliged to reside with one of my guardians. To-day I have seen Mrs Delvile, and—"

"Mrs Delvile?" interrupted Mr Monckton, in a voice of astonishment. "Surely you do not think of removing into that family?"

"What can I do so well? Mrs Delvile is a charming woman, and her conversation would afford me more entertainment and instruction in a single day, than under this roof I should obtain in a twelvemonth."

"Are you serious? Do you really think of making such a change?"

"I really wish it, but I know not yet if it is practicable: on Thursday, however, I am to dine with her, and then, if it is in my power, I will hint to her my desire."

"And can Miss Beverley possibly wish," cried Mr Monckton with earnestness, "to reside in such a house? Is not Mr Delvile the most ostentatious, haughty, and self-sufficient of men? Is not his wife the proudest of women? And is not the whole family odious to all the world?"

"You amaze me!" cried Cecilia; "surely that cannot be their general character? Mr Delvile, indeed, deserves all the censure he can meet for his wearisome parade of superiority; but his lady by no means merits to be included in the same reproach. I have spent this whole morning with her, and though I waited upon her with a strong prejudice in her disfavour, I observed in her no pride that exceeded the bounds of propriety and native dignity."

"Have you often been at the house? Do you know the son, too?"

"I have seen him three or four times."

"And what do you think of him?"

"I hardly know enough of him to judge fairly."

"But what does he seem to you? Do you not perceive in him already all the arrogance, all the contemptuous insolence of his father?"

"O no! far from it indeed; his mind seems to be liberal and noble, open to impressions of merit, and eager to honour and promote it."

"You are much deceived; you have been reading your own mind, and thought you had read his: I would advise you sedulously to avoid the whole family; you will find all intercourse with them irksome and comfortless: such as the father appears at once, the wife and the son will, in a few more meetings, appear also. They are descended from the same stock, and inherit the same self-complacency. Mr Delvile married his cousin, and each of them instigates the other to believe that all birth and rank would be at an end in the world, if their own superb family had not a promise of support from their hopeful Mortimer. Should you precipitately settle yourself in their house, you would very soon be totally weighed down by their united insolence."

Cecilia again and warmly attempted to defend them; but Mr Monckton was so positive in his assertions, and so significant in his insinuations to their discredit, that she was at length persuaded she had judged too hastily, and, after thanking him for his counsel, promised not to take any measures towards a removal without his advice.

This was all he desired; and now, enlivened by finding that his influence with her was unimpaired, and that her heart was yet her own, he ceased his exhortations, and turned the discourse to subjects more gay and general, judiciously cautious neither by tedious admonitions to disgust, nor by fretful solicitude to alarm her. He did not quit her till the evening was far advanced, and then, in returning to his own house, felt all his anxieties and disappointments recompensed by the comfort this long and satisfactory conversation had afforded him. While Cecilia, charmed with having spent the morning with her new acquaintance, and the evening with her old friend, retired to rest better pleased with the disposal of her time than she had yet been since her journey from Suffolk.

CHAPTER VIII

A TETE A TETE.

The two following days had neither event nor disturbance, except some little vexation occasioned by the behaviour of Sir Robert Floyer, who still appeared not to entertain any doubt of the success of his addresses. This impertinent confidence she could only attribute to the officious encouragement of Mr Harrel, and therefore she determined rather to seek than to avoid an explanation with him. But she had, in the mean time, the satisfaction of hearing from Mr Arnott, who, ever eager to oblige her, was frequent in his enquiries, that Mr Belfield was almost entirely recovered.

On Thursday, according to her appointment, she again went to St James' Square, and being shewn into the drawing-room till dinner was ready, found there only young Mr Delvile.

After some general conversation, he asked her how lately she had had any news of Mr Belfield?

"This morning," she answered, "when I had the pleasure of hearing he was quite recovered. Have you seen him again, sir?"

"Yes madam, twice."

"And did you think him almost well?"

"I thought," answered he, with some hesitation, "and I think still, that your enquiries ought to be his cure."

"O," cried Cecilia, "I hope he has far better medicines: but I am afraid I have been misinformed, for I see you do not think him better."

"You must not, however," replied he, "blame those messengers whose artifice has only had your satisfaction in view; nor should I be so malignant as to blast their designs, if I did not fear that Mr Belfield's actual safety may be endangered by your continual deception."

"What deception, sir? I don't at all understand you. How is his safety endangered?"

"Ah madam!" said he smiling, "what danger indeed is there that any man would not risk to give birth to such solicitude! Mr Belfield however, I believe is in none from which a command of yours cannot rescue him."

"Then were I an hard-hearted damsel indeed not to issue it! but if my commands are so medicinal, pray instruct me how to administer them."

"You must order him to give up, for the present, his plan of going into the country, where he can have no assistance, and where his wound must be dressed only by a common servant, and to remain quietly in town till his surgeon pronounces that he may travel without any hazard."

"But is he, seriously, so mad as to intend leaving town without the consent of his surgeon?"

"Nothing less than such an intention could have induced me to undeceive you with respect to his recovery. But indeed I am no friend to those artifices which purchase present relief by future misery: I venture, therefore, to speak to you the simple truth, that by a timely exertion of your influence you may prevent further evil."

"I know not, Sir," said Cecilia, with the utmost surprise, "why you should suppose I have any such influence; nor can I imagine that any deception has been practiced."

"It is possible," answered he, "I may have been too much alarmed; but in such a case as this, no information ought to be depended upon but that of his surgeon. You, madam, may probably know his opinion?"

"Me?—No, indeed? I never saw his surgeon; I know not even who he is."

"I purpose calling upon him to-morrow morning; will Miss Beverley permit me afterwards the honour of communicating to her what may pass?"

"I thank you, sir," said she, colouring very high; "but my impatience is by no means so great as to occasion my giving you that trouble."

Delvile, perceiving her change of countenance, instantly, and with much respect, entreated her pardon for the proposal; which, however, she had no sooner granted, than he said very archly, "Why indeed you have not much right to be angry, since it was your own frankness that excited mine. And thus, you find, like most other culprits, I am ready to cast the blame of the offence upon the offended. I feel, however, an irresistible propensity to do service to Mr Belfield;—shall I sin quite beyond forgiveness if I venture to tell you how I found him situated this morning?"

"No, certainly,—if you wish it, I can have no objection."

"I found him, then, surrounded by a set of gay young men, who, by way of keeping up his spirits, made him laugh and talk without ceasing: he assured me himself that he was perfectly well, and intended to gallop out of town to-morrow morning; though, when I shook hands with him at parting, I was both shocked and alarmed to feel by the burning heat of the skin, that far from discarding his surgeon, he ought rather to call in a physician."

"I am very much concerned to hear this account," said Cecilia; "but I do not well understand what you mean should on my part follow it?"

"That," answered he, bowing, with a look of mock gravity, "I pretend not to settle! In stating the case I have satisfied my conscience, and if in hearing it you can pardon the liberty I have taken, I shall as much honour the openness of your character, as I admire that of your countenance."

Cecilia now, to her no little astonishment, found she had the same mistake to clear up at present concerning Mr Belfield, that only three days before she had explained with respect to the Baronet. But she had no time to speak further upon the subject, as the entrance of Mrs Delvile put an end to their discourse.

That lady received her with the most distinguishing kindness; apologised for not sooner waiting upon her, and repeatedly declared that nothing but indisposition should have prevented her returning the favour of her first visit.

They were soon after summoned to dinner. Mr Delvile, to the infinite joy of Cecilia, was out.

The day was spent greatly to her satisfaction. There was no interruption from visitors, she was tormented by the discussion of no disagreeable subjects, the duel was not mentioned, the antagonists were not hinted at, she was teized with no self-sufficient encouragement, and wearied with no mortifying affability; the conversation at once was lively and rational, and though general, was rendered interesting, by a reciprocation of good-will and pleasure in the conversers.

The favourable opinion she had conceived both of the mother and the son this long visit served to confirm: in Mrs Delvile she found strong sense, quick parts, and high breeding; in Mortimer, sincerity and vivacity joined with softness and elegance; and in both there seemed the most liberal admiration of talents, with an openness of heart that disdained all disguise. Greatly pleased with their manners, and struck with all that was apparent in their characters, she much regretted the prejudice of Mr Monckton, which now, with the promise she had given him, was all that opposed her making an immediate effort towards a change in her abode.

She did not take her leave till eleven o'clock, when Mrs Delvile, after repeatedly thanking her for her visit, said she would not so much encroach upon her good nature as to request another till she had waited upon her in return; but added, that she meant very speedily to pay that debt, in order to enable herself, by friendly and frequent meetings, to enter upon the confidential commission with which her guardian had entrusted her.

Cecilia was pleased with the delicacy which gave rise to this forbearance, yet having in fact nothing either to relate or conceal, she was rather sorry than glad at the delay of an explanation, since she found the whole family was in an error with respect to the situation of her affairs.

BOOK THREE

CHAPTER I

AN APPLICATION.

Cecilia, upon her return home, heard with some surprise that Mr and Mrs Harrel were by themselves in the drawing-room; and, while she was upon the stairs, Mrs Harrel ran out, calling eagerly, "Is that my brother?"

Before she could make an answer, Mr Harrel, in the same impatient tone, exclaimed, "Is it Mr Arnott?"

"No;" said Cecilia, "did you expect him so late?"

"Expect him? Yes," answered Mr Harrel, "I have expected him the whole evening, and cannot conceive what he has done with himself."

"'Tis abominably provoking," said Mrs Harrel, "that he should be out of the way just now when he is wanted. However, I dare say to-morrow will do as well."

"I don't know that," cried Mr Harrel. "Reeves is such a wretch that I am sure he will give me all the trouble in his power."

Here Mr Arnott entered; and Mrs Harrel called out "O brother, we have been distressed for you cruelly; we have had a man here who has plagued Mr Harrel to death, and we wanted you sadly to speak to him."

"I should have been very glad," said Mr Arnott, "to have been of any use, and perhaps it is not yet too late; who is the man?"

"O," cried Mr Harrel, carelessly, "only a fellow from that rascally taylor who has been so troublesome to me lately. He has had the impudence, because I did not pay him the moment he was pleased to want his money, to put the bill into the hands of one Reeves, a griping attorney, who has been here this evening, and thought proper to talk to me pretty freely. I can tell the gentleman I shall not easily forget his impertinence! however, I really wish mean time I could get rid of him."

"How much is the bill, Sir?" said Mr Arnott.

"Why it's rather a round sum; but I don't know how it is, one's bills mount up before one is aware: those fellows charge such confounded sums for tape and buckram; I hardly know what I have had of him, and yet he has run me up a bill of between three and four hundred pound."

Here there was a general silence; till Mrs Harrel said "Brother, can't you be so good as to lend us the money? Mr Harrel says he can pay it again very soon."

"O yes, very soon," said Mr Harrel, "for I shall receive a great deal of money in a little time; I only want to stop this fellow's mouth for the present."

"Suppose I go and talk with him?" said Mr Arnott.

"O, he's a brute, a stock!" cried Mr Harrel, "nothing but the money will satisfy him: he will hear no reason; one might as well talk to a stone."

Mr Arnott now looked extremely distressed; but upon his sister's warmly pressing him not to lose any time, he gently said, "If this person will but wait a week or two, I should be extremely glad, for really just now I cannot take up so much money, without such particular loss and inconvenience, that I hardly know how to do it:—but yet, if he will not be appeased, he must certainly have it."

"Appeased?" cried Mr Harrel, "you might as well appease the sea in a storm! he is hard as iron."

Mr Arnott then, forcing a smile, though evidently in much uneasiness, said he would not fail to raise the money the next morning, and was taking his leave, when Cecilia, shocked that such tenderness and good-nature should be thus grossly imposed upon, hastily begged to speak with Mrs Harrel, and taking her into another room, said, "I beseech you, my dear friend, let not your worthy brother suffer by his generosity; permit me in the present exigence to assist Mr Harrel: my having such a sum advanced can be of no consequence; but I should grieve indeed that your brother, who so nobly understands the use of money, should take it up at any particular disadvantage."

"You are vastly kind," said Mrs Harrel, "and I will run and speak to them about it: but which ever of you lends the money, Mr Harrel has assured me he shall pay it very soon."

She then returned with the proposition. Mr Arnott strongly opposed it, but Mr Harrel seemed rather to prefer it, yet spoke so confidently of his speedy payment, that he appeared to think it a matter of little importance from which he accepted it. A generous contest ensued between Mr Arnott and Cecilia, but as she was very earnest, she at length prevailed, and settled to go herself the next morning into the city, in order to have the money advanced by Mr Briggs, who had the management of her fortune entirely to himself, her other guardians never interfering in the executive part of her affairs.

This arranged, they all retired.

And then, with encreasing astonishment, Cecilia reflected upon the ruinous levity of Mr Harrel, and the blind security of his wife; she saw in their situation danger the most alarming, and in the behaviour of Mr Harrel selfishness the most inexcusable; such glaring injustice to his creditors, such utter insensibility to his friends, took from her all wish of assisting him, though the indignant compassion with which she saw the easy generosity of Mr Arnott so frequently abused, had now, for his sake merely, induced her to relieve him.

She resolved, however, as soon as the present difficulty was surmounted, to make another attempt to open the eyes of Mrs Harrel to the evils which so apparently threatened her, and press her to exert all her influence with her husband, by means both of example and advice, to retrench his expences before it should be absolutely too late to save him from ruin.

She determined also at the same time dial she applied for the money requisite for this debt, to take up enough for discharging her own bill at the bookseller's, and putting in execution her plan of assisting the Hills.

The next morning she arose early, and attended by her servant, set out for the house of Mr Briggs, purposing, as the weather was clear and frosty, to walk through Oxford Road, and then put herself into a chair; and hoping to return to Mr Harrel's by the usual hour of breakfast.

She had not proceeded far, before she saw a mob gathering, and the windows of almost all the houses filling with spectators. She desired her servant to enquire what this meant, and was informed that the people were assembling to see some malefactors pass by in their way to Tyburn.

Alarmed at this intelligence from the fear of meeting the unhappy criminals, she hastily turned down die next street, but found that also filling with people who were running to the scene she was trying to avoid: encircled thus every way, she applied to a maidservant who was standing at the door of a large house, and begged leave to step in till the mob was gone by. The maid immediately consented, and she waited here while she sent her man for a chair.

He soon arrived with one; but just as she returned to the street door, a gentleman, who was hastily entering the house, standing back to let her pass, suddenly exclaimed, "Miss Beverley!" and looking at him, she perceived young Delvile.

"I cannot stop an instant," cried she, running down the steps, "lest the crowd should prevent the chair from going on."

"Will you not first," said he, handing her in, "tell me what news you have heard?"

"News?" repeated she. "No, I have heard none!"

"You will only, then, laugh at me for those officious offers you did so well to reject?"

"I know not what offers you mean!"

"They were indeed superfluous, and therefore I wonder not you have forgotten them. Shall I tell the chairmen whither to go?"

"To Mr Briggs. But I cannot imagine what you mean."

"To Mr Briggs!" repeated he, "O live for ever French beads and Bristol stones! fresh offers may perhaps be made there, impertinent, officious, and useless as mine!"

He then told her servant the direction, and, making his bow, went into the house she had just quitted.

Cecilia, extremely amazed by this short, but unintelligible conversation, would again have called upon him to explain his meaning, but found the crowd encreasing so fast that she could not venture to detain the chair, which with difficulty made its way to the adjoining streets: but her surprize at what had passed so entirely occupied her, that when she stopt at the house of Mr Briggs, she had almost forgotten what had brought her thither.

The foot-boy, who came to the door, told her that his master was at home, but not well.

She desired he might be acquainted that she wished to speak to him upon business, and would wait upon him again at any hour when he thought he should be able to see her.

The boy returned with an answer that she might call again the next week.

Cecilia, knowing that so long a delay would destroy all the kindness of her intention, determined to write to him for the money, and therefore went into the parlour, and desired to have pen and ink.

The boy, after making her wait some time in a room without any fire, brought her a pen and a little ink in a broken tea-cup, saying "Master begs you won't spirt it about, for he's got no more; and all our blacking's as good as gone."

"Blacking?" repeated Cecilia.

"Yes, Miss; when Master's shoes are blacked, we commonly gets a little drap of fresh ink."

Cecilia promised to be careful, but desired him to fetch her a sheet of paper.

"Law, Miss," cried the boy, with a grin, "I dare say master'd as soon give you a bit of his nose! howsever, I'll go ax."

In a few minutes he again returned, and brought in his hand a slate and a black lead pencil; "Miss," cried he, "Master says how you may write upon this, for he supposes you've no great matters to say."

Cecilia, much astonished at this extreme parsimony, was obliged to consent, but as the point of the pencil was very blunt, desired the boy to get her a knife that she might cut it. He obeyed, but said "Pray Miss, take care it ben't known, for master don't do such a thing once in a year, and if he know'd I'd got you the knife, he'd go nigh to give me a good polt of the head."

Cecilia then wrote upon the slate her desire to be informed in what manner she should send him her receipt for 600 pounds, which she begged to have instantly advanced.

The boy came back grinning, and holding up his hands, and said, "Miss, there's a fine piece of work upstairs! Master's in a peck of troubles; but he says how he'll come down, if you'll stay till he's got his things on."

"Does he keep his bed, then? I hope I have not made him rise?"

"No, Miss, he don't keep his bed, only he must get ready, for he wears no great matters of cloaths when he's alone. You are to know, Miss," lowering his voice, "that that day as he went abroad with our sweep's cloaths on, he comed home in sich a pickle you never see! I believe somebody'd knocked him in the kennel; so does Moll; but don't you say as I told you! He's been special bad ever since. Moll and I was as glad as could be, because he's so plaguy sharp; for, to let you know, Miss, he's so near, it's partly a wonder how he lives at all: and yet he's worth a power of money, too."

"Well, well," said Cecilia, not very desirous to encourage his forwardness, "if I want any thing, I'll call for you."

The boy, however, glad to tell his tale, went on.

"Our Moll won't stay with him above a week longer, Miss, because she says how she can get nothing to eat, but just some old stinking salt meat, that's stayed in the butcher's shop so long, it would make a horse sick to look at it. But Moll's pretty nice; howsever, Miss, to let you know, we don't get a good meal so often as once a quarter! why this last week we ha'n't had nothing at all but some dry musty red herrings; so you may think, Miss, we're kept pretty sharp!"

He was now interrupted by hearing Mr Briggs coming down the stairs, upon which, abruptly breaking off his complaints, he held up his finger to his nose in token of secrecy, and ran hastily into the kitchen.

The appearance of Mr Briggs was by no means rendered more attractive by illness and negligence of dress. He had on a flannel gown and night cap; his black beard, of many days' growth, was long and grim, and upon his nose and one of his cheeks was a large patch of brown paper, which, as he entered the room, he held on with both his hands.

Cecilia made many apologies for having disturbed him, and some civil enquiries concerning his health.

"Ay, ay," cried he, pettishly, "bad enough: all along of that trumpery masquerade; wish I had not gone! Fool for my pains."

"When were you taken ill, Sir?"

"Met with an accident; got a fall, broke my head, like to have lost my wig. Wish the masquerade at old Nick! thought it would cost nothing, or would not have gone. Warrant sha'n't get me so soon to another!"

"Did you fall in going home, Sir?"

"Ay, ay, plump in the kennel; could hardly get out of it; felt myself a going, was afraid to tear my cloaths, knew the rascal would make me pay for them, so by holding up the old sack, come bolt on my face! off pops my wig; could not tell what to do; all as dark as pitch!"

"Did not you call for help?"

"Nobody by but scrubs, knew they would not help for nothing. Scrawled out as I could, groped about for my wig, found it at last, all soused in the mud; stuck to my head like Turner's cerate,"

"I hope, then, you got into a hackney coach?"

"What for? to make things worse? was not bad enough, hay?—must pay two shillings beside?"

"But how did you find yourself when you got home, Sir?"

"How? why wet as muck; my head all bumps, my cheek all cut, my nose big as two! forced to wear a plaister; half ruined in vinegar. Got a great cold; put me in a fever; never been well since."

"But have you had no advice, Sir? Should not you send for a physician?"

"What to do, hay? fill me with jallop? can get it myself, can't I? Had one once; was taken very bad, thought should have popt off; began to flinch, sent for the doctor, proved nothing but a cheat! cost me a guinea, gave it at fourth visit, and he never came again!—warrant won't have no more!"

Then perceiving upon the table some dust from the black lead pencil, "What's here?" cried he, angrily, "who's been cutting the pencil? wish they were hanged; suppose it's the boy; deserves to be horsewhipped: give him a good banging."

Cecilia immediately cleared him, by acknowledging she had herself been the culprit.

"Ay, ay," cried he, "thought as much all the time! guessed how it was; nothing but ruin and waste; sending for money, nobody knows why; wanting 600 pounds—what to do? throw it in the dirt? Never heard the like! Sha'n't have it, promise you that," nodding his head, "shan't have no such thing!"

"Sha'n't have it?" cried Cecilia, much surprised, "why not, Sir?"

"Keep it for your husband; get you one soon: won't have no juggling. Don't be in a hurry; one in my eye."

Cecilia then began a very earnest expostulation, assuring him she really wanted the money, for an occasion which would not admit of delay. Her remonstrances, however, he wholly disregarded, telling her that girls knew nothing of the value of money, and ought not to be trusted with it; that he would not hear of such extravagance, and was resolved not to advance her a penny. Cecilia was both provoked and confounded by a refusal so unexpected, and as she thought herself bound in honour to Mr Harrel not to make known the motive of her urgency, she was for some time totally silenced: till recollecting her account with the bookseller, she determined to rest her plea upon that, persuaded that he could not, at least, deny her money to pay her own bills. He heard her, however, with the utmost contempt; "Books?" he cried, "what do you want with books? do no good; all lost time; words get no cash." She informed him his admonitions were now too late, as she had already received them, and must therefore necessarily pay for them. "No, no," cried he, "send 'em back, that's best; keep no such rubbish, won't turn to account; do better without 'em." "That, Sir, will be impossible, for I have had them some time, and cannot expect the bookseller to take them again." "Must, must," cried he, "can't help himself; glad to have 'em too. Are but a minor, can't be made pay a farthing." Cecilia with much indignation heard such fraud recommended, and told him she could by no means consent to follow his advice. But she soon found, to her utter amazement, that he steadily refused to give her any other, or to bestow the slightest attention upon her expostulations, sturdily saying that her uncle had left her a noble estate, and he would take care to see it put in proper hands, by getting her a good and careful husband.

"I have no intention, no wish, Sir," cried she, "to break into the income or estate left me by my uncle; on the contrary, I hold them sacred, and think myself bound in conscience never to live beyond them: but the L10,000 bequeathed me by my Father, I regard as more peculiarly my own property, and therefore think myself at liberty to dispose of it as I please."

"What," cried he, in a rage, "make it over to a scrubby bookseller! give it up for an old pot-hook? no, no, won't suffer it; sha'n't be, sha'n't be, I say! if you want some books, go to Moorfields, pick up enough at an old stall; get 'em at two pence a-piece; dear enough, too."

Cecilia for some time hoped he was merely indulging his strange and sordid humour by an opposition that was only intended to teize her; but she soon found herself extremely mistaken: he was immoveable in obstinacy, as he was incorrigible in avarice; he neither troubled himself with enquiries nor reasoning, but was contented with refusing her as a child might be refused, by peremptorily telling her she did not know what she wanted, and therefore should not have what she asked.

And with this answer, after all that she could urge, she was compelled to leave the house, as he complained that his brown paper plaister wanted fresh dipping in vinegar, and he could stay talking no longer.

The disgust with which this behaviour filled her, was doubled by the shame and concern of returning to the Harrels with her promise unperformed; she deliberated upon every method that occurred to her of still endeavouring to serve them, but could suggest nothing, except trying to prevail upon Mr Delvile to interfere in her favour. She liked not, indeed, the office of solicitation to so haughty a man, but, having no other expedient, her repugnance gave way to her generosity, and she ordered the chairmen to carry her to St James's Square.

CHAPTER II

A PERPLEXITY.

And here, at the door of his Father's house, and just ascending the steps, she perceived young Delvile.

"Again!" cried he, handing her out of the chair, "surely some good genius is at work for me this morning!"

She told him she should not have called so early, now she was acquainted with the late hours of Mrs Delvile, but that she merely meant to speak with his Father, for two minutes, upon business.

He attended her up stairs; and finding she was in haste, went himself with her message to Mr Delvile: and soon returned with an answer that he would wait upon her presently.

The strange speeches he had made to her when they first met in the morning now recurring to her memory, she determined to have them explained, and in order to lead to the subject, mentioned the disagreeable situation in which he had found her, while she was standing up to avoid the sight of the condemned malefactors.

"Indeed?" cried he, in a tone of voice somewhat incredulous, "and was that the purpose for which you stood up?"

"Certainly, Sir;—what other could I have?"

"None, surely!" said he, smiling, "but the accident was singularly opportune."

"Opportune?" cried Cecilia, staring, "how opportune? this is the second time in the same morning that I am not able to understand you!"

"How *should* you understand what is so little intelligible?"

"I see you have some meaning which I cannot fathom, why, else, should it be so extraordinary that I should endeavour to avoid a mob? or how could it be opportune that I should happen to meet with one?"

He laughed at first without making any answer; but perceiving she looked at him with impatience, he half gaily, half reproachfully, said, "Whence is it that young ladies, even such whose principles are most strict, seem universally, in those affairs where their affections are concerned, to think hypocrisy necessary, and deceit amiable? and hold it graceful to disavow to-day, what they may perhaps mean publicly to acknowledge to-morrow?"

Cecilia, who heard these questions with unfeigned astonishment, looked at him with the utmost eagerness for an explanation.

"Do you so much wonder," he continued, "that I should have hoped in Miss Beverley to have seen some deviation from such rules? and have expected more openness and candour in a young lady who has given so noble a proof of the liberality of her mind and understanding?"

"You amaze me beyond measure!" cried she, "what rules, what candour, what liberality, do you mean?"

"Must I speak yet more plainly? and if I do, will you bear to hear me?"

"Indeed I should be extremely glad if you would give me leave to understand you."

"And may I tell you what has charmed me, as well as what I have presumed to wonder at?"

"You may tell me any thing, if you will but be less mysterious."

"Forgive then the frankness you invite, and let me acknowledge to you how greatly I honour the nobleness of your conduct. Surrounded as you are by the opulent and the splendid, unshackled by dependance, unrestrained by authority, blest by nature with all that is attractive, by situation with all that is desirable,—to slight the rich, and disregard the powerful, for the purer pleasure of raising oppressed merit, and giving to

212

desert that wealth in which alone it seemed deficient—how can a spirit so liberal be sufficiently admired, or a choice of so much dignity be too highly extolled?"

"I find," cried Cecilia, "I must forbear any further enquiry, for the more I hear, the less I understand."

"Pardon me, then," cried he, "if here I return to my first question: whence is it that a young lady who can think so nobly, and act so disinterestedly, should not be uniformly great, simple in truth, and unaffected in sincerity? Why should she be thus guarded, where frankness would do her so much honour? Why blush in owning what all others may blush in envying?"

"Indeed you perplex me intolerably," cried Cecilia, with some vexation, "why Sir, will you not be more explicit?"

"And why, Madam," returned he, with a laugh, "would you tempt me to be more impertinent? have I not said strange things already?"

"Strange indeed," cried she, "for not one of them can I comprehend!"

"Pardon, then," cried he, "and forget them all! I scarce know myself what urged me to say them, but I began inadvertently, without intending to go on, and I have proceeded involuntarily, without knowing how to stop. The fault, however, is ultimately your own, for the sight of you creates an insurmountable desire to converse with you, and your conversation a propensity equally incorrigible to take some interest in your welfare."

He would then have changed the discourse, and Cecilia, ashamed of pressing him further, was for some time silent; but when one of the servants came to inform her that his master meant to wait upon her directly, her unwillingness to leave the matter in suspense induced her, somewhat abruptly, to say, "Perhaps, Sir, you are thinking of Mr Belfield?"

"A happy conjecture!" cried he, "but so wild a one, I cannot but marvel how it should occur to you!"

"Well, Sir," said she, "I must acknowledge I now understand your meaning; but with respect to what has given rise to it, I am as much a stranger as ever."

The entrance of Mr Delvile here closed the conversation.

He began with his usual ostentatious apologies, declaring he had so many people to attend, so many complaints to hear, and so many grievances to redress, that it was impossible for him to wait upon her sooner, and not without difficulty that he waited upon her now.

Mean time his son almost immediately retired: and Cecilia, instead of listening to this harangue, was only disturbing herself with conjectures upon what had just passed. She saw that young Delvile concluded she was absolutely engaged to Mr Belfield, and though she was better pleased that any suspicion should fall there than upon Sir Robert Floyer, she was yet both provoked and concerned to be suspected at all. An attack so earnest from almost any other person could hardly have failed being very offensive to her, but in the manners of young Delvile good breeding was so happily blended with frankness, that his freedom seemed merely to result from the openness of his disposition, and even in its very act pleaded its own excuse.

Her reverie was at length interrupted by Mr Delvile's desiring to know in what he could serve her.

She told him she had present occasion for L600, and hoped he would not object to her taking up that sum.

"Six hundred pounds," said he, after some deliberation, "is rather an extraordinary demand for a young lady in your situation; your allowance is considerable, you have yet no house, no equipage, no establishment; your expences, I should imagine, cannot be very great—"

He stopt, and seemed weighing her request.

Cecilia, shocked at appearing extravagant, yet too generous to mention Mr Harrel, had again recourse to her bookseller's bill, which she told him she was anxious to discharge.

"A bookseller's bill?" cried he; "and do you want L600 for a bookseller's bill?"

"No, Sir," said she, stammering, "no,—not all for that,—I have some other—I have a particular occasion—"

"But what bill at all," cried he, with much surprise, "can a young lady have with a bookseller? The Spectator, Tatler and Guardian, would make library sufficient for any female in the kingdom, nor do I think it like a gentlewoman to have more. Besides, if you ally yourself in such a manner as I shall approve and recommend, you will, in all probability, find already collected more books than there can ever be any possible occasion for you to look into. And let me counsel you to remember that a lady, whether so called from birth or only from fortune, should never degrade herself by being put on a level with writers, and such sort of people."

Cecilia thanked him for his advice, but confessed that upon the present occasion it came too late, as the books were now actually in her own possession.

"And have you taken," cried he, "such a measure as this without consulting me? I thought I had assured you my opinion was always at your service when you were in any dilemma."

"Yes, Sir," answered Cecilia; "but I knew how much you were occupied, and wished to avoid taking up your time."

"I cannot blame your modesty," he replied, "and therefore, as you have contracted the debt, you are, in honour, bound to pay it. Mr Briggs, however, has the entire management of your fortune, my many avocations obliging me to decline so laborious a trust; apply, therefore, to him, and, as things are situated, I will make no opposition to your demand."

"I have already, Sir," said Cecilia, "spoke to Mr Briggs, but—"

"You went to him first, then?" interrupted Mr Delvile, with a look of much displeasure.

"I was unwilling, Sir, to trouble you till I found it unavoidable." She then acquainted him with Mr Briggs' refusal, and entreated he would do her the favour to intercede in her behalf, that the money might no longer be denied her.

Every word she spoke his pride seemed rising to resent, and when, she had done, after regarding her some time with apparent indignation, he said, "*I* intercede! *I* become an agent!"

Cecilia, amazed to find him thus violently irritated, made a very earnest apology for her request; but without paying her any attention, he walked up and down the room, exclaiming, "an agent! and to Mr Briggs!—This is an affront I could never have expected! why did I degrade myself by accepting this humiliating office? I ought to have known better!" Then, turning to Cecilia, "Child," he added, "for whom is it you take me, and for what?"

Cecilia again, though affronted in her turn, began some protestations of respect; but haughtily interrupting her, he said, "If of me, and of my rank in life you judge by Mr Briggs or by Mr Harrel, I may be subject to proposals such as these every day; suffer me, therefore, for your better information, to hint to you, that the head of an ancient and honourable house, is apt to think himself somewhat superior to people but just rising from dust and obscurity."

Thunderstruck by this imperious reproof, she could attempt no further vindication; but when he observed her consternation, he was somewhat appeased, and hoping he had now impressed her with a proper sense of his dignity, he more gently said, "You did not, I believe, intend to insult me."

"Good Heaven, Sir; no!" cried Cecilia, "nothing was more distant from my thoughts: if my expressions have been faulty, it has been wholly from ignorance."

"Well, well, we will think then no more of it."

She then said she would no longer detain him, and, without daring to again mention her petition, she wished him good morning.

He suffered her to go, yet, as she left the room, graciously said, "Think no more of my displeasure, for it is over: I see you were not aware of the extraordinary thing you proposed. I am sorry I cannot possibly assist you; on any other occasion you may depend upon my services; but you know Mr Briggs, you have seen him yourself,—judge, then, how a man of any fashion is to accommodate himself with such a person!"

Cecilia concurred, and, courtsying, took her leave.

"Ah!" thought she, in her way home, "how happy is it for me that I followed the advice of Mr Monckton! else I had surely made interest to become an inmate of that house, and then indeed, as he wisely foresaw, I should inevitably have been overwhelmed by this pompous insolence! no family, however amiable, could make amends for such a master of it."

CHAPTER III

AN ADMONITION.

The Harrels and Mr Arnott waited the return of Cecilia with the utmost impatience; she told them with much concern the failure of her embassy, which Mr Harrel heard with visible resentment and discontent, while Mr Arnott, entreating him not to think of it, again made an offer of his services, and declared he would disregard all personal convenience for the pleasure of making him and his sister easy.

Cecilia was much mortified that she had not the power to act the same part, and asked Mr Harrel whether he believed his own influence with Mr Briggs would be more successful.

"No, no," answered he, "the old curmudgeon would but the rather refuse. I know his reason, and therefore am sure all pleas will be vain. He has dealings in the alley, and I dare say games with your money as if it were his own. There is, indeed, one way—but I do not think you would like it—though I protest I hardly know why not—however, 'tis as well let alone."

Cecilia insisted upon hearing what he meant, and, after some hesitation, he hinted that there were means by which, with very little inconvenience, she might borrow the money.

Cecilia, with that horror natural to all unpractised minds at the first idea of contracting a voluntary debt, started at this suggestion, and seemed very ill disposed to listen to it. Mr Harrel, perceiving her repugnance, turned to Mr Arnott, and said, "Well, my good brother, I hardly know how to suffer you to sell out at such a loss, but yet, my present necessity is so urgent—"

"Don't mention it," cried Mr Arnott, "I am very sorry I let you know it; be certain, however, that while I have anything, it is yours and my sister's."

The two gentlemen we then retiring together; but Cecilia, shocked for Mr Arnott, though unmoved by Mr Harrel, stopt them to enquire what was the way by which it was meant she could borrow the money?

Mr Harrel seemed averse to answer, but she would not be refused; and then he mentioned a Jew, of whose honesty he had made undoubted trial, and who, as she was so near being of age, would accept very trifling interest for whatever she should like to take up.

The heart of Cecilia recoiled at the very mention of a *Jew*, and *taking up money upon interest*; but, impelled strongly by her own generosity to emulate that of Mr Arnott, she agreed, after some hesitation, to have recourse to this method.

Mr Harrel then made some faint denials, and Mr Arnott protested he had a thousand times rather sell out at any discount, than consent to her taking such a measure; but, when her first reluctance was conquered, all that he urged served but to shew his worthiness in a stronger light, and only increased her desire of saving him from such repeated imposition.

Her total ignorance in what manner to transact this business, made her next put it wholly into the hands of Mr Harrel, whom she begged to take up 600 pounds, upon such terms as he thought equitable, and to which, what ever they might be, she would sign her name.

He seemed somewhat surprised at the sum, but without any question or objection undertook the commission: and Cecilia would not lessen it, because unwilling to do more for the security of the luxurious Mr Harrel, than for the distresses of the laborious Hills.

Nothing could be more speedy than the execution of this affair, Mr Harrel was diligent and expert, the whole was settled that morning, and, giving to the Jew her bond for the payment at the interest he required, she put into the hands of Mr Harrel L350, for which he gave his receipt, and she kept the rest for her own purposes.

She intended the morning after this transaction to settle her account with the bookseller. When she went into the parlour to breakfast, she was somewhat surprised to see Mr Harrel seated there, in earnest discourse with his wife. Fearful of interrupting a *tete-a-tete* so uncommon, she would have retired, but Mr Harrel, calling after her, said, "O pray come in! I am only telling Priscilla a piece of my usual ill luck. You must know I happen to be in immediate want of L200, though only for three or four days, and I sent to order honest old Aaron to come hither directly with the money, but it so happens that he went out of town the moment he had done with us yesterday, and will not be back again this week. Now I don't believe there is another Jew in the kingdom who will let me have money upon the same terms; they are such notorious rascals, that I hate the very thought of employing them."

Cecilia, who could not but understand what this meant, was too much displeased both by his extravagance and his indelicacy, to feel at all inclined to change the destination of the money she had just received; and therefore coolly agreed that it was unfortunate, but added nothing more.

"O, it is provoking indeed," cried he, "for the extra-interest I must pay one of those extortioners is absolutely so much money thrown away."

Cecilia, still without noticing these hints, began her breakfast. Mr Harrel then said he would take his tea with them: and, while he was buttering some dry toast, exclaimed, as if from sudden recollection, "O Lord, now I think of it, I believe, Miss Beverley, you can lend me this money yourself for a day or two. The moment old Aaron comes to town, I will pay you."

Cecilia, whose generosity, however extensive, was neither thoughtless nor indiscriminate, found something so repulsive in this gross procedure, that instead of assenting to his request with her usual alacrity, she answered very gravely that the money she had just received was already appropriated to a particular purpose, and she knew not how to defer making use of it.

Mr Harrel was extremely chagrined by this reply, which was by no means what he expected; but, tossing down a dish of tea, he began humming an air, and soon recovered his usual unconcern.

In a few minutes, ringing his bell, he desired a servant to go to Mr Zackery, and inform him that he wanted to speak with him immediately.

"And now," said he, with a look in which vexation seemed struggling with carelessness, "the thing is done! I don't like, indeed, to get into such hands, for 'tis hard ever to get out of them when once one begins,—and hitherto I have kept pretty clear. But there's no help for it—Mr Arnott cannot just now assist me—and so the thing must take its course. Priscilla, why do you look so grave?"

"I am thinking how unlucky it is my Brother should happen to be unable to lend you this money."

"O, don't think about it; I shall get rid of the man very soon I dare say—I hope so, at least—I am sure I mean it."

Cecilia now grew a little disturbed; she looked at Mrs. Harrel, who seemed also uneasy, and then, with some hesitation, said "Have you really never, Sir, employed this man before?"

"Never in my life: never any but old Aaron. I dread the whole race; I have a sort of superstitious notion that if once I get into their clutches, I shall never be my own man again; and that induced me to beg your assistance. However, 'tis no great matter."

She then began to waver; she feared there might be future mischief as well as present inconvenience, in his applying to new usurers, and knowing she had now the power to prevent him, thought herself half cruel in refusing to exert it. She wished to consult Mr. Monckton, but found it necessary to take her measures immediately, as the Jew was already sent for, and must in a few moments be either employed or discarded.

Much perplext how to act, between a desire of doing good, and a fear of encouraging evil, she weighed each side hastily, but while still uncertain which ought to preponderate, her kindness for Mrs. Harrel interfered, and, in the hope of rescuing her husband from further bad practices, she said she would postpone her own business for the few days he mentioned, rather than see him compelled to open any new account with so dangerous a set of men.

He thanked her in his usual negligent manner, and accepting the 200 pounds, gave her his receipt for it, and a promise she should be paid in a week.

Mrs. Harrel, however, seemed more grateful, and with many embraces spoke her sense of this friendly good nature. Cecilia, happy from believing she had revived in her some spark of sensibility, determined to avail herself of so favourable a symptom, and enter at once upon the disagreeable task she had set herself, of representing to her the danger of her present situation.

As soon, therefore, as breakfast was done, and Mr Arnott, who came in before it was over, was gone, with a view to excite her attention by raising her curiosity, she begged the favour of a private conference in her own room, upon matters of some importance.

She began with hoping that the friendship in which they had so long lived would make her pardon the liberty she was going to take, and which nothing less than their former intimacy, joined to strong apprehensions for her future welfare, could authorise; "But oh Priscilla!" she continued, "with open eyes to see your danger, yet not warn you of it, would be a reserve treacherous in a friend, and cruel even in a fellow-creature."

"What danger?" cried Mrs Harrel, much alarmed, "do you think me ill? do I look consumptive?"

"Yes, consumptive indeed!" said Cecilia, "but not, I hope, in your constitution."

And then, with all the tenderness in her power, she came to the point, and conjured her without delay to retrench her expences, and change her thoughtless way of life for one more considerate and domestic.

Mrs Harrel, with much simplicity, assured her *she did nothing but what every body else did*, and that it was quite impossible for her to *appear in the world* in any other manner.

"But how are you to appear hereafter?" cried Cecilia, "if now you live beyond your income, you must consider that in time your income by such depredations will be exhausted."

"But I declare to you," answered Mrs Harrel, "I never run in debt for more than half a year, for as soon as I receive my own money, I generally pay it away every shilling: and so borrow what I want till pay day comes round again."

"And that," said Cecilia, "seems a method expressly devised for keeping you eternally comfortless: pardon me, however, for speaking so openly, but I fear Mr Harrel himself must be even still less attentive and accurate in his affairs, or he could not so frequently be embarrassed. And what is to be the result? look but, my dear Priscilla, a little forward, and you will tremble at the prospect before you!"

Mrs Harrel seemed frightened at this speech, and begged to know what she would have them do?

Cecilia then, with equal wisdom and friendliness, proposed a general reform in the household, the public and private expences of both; she advised that a strict examination might be made into the state of their affairs, that all their bills should be called in, and faithfully paid, and that an entire new plan of life should be adopted, according to the situation of their fortune and income when cleared of all incumbrances.

"Lord, my dear!" exclaimed Mrs Harrel, with a look of astonishment, "why Mr Harrel would no more do all this than fly! If I was only to make such a proposal, I dare say he would laugh in my face."

"And why?"

"Why?—why because it would seem such an odd thing—it's what nobody thinks of—though I am sure I am very much obliged to you for mentioning it. Shall we go down stairs? I think I heard somebody come in.

"No matter who comes in," said Cecilia, "reflect for a moment upon my proposal, and, at least, if you disapprove it, suggest something more eligible."

"Oh, it's a very good proposal, that I agree," said Mrs Harrel, looking very weary, "but only the thing is it's quite impossible."

"Why so? why is it impossible?"

"Why because—dear, I don't know—but I am sure it is."

"But what is your reason? What makes you sure of it?"

"Lord, I can't tell—but I know it is—because—I am very certain it is."

Argument such as this, though extremely fatiguing to the understanding of Cecilia, had yet no power to *blunt her purpose*: she warmly expostulated against the weakness of her defence, strongly represented the imprudence of her conduct, and exhorted her by every tie of justice, honour and discretion to set about a reformation.

"Why what can I do?" cried Mrs Harrel, impatiently, "one must live a little like other people. You would not have me stared at, I suppose; and I am sure I don't know what I do that every body else does not do too."

"But were it not better," said Cecilia, with more energy, "to think less of *other people*, and more of *yourself?* to consult your own fortune, and your own situation in life, instead of being blindly guided by those of *other people*? If, indeed, *other people* would be responsible for your losses, for the diminution of your wealth, and for the disorder of your affairs, then might you rationally make their way of life the example of yours: but you cannot flatter yourself such will be the case; you know better; your losses, your diminished fortune, your embarrassed circumstances will be all your own! pitied, perhaps, by some, but blamed by more, and assisted by none!"

"Good Lord, Miss Beverley!" cried Mrs Harrel, starting, "you talk just as if we were ruined!"

"I mean not that," replied Cecilia, "but I would fain, by pointing out your danger, prevail with you to prevent in time so dreadful a catastrophe."

Mrs Harrel, more affronted than alarmed, heard this answer with much displeasure, and after a sullen hesitation, peevishly said, "I must own I don't take it very kind of you to say such frightful things to me; I am sure we only live like the rest of the world, and I don't see why a man of Mr Harrel's fortune should live any worse. As to his having now and then a little debt or two, it is nothing but what every body else has. You only think it so odd, because you a'n't used to it: but you are quite mistaken if you suppose he does not mean to pay, for he told me this morning that as soon as ever he receives his rents, he intends to discharge every bill he has in the world."

"I am very glad to hear it," answered Cecilia, "and I heartily wish he may have the resolution to adhere to his purpose. I feared you would think me impertinent, but you do worse in believing me unkind: friendship and good-will could alone have induced me to hazard what I have said to you. I must, however, have done; though I cannot forbear adding that I hope what has already passed will sometimes recur to you."

They then separated; Mrs Harrel half angry at remonstrances she thought only censorious, and Cecilia offended at her pettishness and folly, though grieved at her blindness.

She was soon, however, recompensed for this vexation by a visit from Mrs Delvile, who, finding her alone, sat with her some time, and by her spirit, understanding and elegance, dissipated all her chagrin.

From another circumstance, also, she received much pleasure, though a little perplexity; Mr Arnott brought her word that Mr Belfield, almost quite well, had actually left his lodgings, and was gone into the country.

She now half suspected that the account of his illness given her by young Delvile, was merely the effect of his curiosity to discover her sentiments of him; yet when she considered how foreign to his character appeared every species of artifice, she exculpated him from the design, and concluded that the impatient spirit of Belfield had hurried him away, when really unfit for travelling. She had no means, however, to hear more of him now he had quitted the town, and therefore, though uneasy, she was compelled to be patient.

In the evening she had again a visit from Mr Monckton, who, though he was now acquainted how much she was at home, had the forbearance to avoid making frequent use of that knowledge, that his attendance might escape observation.

Cecilia, as usual, spoke to him of all her affairs with the utmost openness; and as her mind was now chiefly occupied by her apprehensions for the Harrels, she communicated to him the extravagance of which they were guilty, and hinted at the distress that from time to time it occasioned; but the assistance she had afforded them her own delicacy prevented her mentioning.

Mr Monckton scrupled not from this account instantly to pronounce Harrel a *ruined man*; and thinking Cecilia, from her connection with him, in much danger of being involved in his future difficulties, he most earnestly exhorted her to suffer no inducement to prevail with her to advance him any money, confidently affirming she would have little chance of being ever repaid.

Cecilia listened to this charge with much alarm, but readily promised future circumspection. She confessed to him the conference she had had in the morning with Mrs Harrel, and after lamenting her determined neglect of her affairs, she added, "I cannot but own that my esteem for her, even more than my affection, has lessened almost every day since I have been in her house; but this morning, when I ventured to speak to her with earnestness, I found her powers of reasoning so weak, and her infatuation to luxury and expence so strong, that I have ever since felt ashamed of my own discernment in having formerly selected her for my friend."

"When you gave her that title," said Mr Monckton, "you had little choice in your power; her sweetness and good-nature attracted you; childhood is never troubled with foresight, and youth is seldom difficult: she was lively and pleasing, you were generous and affectionate; your

226

acquaintance with her was formed while you were yet too young to know your own worth, your fondness of her grew from habit, and before the inferiority of her parts had weakened your regard, by offending your judgment, her early marriage separated you from her entirely. But now you meet again the scene is altered; three years of absence spent in the cultivation of an understanding naturally of the first order, by encreasing your wisdom, has made you more fastidious; while the same time spent by her in mere idleness and shew, has hurt her disposition, without adding to her knowledge, and robbed her of her natural excellencies, without enriching her with acquired ones. You see her now with impartiality, for you see her almost as a stranger, and all those deficiencies which retirement and inexperience had formerly concealed, her vanity, and her superficial acquaintance with the world, have now rendered glaring. But folly weakens all bands: remember, therefore, if you would form a solid friendship, to consult not only the heart but the head, not only the temper, but the understanding."

"Well, then," said Cecilia, "at least it must be confessed I have judiciously chosen *you*!"

"You have, indeed, done me the highest honour," he answered.

They then talked of Belfield, and Mr Monckton confirmed the account of Mr Arnott, that he had left London in good health. After which, he enquired if she had seen any thing more of the Delviles?

"Yes," said Cecilia, "Mrs. Delvile called upon me this morning. She is a delightful woman; I am sorry you know her not enough to do her justice."

"Is she civil to you?"

"Civil? she is all kindness!"

"Then depend upon it she has something in view: whenever that is not the case she is all insolence. And Mr Delvile,—pray what do you think of him?"

"O, I think him insufferable! and I cannot sufficiently thank you for that timely caution which prevented my change of habitation. I would not live under the same roof with him for the world!"

"Well, and do you not now begin also to see the son properly?"

"Properly? I don't understand you."

"Why as the very son of such parents, haughty and impertinent."

"No, indeed; he has not the smallest resemblance [to] his father, and if he resembles his mother, it is only what every one must wish who impartially sees her."

"You know not that family. But how, indeed, should you, when they are in a combination to prevent your getting that knowledge? They have all their designs upon you, and if you are not carefully upon your guard, you will be the dupe to them."

"What can you possibly mean?"

"Nothing but what every body else must immediately see; they have a great share of pride, and a small one of wealth; you seem by fortune to be flung in their way, and doubtless they mean not to neglect so inviting an opportunity of repairing their estates."

"Indeed you are mistaken; I am certain they have no such intention: on the contrary, they all even teasingly persist in thinking me already engaged elsewhere."

She then gave him a history of their several suspicions.

"The impertinence of report," she added, "has so much convinced them that Sir Robert Floyer and Mr Belfield fought merely as rivals, that I can only clear myself of partiality for one of them, to have it instantly concluded I feel it for the other. And, far from seeming hurt that I appear to be disposed of, Mr Delvile openly seconds the pretensions of Sir Robert, and his son officiously persuades me that I am already Mr Belfield's."

"Tricks, nothing but tricks to discover your real situation."

He then gave her some general cautions to be upon her guard against their artifices, and changing the subject, talked, for the rest of his visit, upon matters of general entertainment.

CHAPTER IV

AN EVASION.

Cecilia now for about a fortnight passed her time without incident; the Harrels continued their accustomed dissipation, Sir Robert Floyer, without even seeking a private conference, persevered in his attentions, and Mr Arnott, though still silent and humble, seemed only to live by the pleasure of beholding her. She spent two whole days with Mrs Delvile, both of which served to confirm her admiration of that lady and of her son; and she joined the parties of the Harrels, or stayed quietly at home, according to her spirits and inclinations: while she was visited by Mr Monckton often enough to satisfy him with her proceedings, yet too seldom to betray either to herself or to the world any suspicion of his designs.

Her L200 pounds however, which was to have been returned at the end if the first week, though a fortnight was now elapsed, had not even been mentioned; she began to grow very impatient, but not knowing what course to pursue, and wanting courage to remind Mr Harrel of his promise, she still waited the performance of it without speaking.

At this time, preparations were making in the family for removing to Violet-bank to spend the Easter holidays: but Cecilia, who was too much grieved at such perpetual encrease of unnecessary expences to have any enjoyment in new prospects of entertainment, had at present some business of her own which gave her full employment.

The poor carpenter, whose family she had taken under her protection, was just dead, and, as soon as the last duties had been paid him, she sent for his widow, and after trying to console her for the loss she had suffered, assured her she was immediately ready to fulfil the engagement into which she had entered, of assisting her to undertake some better method of procuring a livelihood; and therefore desired to know in what manner she could serve her, and what she thought herself able to do.

The good woman, pouring forth thanks and praises innumerable, answered that she had a Cousin, who had offered, for a certain premium, to take her into partnership in a small haberdasher's shop. "But then, madam," continued she, "it's quite morally impossible I should raise such a sum, or else, to be sure, such a shop as that, now I am grown so poorly, would be quite a heaven upon earth to me: for my strength, madam, is almost all gone away, and when I do any hard work, it's quite a piteous sight to see me, for I am all in a tremble after it, just as if I had an ague, and yet all the time my hands, madam, will be burning like a coal!"

"You have indeed been overworked," said Cecilia, "and it is high time your feeble frame should have some rest. What is the sum your cousin demands?"

"O madam, more than I should be able to get together in all my life! for earn what I will, it goes as fast as it conies, because there's many mouths, and small pay, and two of the little ones that can't help at all;—and there's no Billy, madam, to work for us now!"

"But tell me, what is the sum?"

"Sixty pound, madam."

"You shall have it!" cried the generous Cecilia, "if the situation will make you happy, I will give it you myself."

The poor woman wept her thanks, and was long before she could sufficiently compose herself to answer the further questions of Cecilia, who next enquired what could be done with the children? Mrs Hill, however, hitherto hopeless of such a provision for herself, had for them formed no plan. She told her, therefore, to go to her cousin, and consult upon this subject, as well as to make preparations for her own removal.

The arrangement of this business now became her favourite occupation. She went herself to the shop, which was a very small one in Fetter-lane, and spoke with Mrs Roberts, the cousin; who agreed to take the eldest girl, now sixteen years of age, by way of helper; but said she had room for no other: however, upon Cecilia's offering to raise the premium, she consented that the two little children should also live in the house, where they might be under the care of their mother and sister.

There were still two others to be disposed of; but as no immediate method of providing for them occurred to Cecilia, she determined, for the present, to place them in some cheap school, where they might be taught plain work, which could not but prove a useful qualification for whatever sort of business they might hereafter attempt.

Her plan was to bestow upon Mrs Hill and her children L100 by way of putting them all into a decent way of living; and, then, from time to time, to make them such small presents as their future exigencies or changes of situation might require.

Now, therefore, payment from Mr Harrel became immediately necessary, for she had only L50 of the L600 she had taken up in her own possession, and her customary allowance was already so appropriated that she could make from it no considerable deduction.

There is something in the sight of laborious indigence so affecting and so respectable, that it renders dissipation peculiarly contemptible, and doubles the odium of extravagance: every time Cecilia saw this poor family, her aversion to the conduct and the principles of Mr Harrel encreased, while her delicacy of shocking or shaming him diminished, and she soon acquired for them what she had failed to acquire for herself, the spirit and resolution to claim her debt.

One morning, therefore, as he was quitting the breakfast room, she hastily arose, and following, begged to have a moment's discourse with him. They went together to the library, and after some apologies, and much hesitation, she told him she fancied he had forgotten the L200 which she had lent him.

"The L200," cried he; "O, ay, true!—I protest it had escaped me. Well, but you don't want it immediately?"

"Indeed I do, if you can conveniently spare it."

"O yes, certainly!—without the least doubt!—Though now I think of it—it's extremely unlucky, but really just at this time—why did not you put me in mind of it before?"

"I hoped you would have remembered it yourself."

"I could have paid you two days ago extremely well—however, you shall certainly have it very soon, that you may depend upon, and a day or two can make no great difference to you."

He then wished her good morning, and left her.

Cecilia, very much provoked, regretted that she had ever lent it at all, and determined for the future strictly to follow the advice of Mr. Monckton in trusting him no more.

Two or three days passed on, but still no notice was taken either of the payment or of the debt. She then resolved to renew her application, and be more serious and more urgent with him; but she found, to her utter surprise, this was not in her power, and that though she lived under the same roof with him, she had no opportunity to enforce her claim. Mr. Harrel, whenever she desired to speak with him, protested he was so much hurried he had not a moment to spare: and even when, tired of his excuses, she pursued him out of the room, he only quickened his speed, smiling, however, and bowing, and calling out "I am vastly sorry, but I am so late now I cannot stop an instant; however, as soon as I come back, I shall be wholly at your command."

When he came back, however, Sir Robert Floyer, or some other gentleman, was sure to be with him, and the difficulties of obtaining an audience were sure to be encreased. And by this method, which he constantly practised, of avoiding any private conversation, he frustrated all her schemes of remonstrating upon his delay, since her resentment, however great, could never urge her to the indelicacy of dunning him in presence of a third person.

She was now much perplext herself how to put into execution her plans for the Hills: she knew it would be as vain to apply for money to Mr. Briggs, as for payment to Mr. Harrel. Her word, however, had been given, and her word she held sacred: she resolved, therefore, for the present, to bestow upon them the 50 pounds she still retained, and, if the rest should be necessary before she became of age, to spare it, however inconveniently, from her private allowance, which, by the will of her uncle, was 500 pounds a year, 250 pounds of which Mr Harrel received for her board and accommodations.

Having settled this matter in her own mind, she went to the lodging of Mrs Hill, in order to conclude the affair. She found her and all her children, except the youngest, hard at work, and their honest industry so much strengthened her compassion, that her wishes for serving them grew every instant more liberal.

Mrs Hill readily undertook to make her cousin accept half the premium for the present, which would suffice to fix her, with three of her children, in the shop: Cecilia then went with her to Fetter-lane, and there, drawing up herself an agreement for their entering into partnership, she made each of them sign it and take a copy, and kept a third in her own possession: after which, she gave a promissory note to Mrs Roberts for the rest of the money.

She presented Mrs Hill, also, with 10 pounds to clothe them all decently, and enable her to send two of the children to school; and assured her that she would herself pay for their board and instruction, till she should be established in her business, and have power to save money for that purpose.

She then put herself into a chair to return home, followed by the prayers and blessings of the whole family.

CHAPTER V

AN ADVENTURE.

Never had the heart of Cecilia felt so light, so gay, so glowing as after the transaction of this affair: her life had never appeared to her so important, nor her wealth so valuable. To see five helpless children provided for by herself, rescued from the extremes of penury and wretchedness, and put in a way to become useful to society, and comfortable to themselves; to behold their feeble mother, snatched from the hardship of that labour which, over-powering her strength, had almost destroyed her existence, now placed in a situation where a competent maintenance might be earned without fatigue, and the remnant of her days pass in easy employment— to view such sights, and have power to say *"These deeds are mine!"* what, to a disposition fraught with tenderness and benevolence, could give purer self-applause, or more exquisite satisfaction?

Such were the pleasures which regaled the reflections of Cecilia when, in her way home, having got out of her chair to walk through the upper part of Oxford Street, she was suddenly met by the old gentleman whose emphatical addresses to her had so much excited her astonishment.

He was passing quick on, but stopping the moment he perceived her, he sternly called out "Are you proud? are you callous? are you hard of heart so soon?"

"Put me, if you please, to some trial!" cried Cecilia, with the virtuous courage of a self-acquitting conscience.

"I already have!" returned he, indignantly, "and already I have found you faulty!"

"I am sorry to hear it," said the amazed Cecilia, "but at least I hope you will tell me in what?"

"You refused me admittance," he answered, "yet I was your friend, yet I was willing to prolong the term of your genuine [tranquillity]! I pointed out to you a method of preserving peace with your own soul; I came to you in behalf of the poor, and instructed you how to merit their prayers; you heard me, you were susceptible, you complied! I meant to have repeated the lesson, to have tuned your whole heart to compassion, and to have taught you the sad duties of sympathising humanity. For this purpose I called again, but again I was not admitted! Short was the period of my absence, yet long enough for the completion of your downfall!"

"Good heaven," cried Cecilia, "how dreadful is this language! when have you called, Sir? I never heard you had been at the house. Far from refusing you admittance, I wished to see you."

"Indeed?" cried he, with some softness, "and are you, in truth, not proud? not callous? not hard of heart? Follow me, then, and visit the humble and the poor, follow me, and give comfort to the fallen and dejected!"

At this invitation, however desirous to do good, Cecilia started; the strangeness of the inviter, his flightiness, his authoritative manner, and the uncertainty whither or to whom he might carry her, made her fearful of proceeding: yet a benevolent curiosity to see as well as serve the objects of his recommendation, joined to the eagerness of youthful integrity to clear her own character from the aspersion of hard-heartedness, soon conquered her irresolution, and making a sign to her servant to keep near her, she followed as her conductor led.

He went on silently and solemnly till he came to Swallow-street, then turning into it, he stopt at a small and mean-looking house, knocked at the door, and without asking any question of the man who opened it, beckoned her to come after him, and hastened up some narrow winding stairs.

Cecilia again hesitated; but when she recollected that this old man, though little known, was frequently seen, and though with few people acquainted, was by many personally recognized, she thought it impossible he could mean her any injury. She ordered her servant, however, to come in, and bid him keep walking up and down the stairs till she returned to him. And then she obeyed the directions of her guide.

He proceeded till he came to the second floor, then, again beckoning her to follow him, he opened a door, and entered a small and very meanly furnished apartment.

And here, to her infinite astonishment, she perceived, employed in washing some china, a very lovely young woman, [genteelly] dressed, and appearing hardly seventeen years of age.

The moment they came in, with evident marks of confusion, she instantly gave over her work, hastily putting the basin she was washing upon the table, and endeavouring to hide the towel with which she was wiping it behind her chair.

The old gentleman, advancing to her with quickness, said, "How is he now? Is he better? will he live?"

"Heaven forbid he should not!" answered the young woman with emotion, "but, indeed, he is no better!"

"Look here," said he, pointing to Cecilia, "I have brought you one who has power to serve you, and to relieve your distress: one who is rolling in affluence, a stranger to ill, a novice in the world; unskilled in the miseries she is yet to endure, unconscious of the depravity into which she is to sink! receive her benefactions while yet she is untainted, satisfied that while, she aids you, she is blessing herself!"

The young woman, blushing and abashed, said, "You are very good to me, Sir, but there is no occasion—there is no need—I have not any necessity—I am far from being so very much in want—"

"Poor, simple soul!" interrupted the old man, "and art thou ashamed of poverty? Guard, guard thyself from other shames, and the wealthiest may envy thee! Tell her thy story, plainly, roundly, truly; abate nothing of thy indigence, repress nothing of her liberality. The Poor not impoverished by their own Guilt, are Equals of the Affluent, not enriched by their own Virtue. Come, then, and let me present ye to each other! young as ye both are, with many years and many sorrows to encounter, lighten the burthen of each other's cares, by the heart-soothing exchange of gratitude for beneficence!"

He then took a hand of each, and joining them between his own, "*You,*" he continued, "who, though rich, are not hardened, and you, who though poor, are not debased, why should ye not love, why should ye not cherish each other? The afflictions of life are tedious, its joys are evanescent; ye are now both young, and, with little to enjoy, will find much to suffer. Ye are both, too, I believe, innocent—Oh could ye always remain so!—Cherubs were ye then, and the sons of men might worship you!"

He stopt, checked by his own rising emotion; but soon resuming his usual austerity, "Such, however," he continued, "is not the condition of humanity; in pity, therefore, to the evils impending over both, be kind to each other! I leave you together, and to your mutual tenderness I recommend you!"

Then, turning particularly to Cecilia, "Disdain not," he said, "to console the depressed; look upon her without scorn, converse with her without contempt: like you, she is an orphan, though not like you, an heiress;—like her, you are fatherless, though not like her friendless! If she is awaited by the temptations of adversity, you, also, are surrounded by the corruptions of prosperity. Your fall is most probable, her's most excusable;—commiserate *her* therefore now,—by and by she may commiserate *you?*"

And with these words he left the room.

A total silence for some time succeeded his departure: Cecilia found it difficult to recover from the surprise into which she had been thrown sufficiently for speech: in following her extraordinary director, her imagination had painted to her a scene such as she had so lately quitted, and prepared her to behold some family in distress, some helpless creature in sickness, or some children in want; but of these to see none, to meet but one person, and that one fair, young, and delicate,—an introduction so singular to an object so unthought of, deprived her of all power but that of shewing her amazement.

Mean while the young woman looked scarcely less surprised, and infinitely more embarrassed. She surveyed her apartment with vexation, and her guest with confusion; she had listened to the exhortation of the old man with visible uneasiness, and now he was gone, seemed overwhelmed with shame and chagrin.

Cecilia, who in observing these emotions felt both her curiosity and her compassion encrease, pressed her hand as she parted with it, and, when a little recovered, said, "You must think this a strange intrusion; but the gentleman who brought me hither is perhaps so well known to you, as to make his singularities plead with you their own apology."

"No indeed, madam," she answered, bashfully, "he is very little known to me; but he is very good, and very desirous to do me service:—not but what I believe he thinks me much worse off than I really am, for, I assure you, madam, whatever he has said, I am not ill off at all—hardly."

The various doubts to her disadvantage, which had at first, from her uncommon situation, arisen in the mind of Cecilia, this anxiety to disguise, not display her distress, considerably removed, since it cleared her of all suspicion of seeking by artifice and imposition to play upon her feelings.

With a gentleness, therefore, the most soothing, she replied, "I should by no means have broken in upon you thus unexpectedly, if I had not concluded my conductor had some right to bring me. However, since we are actually met, let us remember his injunctions, and endeavour not to part till, by a mutual exchange of good-will, each has added a friend to the other."

"You are condescending, indeed, madam," answered the young woman, with an air the most humble, "looking as you look, to talk of a friend when you come to such a place as this! up two pair of stairs! no furniture! no servant! every thing in such disorder!—indeed I wonder at Mr. Albany! he should not—but he thinks every body's affairs may be made public, and does not care what he tells, nor who hears him;—he knows not the pain he gives, nor the mischief he may do."

"I am very much concerned," cried Cecilia, more and more surprised at all she heard, "to find I have been thus instrumental to distressing you. I was ignorant whither I was coming, and followed him, believe me, neither from curiosity nor inclination, but simply because I knew not how to refuse him. He is gone, however, and I will therefore relieve you by going too: but permit me to leave behind me a small testimony that the intention of my coming was not mere impertinence."

She then took out her purse; but the young woman, starting back with a look of resentful mortification, exclaimed, "No, madam! you are quite mistaken; pray put up your purse; I am no beggar! Mr Albany has misrepresented me, if he has told you I am."

Cecilia, mortified in her turn at this unexpected rejection of an offer she had thought herself invited to make, stood some moments silent; and then said, "I am far from meaning to offend you, and I sincerely beg your pardon if I have misunderstood the charge just now given to me."

"I have nothing to pardon, madam," said she, more calmly, "except, indeed, to Mr Albany; and to him, 'tis of no use to be angry, for he minds not what I say! he is very good, but he is very strange, for he thinks the whole world made to live in common, and that every one who is poor should ask, and every one who is rich should give: he does not know that there are many who would rather starve."

"And are you," said Cecilia, half-smiling, "of that number?"

"No, indeed, madam! I have not so much greatness of mind. But those to whom I belong have more fortitude and higher spirit. I wish I could imitate them!"

Struck with the candour and simplicity of this speech, Cecilia now felt a warm desire to serve her, and taking her hand, said, "Forgive me, but though I see you wish me gone, I know not how to leave you: recollect, therefore, the charge that has been given to us both, and if you refuse my assistance one way, point out to me in what other I may offer it."

"You are very kind, madam," she answered, "and I dare say you are very good; I am sure you look so, at least. But I want nothing; I do very well, and I have hopes of doing better. Mr Albany is too impatient. He knows, indeed, that I am not extremely rich, but he is much to blame if he supposes me therefore an object of charity, and thinks me so mean as to receive money from a stranger."

"I am truly sorry," cried Cecilia, "for the error I have committed, but you must suffer me to make my peace with you before we part: yet, till I am better known to you, I am fearful of proposing terms. Perhaps you will permit me to leave you my direction, and do me the favour to call upon me yourself?"

"O no, madam! I have a sick relation whom I cannot leave: and indeed, if he were well, he would not like to have me make an acquaintance while I am in this place."

"I hope you are not his only nurse? I am sure you do not look able to bear such fatigue. Has he a physician? Is he properly attended?"

"No, madam; he has no physician, and no attendance at all!"

"And is it possible that in such a situation you can refuse to be assisted? Surely you should accept some help for him, if not for yourself."

"But what will that signify when, if I do, he will not make use of it? and when he had a thousand and a thousand times rather die, than let any one know he is in want?"

"Take it, then, unknown to him; serve him without acquainting him you serve him. Surely you would not suffer him to perish without aid?"

240

"Heaven forbid! But what can I do? I am under his command, madam, not he under mine!"

"Is he your father?—Pardon my question, but your youth seems much to want such a protector."

"No, madam, I have no father! I was happier when I had! He is my brother."

"And what is his illness?"

"A fever."

"A fever, and without a physician! Are you sure, too, it is not infectious?"

"O yes, too sure!"

"Too sure? how so?"

"Because I know too well the occasion of it!"

"And what is the occasion?" cried Cecilia, again taking her hand, "pray trust me; indeed you shall not repent your confidence. Your reserve hitherto has only raised you in my esteem, but do not carry it so far as to mortify me by a total rejection of my good offices."

"Ah madam!" said the young woman, sighing, "you ought to be good, I am sure, for you will draw all out of me by such kindness as this! the occasion was a neglected wound, never properly healed."

"A wound? is he in the army?"

"No,—he was shot through the side in a duel."

"In a duel?" exclaimed Cecilia, "pray what is his name?"

"O that I must not tell you! his name is a great secret now, while he is in this poor place, for I know he had almost rather never see the light again than have it known."

"Surely, surely," cried Cecilia, with much emotion, "he cannot—I hope he cannot be Mr Belfield?"

"Ah Heaven!" cried the young woman, screaming, "do you then know him?"

Here, in mutual astonishment, they looked at each other.

"You are then," said Cecilia, "the sister of Mr Belfield? And Mr Belfield is thus sick, his wound is not yet healed,—and he is without any help!"

"And who, madam, are *you*?" cried she, "and how is it you know him?"

"My name is Beverley."

"Ah!" exclaimed she again, "I fear I have done nothing but mischief! I know very well who you are now, madam, but if my brother discovers that I have betrayed him, he will take it very unkind, and perhaps never forgive me."

"Be not alarmed," cried Cecilia; "rest assured he shall never know it. Is he not now in the country?"

"No, madam, he is now in the very next room."

"But what is become of the surgeon who used to attend him, and why does he not still visit him?"

"It is in vain, now, to hide any thing from you; my brother deceived him, and said he was going out of town merely to get rid of him."

"And what could induce him to act so strangely?"

"A reason which you, madam, I hope, will never know, Poverty!—he would not run up a bill he could not pay."

"Good Heaven!—But what can be done for him? He must not be suffered to linger thus; we must contrive some method of relieving and assisting him, whether he will consent or not."

"I fear that will not be possible. One of his friends has already found him out, and has written him the kindest letter! but he would not answer it, and would not see him, and was only fretted and angry."

"Well," said Cecilia, "I will not keep you longer, lest he should be alarmed by your absence. To-morrow morning, with your leave, I will call upon you again, and then, I hope, you will permit me to make some effort to assist you."

"If it only depended upon me, madam," she answered, "now I have the honour to know who you are, I believe I should not make much scruple, for I was not brought up to notions so high as my brother. Ah! happy had it been for him, for me, for all his family, if he had not had them neither!"

Cecilia then repeated her expressions of comfort and kindness, and took her leave.

This little adventure gave her infinite concern; all the horror which the duel had originally occasioned her, again returned; she accused herself with much bitterness for having brought it on; and finding that Mr Belfield was so cruelly a sufferer both in his health and his affairs, she thought it incumbent upon her to relieve him to the utmost of her ability.

His sister, too, had extremely interested her; her youth, and the uncommon artlessness of her conversation, added to her melancholy situation, and the loveliness of her person, excited in her a desire to serve, and an inclination to love her; and she determined, if she found her as deserving as she seemed engaging, not only to assist her at present, but, if her distresses continued, to received her into her own house in future.

Again she regretted the undue detention of her L200. What she now had to spare was extremely inadequate to what she now wished to bestow, and she looked forward to the conclusion of her minority with encreasing eagerness. The generous and elegant plan of life she then intended to pursue, daily gained ground in her imagination, and credit in her opinion.

CHAPTER VI

A MAN OF GENIUS.

The next morning, as soon as breakfast was over, Cecilia went in a chair to Swallow-street; she enquired for Miss Belfield, and was told to go up stairs: but what was her amazement to meet, just coming out of the room into which she was entering, young Delvile!

They both started, and Cecilia, from the seeming strangeness of her situation, felt a confusion with which she had hitherto been unacquainted. But Delvile, presently recovering from his surprise, said to her, with an expressive smile, "How good is Miss Beverley thus to visit the sick! and how much better might I have had the pleasure of seeing Mr Belfield, had I but, by prescience, known her design, and deferred my own enquiries till he had been revived by hers!"

And then, bowing and wishing her good morning, he glided past her.

Cecilia, notwithstanding the openness and purity of her intentions, was so much disconcerted by this unexpected meeting, and pointed speech, that she had not the presence of mind to call him back and clear herself: and the various interrogatories and railleries which had already passed between them upon the subject of Mr Belfield, made her suppose that what he had formerly suspected he would now think confirmed, and conclude that all her assertions of indifference, proceeded merely from that readiness at hypocrisy upon particular subjects, of which he had openly accused her whole Sex.

This circumstance and this apprehension took from her for a while all interest in the errand upon which she came; but the benevolence of her heart soon brought it back, when, upon going into the room, she saw her new favourite in tears.

"What is the matter?" cried she, tenderly; "no new affliction I hope has happened? Your brother is not worse?"

"No, madam, he is much the same; I was not then crying for him."

"For what then? tell me, acquaint me with your sorrows, and assure yourself you tell them to a friend."

"I was crying, madam, to find so much goodness in the world, when I thought there was so little! to find I have some chance of being again happy, when I thought I was miserable for ever! Two whole years have I spent in nothing but unhappiness, and I thought there was nothing else to be had; but yesterday, madam, brought me you, with every promise of nobleness and protection; and to-day, a friend of my brother's has behaved so generously, that even my brother has listened to him, and almost consented to be obliged to him!"

"And have you already known so much sorrow," said Cecilia, "that this little dawn of prosperity should wholly overpower your spirits? Gentle, amiable girl! may the future recompense you for the past, and may Mr Albany's kind wishes be fulfilled in the reciprocation of our comfort and affection!"

They then entered into a conversation which the sweetness of Cecilia, and the gratitude of Miss Belfield, soon rendered interesting, friendly and unreserved: and in a very short time, whatever was essential in the story or situation of the latter was fully communicated. She gave, however, a charge the most earnest, that her brother should never be acquainted with the confidence she had made.

Her father, who had been dead only two years, was a linen-draper in the city; he had six daughters, of whom herself was the youngest, and only one son. This son, Mr Belfield, was alike the darling of his father, mother, and sisters: he was brought up at Eaton, no expence was spared in his education, nothing was denied that could make him happy. With an excellent understanding he had uncommon quickness of parts, and his progress in his studies was rapid and honourable: his father, though he always meant him for his successor in his business, heard of his improvement with rapture, often saying, "My boy will be the ornament of the city, he will be the best scholar in any shop in London."

He was soon, however, taught another lesson; when, at the age of sixteen, he returned home, and was placed in the shop, instead of applying his talents, as his father had expected, to trade, he both despised and abhorred the name of it; when serious, treating it with contempt, when gay, with derision.

He was seized, also, with a most ardent desire to finish his education, like those of his school-fellows who left Eaton at the same time, at one of the Universities; and, after many difficulties, this petition, at the intercession of his mother, was granted, old Mr Belfield telling him he hoped a little more learning would give him a little more sense, and that when he became a *finished student*, he would not only know the true value of business, but understand how to get money, and make a bargain, better than any man whatsoever within Temple Bar.

These expectations, equally shortsighted, were also equally fallacious with the former: the son again returned, and returned, as his father had hoped, a *finished student*; but, far from being more tractable, or better disposed for application to trade, his aversion to it now was more stubborn, and his opposition more hardy than ever. The young men of fashion with whom he had formed friendships at school, or at the University, and with whom, from the indulgence of his father, he was always able to vie in expence, and from the indulgence of Nature to excel in capacity, earnestly sought the continuance of his acquaintance, and courted and coveted the pleasure of his conversation: but though he was now totally disqualified for any other society, he lost all delight in their favour from the fear they should discover his abode, and sedulously endeavoured to avoid even occasionally meeting them, lest any of his family should at the same time approach him: for of his family, though wealthy, worthy, and independent, he was now so utterly ashamed, that the mortification the most cruel he could receive, was to be asked his address, or told he should be visited.

Tired, at length, of evading the enquiries made by some, and forcing faint laughs at the detection made by others, he privately took a lodging at the west end of the town, to which he thence forward directed all his friends, and where, under various pretences, he contrived to spend the greatest part of his time.

In all his expensive deceits and frolics, his mother was his never-failing confidant and assistant; for when she heard that the companions of her son were men of fashion, some born to titles, others destined to high stations, she concluded he was in the certain road to honour and profit, and frequently distressed herself, without ever repining, in order to enable him to preserve upon equal terms, connections which she believed so conducive to his future grandeur.

In this wild and unsettled manner he passed some time, struggling incessantly against the authority of his father, privately abetted by his mother, and constantly aided and admired by his sisters: till, sick of so desultory a way of life, he entered himself a volunteer in the army.

How soon he grew tired of this change has already been related,[3] as well as his reconciliation with his father, and his becoming a student at the Temple: for the father now grew as weary of opposing, as the young man of being opposed.

Here, for two or three years, he lived in happiness uninterrupted; he extended his acquaintance among the great, by whom he was no sooner known than caressed and admired, and he frequently visited his family, which, though he blushed to own in public, he affectionately loved in private. His profession, indeed, was but little in his thoughts, successive engagements occupying almost all his hours. Delighted with the favour

---

3 Book 1, Chap. II.

of the world, and charmed to find his presence seemed the signal for entertainment, he soon forgot the uncertainty of his fortune, and the inferiority of his rank: the law grew more and more fatiguing, pleasure became more and more alluring, and, by degrees, he had not a day unappropriated to some party or amusement; voluntarily consigning the few leisure moments his gay circle afforded him, to the indulgence of his fancy in some hasty compositions in verse, which were handed about in manuscript, and which contributed to keep him in fashion.

Such was his situation at the death of his father; a new scene was then opened to him, and for some time he hesitated what course to pursue.

Old Mr Belfield, though he lived in great affluence, left not behind him any considerable fortune, after the portions of his daughters, to each of whom he bequeathed L2000, had been deducted from it. But his stock in trade was great, and his business was prosperous and lucrative.

His son, however, did not merely want application and fortitude to become his successor, but skill and knowledge; his deliberation, therefore, was hasty, and his resolution improvident; he determined to continue at the Temple himself, while the shop, which he could by no means afford to relinquish, should be kept up by another name, and the business of it be transacted by an agent; hoping thus to secure and enjoy its emoluments, without either the trouble or the humiliation of attendance.

But this scheme, like most others that have their basis in vanity, ended in nothing but mortification and disappointment: the shop which under old Mr. Belfield had been flourishing and successful, and enriched himself and all his family, could now scarce support the expences of an individual. Without a master, without that diligent attention to its prosperity which the interest of possession alone can give, and the authority of a principal alone can enforce, it quickly lost its fame for the excellence of its goods, and soon after its customers from the report of its declension. The produce, therefore, diminished every month; he was surprised, he was provoked; he was convinced he was cheated, and that his affairs were neglected; but though he threatened from time to time to enquire into the real state of the business, and investigate the cause of its decay, he felt himself inadequate to the task; and now first lamented that early contempt of trade, which by preventing him acquiring some knowledge of it while he had youth and opportunity, made him now ignorant what redress to seek, though certain of imposition and injury.

But yet, however disturbed by alarming suggestions in his hours of retirement, no alteration was made in the general course of his life; he was still the darling of his friends, and the leader in all parties, and still, though his income was lessened, his expences encreased.

Such were his circumstances at the time Cecilia first saw him at the house of Mr. Monckton: from which, two days after her arrival in town, he was himself summoned, by an information that his agent had suddenly left the kingdom.

The fatal consequence of this fraudulent elopement was immediate bankruptcy.

His spirits, however, did not yet fail him; as he had never been the nominal master of the shop, he escaped all dishonour from its ruin, and was satisfied to consign what remained to the mercy of the creditors, so that his own name should not appear in the *Gazette*.

Three of his sisters were already extremely well married to reputable tradesmen; the two elder of those who were yet single were settled with two of those who were married, and Henrietta, the youngest, resided with her mother, who had a comfortable annuity, and a small house at Padington.

Bereft thus through vanity and imprudence of all the long labours of his father, he was now compelled to think seriously of some actual method of maintenance; since his mother, though willing to sacrifice to him even the nourishment which sustained her, could do for him but little, and that little he had too much justice to accept. The law, even to the most diligent and successful, is extremely slow of profit, and whatever, from his connections and abilities might be hoped hereafter, at present required an expence which he was no longer able to support.

It remained then to try his influence with his friends among the great and the powerful.

His canvas proved extremely honourable; every one promised something, and all seemed delighted to have an opportunity of serving him.

Pleased with finding the world so much better than report had made it, he now saw the conclusion of his difficulties in the prospect of a place at court.

Belfield, with half the penetration with which he was gifted, would have seen in any other man the delusive idleness of expectations no better founded; but though discernment teaches us the folly of others, experience singly can teach us our own! he flattered himself that his friends had been more wisely selected than the friends of those who in similar circumstances had been beguiled, and he suspected not the fraud of his vanity, till he found his invitations daily slacken, and that his time was at his own command.

All his hopes now rested upon one friend and patron,

Mr Floyer, an uncle of Sir Robert Floyer, a man of power in the royal household, with whom he had lived in great intimacy, and who at this period had the disposal of a place which he solicited. The only obstacle that seemed in his way was from Sir Robert himself, who warmly exerted his interest in favour of a friend of his own. Mr Floyer, however, assured Belfield of the preference, and only begged his patience till he could find some opportunity of appeasing his nephew.

And this was the state of his affairs at the time of his quarrel at the Opera-house. Already declared opponents of each other, Sir Robert felt double wrath that for *him* Cecilia should reject his civilities; while Belfield, suspecting he presumed upon his known dependence on his uncle to affront him, felt also double indignation at the haughtiness of his behaviour. And thus, slight as seemed to the world the cause of their contest, each had private motives of animosity that served to stimulate revenge.

The very day after this duel, Mr Floyer wrote him word that he was now obliged in common decency to take the part of his nephew, and therefore had already given the place to the friend he had recommended.

This was the termination of his hopes, and the signal of his ruin! To the pain of his wound he became insensible, from the superior pain of this unexpected miscarriage; yet his pride still enabled him to disguise his distress, and to see all the friends whom this accident induced to seek him, while from the sprightliness he forced in order to conceal his anguish, he appeared to them more lively and more entertaining than ever.

But these efforts, when left to himself and to nature, only sunk him the deeper in sadness; he found an immediate change in his way of life was necessary, yet could not brook to make it in sight of those with whom he had so long lived in all the brilliancy of equality. A high principle of honour which still, in the midst of his gay career, had remained uncorrupted, had scrupulously guarded him from running in debt, and therefore, though of little possessed, that little was strictly his own. He now published that he was going out of town for the benefit of purer air, discharged his surgeon, took a gay leave of his friends, and trusting no one with his secret but his servant, was privately conveyed to mean and cheap lodgings in Swallow-street.

Here, shut up from every human being he had formerly known, he purposed to remain till he grew better, and then again to seek his fortune in the army.

His present situation, however, was little calculated to contribute to his recovery; the dismission of the surgeon, the precipitation of his removal, the inconveniencies of his lodgings, and the unseasonable deprivation of long customary indulgencies, were unavoidable delays of his amendment; while the mortification of his present disgrace, and the bitterness of his late disappointment, preyed incessantly upon his mind, robbed him of rest, heightened his fever, and reduced him by degrees to a state so low and dangerous, that his servant, alarmed for his life, secretly acquainted his mother with his illness and retreat.

The mother, almost distracted by this intelligence, instantly, with her daughter, flew to his lodgings. She wished to have taken him immediately to her house at Padington, but he had suffered so much from his first removal, that he would not consent to another. She would then have called in a physician, but he refused even to see one; and she had too long given way to all his desires and opinions, to have now the force of mind for exerting the requisite authority of issuing her orders without consulting him.

She begged, she pleaded, indeed, and Henrietta joined in her entreaties; but sickness and vexation had not rendered him tame, though they had made him sullen: he resisted their prayers, and commonly silenced them by assurances that their opposition to the plan he had determined to pursue, only inflamed his fever, and retarded his recovery.

The motive of an obduracy so cruel to his friends was the fear of a detection which he thought not merely prejudicial to his affairs, but dishonourable to his character: for, without betraying any symptom of his distress, he had taken a general leave of his acquaintance upon pretence of going out of town, and he could ill endure to make a discovery which would at once proclaim his degradation and his deceit.

Mr. Albany had accidentally broken in upon him, by mistaking his room for that of another sick person in the same house, to whom his visit had been intended; but as he knew and reverenced that old gentleman, he did not much repine at his intrusion.

He was not so easy when the same discovery was made by young Delvile, who, chancing to meet his servant in the street, enquired concerning his master's health, and surprising from him its real state, followed him home; where, soon certain of the change in his affairs by the change of his habitation, he wrote him a letter, in which, after apologizing for his freedom, he warmly declared that nothing could make him so happy as being favoured with his commands, if, either through himself or his friends, he could be so fortunate as to do him any service.

Belfield, deeply mortified at this detection of his situation, returned only a verbal answer of cold thanks, and desired he would not speak of his being in town, as he was not well enough to be seen.

This reply gave almost equal mortification to young Delvile, who continued, however, to call at the door with enquiries how he went on, though he made no further attempt to see him.

Belfield, softened at length by the kindness of this conduct, determined to admit him; and he was just come from paying his first visit, when he was met by Cecilia upon the stairs.

His stay with him had been short, and he had taken no notice either of his change of abode, or his pretence of going into the country; he had talked to him only in general terms, and upon general subjects, till he arose to depart, and then he re-urged his offers of service with so much openness and warmth, that Belfield, affected by his earnestness, promised he would soon see him again, and intimated to his delighted mother and sister, that he would frankly consult with him upon his affairs.

Such was the tale which, with various minuter circumstances, Miss Belfield communicated to Cecilia. "My mother," she added, "who never quits him, knows that you are here, madam, for she heard me talking with somebody yesterday, and she made me tell her all that had passed, and that you said you would come again this morning."

Cecilia returned many acknowledgments for this artless and unreserved communication, but could not, when it was over, forbear enquiring by what early misery she had already, though so very young, spent *two years in nothing but unhappiness?*

"Because," she answered, "when my poor father died all our family separated, and I left every body to go and live with my mother at Padington; and I was never a favourite with my mother—no more, indeed, was any body but my brother, for she thinks all the rest of the world only made for his sake. So she used to deny both herself and me almost common necessaries, in order to save up money to make him presents: though, if he had known how it was done, he would only have been angry instead of taking them. However, I should have regarded nothing that had but been for his benefit, for I loved him a great deal more than my own convenience; but sums that would distress us for months to save up, would by him be spent in a day, and then thought of no more! Nor was that all—O no! I had much greater uneasiness to suffer; for I was informed by one of my brothers-in-law how ill every thing went, and that certain ruin would come to my poor brother from the treachery of his agent; and the thought of this was always preying upon my mind, for I did not dare tell it my mother, for fear it should put her out of humour, for, sometimes, she is not very patient; and it mattered little what any of us said to my brother, for he was too gay and too confident to believe his danger."

"Well but," said Cecilia, "I hope, now, all will go better; if your brother will consent to see a physician—"

"Ah, madam! that is the thing I fear he never will do, because of being seen in these bad lodgings. I would kneel whole days to prevail with him, but he is unused to controul, and knows not how to submit to it; and he has lived so long among the great, that he forgets he was not born as high as themselves. Oh that he had never quitted his own family! If he had not been spoilt by ambition, he had the best heart and sweetest disposition in the world. But living always with his superiors, taught him to disdain his own relations, and be ashamed of us all; and yet now, in the hour of his distress—who else comes to help him?"

Cecilia then enquired if she wanted not assistance for herself and her mother, observing that they did not seem to have all the conveniencies to which they were entitled.

"Why indeed, madam," she replied, with an ingenuous smile, "when you first came here I was a little like my brother, for I was sadly ashamed to let you see how ill we lived! but now you know the worst, so I shall fret about it no more."

"But this cannot be your usual way of life; I fear the misfortunes of Mr Belfield have spread a ruin wider than his own."

"No indeed; he took care from the first not to involve us in his hazards, for he is very generous, madam, and very noble in all his notions, and could behave to us all no better about money matters than he has ever done. But from the moment we came to this dismal place, and saw his distress, and that he was sunk so low who used always to be higher than any of us, we had a sad scene indeed! My poor mother, whose whole delight was to think that he lived like a nobleman, and who always flattered herself that he would rise to be as great as the company he kept, was so distracted with her disappointment, that she would not listen to reason, but immediately discharged both our servants, said she and I should do all the work ourselves, hired this poor room for us to live in, and sent to order a bill to be put upon her house at Padington, for she said she would never return to it any more."

"But are you, then," cried Cecilia, "without any servant?"

"We have my brother's man, madam, and so he lights our fires, and takes away some of our litters; and there is not much else to be done, except sweeping the rooms, for we eat nothing but cold meat from the cook shops."

"And how long is this to last?"

"Indeed I cannot tell; for the real truth is, my poor mother has almost lost her senses; and ever since our coming here, she has been so miserable and so complaining, that indeed, between her and my brother, I have almost lost mine too! For when she found all her hopes at an end, and that her darling son, instead of being rich and powerful, and surrounded by friends and admirers, all trying who should do the most for him, was shut up by himself in this poor little lodging, and instead of gaining more, had spent all he was worth at first, with not a creature to come near him, though ill, though confined, though keeping his bed!—Oh madam, had you seen my poor mother when she first cast her eyes upon him in that condition!—indeed you could never have forgotten it!"

"I wonder not at her disappointment," cried Cecilia; "with expectations so sanguine, and a son of so much merit, it might well indeed be bitter."

"Yes, and besides the disappointment, she is now continually reproaching herself for always complying with his humours, and assisting him to appear better than the rest of his family, though my father never approved her doing so. But she thought herself so sure of his rising, that she believed we should all thank her for it in the end. And she always used to say that he was born to be a gentleman, and what a grievous thing it would be to have him made a tradesman."

"I hope, at least, she has not the additional misery of seeing him ungrateful for her fondness, however injudicious it may have been?"

"O no! he does nothing but comfort and cheer her! and indeed it is very good of him, for he has owned to me in private, that but for her encouragement, he could not have run the course he has run, for he should have been obliged to enter into business, whether he had liked it or not. But my poor mother knows this, though he will not tell it her, and therefore she says that unless he gets well, she will punish herself all the rest of her life, and never go back to her house, and never hire another servant, and never eat any thing but bread, nor drink any thing but water!"

"Poor unhappy woman!" cried Cecilia, "how dearly does she pay for her imprudent and short-sighted indulgence! but surely you are not also to suffer in the same manner?"

"No, madam, not by her fault, for she wants me to go and live with one of my sisters: but I would not quit her for the world; I should think myself wicked indeed to leave her now. Besides, I don't at all repine at the little hardships I go through at present, because my poor brother is in so much distress, that all we save may be really turned to account; but when we lived so hardly only to procure him luxuries he had no right to, I must own I used often to think it unfair, and if I had not loved him dearly, I should not have borne it so well, perhaps, as I ought."

Cecilia now began to think it high time to release her new acquaintance by quitting her, though she felt herself so much interested in her affairs, that every word she spoke gave her a desire to lengthen the conversation.

She ardently wished to make her some present, but was restrained by the fear of offending, or of being again refused; she had, however, devised a private scheme for serving her more effectually than by the donation of a few guineas, and therefore, after earnestly begging to hear from her if she could possibly be of any use, she told her that she should not find her confidence misplaced, and promising again to see her soon, reluctantly departed.

CHAPTER VII

AN EXPEDIENT.

The scheme now projected by Cecilia, was to acquaint the surgeon who had already attended Mr. Belfield with his present situation and address, and to desire him to continue his visits, for the payment of which she would herself be accountable.

The raillery of young Delvile, however, had taught her to fear the constructions of the world, and she therefore purposed to keep both the surgeon and Mr Belfield ignorant to whom they were indebted. She was aware, indeed, that whatever might be her management, that high-spirited and unfortunate young man would be extremely hurt to find himself thus detected and pursued; but she thought his life too well worth preserving to let it be sacrificed to his pride, and her internal conviction of being herself the immediate cause of its present danger, gave to her an anxious and restless desire to be herself the means of extricating him from it.

Rupil, the name of the surgeon, she had already heard mentioned by Mr. Arnott, and in getting into her chair, she ordered Ralph, her man, to enquire where he lived.

"I know already where he lives, madam," answered Ralph, "for I saw his name over a door in Cavendish-street, Oxford-road; I took particular notice of it, because it was at the house where you stood up that day on account of the mob that was waiting to see the malefactors go to Tyburn."

This answer unravelled to Cecilia a mystery which had long perplext her; for the speeches of young Delvile when he had surprised her in that situation were now fully explained. In seeing her come out of the surgeon's house, he had naturally concluded she had only entered it to ask news of his patient, Mr. Belfield; her protestations of merely standing up to avoid the crowd, he had only laughed at; and his hints at her reserve and dissimulation, were meant but to reproach her for refusing his offer of procuring her intelligence, at the very time when, to all appearance, she anxiously, though clandestinely, sought it for herself.

This discovery, notwithstanding it relieved her from all suspense of his meaning, gave her much vexation: to be supposed to take an interest so ardent, yet so private, in the affairs of Mr Belfield, might well authorise all suspicions of her partiality for him: and even if any doubt had yet remained, the unlucky meeting upon the stairs at his lodgings, would not fail to dispel it, and confirm the notion of her secret regard. She hoped, however, to have soon some opportunity of clearing up the mistake, and resolved in the mean time to be studiously cautious in avoiding all appearances that might strengthen it.

No caution, however, and no apprehension, could intimidate her active humanity from putting into immediate execution a plan in which she feared any delay might be fatal; and therefore the moment she got home, she wrote the following note to the surgeon.

"To—Rupil, Esq.

March 27, 1779.

"A friend of Mr Belfield begs Mr Rupil will immediately call upon that gentleman, who is in lodgings about the middle of Swallow-street, and insist upon visiting him till he is perfectly recovered. Mr Rupil is entreated not to make known this request, nor to receive from Mr Belfield any return for his attendance; but to attribute the discovery of his residence to accident, and to rest assured he shall be amply recompensed for his time and trouble by the friend who makes this application, and who is willing to

259

give any security that Mr Rupil shall think proper to mention, for the performance of this engagement."

Her next difficulty was in what manner to have this note conveyed; to send her own servant was inevitably betraying herself, to employ any other was risking a confidence that might be still more dangerous, and she could not trust to the penny-post, as her proposal required an answer. After much deliberation, she at length determined to have recourse to Mrs Hill, to whose services she was entitled, and upon whose fidelity she could rely.

The morning was already far advanced, but the Harrels dined late, and she would not lose a day where even an hour might be of importance. She went therefore immediately to Mrs. Hill, whom she found already removed into her new habitation in Fetter-lane, and equally busy and happy in the change of scene and of employment. She gave to her the note, which she desired her to carry to Cavendish-street directly, and either to deliver it into Mr. Rupil's own hands, or to bring it back if he was out; but upon no consideration to make known whence or from whom it came.

She then went into the back part of the shop, which by Mrs. Roberts was called the parlour, and amused herself during the absence of her messenger, by playing with the children.

Mrs. Hill at her return said she had found Mr. Rupil at home, and as she refused to give the letter to the servant, she had been taken into a room where he was talking with a gentleman, to whom, as soon as he had read it, he said with a laugh, "Why here's another person with the same proposal as yours! however, I shall treat you both alike." And then he wrote an answer, which he sealed up, and bid her take care of. This answer was as follows:

"Mr. Rupil will certainly attend Mr. Belfield, whose friends may be satisfied he will do all in his power to recover him, without receiving any recompense but the pleasure of serving a gentleman who is so much beloved."

Cecilia, charmed at this unhoped for success, was making further enquiries into what had passed, when Mrs Hill, in a low voice, said, "There's the gentleman, madam, who was with Mr. Rupil when I gave him the letter. I had a notion he was dodging me all the way I came, for I saw him just behind me, turn which way I would."

Cecilia then looked—and perceived young Delvile! who, after stopping a moment at the door, came into the shop, and desired to be shewn some gloves, which, among other things, were laid in the window.

Extremely disconcerted at the sight of him, she began now almost to fancy there was some fatality attending her acquaintance with him, since she was always sure of meeting, when she had any reason to wish avoiding him.

As soon as he saw he was observed by her, he bowed with the utmost respect: she coloured in returning the salutation, and prepared, with no little vexation, for another attack, and further [raillery], similar to what she had already received from him: but, as soon as he had made his purchase, he bowed to her again, and, without speaking, left the shop.

A silence so unexpected at once astonished and disturbed her; she again desired to hear all that had passed at Mr. Rupil's, and from the relation gathered that Delvile had himself undertaken to be responsible for his attendance upon Mr. Belfield.

A liberality so like her own failed not to impress her with the most lively esteem: but this served rather to augment than lessen the pain with which she considered the clandestine appearance she thus repeatedly made to him. She had no doubt he had immediately concluded she was author of the application to the surgeon, and that he followed her messenger merely to ascertain the fact; while his silence when he had made the discovery, she could only attribute to his now believing that her regard for Mr Belfield was too serious for raillery.

Doubly, however, she rejoiced at the generosity of Mr Rupil, as it rendered wholly unnecessary her further interference: for she now saw with some alarm the danger to which benevolence itself, directed towards a youthful object, might expose her.

CHAPTER VIII

A REMONSTRANCE.

Cecilia returned home so late, that she was summoned to the dining parlour the moment she entered the house. Her morning dress, and her long absence, excited much curiosity in Mrs Harrel, which a quick succession of questions evasively answered soon made general; and Sir Robert Floyer, turning to her with a look of surprise, said, "If you have such freaks as these, Miss Beverley, I must begin to enquire a little more into your proceedings."

"That, Sir," said Cecilia, very coldly, "would ill repay your trouble."

"When we get her to Violet Bank," cried Mr Harrel, "we shall be able to keep a better watch over her."

"I hope so," answered Sir Robert; "though faith she has been so demure, that I never supposed she did any thing but read sermons. However, I find there's no going upon trust with women, any more than with money."

"Ay, Sir Robert," cried Mrs Harrel, "you know I always advised you not to be quite so easy, and I am sure I really think you deserve a little severity, for not being more afraid."

"Afraid of what, madam?" cried the baronet; "of a young lady's walking out without me? Do you think I wish to be any restraint upon Miss Beverley's time in a morning, while I have the happiness of waiting upon her every afternoon?"

Cecilia was thunderstruck by this speech, which not only expressed an open avowal of his pretensions, but a confident security of his success. She was shocked that a man of such principles should even for a moment presume upon her favour, and irritated at the stubbornness of Mr. Harrel in not acquainting him with her refusal.

His intimation of coming to the house for *the happiness of waiting upon her*, made her determine, without losing a moment, to seek herself an explanation with him: while the discovery that he was included in the Easter party, which various other concomitant causes had already rendered disagreeable to her, made her look forward to that purposed expedition with nothing but unwillingness and distaste.

But though her earnestness to conclude this affair made her now put herself voluntarily in the way of the baronet, she found her plan always counteracted by Mr. Harrel, who, with an officiousness too obvious to pass for chance, constantly stopt the progress of any discourse in which he did not himself bear a part. A more passionate admirer might not have been so easily defeated; but Sir Robert, too proud for solicitation, and too indolent for assiduity, was very soon checked, because very soon wearied.

The whole evening, therefore, to her infinite mortification, passed away without affording her any opportunity of making known to him his mistake.

Her next effort was to remonstrate with Mr. Harrel himself; but this scheme was not more easy of execution than the other, since Mr. Harrel, suspecting she meant again to dun him for her money, avoided all separate conversation with her so skilfully, that she could not find a moment to make him hear her.

She then resolved to apply to his lady; but here her success was not better: Mrs. Harrel, dreading another lecture upon economy, peevishly answered to her request of a conference, that she was not very well, and could not talk gravely.

Cecilia, justly offended with them all, had now no resource but in Mr. Monckton, whose counsel for effectually dismissing the baronet, she determined to solicit by the first opportunity.

The moment, therefore, that she next saw him, she acquainted him with the speeches of Sir Robert and the behaviour of Mr. Harrel.

There needed no rhetoric to point out to Mr. Monckton the danger of suffering such expectations, or the impropriety of her present situation: he was struck with both in a manner the most forcible, and spared not for warmth of expression to alarm her delicacy, or add to her displeasure. But chiefly he was exasperated against Mr. Harrel, assuring her there could be no doubt but that he had some particular interest in so strenuously and artfully supporting the pretensions of Sir Robert. Cecilia endeavoured to refute this opinion, which she regarded as proceeding rather from prejudice than justice; but when she mentioned that the baronet was invited to spent the Easter holidays at Violet-Bank, he represented with such energy the consequent constructions of the world, as well as the unavoidable encouragement such intimacy would imply, that he terrified her into an earnest entreaty to suggest to her some way of deliverance.

"There is only one;" answered he, "you must peremptorily refuse to go to Violet Bank yourself. If, after what has passed, you are included in the same party with Sir Robert, you give a sanction yourself to the reports already circulated of your engagements with I and the effect of such a sanction will be more serious than you can easily imagine, since the knowledge that a connection is believed in the world, frequently, if not generally, leads by imperceptible degrees to its real ratification."

Cecilia, with the utmost alacrity, promised implicitly to follow his advice, whatever might be the opposition of Mr Harrel. He quitted her, therefore, with unusual satisfaction, happy in his power over her mind, and anticipating with secret rapture the felicity he had in reserve from visiting her during the absence of the family.

As no private interview was necessary for making known her intention of giving up the Easter party, which was to take place in two days' time, she mentioned next morning her design of spending the holidays in town, when Mr Harrel sauntered into the breakfast room to give some commission to his lady.

At first he only laughed at her plan, gaily rallying her upon her love of solitude; but when he found it was serious, he very warmly opposed it, and called upon Mrs Harrel to join in his expostulations. That lady complied, but in so faint a manner, that Cecilia soon saw she did not wish to prevail; and with a concern, that cost her infinite pain, now finally perceived that not only all her former affection was subsided into indifference, but that, since she had endeavoured to abridge her amusements, she regarded her as a spy, and dreaded her as the censor of her conduct.

Mean while Mr Arnott, who was present, though he interfered not in the debate, waited the event with anxiety; naturally hoping her objections arose from her dislike of Sir Robert, and secretly resolving to be guided himself by her motions. Cecilia at length, tired of the importunities of Mr Harrel, gravely said, that if he desired to hear the reasons which obliged her to refuse his request, she was ready to communicate them.

Mr Harrel, after a little hesitation, accompanied her into another room.

She then declared her resolution not to live under the same roof with Sir Robert, and very openly expressed her vexation and displeasure, that he so evidently persisted in giving that gentleman encouragement.

"My dear Miss Beverley," answered he, carelessly, "when young ladies will not know their own minds, it is necessary some friend should tell it them: you were certainly very favourable to Sir Robert but a short time ago, and so, I dare say, you will be again, when you have seen more of him."

"You amaze me, Sir!" cried Cecilia: "when was I favourable to him? Has he not always and regularly been my aversion?"

"I fancy," answered Mr Harrel, laughing, "you will not easily persuade him to think so; your behaviour at the Opera-house was ill calculated to give him that notion."

"My behaviour at the Opera-house, Sir, I have already explained to you; and if Sir Robert himself has any doubts, either from that circumstance or from any other, pardon me if I say they can only be attributed to your unwillingness to remove them. I entreat you, therefore, to trifle with him no longer, nor to subject me again to the freedom of implications extremely disagreeable to me."

"O fie, fie, Miss Beverley! after all that has passed, after his long expectations, and his constant attendance, you cannot for a moment think seriously of discarding him."

Cecilia, equally surprised and provoked by this speech, could not for a moment tell how to answer it; and Mr Harrel, wilfully misinterpreting her silence, took her hand, and said, "Come, I am sure you have too much, honour to make a fool of such a man as Sir Robert Floyer. There is not a woman in town who will not envy your choice, and I assure you there is not a man in England I would so soon recommend to you."

He would then have hurried her back to the next room; but, drawing away her hand with undisguised resentment, "No, Sir," she cried, "this must not pass! my positive rejection of Sir Robert the instant you communicated to me his proposals, you can neither have forgotten nor mistaken: and you must not wonder if I acknowledge myself extremely disobliged by your unaccountable perseverance in refusing to receive my answer."

"Young ladies who have been brought up in the country," returned Mr Harrel, with his usual negligence, "are always so high flown in their notions, it is difficult to deal with them; but as I am much better acquainted with the world than you can be, you must give me leave to tell you, that if, after all, you refuse Sir Robert, it will be using him very ill."

"Why will you say so, Sir?" cried Cecilia, "when it is utterly impossible you can have formed so preposterous an opinion. Pray hear me, however, finally, and pray tell Sir Robert—"

"No, no," interrupted he, with affected gaiety, "you shall manage it all your own way; I will have nothing to do with the quarrels of lovers."

And then, with a pretended laugh, he hastily left her.

Cecilia was so much incensed by this impracticable behaviour, that instead of returning to the family, she went directly to her own room. It was easy for her to see that Mr Harrel was bent upon using every method he could devise, to entangle her into some engagement with Sir Robert, and though she could not imagine the meaning of such a scheme, the littleness of his behaviour excited her contempt, and the long-continued error of the baronet gave her the utmost uneasiness. She again determined to seek an explanation with him herself, and immovably to refuse joining the party to Violet Bank.

The following day, while the ladies and Mr Arnott were at breakfast, Mr Harrel came into the room to enquire if they should all be ready to set off for his villa by ten o'clock the next day. Mrs Harrel and her brother answered in the affirmative; but Cecilia was silent, and he turned to her and repeated his question.

"Do you think me so capricious, Sir," said she, "that after telling you but yesterday I could not be of your party, I shall tell you to-day that I can?"

"Why you do not really mean to remain in town by yourself?" replied he, "you cannot suppose that will be an eligible plan for a young lady. On the contrary, it will be so very improper, that I think myself, as your Guardian, obliged to oppose it."

Amazed at this authoritative speech, Cecilia looked at him with a mixture of mortification and anger; but knowing it would be vain to resist his power if he was resolute to exert it, she made not any answer.

"Besides," he continued, "I have a plan for some alterations in the house during my absence; and I think your room, in particular, will be much improved by them: but it will be impossible to employ any workmen, if we do not all quit the premises."

This determined persecution now seriously alarmed her; she saw that Mr Harrel would omit no expedient or stratagem to encourage the addresses of Sir Robert, and force her into his presence; and she began next to apprehend that her connivance in his conduct might be presumed upon by that gentleman: she resolved, therefore, as the last and only effort in her power for avoiding him, to endeavour to find an accommodation at the house of Mrs Delvile, during the excursion to Violet Bank: and if, when she returned to Portman-square, the baronet still persevered in his attendance, to entreat her friend Mr Monckton would take upon himself the charge of undeceiving him.

CHAPTER IX

A VICTORY.

As not a moment was now to be lost, Cecilia had no sooner suggested this scheme, than she hastened to St James's-Square, to try its practicability.

She found Mrs Delvile alone, and still at breakfast.

After the first compliments were over, while she was considering in what manner to introduce her proposal, Mrs Delvile herself led to the subject, by saying, "I am very sorry to hear we are so soon to lose you; but I hope Mr Harrel does not intend to make any long stay at his villa; for if he does, I shall be half tempted to come and run away with you from him."

"And that," said Cecilia, delighted with this opening, "would be an honour I am *more* than half tempted to desire."

"Why indeed your leaving London at this time," continued Mrs Delvile, "is, for me, particularly unfortunate, as, if I could now be favoured with your visits, I should doubly value them; for Mr Delvile is gone to spend the holidays at the Duke of Derwent's, whither I was not well enough to accompany him; my son has his own engagements, and there are so few people I can bear to see, that I shall live almost entirely alone."

"If I," cried Cecilia, "in such a situation might hope to be admitted, how gladly for that happiness would I exchange my expedition to Violet Bank!"

"You are very good, and very amiable," said Mrs Devile, "and your society would, indeed, give me infinite satisfaction. Yet I am no enemy

270

to solitude; on the contrary, company is commonly burthensome to me; I find few who have any power to give me entertainment, and even of those few, the chief part have in their manners, situation, or characters, an unfortunate something, that generally renders a near connection with them inconvenient or disagreeable. There are, indeed, so many drawbacks to regard and intimacy, from pride, from propriety, and various other collateral causes, that rarely as we meet with people of brilliant parts, there is almost ever some objection to our desire of meeting them again. Yet to live wholly alone is chearless and depressing; and with you, at least," taking Cecilia's hand, "I find not one single obstacle to oppose to a thousand inducements, which invite me to form a friendship that I can only hope may be as lasting, as I am sure it will be pleasant."

Cecilia expressed her sense of this partiality in the warmest terms; and Mrs Delvile, soon discovering by her manner that she took not any delight in her intended visit to Violet Bank, began next to question her whether it would be possible for her to give it up.

She instantly answered in the affirmative.

"And would you really be so obliging," cried Mrs Delvile, with some surprise, "as to bestow upon me the time you had destined for this gay excursion?"

"Most willingly," answered Cecilia, "if you are so good as to wish it."

"But can you also—for you must by no means remain alone in Portman Square—manage to live entirely in my house till Mr Barrel's return?"

To this proposal, which was what she most desired, Cecilia gave a glad assent; and Mrs Delvile, extremely pleased with her compliance, promised to have an apartment prepared for her immediately.

She then hastened home, to announce her new plan.

This she took occasion to do when the family was assembled at dinner. The surprize with which she was heard was very general: Sir Robert seemed at a loss what conclusion to draw from her information; Mr Arnott was half elated with pleasure, and half depressed with apprehension; Mrs

Harrel wondered, without any other sensation; and Mr Harrel himself was evidently the most concerned of the party.

Every effort of persuasion and importunity he now essayed to prevail upon her to give up this scheme, and still accompany them to the villa; but she coolly answered that her engagement with Mrs Delvile was decided, and she had appointed to wait upon her the next morning.

When her resolution was found so steady, a general ill humour took place of surprise: Sir Robert now had the air of a man who thought himself affronted; Mr Arnott was wretched from a thousand uncertainties; Mrs Harrel, indeed, was still the most indifferent; but Mr Harrel could hardly repress his disappointment and anger.

Cecilia, however, was all gaiety and pleasure: in removing only from the house of one guardian to another, she knew she could not be opposed; and the flattering readiness with which Mrs Delvile had anticipated her request, without enquiring into her motives, had relieved her from a situation which now grew extremely distressing, without giving to her the pain of making complaints of Mr Harrel. The absence of Mr Delvile contributed to her happiness, and she much rejoiced in having now the prospect of a speedy opportunity to explain to his son, whatever had appeared mysterious in her conduct respecting Mr Belfield. If she had any thing to regret, it was merely the impossibility, at this time, of waiting for the counsel of Mr Monckton.

The next morning, while the family was in the midst of preparation for departure, she took leave of Mrs Harrel, who faintly lamented the loss of her company, and then hastily made her compliments to Mr Harrel and Mr Arnott, and putting herself into a chair, was conveyed to her new habitation.

Mrs Delvile received her with the most distinguished politeness; she conducted her to the apartment which had been prepared for her, led her to the library, which she desired her to make use of as her own, and gave her the most obliging charges to remember that she was in a house of which she had the command.

Young Delvile did not make his appearance till dinner time. Cecilia, from recollecting the strange situations in which she had lately been seen by him, blushed extremely when she first met his eyes; but finding him gay and easy, general in his conversation, and undesigning in his looks, she soon recovered from her embarrassment, and passed the rest of the day without restraint or uneasiness.

Every hour she spent with Mrs Delvile, contributed to raise in her esteem the mind and understanding of that lady. She found, indeed, that it was not for nothing she was accused of pride, but she found at the same time so many excellent qualities, so much true dignity of mind, and so noble a spirit of liberality, that however great was the respect she seemed to demand, it was always inferior to what she felt inclined to pay.

Nor was young Delvile less rapid in the progress he made in her favour; his character, upon every opportunity of shewing it, rose in her opinion, and his disposition and manners had a mingled sweetness and vivacity that rendered his society attractive, and his conversation spirited.

Here, therefore, Cecilia experienced that happiness she so long had coveted in vain: her life was neither public nor private, her amusements were neither dissipated nor retired; the company she saw were either people of high rank or strong parts, and their visits were neither frequent nor long. The situation she quitted gave a zest to that into which she entered, for she was now no longer shocked by extravagance or levity, no longer tormented with addresses which disgusted her, nor mortified by the ingratitude of the friend she had endeavoured to serve. All was smooth and serene, yet lively and interesting.

Her plan, however, of clearing to young Delvile his mistakes concerning Belfield, she could not put in execution; for he now never led to the subject, though he was frequently alone with her, nor seemed at all desirous to renew his former raillery, or repeat his enquiries. She wondered at this change in him, but chose rather to wait the revival of his own curiosity, than to distress or perplex herself by contriving methods of explanation.

Situated thus happily, she had now one only anxiety, which was to know whether, and in what manner, Mr Belfield had received his surgeon, as well as the actual state of his own and his sister's affairs: but the fear of again encountering young Delvile in suspicious circumstances, deterred her at present from going to their house. Yet her natural benevolence, which partial convenience never lulled to sleep, impressing her with an apprehension that her services might be wanted, she was induced to write to Miss Belfield, though she forbore to visit her.

Her letter was short, but kind and to the purpose: she apologized for her officiousness, desiring to know if her brother was better, and entreated her, in terms the most delicate, to acquaint her if yet she would accept from her any assistance.

She sent this letter by her servant, who, after waiting a considerable time, brought her the following answer.

To Miss Beverley.

Ah madam! your goodness quite melts me! we want nothing, however, yet, though I fear we shall not say so much longer. But though I hope I shall never forget myself so as to be proud and impertinent, I will rather struggle with any hardship than beg, for I will not disoblige my poor brother by any fault that I can help, especially now he is fallen so low. But, thank heaven, his wound has at last been dressed, for the surgeon has found him out, and he attends him for nothing; though my brother is willing to part with every thing he is worth in the world, rather than owe that obligation to him: yet I often wonder why he hates so to be obliged, for when he was rich himself he was always doing something to oblige other people. But I fear the surgeon thinks him very bad! for he won't speak to us when we follow him down stairs.

I am sadly ashamed to send this bad writing, but I dare not ask my brother for any help, because he would only be angry that I wrote any thing about him at all; but indeed I have seen too little good come of pride to think of imitating it; and as I have not his genius, I am sure there is no need I should have his defects: ill, therefore, as I write, you, madam, who have so much goodness and gentleness, would forgive it, I believe, if it was worse, almost. And though we are not in need of your kind offers, it is a great comfort to me to think there is a lady in the world that, if we come to be quite destitute, and if the proud heart of my poor unhappy brother should be quite broke down, will look upon our distress with pity, and generously help us from quite sinking under it.—I remain, Madam, with the most humble respect, your ever most obliged humble servant, HENRIETTA BELFIELD.

Cecilia, much moved by the simplicity of this letter, determined that her very first visit from Portman-square should be to its fair and innocent writer. And having now an assurance that she was in no immediate distress, and that her brother was actually under Mr Rupil's care, she dismissed from her mind the only subject of uneasiness that at present had endeavoured to disturb it, and gave herself wholly up to the delightful serenity of [unalloyed] happiness.

Few are the days of felicity unmixed which we acknowledge while we experience, though many are those we deplore, when by sorrow taught their value, and by misfortune, their loss. Time with Cecilia now glided on with such rapidity, that before she thought the morning half over, the evening was closed, and ere she was sensible the first week was past, the second was departed for ever. More and more pleased with the inmates of her new habitation, she found in the abilities of Mrs Delvile sources inexhaustible of entertainment, and, in the disposition and sentiments of her son something so concordant to her own, that almost every word he spoke shewed the sympathy of their minds, and almost every look which caught her eyes was a reciprocation of intelligence. Her heart, deeply wounded of late by unexpected indifference, and unreserved mortification, was now, perhaps, more than usually susceptible of those penetrating and exquisite pleasures which friendship and kindness possess the highest powers of bestowing. Easy, gay, and airy, she only rose to happiness, and only retired to rest; and not merely heightened was her present enjoyment by her past disappointment, but, carrying her retrospection to her earliest remembrance, she still found her actual situation more peculiarly adapted to her taste and temper, than any she had hitherto at any time experienced.

The very morning that the destined fortnight was elapsed, she received a note from Mrs Harrel, with information of her arrival in town, and an entreaty that she would return to Portman-square.

Cecilia, who, thus happy, had forgot to mark the progress of time, was now all amazement to find the term of her absence so soon past. She thought of going back with the utmost reluctance, and of quitting her new abode with the most lively regret. The representations of Mr Monckton daily lost their force, and notwithstanding her dislike of Mr Delvile, she had no wish so earnest as that of being settled in his family for the rest of her minority.

To effect this was her next thought; yet she knew not how to make the proposal, but from the uncommon partiality of Mrs Delvile, she hoped, with a very little encouragement, she would lead to it herself.

Here, however, she was disappointed; Mrs Delvile, when she heard of the summons from the Harrels, expressed her sorrow at losing her in terms of the most flattering regret, yet seemed to think the parting indispensable, and dropt not the most distant hint of attempting to prevent it.

Cecilia, vexed and disconcerted, then made arrangements for her departure, which she fixed for the next morning.

The rest of this day, unlike every other which for the last fortnight had preceded it, was passed with little appearance, and no reality of satisfaction: Mrs Delvile was evidently concerned, her son openly avowed his chagrin, and Cecilia felt the utmost mortification; yet, though every one was discontented, no effort was made towards obtaining any delay.

The next morning during breakfast, Mrs Delvile very elegantly thanked her for granting to her so much of her time, and earnestly begged to see her in future whenever she could be spared from her other friends; protesting she was now so accustomed to her society, that she should require both long and frequent visits to soften the separation. This request was very eagerly seconded by young Delvile, who warmly spoke his satisfaction that his mother had found so charming a friend, and unaffectedly joined in her entreaties that the intimacy might be still more closely cemented.

Cecilia had no great difficulty in according her compliance to those demands, of which the kindness and cordiality somewhat lessened her disturbance at the parting.

When Mrs Harrel's carriage arrived, Mrs Delvile took a most affectionate leave of her, and her son attended her to the coach.

In her way down stairs, he stopt her for a few moments, and in some confusion said "I wish much to apologize to Miss Beverley, before her departure, for the very gross mistake of which I have been guilty. I know not if it is possible she can pardon me, and I hardly know myself by what perversity and blindness I persisted so long in my error."

"O," cried Cecilia, much rejoiced at this voluntary explanation, "if you are but convinced you were really in an error, I have nothing more to wish. Appearances, indeed, were so strangely against me, that I ought not, perhaps, to wonder they deceived you."

"This is being candid indeed," answered he, again leading her on: "and in truth, though your anxiety was obvious, its cause was obscure, and where any thing is left to conjecture, opinion interferes, and the judgment is easily warped. My own partiality, however, for Mr Belfield, will I hope plead my excuse, as from that, and not from any prejudice against the Baronet, my mistake arose: on the contrary, so highly I respect your taste and your discernment, that your approbation, when known, can scarcely fail of securing mine."

Great as was the astonishment of Cecilia at the conclusion of this speech; she was at the coach door before she could make any answer: but Delvile, perceiving her surprise, added, while he handed her in, "Is it possible—but no, it is *not* possible I should be again mistaken. I forbore to speak at all, till I had information by which I could not be misled."

"I know not in what unaccountable obscurity," cried Cecilia, "I, or my affairs, may be involved, but I perceive that the cloud which I had hoped was dissipated, is thicker and more impenetrable than ever."

Delvile then bowed to her with a look that accused her of insincerity, and the carriage drove away.

Teazed by these eternal mistakes, and provoked to find that though the object of her supposed partiality was so frequently changed, the notion of her positive engagement with one of the duelists was invariable, she resolved with all the speed in her power, to commission Mr Monckton to wait upon Sir Robert Floyer, and in her own name give a formal rejection to his proposals, and desire him thenceforward to make known, by every opportunity, their total independence of each other: for sick of debating with Mr Harrel, and detesting all intercourse with Sir Robert, she now dropt her design of seeking an explanation herself.

She was received by Mrs Harrel with the same coldness with which she had parted from her. That lady appeared now to have some uneasiness upon her mind, and Cecilia endeavoured to draw from her its cause; but far from seeking any alleviation in friendship, she studiously avoided her, seeming pained by her conversation, and reproached by her sight. Cecilia perceived this encreasing reserve with much concern, but with more indignation, conscious that her good offices had merited a better reception, and angry to find that her advice had not merely failed of success, but even exposed her to aversion.

Mr Harrel, on the contrary, behaved to her with unusual civility, seemed eager to oblige her, and desirous to render his house more agreeable to her than ever. But in this he did not prosper; for Cecilia, immediately upon her return, looking in her apartment for the projected alterations, and finding none had been made, was so disgusted by such a detection of duplicity, that he sunk yet lower than before in her opinion, and she repined at the necessity she was under of any longer continuing his guest.

The joy of Mr Arnott at again seeing her, was visible and sincere; and not a little was it encreased by finding that Cecilia, who sought not more to avoid Mr Harrel and Sir Robert, than she was herself avoided by Mrs Harrel, talked with pleasure to nobody else in the house, and scarcely attempted to conceal that he was the only one of the family who possessed any portion of her esteem.

Even Sir Robert appeared now to have formed a design of paying her rather more respect than he had hitherto thought necessary; but the violence he did himself was so evident, and his imperious nature seemed so repugnant to the task, that his insolence, breaking forth by starts, and checked only by compulsion, was but the more conspicuous from his inadequate efforts to disguise it.

BOOK IV.

CHAPTER I

A COMPLAINT.

As Cecilia now found herself cleared, at least, of all suspicions of harbouring too tender a regard for Mr Belfield, her objections to visiting his sister were removed, and the morning after her return to Mr Harrel's, she went in a chair to Swallow-street.

She sent her servant up stairs to enquire if she might be admitted, and was immediately taken into the room where she had twice before been received.

In a few minutes Miss Belfield, softly opening and shutting the door of the next apartment, made her appearance. She looked thin and pale, but much gratified by the sight of Cecilia. "Ah madam!" she cried, "you are good indeed not to forget us! and you can little think how it cheers and consoles me, that such a lady as you can condescend to be kind to me. It is quite the only pleasure that I have now in the whole world."

"I grieve that you have no greater;" cried Cecilia, "you seem much fatigued and harassed. How is your brother? I fear you neglect your own health, by too much attention to his."

"No, indeed, madam; my mother does everything for him herself, and hardly suffers anybody else to go near him."

"What, then, makes you so melancholy?" said Cecilia, taking her hand; "you do not look well; your anxiety, I am sure, is too much for your strength."

"How should I look well, madam," answered she, "living as I live? However, I will not talk of myself, but of my brother,—O he is so ill! Indeed I am sadly, sadly afraid he will never be well again!"

"What does his surgeon say? You are too tender, and too much frightened to be any judge."

"It is not that I think myself he will die of his wound, for Mr Rupil says the wound is almost nothing; but he is in a constant fever, and so thin, and so weak, that indeed it is almost impossible he should recover!"

"You are too apprehensive," said Cecilia, "you know not what effect the country air may have upon him; there are many, many expedients that with so young a man may yet be successful."

"O no, the country air can do nothing for him! for I will not deceive you, madam, for that would be doubly a fault when I am so ready in blaming other people for wearing false appearances: besides, you are so good and so gentle, that it quite composes me to talk with you. So I will honestly speak the truth, and the whole truth at once; my poor brother is lost—O I fear for ever lost!—all by his own unhappy pride! He forgets his father was a tradesman, he is ashamed of all his family, and his whole desire is to live among the grandest people, as if he belonged to no other. And now that he can no longer do that, he takes the disappointment so to heart that he cannot get the better of it; and he told me this morning that he wished he was dead, for he did not know why he should live only to see his own ruin! But when he saw how I cried at his saying so, he was very sorry indeed, for he has always been the kindest brother in the world, when he has been away from the great folks who have spoilt him: 'But why,' said he, 'Henrietta, why would you have me live, when instead of raising you and my poor mother into an higher station, I am sunk so low, that I only help to consume your own poor pittances to support me in my disgrace!'"

"I am sorry indeed," said Cecilia, "to find he has so deep a sense of the failure of his expectations: but how happens it that you are so much wiser? Young and inexperienced as you are, and early as you must have been accustomed, from your mother as well as from Mr Belfield, to far other doctrine, the clearness of your judgment, and the justness of your remarks, astonish as much as they charm me."

"Ah madam! Brought up as I have been brought up, there is little wonder I should see the danger of an high education, let me be ever so ignorant of everything else; for I, and all my sisters, have been the sufferers the whole time: and while we were kept backward, that he might be brought forward, while we were denied comforts, that he might have luxuries, how could we help seeing the evil of so much vanity, and wishing we had all been brought up according to our proper station? instead of living in continual inconvenience, and having one part of a family struggling with distress, only to let another part of it appear in a way he had no right to!"

"How rationally," said Cecilia, "have you considered this subject! and how much do I honour you for the affection you retain for your brother, notwithstanding the wrongs you have suffered to promote his elevation!"

"Indeed he deserves it; take but from him that one fault, pride, and I believe he has not another: and humoured and darling child as from his infancy he has always been, who at that can wonder, or be angry?"

"And he has still no plan, no scheme for his future destination?"

"No, madam, none at all; and that it is makes him so miserable, and being so miserable makes him so ill, for Mr Rupil says that with such uneasiness upon his mind, he can never, in his present low state, get well. O it is melancholy to see how he is altered! and how he has lost all his fine spirits! he that used to be the life of us all!—And now he hardly ever speaks a word, or if he does, he says something so sorrowful that it cuts us to the soul! But yesterday, when my mother and I thought he was asleep, he lifted up his head, and looked at us both with the tears in his eyes, which almost broke our hearts to see, and then, in a low voice, he said 'What a lingering illness is this! Ah, my dear mother, you and poor Henrietta ought to wish it quicker over! for should I recover, my life, hereafter, will but linger like this illness.' And afterwards he called out, 'what on earth is to become of me? I shall never have health for the army, nor interest, nor means; what am I to do? subsist in the very prime of my life upon the bounty of a widowed mother! or, with such an education, such connections as mine, enter at last into some mean and sordid business?'"

"It seems, then," said Cecilia, "he now less wants a physician than a friend."

"He has a friend, madam, a noble friend, would he but accept his services; but he never sees him without suffering fresh vexation, and his fever encreases after every visit he pays him."

"Well," said Cecilia, rising, "I find we shall not have an easy task to manage him; but keep up your spirits, and assure yourself he shall not be lost, if it be possible to save him."

She then, though with much fearfulness of offending, once more made an offer of her purse. Miss Belfield no longer started at the proposal; yet, gratefully thanking her, said she was not in any immediate distress, and did not dare risk the displeasure of her brother, unless driven to it by severer necessity. Cecilia, however, drew from her a promise that she would apply to her in any sudden difficulty, and charged her never to think herself without a banker while her direction was known to her.

She then bid her adieu, and returned home; meditating the whole way upon some plan of employment and advantage for Mr Belfield, which by clearing his prospects, might revive his spirits, and facilitate his recovery: for since his mind was so evidently the seat of his disease, she saw that unless she could do more for him, she had yet done nothing.

Her meditation, however, turned to no account; she could suggest nothing, for she was ignorant what was eligible to suggest. The stations and employments of men she only knew by occasionally hearing that such were their professions, and such their situations in life; but with the means and gradations by which they arose to them she was wholly unacquainted.

Mr Monckton, her constant resource in all cases of difficulty, immediately occurred to her as her most able counsellor, and she determined by the first opportunity to consult with him upon the subject, certain of advice the most judicious from his experience, and knowledge of the world.

But though she rested upon him her serious expectations of assistance, another idea entered her mind not less pleasant, though less promising of utility: this was to mention her views to young Delvile. He was already, she knew, well informed of the distress of Mr Belfield, and she hoped, by openly asking his opinion, to confirm to him her freedom from any engagement with that gentleman, and convince him, at the same time, by her application to himself, that she was equally clear of any tie with the Baronet.

CHAPTER II

A SYMPATHY.

The next day Cecilia had appointed to spend in St James'-square; and she knew by experience that in its course, she should in all probability find some opportunity of speaking with Delvile alone.

This accordingly happened; for in the evening Mrs Delvile quitted the room for a few moments to answer a letter. Cecilia then, left with her son, said, after a little hesitation, "Will you not think me very strange if I should take the liberty to consult you upon some business?"

"I already think you very strange," answered he; "so strange that I know not any one who at all resembles you. But what is this consultation in which you will permit me to have a voice?"

"You are acquainted, I believe, with the distress of Mr Belfield?"

"I am; and I think his situation the most melancholy that can be imagined. I pity him with my whole soul, and nothing would give me greater joy than an opportunity of serving him."

"He is, indeed, much to be compassionated," returned Cecilia; "and if something is not speedily done for him, I fear he will be utterly lost. The agitation of his mind baffles all the power of medicine, and till that is relieved, his health can never be restored. His, spirit, probably always too high for his rank in life, now struggles against every attack of sickness and of poverty, in preference to yielding to his fate, and applying to his friends for their interest and assistance. I mean not to vindicate his obduracy, yet I wish it were possible it could be surmounted. Indeed I dread to think what may become of him! feeling at present nothing but wretchedness and pain, looking forward in future to nothing but ruin and despair!"

"There is no man," cried young Delvile, with emotion, "who might not rather envy than pity sufferings which give rise to such compassion!"

"Pecuniary assistance he will not accept," she continued, "and, indeed, his mind is superior to receiving consolation from such temporary relief; I wish him, therefore, to be put into some way of life by which his own talents, which have long enough amused the world, may at length become serviceable to himself. Do you think, Sir, this is possible?"

"How do I rejoice," cried Delvile, colouring with pleasure while he spoke, "in this flattering concurrence of our opinions! see, madam," taking from his pocket a letter, "how I have been this very morning occupied, in endeavouring to procure for Mr Belfield some employment by which his education might be rendered useful, and his parts redound to his own credit and advantage."

He then broke the seal, and put into her hand a letter to a nobleman, whose son was soon going abroad, strongly recommending Belfield to him in capacity of a tutor.

A sympathy of sentiment so striking impressed them at the same moment with surprise and esteem; Delvile earnestly regarded her with eyes of speaking admiration, while the occasion of his notice rendered it too pleasant to distress her, and filled her with an inward satisfaction which brightened her whole countenance.

She had only time, in a manner that strongly marked her approbation, to return the letter, before Mrs Delvile again made her appearance.

During the rest of the evening but little was said; Cecilia was not talkative, and young Delvile was so absent, that three times his mother reminded him of an engagement to meet his father, who that night was expected at the Duke of Derwent's house in town, before he heard that she spoke to him, and three times more before, when he had heard, he obeyed.

Cecilia, when she came back to Mr Barrel's, found the house full of company. She went into the drawing-room, but did not remain there long: she was grave and thoughtful, she wished to be alone, and by the earliest opportunity, stole away to her own apartment.

Her mind was now occupied by new ideas, and her fancy was busied in the delineation of new prospects. She had been struck from her first meeting young Delvile with an involuntary admiration of his manners and conversation; she had found upon every succeeding interview something further to approve, and felt for him a rising partiality which made her always see him with pleasure, and never part from him without a wish to see him again. Yet, as she was not of that inflammable nature which is always ready to take fire, as her passions were under the controul of her reason, and she suffered not her affections to triumph over her principles, she started at her danger the moment she perceived it, and instantly determined to give no weak encouragement to a prepossession which neither time nor intimacy had justified. She denied herself the deluding satisfaction of dwelling upon the supposition of his worth, was unusually assiduous to occupy all her time, that her heart might have less leisure for imagination; and had she found that his character degenerated from the promise of his appearance, the well regulated purity of her mind would soon have enabled her to have driven him wholly from her thoughts.

Such was her situation when the circumstances of her affairs occasioned her becoming an inmate of his house; and here she grew less guarded, because less clear-sighted to the danger of negligence, for the frequency of their conversation allowed her little time to consider their effects. If at first she had been pleased with his deportment and elegance, upon intimacy she was charmed with his disposition and his behaviour; she found him manly, generous, open-hearted and amiable, fond of literature, delighting in knowledge, kind in his temper, and spirited in his actions.

Qualities such as these, when recommended by high birth, a striking figure, and polished manners, formed but a dangerous companion for a young woman, who, without the guard of any former prepossession, was so fervent an admirer of excellence as Cecilia. Her heart made no resistance, for the attack was too gentle and too gradual to alarm her vigilance, and therefore, though always sensible of the pleasure she received from his society, it was not till she returned to Portman-square, after having lived under the same roof with him for a fortnight, that she was conscious her happiness was no longer in her own power.

Mr Harrel's house, which had never pleased her, now became utterly disgustful; she was wearied and uncomfortable, yet, willing to attribute her uneasiness to any other than the true cause, she fancied the house itself was changed, and that all its inhabitants and visitors were more than unusually disagreeable: but this idle error was of short duration, the moment of self-conviction was at hand, and when Delvile presented her the letter he had written for Mr Belfield, it flashed in her eyes!

This detection of the altered state of her mind opened to her views and her hopes a scene entirely new, for neither the exertion of the most active benevolence, nor the steady course of the most virtuous conduct, sufficed any longer to wholly engage her thoughts, or constitute her felicity; she had purposes that came nearer home, and cares that threatened to absorb in themselves that heart and those faculties which hitherto had only seemed animated for the service of others.

Yet this loss of mental freedom gave her not much uneasiness, since the choice of her heart, though involuntary, was approved by her principles, and confirmed by her judgment. Young Delvile's situation in life was just what she wished, more elevated than her own, yet not so exalted as to humble her with a sense of inferiority; his connections were honourable, his mother appeared to her the first of women, his character and disposition seemed formed to make her happy, and her own fortune was so large, that to the state of his she was indifferent.

Delighted with so flattering a union of inclination with propriety, she now began to cherish the partiality she at first had repressed, and thinking the future destination of her life already settled, looked forward with grateful joy to the prospect of ending her days with the man she thought most worthy to be entrusted with the disposal of her fortune.

She had not, indeed, any certainty that the regard of young Delvile was reciprocal, but she had every reason to believe he greatly admired her, and to suspect that his mistaken notion of her prior engagement, first with Mr Belfield, and afterwards with Sir Robert Floyer, made him at present check those sentiments in her favour which, when that error was removed, she hoped to see I encouraged.

Her purpose, therefore, was quietly to wait an explanation, which she rather wished retarded than forwarded, that her leisure and opportunity might be more for investigating his character, and saving herself from repentance.

CHAPTER III

A CONFLICT.

The day following this happy intellectual arrangement, Cecilia was visited by Mr Monckton. That gentleman, who had enquired for her immediately after the Harrels went to their villa, and who had flattered himself with reaping much advantage from their absence, by frequent meetings and confidential discourses, suffered the severest mortification when he found that her stay in town rendered her not the less inaccessible to him, since he had no personal acquaintance with the Delviles, and could not venture to present himself at their house.

He was now received by her with more than usual pleasure; the time had seemed long to her since she had conversed with him, and she was eager to ask his counsel and assistance in her affairs. She related to him the motives which had induced her to go to St James'-square, and the incorrigible obstinacy with which Mr Harrel still continued to encourage the addresses of Sir Robert Floyer; she earnestly entreated him to become her agent in a business to which she was unequal, by expostulating in her cause with Mr Harrel, and by calling upon Sir Robert himself to insist upon his foregoing his unauthorised pretensions.

Mr Monckton listened eagerly to her account and request, and when she had finished, assured her he would deliberate upon each circumstance of the affair, and then maturely weigh every method he could devise, to extricate her from an embarrassment which now grew far too serious to be safely neglected.

"I will not, however," continued he, "either act or give my opinion without further enquiry, as I am confident there is a mystery in this business which lies deeper than we can at present fathom. Mr Harrel has doubtless purposes of his own to answer by this pretended zeal for Sir Robert; nor is it difficult to conjecture what they may be. Friendship, in a man of his light cast, is a mere cover, a mere name, to conceal a connection which has its basis solely in the licentious convenience of borrowing money, going to the same gaming house, and mutually communicating and boasting their mutual vices and intrigues, while, all the time, their regard for each other is equally hollow with their regard for truth and integrity."

He then cautioned her to be extremely careful with respect to any money transactions with Mr Harrel, whose splendid extravagance he assured her was universally known to exceed his fortune.

The countenance of Cecilia during this exhortation was testimony sufficient to the penetrating eyes of Mr Monckton that his advice came not too soon: a suspicion of the real state of the case speedily occurred to him, and he questioned her minutely upon the subject. She endeavoured to avoid making him any answer, but his discernment was too keen for her inartificial evasion, and he very soon gathered all the particulars of her transactions with Mr Harrel.

He was less alarmed at the sum she had lent him, which was rather within his expectations, than at the method she had been induced to take to procure it. He represented to her in the strongest manner the danger of imposition, nay of ruin, from the extortions and the craft of money-lenders; and he charged her upon no consideration to be tempted or persuaded again to have recourse to such perilous expedients.

She promised the most attentive observance of his advice: and then told him the acquaintance she had made with Miss Belfield, and her sorrow for the situation of her brother; though, satisfied for the present with the plan of young Delvile, she now gave up her design of soliciting his counsel.

In the midst of this conversation, a note was delivered to her from Mr Delvile senior, acquainting her with his return to town, and begging the favour of her to call in St James's-square the next morning, as he wished to speak to her upon some business of importance.

The eager manner in which Cecilia accepted this invitation, and her repeated and earnest exclamation of wonder at what Mr Delvile could have to say, past not unnoticed by Mr Monckton; he instantly turned the discourse from the Belfields, the Harrels, and the Baronet, to enquire how she had spent her time during her visit in St James's-square, and what was her opinion of the family after her late opportunities of intimacy?

Cecilia answered that she had yet seen nothing more of Mr Delvile, who had been absent the whole time, but with equal readiness and pleasure she replied to all his questions concerning his lady, expatiating with warmth and fervour upon her many rare and estimable qualities.

But when the same interrogatories were transferred to the son, she spoke no longer with the same ease, nor with her usual promptitude of sincerity; she was embarrassed, her answers were short, and she endeavoured to hasten from the subject.

Mr Monckton remarked this change with the most apprehensive quickness, but, forcing a smile, "Have you yet," he said, "observed the family compact in which those people are bound to besiege you, and draw you into their snares?"

"No, indeed," cried Cecilia, much hurt by the question, "I am sure no such compact has been formed; and I am sure, too, that if you knew them better, you would yourself be the first to admire and do them justice."

"My dear Miss Beverley," cried he, "I know them already; I do not, indeed, visit them, but I am perfectly acquainted with their characters, which have been drawn to me by those who are most closely connected with them, and who have had opportunities of inspection which I hope will never fall to your share, since I am satisfied the trial would pain, though the proof would convince you."

"What then have you heard of them?" cried Cecilia, with much earnestness: "It is, at least, not possible any ill can be said of Mrs Delvile."

"I beg your pardon," returned he. "Mrs Delvile is not nearer perfection than the rest of her family, she has only more art in disguising her foibles; because, tho' she is the daughter of pride, she is the slave of interest."

"I see you have been greatly misinformed," said Cecilia warmly; "Mrs Delvile is the noblest of women! she may, indeed, from her very exaltation, have enemies, but they are the enemies of envy, not of resentment, enemies raised by superior merit, not excited by injury or provocation!"

"You will know her better hereafter," said Mr Monckton calmly, "I only hope your knowledge will not be purchased by the sacrifice of your happiness."

"And what knowledge of her, Sir," cried Cecilia, starting, "can have power to put my happiness in any danger?"

"I will tell you," answered he, "with all the openness you have a claim to from my regard, and then leave to time to shew if I am mistaken. The Delvile family, notwithstanding its ostentatious magnificence, I can solemnly assure you, is poor in every branch, alike lineal and collateral."

"But is it therefore the less estimable?"

"Yes, because the more rapacious. And while they count on each side Dukes, Earls and Barons in their genealogy, the very wealth with which, through your means, they project the support of their insolence, and which they will grasp with all the greediness of avarice, they will think honoured by being employed in their service, while the instrument, all amiable as she is, by which they attain it, will be constantly held down as the disgrace of their alliance."

Cecilia, stung to the soul by this speech, rose from her chair, unwilling to answer it, yet unable to conceal how much it shocked her. Mr Monckton, perceiving her emotion, followed her, and taking her hand, said, "I would not give this warning to one I thought too weak to profit from it; but as I am well informed of the use that is meant to be made of your fortune, and the abuse that will follow of yourself, I think it right to prepare you for their artifices, which merely to point out, may render abortive."

Cecilia, too much disturbed to thank him, drew back her hand, and continued silent. Mr Monckton, reading through her displeasure the state of her affections, saw with terror the greatness of the danger which threatened him. He found, however, that the present was no time for enforcing objections, and perceiving he had already gone too far, though he was by no means disposed to recant, he thought it most prudent to retreat, and let her meditate upon his exhortation while its impression was yet strong in her mind.

He would now, therefore, have taken leave; but Cecilia, endeavouring to recollect herself, and fully persuaded that however he had shocked her, he had only her interest in view, stopt him, saying, "You think me, perhaps, ungrateful, but believe me I am not; I must, however, acknowledge that your censure of Mrs Delvile hurts me extremely. Indeed I cannot doubt her worthiness, I must still, therefore, plead for her, and I hope the time may come when you will allow I have not pleaded unjustly."

"Justly or unjustly," answered Mr Monckton, "I am at least sure you can never plead vainly. I give up, therefore, to your opinion my attack of Mrs Delvile, and am willing from your commendations to suppose her the best of the race. Nay, I will even own that perhaps Mr Delvile himself, as well as his lady, might pass through life and give but little offence, had they only themselves to think of, and no son to stimulate their arrogance."

"Is the son, then," said Cecilia faintly, "so much the most culpable?"

"The son, I believe," answered he, "is at least the chief incentive to insolence and ostentation in the; parents, since it is for his sake they covet with such avidity honours and riches, since they plume themselves upon regarding him as the support of their name and, family, and since their pride in him even surpasses their pride in their lineage and themselves."

"Ah!" thought Cecilia, "and of such a son who could help being proud!"

"Their purpose, therefore," he continued, "is to, secure through his means your fortune, which they will no sooner obtain, than, to my certain knowledge, they mean instantly, and most unmercifully, to employ it in repairing all their dilapidated estates."

And then he quitted the subject; and, with that guarded warmth which accompanied all his expressions, told her he would carefully watch for her honour and welfare, and, repeating his promise of endeavouring to discover the tie by which Mr Harrel seemed bound to the Baronet, he left her—a prey himself to an anxiety yet more severe than that with which he had filled her! He now saw all his long cherished hopes in danger of final destruction, and suddenly cast upon the brink of a precipice, where, while he struggled to protect them from falling, his eyes were dazzled by beholding them totter.

Mean while Cecilia, disturbed from the calm of soft serenity to which she had yielded every avenue of her soul, now looked forward with distrust and uneasiness, even to the completion of the views which but a few minutes before had comprised all her notions of felicity. The alliance which so lately had seemed wholly unexceptionable, now appeared teeming with objections, and threatening with difficulties. The representations of Mr Monckton had cruelly mortified her; well acquainted with his knowledge of the world, and wholly unsuspicious of his selfish motives, she gave to his assertions involuntary credit, and even while she attempted to combat them, they made upon her mind an impression scarce ever to be erased.

Full, therefore, of doubt and inquietude, she passed the night in discomfort and irresolution, now determining to give way to her feelings, and now to be wholly governed by the counsel of Mr Monckton.

CHAPTER IV

AN EXPECTATION.

In this disposition of mind Cecilia the next morning obeyed the summons of Mr Delvile, and for the first time went to St James'-square in a humour to look for evil instead of good, and meanness instead of nobleness.

She was shewn into an apartment where she found Mr Delvile alone, and was received by him, as usual, with the most stately solemnity.

When she was seated, "I have given you, Miss Beverley," said he, "the trouble of calling, in order to discuss with you the internal state of your affairs; a duty which, at this juncture, I hold to be incumbent upon my character. The delicacy due to your sex would certainly have induced me to wait upon you myself for this purpose, but for the reasons I have already hinted to you, of fearing the people with whom you live might think it necessary to return my visit. Persons of low origin are commonly in those matters the most forward. Not, however, that I would prejudice you against them; though, for myself, it is fit I remember that a general and indiscriminate acquaintance, by levelling all ranks, does injury to the rites of society."

Ah! thought Cecilia, how infallible is Mr Monckton! and how inevitably, in a family of which Mr Delvile is the head, should I be cruelly *held down, as the disgrace of their alliance*!

"I have applied," continued he, "to Mrs Delvile, to know if the communication which I had recommended to you, and to which she had promised her attention, had yet passed; but I am informed you have not spoken to her upon the subject."

"I had nothing, Sir, to communicate," answered Cecilia, "and I had hoped, as Mrs Delvile made no enquiries, she was satisfied she had nothing to hear."

"With respect to enquiries," said Mr Delvile, "I fear you are not sufficiently aware of the distance between a lady of Mrs Delvile's rank, both by birth and alliance, and such a young woman as Mrs Harrel, whose ancestors, but a short time since, were mere Suffolk farmers. But I beg your pardon;—I mean not any reflection upon yours: I have always heard they were very worthy people. And a farmer is certainly a very respectable person. Your father, I think, no more than the Dean your uncle, did nothing in that way himself?"

"No, Sir," said Cecilia, drily, and much provoked by this contemptuous courtesy.

"I have always been told he was a very good sort of man: I knew none of the family myself, but the Dean. His connections with the Bishop of—, my relation, put him often in my way. Though his naming me for one of his trustees, I must own, was rather extraordinary; but I mean not to hurt you; on the contrary, I should be much concerned to give you any uneasiness."

Again Mr Monckton arose in the mind of Cecilia, and again she acknowledged the truth of his strictures; and though she much wondered in what an harangue so pompous was to end, her disgust so far conquered her curiosity, that without hearing it, she wished herself away.

"To return," said he, "to my purpose. The present period of your life is such as to render advice particularly seasonable; I am sorry, therefore, as I before said, you have not disclosed your situation to Mrs Delvile. A young lady on the point of making an establishment, and with many engagements in her power, is extremely liable to be mistaken in her judgment, and therefore should solicit instruction from those who are able to acquaint her what connection would be most to her advantage.

One thing, however, I am happy to commend, the young man who was wounded in the duel—I cannot recollect his name—is, I hear, totally out of the question."

What next? thought Cecilia; though still she gave him no interruption, for the haughtiness of his manner was repulsive to reply.

"My design, therefore, is to speak to you of Sir Robert Floyer. When I had last the pleasure of addressing you upon this subject, you may probably remember my voice was in his favour; but I then regarded him merely as the rival of an inconsiderable young man, to rescue you from whom he appeared an eligible person. The affair is now altered, that young man is thought of no more, and another rival comes forward, to whom Sir Robert is as inconsiderable as the first rival was to Sir Robert."

Cecilia started at this information, livelier sensations stimulated her curiosity, and surmises in which she was most deeply interested quickened her attention.

"This rival," proceeded he, "I should imagine no young lady would a moment hesitate in electing; he is every way the superior of Sir Robert except in fortune, and the deficiencies of that the splendour of your own may amply supply."

The deepest crimson now tinged the cheeks of Cecilia; the prophecy of Mr Monckton seemed immediately fulfilling, and she trembled with a rising conflict between her approbation of the offer, and her dread of its consequences.

"I know not, indeed," continued he, "in what estimation you may have been accustomed to hold rank and connection, nor whether you are impressed with a proper sense of their superiority and value; for early prejudices are not easily rooted out, and those who have lived chiefly with monied people, regard even birth itself as unimportant when compared with wealth."

The colour which first glowed in the cheeks of Cecilia from expectation, now rose yet higher from resentment: she thought herself already insulted by a prelude so ostentatious and humiliating to the proposals which were to follow; and she angrily determined, with whatever pain to her heart, to assert her own dignity by refusing them at once, too well satisfied by what she now saw of the present, that Mr Monckton had been just in his prediction of the future.

"Your rejection, therefore," continued he, "of this honourable offer, may perhaps have been merely the consequence of the principles in which you have been educated.—"

"Rejection?" interrupted Cecilia, amazed, "what rejection, Sir?"

"Have you not refused the proposals of my Lord Ernolf for his son?"

"Lord Ernolf? never! nor have I ever seen either his Lordship or his son but in public."

"That," replied Mr Delvile, "is little to the purpose; where the connexion is a proper one, a young lady of delicacy has only to accede to it. But though this rejection came not immediately from yourself, it had doubtless your concurrence."

"It had not, Sir, even my knowledge."

"Your alliance then with Sir Robert Floyer is probably nearer a conclusion than I had imagined, for otherwise Mr Harrel would not, without consulting you, have given the Earl so determinate an answer."

"No, Sir," said Cecilia, impatiently, "my alliance with him was never more distant, nor do I mean it should ever approach more near."

She was now little disposed for further conversation. Her heroic design of refusing young Delvile by no means reconciled her to the discovery she now made that he had not meant to address her; and though she was provoked and fretted at this new proof that Mr Harrel scrupled neither assertions nor actions to make her engagement with Sir Robert credited, her disappointment in finding that Mr Delvile, instead of pleading the cause of his son, was exerting his interest for another person, affected her so much more nearly, that notwithstanding he still continued his parading harangue, she scarcely knew even the subject of his discourse, and seized the first opportunity of a cessation to rise and take her leave.

He asked her if she would not call upon Mrs Delvile; but desirous to be alone, she declined the invitation; he then charged her to proceed no further with Sir Robert till he had made some enquiries concerning Lord Ernolf, and graciously promising his protection and counsel, suffered her to depart.

Cecilia now perceived she might plan her rejections, or study her dignity at her leisure, for neither Mr Delvile nor his son seemed in any haste to put her fortitude to the proof. With regard, therefore, to their plots and intentions, Mr Monckton she found was wrong, but with respect to their conduct and sentiments, she had every reason to believe him right: and though her heart refused to rejoice in escaping a trial of its strength, her judgment was so well convinced that his painting was from the life, that she determined to conquer her partiality for young Delvile, since she looked forward to nothing but mortification in a connexion with his family.

CHAPTER V

AN AGITATION.

With this intention, and every faculty of her mind absorbed in reflecting upon the reasons which gave rise to it, she returned to Portman-square.

As her chair was carried into the hall, she observed, with some alarm, a look of consternation among the servants, and an appearance of confusion in the whole house. She was proceeding to her own room, intending to enquire of her maid if any evil had happened, when she was crossed upon the stairs by Mr Harrel, who passed her with an air so wild and perturbed, that he hardly seemed to know her.

Frightened and amazed, she stopt short, irresolute which way to go; but, hastily returning, he beckoned her to follow him.

She obeyed, and he led her to the library. He then shut the door, and abruptly seizing her hand, called out, "Miss Beverley, I am ruined!—I am undone!—I am blasted for ever!"

"I hope not, Sir!" said Cecilia, extremely terrified, "I hope not! Where is Mrs Harrel?"

"O I know not! I know not!" cried he, in a frantic manner, "but I have not seen her,—I cannot see her,—I hope I shall never see her more!—"

"O fie! fie!" said Cecilia, "let me call her, I beg; you should consult with her in this distress, and seek comfort from her affection."

"From her affection?" repeated he, fiercely, "from her hatred you mean! do you not know that she, too, is ruined? Oh past redemption ruined!—and yet that I should hesitate, that I should a moment hesitate to conclude the whole business at once!"

"How dreadful!" cried Cecilia, "what horrible thing has happened?"

"I have undone Priscilla!" cried he, "I have blasted my credit! I have destroyed—no, not yet quite destroyed myself!"

"O yet nor ever!" cried Cecilia, whose agitation now almost equalled his own, "be not so desperate, I conjure you! speak to me more intelligibly,—what does all this mean? How has it come to pass?"

"My debts!—my creditors!—one way only," striking his hand upon his forehead, "is left for me!"

"Do not say so, Sir!" said Cecilia, "you shall find many ways; pray have courage! pray speak calmly; and if you will but be more prudent, will but, in future, better regulate your affairs, I will myself undertake—"

She stopt; checked in the full career of her overflowing compassion, by a sense of the worthlessness of its object; and by the remembrance of the injunctions of Mr Monckton.

"What will you undertake?" cried he, eagerly, "I know you are an angel!—tell me, what will you undertake?"

"I will,—" said Cecilia, hesitating, "I will speak to Mr Monckton,—I will consult—"

"You may as well consult with every cursed creditor in the house!" interrupted he; "but do so, if you please; my disgrace must perforce reach him soon, and a short anticipation is not worth begging off."

"Are your creditors then actually in the house?"

"O yes, yes! and therefore it is high time I should be out of it!—Did you not see them?—Do they not line the hall?—They threaten me with three executions before night!—three executions unless I satisfy their immediate demands!—"

"And to what do their demands amount?"

"I know not!—I dare not ask!—to some thousand pounds, perhaps,—and I have not, at this minute, forty guineas in the house!"

"Nay, then," cried Cecilia, retreating, "I can indeed do nothing! if their demands are so high, I *ought* to do nothing."

She would then have quitted him, not more shocked at his situation, than indignant at the wilful extravagance which had occasioned it.

"Stay," cried he, "and hear me!" then, lowering his voice, "seek out," he continued, "your unfortunate friend,—go to the poor ruined Priscilla,—prepare her for tidings of horror! and do not, though you renounce Me, do not abandon Her!"

Then, fiercely passing her, he was himself leaving the room; but Cecilia, alarmed by the fury of his manner, called out, "What is it you mean? what tidings of horror? whither are you going?"

"To hell!" cried he, and rushed out of the apartment.

Cecilia screamed aloud, and conjuring him to hear her, ran after him; he paid her no regard, but, flying faster than she had power to pursue, reached his own dressing-room, shut himself into it with violence, and just as she arrived at the door, turned the key, and bolted it.

Her terror was now inexpressible; she believed him in the very act of suicide, and her refusal of assistance seemed the signal for the deed: her whole fortune, at that moment, was valueless and unimportant to her, compared with the preservation of a fellow-creature: she called out with all the vehemence of agony to beg he would open the door, and eagerly promised by all that was sacred to do everything in her power to save him.

At these words he opened it; his face was totally without colour, and he grasped a razor in his hand.

"You have stopt me," said he, in a voice scarce audible, "at the very moment I had gathered courage for the blow: but if indeed you will assist me, I will shut this up,—if not, I will steep it in my blood!"

"I will! I will!" cried Cecilia, "I will do every thing you desire!"

"And quickly?"

"Immediately."

"Before my disgrace is known? and while all may yet be hushed up?"

"Yes, yes! all—any—every thing you wish!"

"Swear, then!"

Here Cecilia drew back; her recollection returned as her terror abated, and her repugnance to entering into an engagement for she knew not what, with a man whose actions she condemned, and whose principles she abhorred, made all her fright now give way to indignation, and, after a short pause, she angrily answered, "No, Sir, I will not swear!—but yet, all that is reasonable, all that is friendly—"

"Hear me swear, then!" interrupted he, furiously, "which at this moment I do, by every thing eternal, and by every thing infernal, that I will not outlive the seizure of my property, and that the moment I am informed there is an execution in my house, shall be the last of my existence!"

"What cruelty! what compulsion! what impiety!" cried Cecilia: "give me, however, that horrible instrument, and prescribe to me what conditions you please."

A noise was now heard below stairs, at which Cecilia, who had not dared call for help lest he should quicken his desperation, was secretly beginning to rejoice, when, starting at the sound, he exclaimed, "I believe you are too late!—the ruffians have already seized my house!" then, endeavouring to force her out of the room, "Go," he cried, "to my wife;—I want to be alone!"

"Oh give me first," cried she, "that weapon, and I will take what oath you please!"

"No, no!—go,—leave me,—" cried he, almost breathless with emotion, "I must not now be trifled with."

"I do not trifle! indeed I do not!" cried Cecilia, holding by his arm: "try, put me to the proof!"

"Swear, solemnly swear, to empty my house of these creditors this moment!"

"I do swear," cried she, with energy, "and Heaven prosper me as I am sincere!"

"I see, I see you are an angel!" cried he, rapturously, "and as such I worship and adore you! O you have restored me to life, and rescued me from perdition!"

"Give me, then, that fatal instrument!"

"That instrument," returned he, "is nothing, since so many others are in my power; but you have now taken from me all desire of using them. Go, then, and stop those wretches from coming to me,—send immediately for the Jew!—he will advance what money you please,—my man knows where to find him; consult with Mr Arnott,—speak a word of comfort to Priscilla,—but do nothing, nothing at all, till you have cleared my house of those cursed scoundrels!"

Cecilia, whose heart sunk within her at the solemn promise she had given, the mention of the Jew, and the arduous task she had undertaken, quitted him without reply, and was going to her own room, to compose her hurried spirits, and consider what steps she had to take, when hearing the noise in the hall grow louder, she stopt to listen, and catching some words that greatly alarmed her, went half way down stairs, when she was met by Davison, Mr Harrel's man, of whom she enquired into the occasion of the disturbance.

He answered that he must go immediately to his master, for the bailiffs were coming into the house.

"Let him not know it if you value his life!" cried she, with new terror. "Where is Mr Arnott? call him to me,—beg him to come this moment;— I will wait for him here."

The man flew to obey her; and Cecilia, finding she had time neither for deliberation nor regret, and dreading lest Mr Harrel, by hearing of the arrival of the bailiffs, should relapse into despair, determined to call to her aid all the courage, prudence, and judgment she possessed, and, since to act she was compelled, endeavour with her best ability, to save his credit, and retrieve his affairs.

The moment Mr Arnott came, she ordered Davison to hasten to his master, and watch his motions.

Then, addressing Mr Arnott, "Will you. Sir," she said, "go and tell those people that if they will instantly quit the house, every thing shall be settled, and Mr Harrel will satisfy their demands?"

"Ah madam!" cried Mr Arnott, mournfully, "and how? he has no means to pay them, and I have none—without ruin to myself,—to help him!"

"Send them but away," said Cecilia, "and I will myself be your security that your promise shall not be disgraced."

"Alas, madam," cried he, "what are you doing? well as I wish to Mr Harrel, miserable as I am for my unfortunate sister, I yet cannot bear that such goodness, such beneficence should be injured!"

Cecilia, however, persisted, and with evident reluctance he obeyed her.

While she waited his return, Davison came from Mr Harrel, who had ordered him to run instantly for the Jew.

Good Heaven, thought Cecilia, that a man so wretchedly selfish and worldly, should dare, with all his guilt upon his head,

To rush unlicenced on eternity![4]

Mr Arnott was more than half an hour with the people; and when, at last, he returned, his countenance immediately proclaimed the ill success of his errand. The creditors, he said, declared they had so frequently been deceived, that they would not dismiss the bailiffs, or retire themselves, without actual payment.

"Tell them, then, Sir," said Cecilia," to send me their accounts, and, if it be possible, I will discharge them directly."

Mr Arnott's eyes were filled with tears at this declaration, and he protested, be the consequence to himself what it might, he would pay away every shilling he was worth, rather than witness such injustice.

---

4 Mason's Elfrida

"No," cried Cecilia, exerting more spirit, that she might shock him less, "I did not save Mr Harrel, to destroy so much better a man! you have suffered but too much oppression already; the present evil is mine; and from me, at least, none I hope will ever spread to Mr Arnott."

Mr Arnott could not bear this; he was struck with grief, with admiration, and with gratitude, and finding his tears now refused to be restrained, he went to execute her commission in silent dejection.

The dejection, however, was encreased, though his tears were dispersed, when he returned; "Oh madam!" he cried, "all your efforts, generous as they are, will be of no avail! the bills even now in the house amount to more than L7000!"

Cecilia, amazed and confounded, started and clasped her hands, calling out, "What must I do! to what have I bound myself! and how can I answer to my conscience,—to my successors, such a disposal, such an abuse of so large a part of my fortune!"

Mr Arnott could make no answer; and they stood looking at each other in silent irresolution, till Davison brought intelligence that the Jew was already come, and waited to speak with her.

"And what can I say to him?" cried she, more and more agitated; "I understand nothing of usury; how am I to deal with him?"

Mr Arnott then confessed that he should himself have instantly been bail for his brother, but that his fortune, originally not large, was now so much impaired by the many debts which from time to time he had paid for him, that as he hoped some day to have a family of his own, he dare not run a risk by which he might be utterly ruined, and the less, as his sister had at Violet Bank been prevailed upon to give up her settlement.

This account, which explained the late uneasiness of Mrs Harrel, still encreased the distress of Cecilia; and every moment she obtained for reflection, augmented her reluctance to parting with *so* large a sum of money for so worthless an object, and added strength to her resentment for the unjustifiable menaces which had extorted from her such a promise. Yet not an instant would she listen to Mr Arnott's offer of fulfilling her engagement, and charged him, as he considered her own self-esteem worth her keeping, not to urge to her a proposal so ungenerous and selfish.

Davison now came again to hasten her, and said that the Jew was with his master, and they both impatiently expected her.

Cecilia, half distracted with her uncertainty how to act, changed colour at this message, and exclaimed "Oh Mr Arnott, run I beseech you for Mr Monckton! bring him hither directly,—if any body can save me it is him; but if I go back to Mr Harrel, I know it will be all over!"

"Certainly," said Mr Arnott, "I will run to him this moment."

"Yet no!—stop!—" cried the trembling Cecilia, "he can now do me no good,—his counsel will arrive too late to serve me,—it cannot call back the oath I have given! it cannot, compulsatory as it was, make me break it, and not be miserable for ever!"

This idea sufficed to determine her; and the apprehension of self-reproach, should the threat of Mr Harrel be put in execution, was more insupportable to her blameless and upright mind, than any loss or diminution which her fortune could sustain.

Slowly however, with tardy and unwilling steps, her judgment repugnant, and her spirit repining, she obeyed the summons of Mr Harrel, who, impatient of her delay, came forward to meet her.

"Miss Beverley," he cried, "there is not a moment to be lost; this good man will bring you any sum of money, upon a proper consideration, that you will command; but if he is not immediately commissioned, and these cursed fellows are not got out of my house, the affair will be blown,"— "and what will follow," added he, lowering his voice, "I will not again frighten you by repeating, though I shall never recant."

Cecilia turned from him in horror; and, with a faltering voice and heavy heart, entreated Mr Arnott to settle for her with the Jew.

Large as was the sum, she was so near being of age, and her security was so good, that the transaction was soon finished: 7500 pounds was received of the Jew, Mr Harrel gave Cecilia his bond for the payment, the creditors were satisfied, the bailiffs were dismissed, and the house was soon restored to its customary appearance of splendid gaiety.

Mrs Harrel, who during this scene had shut herself up in her own room to weep and lament, now flew to Cecilia, and in a transport of joy and gratitude, thanked her upon her knees for thus preserving her from utter ruin: the gentle Mr Arnott seemed uncertain whether most to grieve or rejoice; and Mr Harrel repeatedly protested she should have the sole guidance of his future conduct.

This promise, the hope of his amendment, and the joy she had expanded, somewhat revived the spirits of Cecilia; who, however, deeply affected by what had passed, hastened from them all to her own room.

She had now parted with 8050 pounds to Mr Harrel, without any security when or how it was to be paid; and that ardour of benevolence which taught her to value her riches merely as they enabled her to do good and generous actions, was here of no avail to console or reward her, for her gift was compelled, and its receiver was all but detested. "How much better," cried she, "would this have been bestowed upon the amiable Miss Belfield! or upon her noble-minded, though proud-spirited brother! and how much less a sum would have made the virtuous and industrious Hills easy and happy for life! but here, to become the tool of the extravagance I abhor! to be made responsible for the luxury I condemn! to be liberal in opposition to my principles, and lavish in defiance of my judgment!— Oh that my much-deceived Uncle had better known to what dangerous hands he committed me! and that my weak and unhappy friend had met with a worthier protector of her virtue and safety!"

As soon, however, as she recovered from the first shock of her reflections, she turned her thoughts from herself to the formation of some plan that might, at least, render her donation of serious and lasting use. The signal service she had just done them gave her at present an ascendency over the Harrels, which she hoped, if immediately exerted, might prevent the return of so calamitous a scene, by engaging them both to an immediate change of conduct. But unequal herself to contriving expedients for this purpose that might not easily be controverted, she determined to send the next morning a petition to Mr Monckton to call upon her, reveal to him the whole transaction, and entreat him to suggest to her what, with most probability of success, she might offer to their consideration.

While this was passing in her mind, on the evening of the day in which she had so dearly purchased the right of giving counsel, she was summoned to tea.

She found Mr Harrel and his lady engaged in earnest discourse; as soon as she appeared, the former said, "My dear Miss Beverley, after the extraordinary kindness you have shewn me this morning, you will not, I am sure, deny me one trifling favour which I mean to ask this evening."

"No," said Mrs Harrel, "that I am sure she will not, when she knows that our future appearance in the world depends upon her granting it."

"I hope, then," said Cecilia, "I shall not wish to refuse it."

"It is nothing in the world," said Mr Harrel, "but to go with us to-night to the Pantheon."

Cecilia was struck with the utmost indignation at this proposal; that the man who in the morning had an execution in his house, should languish in the evening for the amusement of a public place,—that he who but a few hours before was plunging uncalled into eternity, should, while the intended instrument of death was yet scarce cold from the grasp of his hand, deliberately court a return of his distress, by instantly recurring to the methods which had involved him in it, irritated and shocked her beyond even a wish of disguising her displeasure, and therefore, after an expressive silence, she gave a cold, but absolute denial.

"I see," said Mr Harrel, somewhat confused, "you do not understand the motives of our request. The unfortunate affair of this morning is very likely to spread presently all over the town; the only refutation that can be given to it, is by our all appearing in public before any body knows whether to believe it or not."

"Do, my dearest friend," cried his lady, "oblige me by your compliance; indeed our whole reputation depends upon it. I made an engagement yesterday to go with Mrs Mears, and if I disappoint her, every body will be guessing the reason."

"At least," answered Cecilia, "my going can answer no purpose to you: pray, therefore, do not ask me; I am ill disposed for such sort of amusement, and have by no means your opinion of its necessity."

"But if we do not *all* go," said Mr Harrel, "we do almost nothing: you are known to live with us, and, your appearance at this critical time is important to our credit. If this misfortune gets wind, the consequence is that every dirty tradesman in town to whom I owe a shilling, will be forming the same cursed combination those scoundrels formed this morning, of coming in a body, and waiting for their money, or else bringing an execution into my house. The only way to silence report is by putting a good face upon the matter at once, and shewing ourselves to the world as if nothing had happened. Favour us, therefore, to-night with your company, which is really important to us, or ten to one, but in another fortnight, I shall be just in the same scrape."

Cecilia, however incensed at this intelligence that his debts were still so numerous, felt now so much alarmed at the mention of an execution, as if she was in actual danger of ruin herself. Terrified, therefore, though not convinced, she yielded to their persuasions, and consented to accompany them.

They soon after separated to make some alteration in their dress, and then, calling in their way for Mrs Mears, they proceeded to the Pantheon.

CHAPTER VI

A MAN OF THE TON.

At the door of the Pantheon they were joined by Mr Arnott and Sir Robert Floyer, whom Cecilia now saw with added aversion: they entered the great room during the second apt of the Concert, to which as no one of the party but herself had any desire to listen, no sort of attention was paid; the ladies entertaining themselves as if no Orchestra was in the room, and the gentlemen, with an equal disregard to it, struggling for a place by the fire, about which they continued hovering till the music was over.

Soon after they were seated, Mr Meadows, sauntering towards them, whispered something to Mrs Mears, who, immediately rising, introduced him to Cecilia; after which, the place next to her being vacant, he cast himself upon it, and lolling as much at his ease as his situation would permit, began something like a conversation with her.

"Have you been long in town, ma'am?"

"No, Sir."

"This is not your first winter?"

"Of being in town, it is."

"Then you have something new to see; O charming! how I envy you!—Are you pleased with the Pantheon?"

"Very much; I have seen no building at all equal to it."

"You have not been abroad. Travelling is the ruin of all happiness! There's no looking at a building here after seeing Italy."

"Does all happiness, then, depend upon the sight of buildings?" said Cecilia, when, turning towards her companion, she perceived him yawning, with such evident inattention to her answer, that not chusing to interrupt his reverie, she turned her head another way.

For some minutes he took no notice of this; and then, as if suddenly recollecting himself, he called out hastily, "I beg your pardon, ma'am, you were saying something?"

"No, Sir, nothing worth repeating." "O pray don't punish me so severely as not to let me hear it!"

Cecilia, though merely not to seem offended at his negligence, was then again beginning an answer, when, looking at him as she spoke, she perceived that he was biting his nails with so absent an air, that he appeared not to know he had asked any question. She therefore broke off, and left him to his cogitation.

Sometime after he addressed her again, saying, "Don't you find this place extremely tiresome, ma'am?"

"Yes, Sir," said she, half laughing, "it is, indeed, not very entertaining!"

"Nothing is entertaining," answered he, "for two minutes together. Things are so little different one from another, that there is no making pleasure out of any thing. We go the same dull round for ever; nothing new, no variety! all the same thing over again! Are you fond of public places, ma'am?"

"Yes, Sir, *soberly*, as Lady Grace says."

"Then I envy you extremely, for you have some amusement always in your own power. How desirable that is!"

"And have not you the same resources?"

"O no! I am tired to death! tired of every thing! I would give the universe for a disposition less difficult to please. Yet, after all, what is there to give pleasure? When one has seen one thing, one has seen every thing. O, 'tis heavy work! Don't you find it so, ma'am?"

This speech was ended with so violent a fit of yawning, that Cecilia would not trouble herself to answer it: but her silence, as before, passed wholly unnoticed, exciting neither question nor comment.

A long pause now succeeded, which he broke at last, by saying, as he writhed himself about upon his seat, "These forms would be much more agreeable if there were backs to them. 'Tis intolerable to be forced to sit like a school-boy. The first study of life is ease. There is, indeed, no other study that pays the trouble of attainment. Don't you think so, ma'am?"

"But may not even that," said Cecilia, "by so much study, become labour?"

"I am vastly happy you think so."

"Sir?"

"I beg your pardon, ma'am, but I thought you said—I really beg your pardon, but I was thinking of something else."

"You did very right, Sir," said Cecilia, laughing, "for what I said by no means merited any attention."

"Will you do me the favour to repeat it?" cried he, taking out his glass to examine some lady at a distance.

"O no," said Cecilia, "that would be trying your patience too severely."

"These glasses shew one nothing but defects," said he; "I am sorry they were ever invented. They are the ruin of all beauty; no complexion can stand them. I believe that solo will never be over; I hate a solo; it sinks, it depresses me intolerably."

"You will presently, Sir," said Cecilia, looking at the bill of the concert, "have a full piece; and that, I hope, will revive you."

"A full piece! oh insupportable! it stuns, it fatigues, it overpowers me beyond endurance! no taste in it, no delicacy, no room for the smallest feeling."

"Perhaps, then, you are only fond of singing?"

"I should be, if I could hear it; but we are now so miserably off in voices, that I hardly ever attempt to listen to a song, without fancying myself deaf from the feebleness of the performers. I hate every thing that requires attention. Nothing gives pleasure that does not force its own way."

"You only, then, like loud voices, and great powers?"

"O worse and worse!—no, nothing is so disgusting to me. All my amazement is that these people think it worth while to give Concerts at all; one is sick to death of music."

"Nay," cried Cecilia, "if it gives no pleasure, at least it takes none away; for, far from being any impediment to conversation, I think every body talks more during the performance than between the acts. And what is there better you could substitute in its place?"

Cecilia, receiving no answer to this question, again looked round to see if she had been heard; when she observed her new acquaintance, with a very thoughtful air, had turned from her to fix his eyes upon the statue of Britannia.

Very soon after, he hastily arose, and seeming entirely to forget that he had spoke to her, very abruptly walked away.

Mr Gosport, who was advancing to Cecilia, and had watched part of this scene, stopt him as he was retreating, and said "Why Meadows, how's this? are you caught at last?"

"O worn to death! worn to a thread!" cried he, stretching himself, and yawning; "I have been talking with a young lady to entertain her! O such heavy work! I would not go through it again for millions!

"What, have you talked yourself out of breath?"

"No; but the effort! the effort!—O, it has unhinged me for a fortnight!—Entertaining a young lady!—one had better be a galley-slave at once!"

"Well but, did she not pay your toils? She is surely a sweet creature."

"Nothing can pay one for such insufferable exertion! though she's well enough, too—better than the common run,—but shy, quite too shy; no drawing her out"

"I thought that was to your taste. You commonly hate much volubility. How have I heard you bemoan yourself when attacked by Miss Larolles!"

"Larolles? O distraction! She talks me into a fever in two minutes. But so it is for ever! nothing but extremes to be met with! common girls are too forward, this lady is too reserved—always some fault! always some drawback! nothing ever perfect!"

"Nay, nay," cried Mr Gosport, "you do not know her; she is perfect enough in all conscience."

"Better not know her, then," answered he, again yawning, "for she cannot be pleasing. Nothing perfect is natural;—I hate every thing out of nature."

He then strolled on, and Mr Gosport approached Cecilia.

"I have been wishing," cried he, "to address you this half hour, but as you were engaged with Mr Meadows, I did not dare advance."

"O, I see your malice!" cried Cecilia; "you were determined to add weight to the value of your company, by making me fully sensible where the balance would preponderate."

"Nay, if you do not admire Mr Meadows," cried he, "you must not even whisper it to the winds."

"Is he, then, so very admirable?"

"O, he is now in the very height of fashionable favour: his dress is a model, his manners are imitated, his attention is courted, and his notice is envied."

"Are you not laughing?"

"No, indeed; his privileges are much more extensive than I have mentioned: his decision fixes the exact limits between what is vulgar and what is elegant, his praise gives reputation, and a word from him in public confers fashion!"

"And by what wonderful powers has he acquired such influence?"

"By nothing but a happy art in catching the reigning foibles of the times, and carrying them to an extreme yet more absurd than any one had done before him. Ceremony, he found, was already exploded for ease, he, therefore, exploded ease for indolence; devotion to the fair sex, had given way to a more equal and rational intercourse, which, to push still farther, he presently exchanged for rudeness; joviality, too, was already banished for philosophical indifference, and that, therefore, he discarded, for weariness and disgust."

"And is it possible that qualities such as these should recommend him to favour and admiration?"

"Very possible, for qualities such as these constitute the present taste of the times. A man of the *Ton*, who would now be conspicuous in the gay world, must invariably be insipid, negligent, and selfish."

"Admirable requisites!" cried Cecilia; "and Mr Meadows, I acknowledge, seems to have attained them all."

"He must never," continued Mr Gosport, "confess the least pleasure from any thing, a total apathy being the chief ingredient of his character: he must, upon no account, sustain a conversation with any spirit, lest he should appear, to his utter disgrace, interested in what is said: and when he is quite tired of his existence, from a total vacuity of ideas, he must affect a look of absence, and pretend, on the sudden, to be wholly lost in thought."

"I would not wish," said Cecilia, laughing, "a more amiable companion!"

"If he is asked his opinion of any lady," he continued, "he must commonly answer by a grimace; and if he is seated next to one, he must take the utmost pains to shew by his listlessness, yawning, and inattention, that he is sick of his situation; for what he holds of all things to be most gothic, is gallantry to the women. To avoid this is, indeed, the principal solicitude of his life. If he sees a lady in distress for her carriage, he is to enquire of her what is the matter, and then, with a shrug, wish her well through her fatigues, wink at some bye-stander, and walk away. If he is in a room where there is a crowd of company, and a scarcity of seats, he must early ensure one of the best in the place, be blind to all looks of fatigue, and deaf to all hints of assistance, and seeming totally to forget himself, lounge at his ease, and appear an unconscious spectator of what is going forward. If he is at a ball where there are more women than men, he must decline dancing at all, though it should happen to be his favourite amusement, and smiling as he passes the disengaged young ladies, wonder to see them sit still, and perhaps ask them the reason!"

"A most alluring character indeed!" cried Cecilia; "and pray how long have these been the accomplishments of a fine gentleman?"

"I am but an indifferent chronologer of the modes," he answered, "but I know it has been long enough to raise just expectations that some new folly will be started soon, by which the present race of INSENSIBLISTS may be driven out. Mr Meadows is now at the head of this sect, as Miss Larolles is of the VOLUBLE, and Miss Leeson of the SUPERCILIOUS. But this way comes another, who, though in a different manner, labours with the same view, and aspires at the same reward, which stimulate the ambition of this happy *Triplet*, that of exciting wonder by peculiarity, and envy by wonder."

This description announced Captain Aresby; who, advancing from the fire-place, told Cecilia how much he rejoiced in seeing her, said he had been *reduced to despair* by so long missing that honour, and that he had feared she *made it a principle* to avoid coming in public, having sought her in vain *partout*.

He then smiled, and strolled on to another party.

"And pray of what sect," said Cecilia, "is this gentleman?"

"Of the sect of JARGONISTS," answered Mr Gosport; "he has not an ambition beyond paying a passing compliment, nor a word to make use of that he has not picked up at public places. Yet this dearth of language, however you may despise it, is not merely owing to a narrow capacity: foppery and conceit have their share in the limitation, for though his phrases are almost always ridiculous or misapplied, they are selected with much study, and introduced with infinite pains."

"Poor man!" cried Cecilia, "is it possible it can cost him any trouble to render himself so completely absurd?"

"Yes; but not more than it costs his neighbours to keep him in countenance. Miss Leeson, since she has presided over the sect of the SUPERCILIOUS, spends at least half her life in wishing the annihilation of the other half; for as she must only speak in her own Coterie, she is compelled to be frequently silent, and therefore, having nothing to think of, she is commonly gnawn with self-denial, and soured with want of amusement: Miss Larolles, indeed, is better off, for in talking faster than she thinks, she has but followed the natural bent of her disposition: as to this poor JARGONIST, he has, I must own, rather a hard task, from the continual restraint of speaking only out of his own [Lilliputian] vocabulary, and denying himself the relief of ever uttering one word by the call of occasion but what hardship is that, compared with what is borne by Mr Meadows? who, since he commenced INSENSIBLIST, has never once dared to be pleased, nor ventured for a moment to look in good humour!"

"Surely, then," said Cecilia, "in a short time, the punishment of this affectation will bring its cure."

"No; for the trick grows into habit, and habit is a second nature. A secret idea of fame makes his forbearance of happiness supportable to him: for he has now the self-satisfaction of considering himself raised to that highest pinnacle of fashionable refinement which is built upon apathy and scorn, and from which, proclaiming himself superior to all possibility of enjoyment, he views the whole world with contempt! holding neither beauty, virtue, wealth, nor power of importance sufficient to kindle the smallest emotion!"

"O that they could all round listen to you!" cried Cecilia; "they would soon, I think, sicken of their folly, if they heard it thus admirably exposed."

"No; they would but triumph that it had obtained them so much notice!—But pray do you see that gentleman, or don't you chuse to know him, who has been bowing to you this half hour?"

"Where?" cried Cecilia, and, looking round, perceived Mr Morrice; who, upon her returning his salutation, instantly approached her, though he had never ventured to shew himself at Mr Harrel's, since his unfortunate accident on the evening of the masquerade.

Entirely casting aside the easy familiarity at which he had latterly arrived, he enquired after her health with the most fearful diffidence, and then, bowing profoundly, was modestly retiring; when Mrs Harrel perceiving him, smiled with so much good-humour, that he gathered courage to return and address her, and found her, to his infinite delight, as obliging and civil as ever.

The Concert was now over; the ladies arose, and the gentlemen joined them. Morrice, at sight of Mr Harrel, was again shrinking; but Mr Harrel, immediately shaking hands with him, enquired what had kept him so long from Portman-Square? Morrice then, finding, to his great surprise, that no one had thought more of the mischief but himself who had committed it, joyously discarded his timidity, and became as sprightly as before his mortification.

A motion was now made for going to the tea-room; and as they walked on, Cecilia, in looking up to examine the building, saw in one of the galleries young Delvile, and almost at the same time caught his eye.

Scarcely now did a moment elapse before he joined her. The sight of him, strongly reviving in her mind the painful contrariety of opinion with which she had lately thought of him, the sentiments so much in his favour which but a few days before she had encouraged, and which it was only that morning she had endeavoured to crush, made her meet him with a kind of melancholy that almost induced her to lament he was amiable, and repine that she knew none like him.

His appearance, meantime, was far different; he seemed enchanted at the sight of her, he flew eagerly to meet her, and his eyes sparkled with pleasure as he approached her; a pleasure neither moderate nor disguised, but lively, unrestrained, and expressive.

Cecilia, whose plans since she had last seen him had twice varied, who first had looked forward to being united with him for ever, and afterwards had determined to avoid with him even a common acquaintance, could not, while these thoughts were all recurring to her memory, receive much delight from observing his gaiety, or feel at all gratified by his unembarrassed manners. The openness of his attentions, and the frankness of his admiration, which hitherto had charmed her as marks of the sincerity of his character, now shocked her as proofs of the indifference of his heart, which feeling for her a mere common regard, that affected neither his spirits nor his peace, he manifested without scruple, since it was not accompanied with even a wish beyond the present hour.

She now, too, recollected that such had always been his conduct, one single and singular moment excepted, when, as he gave to her his letter for Mr Belfield, he seemed struck as she was herself by the extraordinary co-incidence of their ideas and proceedings: that emotion, however, she now regarded as casual and transitory, and seeing him so much happier than herself, she felt ashamed of her delusion, and angry at her easy captivation.

Reflections such as these, though they added fresh motives to her resolution of giving up all thoughts of his alliance, were yet so humiliating, that they robbed her of all power of receiving pleasure from what was passing, and made her forget that the place she was in was even intended for a place of entertainment.

Young Delvile, after painting in lively colours the loss his house had sustained by her quitting it, and dwelling with equal force upon the regret of his mother and his own, asked in a low voice if she would do him so much honour as to introduce him to Mr Harrel; "As the son," added he, "of a brother guardian, I think I have a kind of claim to his acquaintance."

Cecilia could not refuse, though as the request was likely to occasion more frequent meetings, she persuaded herself she was unwilling to comply. The ceremony therefore past, and was again repeated with Mrs Harrel, who, though she had several times seen him, had never been formally made known to him.

The Harrels were both of them much pleased at this mark of civility in a young man whose family had prepared them rather to expect his scorn, and expressed their wishes that he would drink his tea in their party; he accepted their invitation with alacrity, and turning to Cecilia, said, "Have I not skilfully timed my introduction! But though you have done me this honour with Mr and Mrs Harrel, I must not yet, I presume, entreat you to extend it to a certain happy gentleman of this company;" glancing his eyes toward Sir Robert Floyer.

"No, Sir," answered she, with quickness, "yet, nor ever!"

They were now at the door leading down stairs to the tea-room. Cecilia saw that Sir Robert, who had hitherto been engaged with some gentlemen, seemed to be seeking her; and the remembrance of the quarrel which had followed her refusal of his assistance at the Opera-house, obliged her to determine, should he offer it again, to accept it: but the same brutality which forced this intention, contributed to render it repugnant to her, and she resolved if possible to avoid him, by hurrying down stairs before he reached her. She made, therefore, a sudden attempt to slip through the crowd, and as she was light and active, she easily succeeded; but though her hasty motion separated her from the rest of her party, Delvile, who was earnestly looking at her, to discover her meaning in the disclaiming speech she made about Sir Robert, saw into her design, but suffered her not to go alone; he contrived in a moment to follow and join her, while she was stopping at the foot of the stairs for Mrs Harrel.

"Why what a little thief you are," cried he, "to run away from us thus! what do you think Sir Robert will say? I saw him looking for you at the very instant of your flight."

"Then you saw at the same time," said Cecilia, "the reason of it."

"Will you give me leave," cried he, laughing, "to repeat this to my Lord Ernolf?"

"You may repeat it, Sir, if you please," said Cecilia, piqued that he had not rather thought of himself than of Lord Ernolf, "to the whole Pantheon."

"And if I should, "cried he, "half of it, at least, would thank me; and to obtain the applause of so noble an assembly, what would it signify that Sir Robert should cut my throat?"

"I believe," said Cecilia, deeply mortified by a raillery that shewed so little interest in her avowal of indifference, "you are determined to make me as sick of that man's name, as I am of his conversation."

"And is it possible," exclaimed Delvile, in a tone of surprise, "that such can be your opinion, and yet, situated as you are, the whole world at your command, and all mankind at your devotion—but I am answering you seriously, when you are only speaking by rule."

"What rule, Sir?"

"That which young ladies, upon certain occasions, always prescribe themselves."

Here they were interrupted by the arrival of the rest of the company; though not before Cecilia had received some little consolation for her displeasure, by finding that young Delvile still supposed she was engaged, and flattering herself his language would be different were he informed of the contrary.

Morrice now undertook to procure them a table for tea, which, as the room was very full, was not easily done; and while they were waiting his success, Miss Larolles, who from the stairs had perceived Cecilia, came running up to her, and taking her hand, called out "Lord, my dear creature, who'd have thought of seeing you here? I was never so surprised in my life! I really thought you was gone into a convent, it's so extreme long since I've seen you. But of all things in the world, why was you not at Lady Nyland's last assembly? I thought of asking Mrs Harrel fifty times why you did not come, but it always went out of my head. You've no notion how excessively I was disappointed."

"You are very obliging," said Cecilia laughing, "but I hope, since you so often forgot it, the disappointment did [not] much lessen your entertainment."

"O Lord no! I was never so happy in my life. There was such a crowd, you could not move a finger. Every body in the world was there. You've no idea how delightful it was. I thought verily I should have fainted with the heat."

"That was delightful indeed! And how long did you stay?"

"Why we danced till three in the morning. We began with Cotillons, and finished with country dances. It was the most elegant thing you ever saw in your life; every thing quite in a style. I was so monstrously fatigued, I could hardly get through the last dance. I really thought I should have dropt down dead. Only conceive dancing five hours in such a monstrous crowd! I assure you when I got home my feet were all blisters. You have no idea how they smarted."

"And whence comes it," cried young Delvile, "that *you* partake so little of these delights?"

"Because I fear," answered Cecilia, "I came too late into the school of fashion to be a ductile pupil."

"Do you know," continued Miss Larolles, "Mr Meadows has not spoke one word to me all the evening! Though I am sure he saw me, for I sat at the outside on purpose to speak to a person or two, that I knew would be strolling about; for if one sits on the inside, there's no speaking to a creature, you know, so I never do it at the Opera, nor in the boxes at Ranelagh, nor any where. It's the shockingest thing you can conceive to be made sit in the middle of those forms; one might as well be at home, for nobody can speak to one."

"But you don't seem to have had much better success," said Cecilia, "in keeping at the outside."

"O yes I have, for I got a little chat with two or three people as they were passing, for, you know, when one sits there, they can't help saying something; though I assure you all the men are so exceedingly odd they don't care whether they speak to one or no. As to Mr Meadows, he's really enough to provoke one to death. I suppose he's in one of his absent fits. However, I assure you I think it's extreme impertinent of him, and so I shall tell Mr Sawyer, for I know he'll make a point of telling him of it again."

"I rather think," said Cecilia, "the best would be to return the compliment in kind, and when he next recollects you, appear to have forgotten him."

"O Lord, that's a very good notion! so I will, I declare. But you can't conceive how glad I am the Concert's over; for I assure you, though I sat as near the fire as possible, I was so extreme cold you've no idea, for Mr Meadows never would let me have the least peep at it. I declare I believe he does it on purpose to plague one, for he grows worse and worse every day. You can't think how I hate him!"

"Not easily, I believe indeed!" said Cecilia, archly.

"O do but look!" resumed the fair VOLUBLE, "if there is not Mrs Mears in her old red gown again! I begin to think she'll never have another. I wish she was to have an execution in her house, if it was only to get rid of it! I am so fatigued with the sight of it you can't conceive."

Mr Morrice now brought intelligence that he had secured one side of a table which would very well accommodate the ladies; and that the other side was only occupied by one gentleman, who, as he was not drinking tea himself, would doubtless give up his place when the party appeared.

Miss Larolles then ran back to her own set, and the rest followed Mr Morrice; Mrs Harrell, Mrs Mears and Cecilia took their places. The gentleman opposite to them proved to be Mr Meadows: Morrice, therefore, was much deceived in his expectations, for, far from giving up his place, he had flung himself all along upon the form in such a lounging posture, while he rested one arm upon the table, that, not contented with merely keeping his own seat, he filled up a space meant for three.

Mr Harrel had already walked off to another party: Delvile stood aloof for some minutes, expecting Sir Robert Floyer would station himself behind Cecilia; but Sir Robert, who would scarce have thought such a condescension due to a princess, disdained any appearance of assiduity, even while he made it his care to publish his pretensions: and therefore, finding no accommodation to please him, he stalked towards some gentlemen in another part of the room. Delvile then took the post he had neglected, and Mr Arnott, who had not had courage to make any effort in his own favour, modestly stood near him. Cecilia contrived to make room for Mr Gosport next to herself, and Morrice was sufficiently happy in being allowed to call the waiters, superintend, the provisions, and serve the whole party.

The task of making tea fell upon Cecilia, who being somewhat incommoded by the vicinity of her neighbours, Mrs Mears called out to Mr Meadows "Do pray, Sir, be so good as to make room for one of us at your side."

Mr Meadows, who was indolently picking his teeth, and examining them with a tooth pick case glass, did not, at first, seem to hear her; and when she repeated her request, he only looked at her, and said "umph?"

"Now really, Mr Meadows," said she, "when you see any ladies in such distress, I wonder how you can forbear helping them."

"In distress, are you?" cried he, with a vacant smile, "pray, what's the matter?"

"Don't you see? we are so crowded we can hardly sit."

"Can't you?" cried he, "upon my honour it's very shameful that these people don't contrive some seats more convenient"

"Yes," said Mrs Mears; "but if you would be so kind as to let somebody else sit by you we should not want any contrivance."

Here Mr Meadows was seized with a furious fit of yawning, which as much diverted Cecilia and Mr Gosport, as it offended Mrs Mears, who with great displeasure added, "Indeed, Mr Meadows, it's very strange that you never hear what's said to you."

"I beg your pardon," said he, "were you speaking to me?" and again began picking his teeth.

Morrice, eager to contrast his civility with the inattention of Mr Meadows, now flew round to the other side of the table, and calling out "let *me* help you, Miss Beverley, I can make tea better than anybody," he lent over that part of the form which Mr Meadows had occupied with one of his feet, in order to pour it out himself: but Mr Meadows, by an unfortunate removal of his foot, bringing him forwarder than he was prepared to go, the tea pot and its contents were overturned immediately opposite to Cecilia.

Young Delvile, who saw the impending evil, from an impetuous impulse to prevent her suffering by it, hastily drew her back, and bending down before her, secured her preservation by receiving himself the mischief with which she was threatened.

Mrs Mears and Mrs Harrel vacated their seats in a moment, and Mr Gosport and Mr Arnott assisted in clearing the table, and removing Cecilia, who was very slightly hurt, and at once surprised, ashamed, and pleased at the manner in which she had been saved.

Young Delvile, though a sufferer from his gallantry, the hot water having penetrated through his coat to his arm and shoulder, was at first insensible to his situation, from an apprehension that Cecilia had not wholly escaped; and his enquiries were so eager and so anxious, made with a look of such solicitude, and a voice of such alarm, that, equally astonished and gratified, she secretly blest the accident which had given birth to his uneasiness, however she grieved for its consequence to himself.

But no sooner was he satisfied of her safety, than he felt himself obliged to retire; yet attributing to inconvenience what was really the effect of pain, he hurried away with an appearance of sport, saying, "There is something I must own, rather *unknightly* in quitting the field for a wet jacket, but the company, I hope, will only give me credit for flying away to Ranelagh. So

"Like a brave general after being beat,
I'll exult and rejoice in a prudent retreat."[5]

He then hastened to his carriage: and poor Morrice, frightened and confounded at the disaster he had occasioned, sneaked after him with much less ceremony. While Mr Meadows, wholly unconcerned by the distress and confusion around him, sat quietly picking his teeth, and looking on, during the whole transaction, with an unmeaning stare, that made it doubtful whether he had even perceived it.

Order being now soon restored, the ladies finished their tea, and went up stairs. Cecilia, to whom the late accident had afforded much new and interesting matter for reflection, wished immediately to have returned home, but she was not the leader of the party, and therefore could not make the proposal.

They then strolled through all the apartments, and having walked about till the fashionable time of retiring, they were joined by Sir Robert Floyer, and proceeded to the little room near the entrance to the great one, in order to wait for their carriages.

Here Cecilia again met Miss Larolles, who came to make various remarks, and infinite ridicule, upon sundry unfashionable or uncostly articles in the dresses of the surrounding company; as well as to complain, with no little resentment, that Mr Meadows was again standing before the fire!

Captain Aresby also advanced, to tell her he was quite *abattu* by having so long lost sight of her, to hope she *would make a renounce* of mortifying the world by discarding it, and to protest he had waited for his carriage till he was actually upon the point of being [*accable.*]

In the midst of this *jargon*, to which the fulness of Cecilia's mind hardly permitted her to listen, there suddenly appeared at the door of

---

5 Smart

the apartment, Mr Albany, who, with his usual austerity of countenance, stopt to look round upon the company.

"Do you see," cried Mr Gosport to Cecilia, "who approaches? your poor *sycophants* will again be taken to task, and I, for one, tremble at the coming storm!"

"O Lord," cried Miss Larolles, "I wish I was safe in my chair! that man always frightens me out of my senses. You've no notion what disagreeable things he says to one. I assure you I've no doubt but he's crazy; and I'm always in the shockingest fright in the world for fear he should be taken with a fit while I'm near him."

"It is really a petrifying thing," said the Captain, "that one can go to no *spectacle* without the *horreur* of being *obsede* by that person! if he comes this way, I shall certainly make a renounce, and retire."

"Why so?" said Sir Robert, "what the d—l do you mind him for?"

"O he is the greatest bore in nature!" cried the Captain, "and I always do *mon possible* to avoid him; for he breaks out in such barbarous phrases, that I find myself *degoute* with him in a moment."

"O, I assure you," said Miss Larolles, "he attacks one sometimes in a manner you've no idea. One day he came up to me all of a sudden, and asked me what good I thought I did by dressing so much? Only conceive how shocking!"

"O, I have had the *horreur* of questions of that sort from him *sans fin*," said the Captain; "once he took the liberty to ask me, what service I was of to the world! and another time, he desired me to inform him whether I had ever made any poor person pray for me! and, in short, he has so frequently inconvenienced me by his impertinences, that he really bores me to a degree."

"That's just the thing that makes him hunt you down," said Sir Robert; "if he were to ask me questions for a month together, I should never trouble myself to move a muscle."

"The matter of his discourse," said Mr Gosport, "is not more singular than the manner, for without any seeming effort or consciousness, he runs into blank verse perpetually. I have made much enquiry about him, but all I am able to learn, is that he was certainly confined, at one part of his life, in a private mad-house: and though now, from not being mischievous, he is set at liberty, his looks, language, and whole behaviour, announce the former injury of his intellects."

"O Lord," cried Miss Larolles, half-screaming, "what shocking notions you put in one's head! I declare I dare say I sha'n't get safe home for him, for I assure you I believe he's taken a spite to me! and all because one day, before I knew of his odd ways, I happened to fall a laughing at his going about in that old coat. Do you know it put him quite in a passion! only conceive how ill-natured!"

"O he has distressed me," exclaimed the Captain, with a shrug, "*partout*! and found so much fault with every thing I have done, that I should really be glad to have the honour to cut, for the moment he comes up to me, I know what I have to expect!"

"But I must tell you," cried Miss Larolles, "how monstrously he put me in a fright one evening when I was talking with Miss Moffat. Do you know, he came up to us, and asked what we were saying! and because we could not think in a minute of something to answer him, he said he supposed we were only talking some scandal, and so we had better go home, and employ ourselves in working for the poor! only think how horrid! and after that, he was so excessive impertinent in his remarks, there was quite no bearing him. I assure you he cut me up so you've no notion."

Here Mr Albany advanced; and every body but Sir Robert moved out of the way.

Fixing his eyes upon Cecilia, with an expression *more in sorrow than in anger*, after contemplating her some time in silence, he exclaimed, "Ah lovely, but perishable flower! how long will that ingenuous countenance, wearing, because wanting no disguise, look responsive of the whiteness of the region within? How long will that air of innocence irradiate your whole appearance? unspoilt by prosperity, unperverted by power! pure

333

in the midst of surrounding depravity! unsullied in the tainted air of infectious perdition!"

The confusion of Cecilia at this public address, which drew upon her the eyes and attention of all the company, was inexpressible; she arose from her seat, covered with blushes, and saying, "I fancy the carriage must be ready," pressed forward to quit the room, followed by Sir Robert, who answered, "No, no, they'll call it when it comes up. Arnott, will you go and see where it is?"

Cecilia stopt, but whispered Mrs Harrel to stand near her.

"And whither," cried Albany indignantly, "whither wouldst thou go? Art thou already disdainful of my precepts? and canst thou not one short moment spare from the tumultuous folly which encircles thee? Many and many are the hours thou mayst spend with such as these; the world, alas! is full of them; weary not then, so soon, of an old man that would admonish thee,—he cannot call upon thee long, for soon he will be called upon himself!"

This solemn exhortation extremely distressed her; and fearing to still further offend him by making another effort to escape, she answered in a low voice, "I will not only hear, but thank you for your precepts, if you will forbear to give them before so many witnesses."

"Whence," cried he sternly, "these vain and superficial distinctions? Do you not dance in public? What renders you more conspicuous? Do you not dress to be admired, and walk to be observed? Why then this fantastical scruple, unjustified by reason, unsupported by analogy? Is folly only to be published? Is vanity alone to be exhibited? Oh slaves of senseless contradiction! Oh feeble followers of yet feebler prejudice! daring to be wicked, yet fearing to be wise; dauntless in levity, yet shrinking from the name of virtue!"

The latter part of this speech, during which he turned with energy to the whole company, raised such a general alarm, that all the ladies hastily quitted the room, and all the gentlemen endeavoured to enter it, equally curious to see the man who made the oration, and the lady to whom it was addressed. Cecilia, therefore, found her situation unsupportable; "I must go," she cried, "whether there is a carriage or not! pray, Mrs Harrel, let us go!"

Sir Robert then offered to take her hand, which she was extremely ready to give him; but while the crowd made their passage difficult, Albany, following and stopping her, said, "What is it you fear? a miserable old man, worn out by the sorrows of that experience from which he offers you counsel? What, too, is it you trust? a libertine wretch, coveting nothing but your wealth, for the gift of which he will repay you by the perversion of your principles!"

"What the d—l do you mean by that?" cried the Baronet.

"To shew," answered he, austerely, "the inconsistency of false delicacy; to show how those who are too timid for truth, can fearless meet licentiousness."

"For Heaven's sake, Sir," cried Cecilia, "say no more to me now: call upon me in Portman-square when you please,—reprove me in whatever you think me blameable, I shall be grateful for your instructions, and bettered, perhaps, by your care;—but lessons and notice thus public can do me nothing but injury."

"How happy," cried he, "were no other injury near thee! spotless were then the hour of thy danger, bright, fair and refulgent thy passage to security! the Good would receive thee with praise, the Guilty would supplicate thy prayers, the Poor would follow thee with blessings, and Children would be taught by thy example!"

He then quitted her, every body making way as he moved, and proceeded into the great room. Mrs Harrel's carriage being announced at the same time, Cecilia lost not an instant in hastening away.

Sir Robert, as he conducted her, disdainfully laughed at the adventure, which the general licence allowed to Mr Albany prevented his resenting, and which therefore he scorned to appear moved at.

Miss Harrel could talk of nothing else, neither was Cecilia disposed to change the subject, for the remains of insanity which seemed to hang upon him were affecting without being alarming, and her desire to know more of him grew every instant stronger.

This desire, however, outlived not the conversation to which it gave rise; when she returned to her own room, no vestige of it remained upon her mind, which a nearer concern and deeper interest wholly occupied.

The behaviour of young Delvile had pained, pleased, and disturbed her; his activity to save her from mischief might proceed merely from gallantry or good nature; upon that, therefore, she dwelt little: but his eagerness, his anxiety, his insensibility to himself, were more than good breeding could claim, and seemed to spring from a motive less artificial.

She now, therefore, believed that her partiality was returned; and this belief had power to shake all her resolves, and enfeeble all her objections. The arrogance of Mr Delvile lessened in her reflections, the admonitions of Mr Monckton abated in their influence. With the first she considered that though connected she need not live, and for the second, though she acknowledged the excellence of his judgment, she concluded him wholly ignorant of her sentiments of Delvile; which she imagined, when once revealed, would make every obstacle to the alliance seem trifling, when put in competition with mutual esteem and affection.

CHAPTER VII

A REPROOF.

The attention of Cecilia to her own affairs, did not make her forgetful of those of the Harrels: and the morning after the busy day which was last recorded, as soon as she quitted the breakfast-room, she began a note to Mr Monckton, but was interrupted with information that he was already in the house.

She went to him immediately, and had the satisfaction of finding him alone: but desirous as she was to relate to him the transactions of the preceding day, there was in his countenance a gravity so unusual, that her impatience was involuntarily checked, and she waited first to hear if he had himself any thing to communicate.

He kept her not long in suspence; "Miss Beverley," he said, "I bring you intelligence which though I know you will be very sorry to hear, it is absolutely necessary should be told you immediately: you may otherwise, from however laudable motives, be drawn into some action which you may repent for life."

"What now!" cried Cecilia, much alarmed.

"All that I suspected," said he, "and more than I hinted to you, is true; Mr Harrel is a ruined man! he is not worth a groat, and he is in debt beyond what he ever possessed."

Cecilia made no answer: she knew but too fatally the desperate state of his affairs, yet that *his debts were more than he had ever possessed*, she had not thought possible.

"My enquiries," continued he, "have been among principals, and such as would not dare deceive me. I hastened, therefore, to you, that this timely notice might enforce the injunctions I gave you when I had the pleasure of seeing you last, and prevent a misjudging generosity from leading you into any injury of your own fortune, for a man who is past all relief from it, and who cannot be saved, even though you were to be destroyed for his sake."

"You are very good," said Cecilia, "but your counsel is now too late!" She then briefly acquainted him with what passed, and with how large a sum she had parted.

He heard her with rage, amazement, and horror: and after inveighing against Mr Harrel in the bitterest terms, he said, "But why, before you signed your name to so base an imposition, could you not send for me?"

"I wished, I meant to have done it," cried she, "but I thought the time past when you could help me: how, indeed, could you have saved me? my word was given, given with an oath the most solemn, and the first I have ever taken in my life."

"An oath so forced," answered he, "the most delicate conscience would have absolved you from performing. You have, indeed, been grossly imposed upon, and pardon me if I add unaccountably to blame. Was it not obvious that relief so circumstanced must be temporary? If his ruin had been any thing less than certain, what tradesmen would have been insolent? You have therefore deprived yourself of the power of doing good to a worthier object, merely to grant a longer date to extravagance and villainy."

"Yet how," cried Cecilia, deeply touched by this reproof, "how could I do otherwise! Could I see a man in the agonies of despair, hear him first darkly hint his own destruction, and afterwards behold him almost in the very act of suicide, the instrument of self-murder in his desperate hand—and yet, though he put his life in my power, though he told me I could preserve him, and told me he had no other reliance or resource, could I leave him to his dreadful despondence, refuse my assisting hand to raise him from perdition, and, to save what, after all, I am well able to spare, suffer a fellow-creature, who flung himself upon my mercy, to offer up his last accounts with an action blacker than any which had preceded it?—No, I cannot repent what I have done, though I lament, indeed, that the object was not more deserving."

"Your representation," said Mr Monckton, "like every thing else that I ever heard you utter, breathes nothing but benevolence and goodness: but your pity has been abused, and your understanding imposed upon. Mr Harrel had no intention to destroy himself; the whole was an infamous trick, which, had not your generosity been too well known, would never have been played."

"I cannot think quite so ill of him," said Cecilia, "nor for the world would I have risked my own future reproaches by trusting to such a suspicion, which, had it proved wrong, and had Mr Harrel, upon my refusal committed the fatal deed, would have made his murder upon my own conscience rest for ever! surely the experiment would have been too hazardous, when the consequence had all my future peace in its power.

"It is impossible not to revere your scruples," said Mr Monckton, "even while I consider them as causeless; for causeless they undoubtedly were: the man who could act so atrocious a part, who could so scandalously pillage a young lady who was his guest and his ward, take advantage of her temper for the plunder of her fortune, and extort her compliance by the basest and most dishonourable arts, meant only to terrify her into compliance, for he can be nothing less than a downright and thorough scoundrel, capable of every species of mean villainy."

He then protested he would at least acquaint her other guardians with what had passed, whose business it would be to enquire if there was any chance of redress.

Cecilia, however, had not much trouble in combating this proposal; for though her objections, which were merely those of punctilious honour and delicacy, weighed nothing with a man who regarded them as absurdities, yet his own apprehensions of appearing too officious in her affairs, forced him, after a little deliberation, to give up the design.

"Besides," said Cecilia, "as I have his bond for what I have parted with, I have, at least, no right to complain, unless, after he receives his rents, he refuses to pay me."

"His bonds! his rents!" exclaimed Mr Monckton, "what is a man's bond who is not worth a guinea? and what are his rents, when all he ever owned must be sold before they are due, and when he will not himself receive a penny from the sale, as he has neither land, house, nor possession of any sort that is not mortgaged?"

"Nay, then," said Cecilia, "if so, it is indeed all, over! I am sorry, I am grieved!—but it is past, and nothing, therefore, remains, but that I try to forget I ever was richer!"

"This is very youthful philosophy," said Mr Monckton; "but it will not lessen your regret hereafter, when the value of money is better known to you."

"If I shall dearly buy my experience," said Cecilia, "let me be the more attentive to making good use of it; and, since my loss seems irremediable to myself, let me at least endeavour to secure its utility to Mr Harrel."

She then told him her wish to propose to that gentleman some scheme of reformation, while yesterday's events were yet recent in his mind: but Mr Monckton, who had hardly patience to hear her, exclaimed, "He is a wretch, and deserves the full force of the disgrace he is courting. What is now most necessary is to guard you from his further machinations, for you may else be involved in ruin as deep as his own. He now knows the way to frighten you, and he will not fail to put it in practice."

"No, Sir," answered Cecilia, "he would vainly apply to me in future: I cannot repent that I ventured not yesterday to brave his menaces, but too little is the comfort I feel from what I have bestowed, to suffer any consideration to make me part with more."

"Your resolution," answered he, "will be as feeble as your generosity will be potent: depend nothing upon yourself, but instantly quit his house.

You will else be made responsible for every debt that he contracts; and whatever may be his difficulties hereafter, he will know that to extricate himself from them, he has but to talk of dying, and to shew you a sword or a pistol."

"If so, then," said Cecilia, looking down while she spoke, "I suppose I must again go to Mr Delvile's."

This was by no means the purpose of Mr Monckton, who saw not more danger to her fortune with one of her guardians, than to her person with the other. He ventured, therefore, to recommend to her a residence with Mr Briggs, well knowing that his house would be a security against her seeing any man equal to himself, and hoping that under his roof he might again be as unrivalled in her opinion and esteem, as he formerly was in the country.

But here the opposition of Cecilia was too earnest for any hope that it might be surmounted; for, added to her dislike of Mr Briggs, her repugnance to such an habitation was strongly, though silently increased, by her secret inclination to return to St James's-square.

"I mention not Mr Briggs as an eligible host," said Mr Monckton, after listening to her objections, "but merely as one more proper for you than Mr Delvile, with whom your fixing at present would but be ill thought of in the world."

"Ill thought of, Sir? Why so?"

"Because he has a son; for whose sake alone it would be universally concluded you changed your abode: and to give any pretence for such a report, would by no means accord with the usual delicacy of your conduct."

Cecilia was confounded by this speech: the truth of the charge she felt, and the probability of the censure she did not dare dispute.

He then gave her a thousand exhortations to beware of the schemes and artifices of Mr Harrel, which he foresaw would be innumerable. He told her, too, that with respect to Sir Robert Floyer, he thought she had better suffer the report to subside of itself, which in time it must necessarily do, than give to it so much consequence as to send a message to the Baronet, from which he might pretend to infer that hitherto she had been wavering, or she would have sent to him sooner.

But the real motive of this advice was, that as he found Sir Robert by no means to be dreaded, he hoped the report, if generally circulated and credited, might keep off other pretenders, and intimidate or deceive young Delvile.

The purport for which Cecilia had wished this conference was, however, wholly unanswered; Mr Monckton, enraged by the conduct of Mr Harrel, refused to talk of his affairs, and could only mention him with detestation: but Cecilia, less severe in her judgment, and more tender in her heart, would not yet give up the hope of an amendment she so anxiously wished; and having now no other person to whom she could apply, determined to consult with Mr Arnott, whose affection for his sister would give him a zeal in the affair that might somewhat supply the place of superior abilities. There was, indeed, no time to be lost in making the projected attempt, for no sooner was the immediate danger of suffering removed, than the alarm wore away, and the penitence was forgotten; every thing went on as usual, no new regulations were made, no expences abated, no pleasures forborn, not a thought of hereafter admitted: and ruinous and terrible as had been the preceding storm, no trace of it was visible in the serenity of the present calm.

An occasion of discussion with Mr Arnott very speedily offered. Mr Harrel said he had observed in the looks of his friends at the Pantheon much surprise at the sight of him, and declared he should take yet another measure for removing all suspicion. This was to give a splendid entertainment at his own house to all his acquaintance, to which he meant to invite every body of any consequence he had ever seen, and almost every body he had ever heard of, in his life.

Levity so unfeeling, and a spirit of extravagance so irreclaimable, were hopeless prognostics; yet Cecilia would not desist from her design. She therefore took the earliest opportunity of speaking with Mr Arnott upon the subject, when she openly expressed her uneasiness at the state of his brother's affairs, and warmly acknowledged her displeasure at his dissipated way of life.

Mr Arnott soon shewed that example was all he wanted to declare the same sentiments. He owned he had long disapproved the conduct of Mr Harrel, and trembled at the situation of his sister. They then considered what it was possible to propose that might retrieve their affairs, and concluded that entirely to quit London for some years, was the only chance that remained of saving them from absolute destruction.

Mr Arnott, therefore, though fearfully, and averse to the talk, told his sister their mutual advice. She thanked him, said she was much obliged to him, and would certainly consider his proposal, and mention it to Mr Harrel.—Parties of pleasure, however, intervened, and the promise was neglected.

Cecilia then again spoke herself. Mrs Harrel, much softened by her late acts of kindness, was no longer offended by her interference, but contented herself with confessing that she quite hated the country, and could only bear to live in it in summer time. And when Cecilia very earnestly expostulated on the weakness of such an objection to a step absolutely necessary for her future safety and happiness, she said, *she could do no worse than that if already ruined*, and therefore that she thought *it would be very hard to expect from her such a sacrifice before-hand.*

It was in vain Cecilia remonstrated: Mrs Harrel's love of pleasure was stronger than her understanding, and therefore, though she listened to her with patience, she concluded with the same answer she had begun.

Cecilia then, though almost heartless, resolved upon talking with Mr Harrel himself: and therefore, taking an opportunity which he had not time to elude, she ingenuously told him her opinion of his danger, and of the manner in which it might be avoided.

He paid unusual attention to her advice, but said she was much mistaken with respect to his affairs, which he believed he should now very speedily retrieve, as he had had the preceding night an uncommon *run of luck*, and flattered himself with being able very shortly to pay all his debts, and begin the world again upon a new score.

This open confession of gaming was but a new shock to Cecilia, who scrupled not to represent to him the uncertainty of so hazardous a reliance, and the inevitable evils of so destructive a practice.

She made not, however, the least impression upon his mind; he assured her he doubted not giving her shortly a good account of himself, and that living in the country was a resource of desperation which need not be anticipated.

Cecilia, though grieved and provoked by their mutual folly and blindness, could proceed no further: advice and admonition she spared not, but authority she had none to use. She regretted her ineffectual attempt to Mr Arnott, who was yet more cruelly afflicted at it; but though they conversed upon the subject by every opportunity, they were equally unable to relate any success from their efforts, or to devise any plan more likely to ensure it.

CHAPTER VIII

A MISTAKE.

Mean time young Delvile failed not to honour Cecilia's introduction of him to Mr Harrel, by waiting upon that gentleman as soon as the ill effects of his accident at the Pantheon permitted him to leave his own house. Mr Harrel, though just going out when he called, was desirous of being upon good terms with his family, and therefore took him up stairs to present him to his lady, and invited him to tea and cards the next evening.

Cecilia, who was with Mrs Harrel, did not see him without emotion; which was not much lessened by the task of thanking him for his assistance at the Pantheon, and enquiring how he had himself fared. No sign, however, of emotion appeared in return, either when he first addressed, or afterwards answered her: the look of solicitude with which she had been so much struck when they last parted was no longer discernible, and the voice of sensibility which had removed all her doubts, was no longer to be heard. His general ease, and natural gaiety were again unruffled, and though he had never seemed really indifferent to her, there was not the least appearance of any added partiality.

Cecilia felt an involuntary mortification as she observed this change: yet, upon reflection, she still attributed his whole behaviour to his mistake with respect to her situation, and therefore was but the more gratified by the preference he occasionally betrayed.

The invitation for the next evening was accepted, and Cecilia, for once, felt no repugnance to joining the company. Young Delvile again was in excellent spirits; but though his chief pleasure was evidently derived from conversing with her, she had the vexation to observe that he seemed to think her the undoubted property of the Baronet, always retreating when he approached, and as careful, when next her, to yield his place if he advanced, as, when he was distant, to guard it from all others.

But when Sir Robert was employed at cards, all scruples ceasing, he neglected not to engross her almost wholly. He was eager to speak to her of the affairs of Mr Belfield, which he told her wore now a better aspect. The letter, indeed, of recommendation which he had shewn to her, had failed, as the nobleman to whom it was written had already entered into an engagement for his son; but he had made application elsewhere which he believed would be successful, and he had communicated his proceedings to Mr Belfield, whose spirits he hoped would recover by this prospect of employment and advantage. "It is, however, but too true," he added, "that I have rather obtained his consent to the steps I am taking, than his approbation of them: nor do I believe, had I previously consulted him, I should have had even that. Disappointed in his higher views, his spirit is broken, and he is heartless and hopeless, scarce condescending to accept relief, from the bitter remembrance that he expected preferment. Time, however, will blunt this acute sensibility, and reflection will make him blush at this unreasonable delicacy. But we must patiently soothe him till he is more himself, or while we mean to serve, we shall only torment him. Sickness, sorrow, and poverty have all fallen heavily upon him, and they have all fallen at once: we must not, therefore, wonder to find him intractable, when his mind is as much depressed, as his body is enervated."

Cecilia, to whom his candour and generosity always gave fresh delight, strengthened his opinions by her concurrence, and confirmed his designs by the interest which she took in them.

From this time, he found almost daily some occasion for calling in Portman-square. The application of Cecilia in favour of Mr Belfield gave him a right to communicate to her all his proceedings concerning him; and he had some letter to shew, some new scheme to propose, some refusal to lament, or some hope to rejoice over, almost perpetually: or even when these failed, Cecilia had a cold, which he came to enquire after, or Mrs Harrel gave him an invitation, which rendered any excuse unnecessary. But though his intimacy with Cecilia was encreased, though his admiration of her was conspicuous, and his fondness for her society seemed to grow with the enjoyment of it, he yet never manifested any doubt of her engagement with the Baronet, nor betrayed either intention or desire to supplant him. Cecilia, however, repined not much at the mistake, since she thought it might be instrumental to procuring her a more impartial acquaintance with his character, than she could rationally expect, if, as she hoped, the explanation of his error should make him seek her good opinion with more study and design.

To satisfy herself not only concerning the brother but the sister, she again visited Miss Belfield, and had the pleasure of finding her in better spirits, and hearing that the *noble friend* of her brother, whom she had already mentioned, and whom Cecilia had before suspected to be young Delvile, had now pointed out to him a method of conduct by which his affairs might be decently retrieved, and himself creditably employed. Miss Belfield spoke of the plan with the highest satisfaction; yet she acknowledged that her mother was extremely discontented with it, and that her brother himself was rather led by shame than inclination to its adoption. Yet he was evidently easier in his mind, though far from happy, and already so much better, that Mr Rupil said he would very soon be able to leave his room.

Such was the quiet and contented situation of Cecilia, when one evening, which was destined for company at home, while she was alone in the drawing-room, which Mrs Harrel had just left to answer a note, Sir Robert Floyer accidentally came up stairs before the other gentlemen.

"Ha!" cried he, the moment he saw her, "at last have I the good fortune to meet with you alone! this, indeed, is a favour I thought I was always to be denied."

He was then approaching her; but Cecilia, who shrunk involuntarily at the sight of him, was retreating hastily to quit the room, when suddenly recollecting that no better opportunity might ever offer for a final explanation with him, she irresolutely stopt; and Sir Robert, immediately following, took her hand, and pressing it to his lips as she endeavoured to withdraw it, exclaimed, "You are a most charming creature!" when the door was opened, and young Delvile at the same moment was announced and appeared.

Cecilia, colouring violently, and extremely chagrined, hastily disengaged herself from his hold. Delvile seemed uncertain whether he ought not to retire, which Sir Robert perceiving, bowed to him with an air of mingled triumph and vexation, and said, "Sir your most obedient!"

The doubt, however, in which every one appeared of what was next to be done, was immediately removed by the return of Mrs Harrel, and the arrival at almost the same moment of more company.

The rest of the evening was spent, on the part of Cecilia, most painfully: the explanation she had planned had ended in worse than nothing, for by suffering the Baronet to detain her, she had rather shewn a disposition to oblige, than any intention to discard him; and the situation in which she had been surprised by young Delvile, was the last to clear the suspicions she so little wished him to harbour: while, on his part, the accident seemed to occasion no other alteration than that of rendering him more than usually assiduous to give way to Sir Robert whenever he approached her.

Nor was Sir Robert slack in taking advantage of this attention: he was highly in spirits, talked to her with more than common freedom, and wore the whole evening an air of exulting satisfaction.

Cecilia, provoked by this presumption, hurt by the behaviour of young Delvile, and mortified by the whole affair, determined to leave this mistake no longer in the power of accident, but to apply immediately to Mr Delvile senior, and desire him, as her guardian, to wait upon Sir Robert himself, and acquaint him that his perseverance in pursuing her was both useless and offensive: and by this method she hoped at once to disentangle herself for ever from the Baronet, and to discover more fully the sentiments of young Delvile: for the provocation she had just endured, robbed her of all patience for waiting the advice of Mr Monckton.

CHAPTER IX

AN EXPLANATION.

The following morning, therefore, Cecilia went early to St James's-square: and, after the usual ceremonies of messages and long waiting, she was shewn into an apartment where she found Mr Delvile and his son.

She rejoiced to see them together, and determined to make known to them both the purport of her visit: and therefore, after some apologies and a little hesitation, she told Mr Delvile, that encouraged by his offers of serving her, she had taken the liberty to call upon him with a view to entreat his assistance.

Young Delvile, immediately arising, would have quitted the room; but Cecilia, assuring him she rather desired what she had to say should be known than kept secret, begged that he would not disturb himself.

Delvile, pleased with this permission to hear her, and curious to know what would follow, very readily returned to his seat.

"I should by no means," she continued, "have thought of proclaiming even to the most intimate of my friends, the partiality which Sir Robert Floyer has been pleased to shew me, had he left to me the choice of publishing or concealing it: but, on the contrary, his own behaviour seems intended not merely to display it, but to insinuate that it meets with my approbation. Mr Harrel, also, urged by too much warmth of friendship, has encouraged this belief; nor, indeed, do I know at present where the mistake stops, nor what it is report has not scrupled to affirm. But I think

I ought no longer to neglect it, and therefore I have presumed to solicit your advice in what manner I may most effectually contradict it."

The extreme surprise of young Delvile at this speech was not more evident than pleasant to Cecilia, to whom it accounted for all that had perplext her in his conduct, while it animated every expectation she wished to encourage."

"The behaviour of Mr Harrel," answered Mr Delvile, "has by no means been such as to lead me to forget that his father was the son of a steward of Mr Grant, who lived in the neighbourhood of my friend and relation the Duke of Derwent: nor can I sufficiently congratulate myself that I have always declined acting with him. The late Dean, indeed, never committed so strange an impropriety as that of nominating Mr Harrel and Mr Briggs coadjutors with Mr Delvile. The impropriety, however, though extremely offensive to me, has never obliterated from my mind the esteem I bore the Dean: nor can I possibly give a greater proof of it than the readiness I have always shewn to offer my counsel and instruction to his niece. Mr Harrel, therefore, ought certainly to have desired Sir Robert Floyer to acquaint me with his proposals before he gave to him any answer."

"Undoubtedly, Sir," said Cecilia, willing to shorten this parading harangue, "but as he neglected that intention, will you think me too impertinent should I entreat the favour of you to speak with Sir Robert yourself, and explain to him the total inefficacy of his pursuit, since my determination against him is unalterable?"

Here the conference was interrupted by the entrance of a servant who said something to Mr Delvile, which occasioned his apologizing to Cecilia for leaving her for a few moments, and ostentatiously assuring her that no business, however important, should prevent his thinking of her affairs, or detain him from returning to her as soon as possible.

The astonishment of young Delvile at the strength of her last expression kept him silent some time after his father left the room; and then, with a countenance that still marked his amazement, he said "Is it possible, Miss Beverley, that I should twice have been thus egregiously deceived? or rather, that the whole town, and even the most intimate of your friends, should so unaccountably have persisted in a mistake."

"For the town," answered Cecilia, "I know not how it can have had any concern in so small a matter; but for my intimate friends, I have too few to make it probable they should ever have been so strangely misinformed."

"Pardon me," cried he, "it was from one who ought to know, that I had myself the intelligence."

"I entreat you, then," said Cecilia, "to acquaint me who it was?"

"Mr Harrel himself; who communicated it to a lady in my hearing, and at a public place."

Cecilia cast up her eyes in wonder and indignation at a proof so incontrovertible of his falsehood, but made not any answer.

"Even yet," continued he, "I can scarcely feel undeceived; your engagement seemed so positive, your connection so irretrievable,—so,— so *fixed*, I mean.—"

He hesitated, a little embarrassed; but then suddenly exclaimed, "Yet whence, if to *neither* favourable, if indifferent alike to Sir Robert and to Belfield, whence that animated apprehension for their safety at the Opera-house? whence that never to be forgotten *oh stop him! good God! will nobody stop him!*—Words of anxiety so tender! and sounds that still vibrate in my ear!"

Cecilia, struck with amazement in her turn at the strength of his own expressions, blushed, and for a few minutes hesitated how to answer him: but then, to leave nothing that related to so disagreeable a report in any doubt, she resolved to tell him ingenuously the circumstances that had occasioned her alarm: and therefore, though with some pain to her modesty, she confessed her fears that she had herself provoked the affront, though her only view had been to discountenance Sir Robert, without meaning to shew any distinction to Mr Belfield.

Delvile, who seemed charmed with the candour of this explanation, said, when she had finished it, "You are then at liberty?—Ah madam!— how many may rue so dangerous a discovery!"

"Could you think," said Cecilia, endeavouring to speak with her usual ease, "that Sir Robert Floyer would be found so irresistible?"

"Oh no!" cried he, "far otherwise; a thousand times I have wondered at his happiness; a thousand times, when I have looked at you, and listened to you, I have thought it impossible!—yet my authority seemed indisputable. And how was I to discredit what was not uttered as a conjecture, but asserted as a fact? asserted, too, by the guardian with whom you lived? and not hinted as a secret, but affirmed as a point settled?"

"Yet surely," said Cecilia, "you have heard me make use of expressions that could not but lead you to suppose there was some mistake, whatever might be the authority which had won your belief."

"No," answered he, "I never supposed any mistake, though sometimes I thought you repented your engagement. I concluded, indeed, you had been unwarily drawn in, and I have even, at times, been tempted to acknowledge my suspicions to you, state your independence, and exhort you—as a *friend*, exhort you—to use it with spirit, and, if you were shackled unwillingly, incautiously, or unworthily, to break the chains by which you were confined, and restore to yourself that freedom of choice upon the use of which all your happiness must ultimately depend. But I doubted if this were honourable to the Baronet,—and what, indeed, was my right to such a liberty? none that every man might not be proud of, a wish to do honour to myself, under the officious pretence of serving the most amiable of women."

"Mr Harrel," said Cecilia, "has been so strangely bigoted to his friend, that in his eagerness to manifest his regard for him, he seems to have forgotten every other consideration; he would not, else, have spread so widely a report that could so ill stand enquiry."

"If Sir Robert," returned he, "is himself deceived while he deceives others, who can forbear to pity him? for my own part, instead of repining that hitherto I have been mistaken, ought I not rather to bless an error that may have been my preservative from danger?"

Cecilia, distressed in what manner to support her part in the conversation, began now to wish the return of Mr Delvile; and, not knowing what else to say, she expressed her surprise at his long absence.

"It is not, indeed, well timed," said young Delvile, "just now,—at the moment when—" he stopt, and presently exclaiming "Oh dangerous interval!" he arose from his seat in manifest disorder.

Cecilia arose too, and hastily ringing the bell, said, "Mr Delvile I am sure is detained, and therefore I will order my chair, and call another time."

"Do I frighten you away?" said he, assuming an appearance more placid.

"No," answered she, "but I would not hasten Mr Delvile."

A servant then came, and said the chair was ready.

She would immediately have followed him, but young Delvile again speaking, she stopt a moment to hear him. "I fear," said he, with much hesitation, "I have strangely exposed myself—and that you cannot—but the extreme astonishment—" he stopt again in the utmost confusion, and then adding, "you will permit me to attend you to the chair," he handed her down stairs, and in quitting her, bowed without saying a word more.

Cecilia, who was almost wholly indifferent to every part of the explanation but that which had actually passed, was now in a state of felicity more delightful than any she had ever experienced. She had not a doubt remaining of her influence over the mind of young Delvile, and the surprise which had made him rather betray than express his regard, was infinitely more flattering and satisfactory to her than any formal or direct declaration. She had now convinced him she was disengaged, and in return, though without seeming to intend it, he had convinced her of the deep interest which he took in the discovery. His perturbation, the words which escaped him, and his evident struggle to say no more, were proofs just such as she wished to receive of his partial admiration, since while they satisfied her heart, they also soothed her pride, by shewing a diffidence of success which assured her that her own secret was still sacred, and that no weakness or inadvertency on her part had robbed her of the power of mingling dignity with the frankness with which she meant to receive his addresses. All, therefore, that now employed her care, was to keep off any indissoluble engagement till each should be better known to the other.

For this reserve, however, she had less immediate occasion than she expected; she saw no more of young Delvile that day; neither did he appear the next. The third she fully expected him,—but still he came not. And while she wondered at an absence so uncommon, she received a note from Lord Ernolf, to beg permission to wait upon her for two minutes, at any time she would appoint.

She readily sent word that she should be at home for the rest of the day, as she wished much for an opportunity of immediately finishing every affair but one, and setting her mind at liberty to think only of that which she desired should prosper.

Lord Ernolf was with her in half an hour. She found him sensible and well bred, extremely desirous to promote her alliance with his son, and apparently as much pleased with herself as with her fortune. He acquainted her that he had addressed himself to Mr Harrel long since, but had been informed that she was actually engaged to Sir Robert Floyer: he should, therefore, have forborn taking up any part of her time, had he not, on the preceding day, while on a visit at Mr Delvile's, been assured that Mr Harrel was mistaken, and that she had not yet declared for any body. He hoped, therefore, that she would allow his son the honour of waiting upon her, and permit him to talk with Mr Briggs, who he understood was her acting guardian, upon such matters as ought to be speedily adjusted.

Cecilia thanked him for the honour he intended her, and confirmed the truth of the account he had heard in St James'-square, but at the same time told him she must decline receiving any visits from his lordship's son, and entreated him to take no measure towards the promotion of an affair which never could succeed.

He seemed much concerned at her answer, and endeavoured for some time to soften her, but found her so steady, though civil in her refusal, that he was obliged, however unwillingly, to give up his attempt.

Cecilia, when he was gone, reflected with much vexation on the readiness of the Delviles to encourage his visit; she considered, however, that the intelligence he had heard might possibly be gathered in general conversation; but she blamed herself that she had not led to some enquiry what part of the family he had seen, and who was present when the information was given him.

Mean while she found that neither coldness, distance, nor aversion were sufficient to repress Sir Robert Floyer, who continued to persecute her with as much confidence of success as could have arisen from the utmost encouragement. She again, though with much difficulty, contrived to speak with Mr Harrel upon the subject, and openly accused him of spreading a report abroad, as well as countenancing an expectation at home, that had neither truth nor justice to support them.

Mr Harrel, with his usual levity and carelessness, laughed at the charge, but denied any belief in her displeasure, and affected to think she was merely playing the coquet, while Sir Robert was not the less her decided choice.

Provoked and wearied, Cecilia resolved no longer to depend upon any body but herself for the management of her own affairs, and therefore, to conclude the business without any possibility of further cavilling, she wrote the following note to Sir Robert herself.

To Sir Robert Floyer, Bart.

Miss BEVERLEY presents her compliments to Sir Robert Floyer, and as she has some reason to fear Mr Harrel did not explicitly acquaint him with her answer to the commission with which he was entrusted, she thinks it necessary, in order to obviate any possible misunderstanding, to take this method of returning him thanks for the honour of his good opinion, but of begging at the same time that he would not lose a moment upon her account, as her thanks are all she can now, or ever, offer in return.

Portman-square, May 11th, 1779.

To this note Cecilia received no answer: but she had the pleasure to observe that Sir Robert forbore his usual visit on the day she sent it, and, though he appeared again the day following, he never spoke to her and seemed sullen and out of humour.

Yet still young Delvile came not, and still, as her surprise encreased, her tranquillity was diminished. She could form no excuse for his delay, nor conjecture any reason for his absence. Every motive seemed to favour his seeking, and not one his shunning her: the explanation which had so lately passed had informed him he had no rival to fear, and the manner in which he had heard it assured her the information was not indifferent to him; why, then, so assiduous in his visits when he thought her engaged, and so slack in all attendance when he knew she was at liberty?

Made in the USA